Time, Forward!

》》》》》》》》》》 《《《《《《《《《《

Valentine Kataev

TIME, FORWARD!

TRANSLATED FROM THE RUSSIAN BY

CHARLES MALAMUTH

NORTHWESTERN UNIVERSITY PRESS

EVANSTON, ILLINOIS

》》》》》》》》》》 《《《《《《《《《《

Northwestern University Press

Evanston, Illinois 60208-4210

Printed in the United States of America

ISBN 0-8101-1247-7

Library of Congress Cataloging-in-Publication Data

Kataev, Valentine, 1897–

    [Vremia, vpered! English]

    Time, forward! / Valentine Kataev ; translated by Charles Malamuth.

        p.   cm.—(European classics)

    Originally published: New York : Holt, Rinehart and Winston, 1961.

    ISBN 0-8101-1247-7 (paper ; alk. paper)

    I. Malamuth, Charles, 1899–1965. II. Title. III. Series: European classics
(Evanston, Ill.)

PG3476.K4V713 1995   95-23933

891.73'42—dc20   CIP

FOREWORD

Valentin Kataev's career as a writer spans a half century, and he is still writing, and even publishing, important literary works. He has exhibited a rare talent not only for literature but for survival, having practiced his craft during the relative freedom of the twenties, under the icy rigors of Stalin, in the liberal period of the mid-sixties, and even under Brezhnev. While a certain sensitivity to external pressures can often be detected in his work, Kataev never abandons the craft of literature. In fact each of his important works is striking and innovative in both style and form. *The Embezzlers* (1927), a novel of the NEP period, satirizes the Soviet bureaucracy in the person of two officials who defraud the Soviet state; told for the most part from the viewpoint of the absconding and drunken officials, the novel is a kind of absurd travelogue in which all events are refracted through an alcoholic haze. *Peace Is Where the Tempests Blow* (1936) describes the events of 1905 as apprehended by children who witnessed them.

Kataev's work of the sixties and seventies is also original and arresting. *A Little Iron Door in the Wall* (1964), a study of Lenin in Paris, Capri, and other foreign parts, is a parody of Soviet Lenin hagiography so subtle in its ironies that it was even published in the USSR; very few readers have understood it. Like the Spanish painter Velasquez, whose traditional canvases depicted court personages in their regal ambience and rich garments while at the same time revealing them as dull fools, so Kataev, never once abandoning the proper hagiographic stance, manages to contrive a dismal portrait of Lenin as a hard-headed and narrow dogmatist, indifferent to higher Parisian culture but fascinated by music halls and the guillotine.* *The Holy Well* (1966), *The Grass of Oblivion* (1967), and *The Graveyard in Skulyani* (1975) are all experiments in the treatment of time which use the technique of abrupt juxtaposition—the montage—to develop startling temporal interrelationships.

Time, Forward! (1932), reprinted here, is an important historical document as well as a literary performance of the first order, probably the best of the Soviet "industrial" novels. It describes the build-

*I am indebted to Dodona Kiziria, who pointed this out to me.

ing of the huge metallurgical plant at Magnitogorsk in the Ural mountains and succeeds in conveying the atmosphere of feverish hurry, of time itself made to move faster, in which industrial projects were undertaken during the First Five-Year Plan (1928-1932). The principal text upon which the novel is based is an address delivered by Stalin in 1931 in which he characteristically distorts the facts of Russian history for his own purposes: "Russia . . . was beaten by Mongol khans, . . . by Turkish beks . . . by Swedish feudal lords. She was beaten by the Polish and Lithuanian gentry . . ."; from this he draws the important conclusion that Russia must liquidate her industrial backwardness or be beaten again and again.

The central event in *Time, Forward!* is a successful attempt by a brigade of workmen at Magnitogorsk, in competition with a brigade working in Kharkov, to break the world's time record for pouring concrete. The vivid action reveals the mechanisms developed in the USSR during the First Five-Year Plan in an effort to motivate workers to outdo themselves: shock brigades, socialist competition, Stakhanovism, slogans, public acclaim of "heroes of labor" and opprobrium for "shirkers." The dominant image is the speeding up of time in the Soviet Union, where a century's work must be done in ten years. Kataev utilizes techniques learned from the cinema to suggest the confusion of "normal" space and time concepts under revolutionary pressures. Objects and persons are shown always in motion; landscapes are seen through the windows of moving trains. The camera eye itself is constantly in motion: the metallurgical plant seen from a distance is a tiny object; then in a sudden closeup it becomes a huge, unencompassable mass; and when the camera moves inside the structure, the interior dimensions are enormous beyond belief. The great plant itself, a twentieth-century industrial giant rising out of a primitive steppe wilderness, is presented as order growing out of chaos, and the naive eye of the camera distinguishes, only with some difficulty, evidences of plan and purpose in the tumble of freight cars, cement-mixers, iron girders, barracks, and sheer junk. Kataev's literary celebration of modern socialist industry is a first-rate modern novel.

EDWARD J. BROWN

Time, Forward!

PRINCIPAL CHARACTERS

SEROSHEVSKY, *chief engineer in charge of the entire construction*

NALBANDOV, GEORGI NIKOLAYEVICH, *assistant chief of the construction*

MARGULIES, DAVID LVOVICH, *engineer in charge of the sixth sector*

KORNEYEV, *superintendent of the sixth sector*

MOSYA, *foreman in charge of the shift*

ISHCHENKO (KONSTANTIN, KOSTYA)
KHANUMOV
YERMAKOV
brigadiers, or pace-setters, each in charge of a shock-brigade

SMETANA
OLGA TREGUBOVA
NEFEDOV
Communist Youth members of Ishchenko's shock-brigade

SAYENKO, *a kulak's son*
ZAGIROV, *the Tatar*
recalcitrant members of Ishchenko's brigade

FOMA YEGOROVICH (THOMAS GEORGE BIXBY), *an American engineer*

ILYUSHCHENKO, *testing engineer at the construction laboratory*

KUTAISOV, *editor*
SLOBODKIN, *a poet*
TRIGER, *secretary*
of the editorial staff of the local travelling edition of the "Komsomolskaya Pravda"

VINKICH, *correspondent of the Russian Telegraphic Agency*

GEORGI VASILYEVICH, *famous novelist*

SEMECHKIN, *correspondent of the regional newspaper*

FILONOV, *secretary of the construction's Communist Party nucleus*

FYENYA, *Ishchenko's wife*

SHURA SOLDATOVA, *in charge of the art shop*

KLAVA, *Korneyev's sweetheart*

RAY ROUPE, *a wealthy American tourist*

LEONARD DARLEY, *an American correspondent*

KATYA, *Margulies's sister in Moscow*

PROFESSOR SMOLENSKY, *of the Institute of Construction in Moscow*

I

The first chapter is omitted for the time being.

II

THE alarm clock rattled like a tin of bonbons. The alarm clock was cheap, painted, brown, of Soviet manufacture.

Half-past six.

The clock was accurate, but Margulies did not depend on it. He was not asleep. He always rose at six and was always ahead of time. There had never yet been an occasion when the alarm clock had actually awakened him.

Margulies could not really have faith in so simple a mechanism as a timepiece; could not entrust to it so precious a thing as time.

Three hundred and six divided by eight. Then sixty divided by thirty-eight and two-tenths. Margulies calculated this in his mind instantly.

The result—one and approximately five-tenths.

The figures had the following significance:

Three hundred and six was the number of mixtures. Eight was the number of working hours. Sixty was the number of minutes in an hour. Thus the concrete mixers of Kharkov made one mixture in one and approximately five-tenths of a minute, that is, in ninety seconds. From these ninety seconds deduct the sixty seconds of compulsory minimum necessary for each mixture according to the book of instructions. There remained thirty seconds.

Thirty seconds in which to wheel up the material, to load, and to lift the scoop!

Theoretically it was possible. But—practically? That was the question that had to be answered.

3

Until now the best brigades of concrete mixers on the construction made no more than two hundred mixtures per shift. This was regarded as an excellent record. Now the situation had altered radically.

With a safety razor blade, Margulies sharpened his yellow pencil. He sharpened it with the smartness and careless dexterity of a young engineer, removing long, amazingly thin and polished slivers.

On the hill, ore was being blasted. Frequent uneven explosions followed each other.

The air broke softly—like a slate.

Margulies browsed through about five thick books with stiff bindings and silver titles, making notes and calculations on the margins of a yellowed newspaper.

The newspaper dispatch explained virtually nothing. Its figures were too inaccurate. Moreover, the necessary sixty seconds taken from the official book of reference likewise seemed highly debatable.

Naked and dirty, Margulies sat before the wobbly little hotel table. The little round table was unsuitable for work. Margulies sat there, wrapped in a soiled sheet and looking like a Bedouin.

Stinging flies swirled around him in loops and rummaged in his rearing shock of hair. He removed the spectacles from his large nose and placed them before him on the tablecloth with the shafts down, so that they looked like a tortoise shell cabriolet. He struck his shoulders, his neck, his head. The assassinated flies fell on the newspaper.

Much was not clear.

The labor front? Transportation? The capacity of the machinery? The number of men? The distance to the place where the concrete must be poured? The height to which the scoop would have to be lifted? All of this was unknown. It had to be guessed at. Margulies tentatively sketched several of the more likely variants.

He pulled on his trousers, shoved his feet into boots with sharp noses and roomy legs, and wound around his neck a dirty towel ribbed like a waffle.

The canvas curtains flew out of the room into the corridor after Margulies. He did not even attempt to shove them back. That was impossible. Lifted by the draught, the curtains flapped, flew, swirled, raged.

Margulies had studied their behaviour thoroughly. He simply slammed the door on them. They hung outside like grey flags.

The hotel stood at the crossing of four winds. In the language of seafaring men, this point is called "the rose of winds."

Four winds—the western, the southern, the eastern, and the northern—joined on the outside in order to fight together against man. They lifted monstrous storms of dust. Oblique, driving towers of whirlwinds hid the sun. Dense and rusty, they seemed like mounds of camel's wool. The soot of the eclipse spread over the earth. The cyclone knocked automobiles and trains together, tore down tents, blinded, burned, shook scaffoldings and steel constructions. The winds raged.

At the same time, their younger brothers, the household draughts, made mischief inside the hotel. They blew the curtains out of the room, tore off hooks with bits of wood clinging to them, broke glass and flung shaving tackle from the window sills.

Three men stood at one end of the corridor before the closed lavatory.

They had already forgotten why they had come there, and were arguing about various affairs, holding forth towels and toothbrushes on the palms of their hands as corroborating evidence. They were in a hurry, however, and might separate at any moment.

The corridor was two rows of door handles, two rows of fat test tubes filled with greenish methyl alcohol.

Chambermaids in white smocks were sweeping the yellow floor with sawdust.

The square window represented a transverse section of the corridor in all its height and breadth. It revealed the east. Masses of dust, yellowish, like burnt aluminum, paced across the checkered screen of the window. The dust darkened the landscape.

Smiling near-sightedly, Margulies approached the engineers.

"What are you talking about?"

The strong white sun burned in the window with the speed of magnesium ribbons, but, having penetrated into the hallway, it immediately lost its principal allies—dust and wind. It lost its wild steppe-like ferocity. Rendered harmless by the glass, it spread itself over the entire length of the xylonite floor painted ochre. It pretended to be tame and good-natured, like a kitten. It gazed perfidiously into one's eyes, reminded one of a fine, early morning, of lilacs, perhaps even of dew.

Margulies squinted and lisped slightly. Large-nosed, spectacled and stubby, he looked like an *externe*.[1]

A fat fellow in an Ukrainian shirt open at the throat turned from him with aversion.

"We were saying," he said rapidly, facing the others, and overtly ignoring Margulies, "we were saying that the lavatories have been closed on all five floors because of a break in the water system, and so I ask you please to go out into the open air until the wind . . ."

With disgust he openly turned away from all of them, and without pausing, addressed himself exclusively to Margulies.

". . . and as for all these tricks, if anybody in my sector attempts two hundred and six—not to speak of three hundred and six—then I will take that son-of-a-bitch and I'll kick him out, and I won't let him come within the range of a cannon shot, even if he is a thrice qualified engineer! You may depend on that!"

He angrily turned his back on the entire assembly and took several steps down the stairway. But immediately, catching his breath, he returned and added rapidly:

"This is a construction, not a stunt."

Again he made as if to depart and again returned from the

---

[1] *Externes,* a class unknown since the Bolshevik revolution, were students who passed examinations for various classes of the gymnasia in preparation for the right to matriculate at the University.

middle of the stairway. That was his way of conducting a conversation.

"I congratulate you," said Margulies, apropos of the accident to the water system, and trotted down the stairs.

He realised at once that the record set by Kharkov was already known all over the construction. He expected that. There was no time to lose.

Below, at the table of the passport clerk, the new arrivals sat on bundles and suitcases. There were about forty of them. They had spent the night there. The hotel of two hundred and fifty rooms did not have a spare bed. Nevertheless, new people continued to arrive every day.

Stumbling over baggage, over bicycles, stepping on people's feet, Margulies made his way to the telephone.

It seemed that Korneyev had not yet left the sector and, even though he had not slept for twenty-four hours, had no intention of leaving. The telephone operator from the central station told Margulies this, immediately recognising his voice, and addressing him by his name and patronymic—David Lvovich. The telephone operator at the central station was in touch with the progress of concrete laying on the sixth sector. There was nothing strange about that. For the moment, Engineer Margulies's sector was regarded as one of the most important.

"I'll connect you with the nucleus," [2] the telephone operator said in a business-like manner. "It seems Korneyev is there. His wife has just phoned him. By the way, she is leaving to-day for Moscow to return to that other husband of hers. Poor Korneyev! By the way, what do you think of Kharkov? Three hundred and six in one shift! That's simply phenomenal. Well, so long! Here's the nucleus of the sixth sector."

An old man in a cotton Tolstoyan shirt removed from the window of the Post Office Department and State Labor Savings Bank a shabby cardboard with the inscription "Closed." The bank was in the vestibule. The old man looked out of the win-

[2] *Nucleus*—a Communist nucleus is the smallest unit of Communist Party organisation in a given industrial or territorial community.

dow like a cuckoo and went about his affairs. Next to him, a bare-footed girl with straight hair was laying out various newspapers and magazines on the counter.

A foreigner walked up and bought an "Izvestya" and a "Pravda." A fat man in an Ukrainian shirt bought "Humanité" and a "Berliner Tageblatt." An old lady selected a "Murzilka." A boy bought "Pod Znamenem Marksizma." The tin box began to fill with coppers.

Outside, through the black crêpe of floating dust, burned the quicksilver bullet of the thermometer. Smudge-nosed cab drivers in goggles that looked like tin cans came in. They brought dry earth into the hotel. They stamped their bast shoes and boots along the stairways, made out the room numbers with great difficulty, and pounded on the doors.

After talking with Korneyev, Margulies again called the station and ordered a connection with Moscow for nine o'clock. Then he ran back to his room. He quickly finished dressing: a striped shirt, a soft collar, a necktie, a double-breasted blue coat that was too large for him.

The evening before he had found no time to wash himself. This morning there was no water. Standing in front of the cheap Slavic cupboard with its effort at luxury, he removed black particles from the corners of his eyes. The *eau de cologne* had dried up. He spat on a towel, and rubbed his large nose and his long hairy nostrils. He pulled on a roomy worsted cap. It assumed the round shape of his stiff, rearing mop of hair.

The alarm clock indicated ten minutes of seven.

Margulies ran out of his room, bumping his shoulder against the fire extinguisher, and hurried down to the dining room. On the counter were sandwiches of dried sturgeon and eggs, but there was a long line of breakfasters. He made a gesture of impatience. He would eat at the sector.

In the doorway he was stopped by a cross-eyed fellow in a yellow football sweater with a black collar.

"Well, Margulies, when are you going to show up Kharkov?"

Margulies squinted officiously.

"We'll see about that later."

"Come on and show us!"

At the entrance to the hotel stood woven Ural carts. They were waiting for the engineers. Horses' tails swished. Gaily decorated shafts glistened. There was an intensely strong odour of horses.

"Hey, Bosses," Margulies shouted in his thin voice. "Who's going to the sixth sector?"

The drivers were silent.

"Kustanayev has an outfit for the sixth," an old Kirghiz replied after a moment of silence. He wore the velvet cap of a magician.

"And where is Kustanayev?"

"Kustanayev went to the hospital."

"Fine!"

The sixth sector was not very far, not more than two kilometres. Margulies squinted and began to walk, digging clumsily into the earth with his toes, walking against the sun and the wind to the crossing. But first he turned into a small wooden house with a high wooden chimney and two open doors. This little house was permeated with the odour of newspapers baked in the sun. Margulies climbed up on a large box and yielded to the exactions of nature.

"They certainly find out news quickly here," he thought, cracking his long fingers.

Crowds of telegraph poles wandered against the wind and the clouds of black dust.

III

EVERYTHING moved from its place. Everything walked. The trees walked. The groves waded across the river in flood.

It was May. One tree was left behind. It had stopped in astonishment, up to its knees in deep water. It turned its head in the direction of the flickering train; it was blooming and shaggy, like a new recruit.

We move like a shadow from the west to the east.

To the east go clouds, elevators, fences, Mordovian sarafans, water pumps, caterpillars, echelons, churches, minarets.

Incandescent sands are piled with wood. Kindling and boats are strewn on the shore. A tug-boat struggles against the swollen water.

The water is swollen like a seine. The water glistens with the bright loops of the net. The net is boiling. The net is pulled by a tangled little boat. Its paddles beat, it blows up its red gills; it bends. It is driven under the bridge.

Stone piers wander stubbornly against the stream, their snouts dipped in the water. The yoke of froth is boiling around their shining necks. The armoured bars of the bridge rise up with the thunder of kilometres. The crossed beams strike the eye with light and shadow.

We are crossing the Volga.

The revolution marches to the east in order to reach the west. No power in the world can stop it. It will reach the west.

Saratov—Ufa.

Road of lilies of the valley and of nightingales! The nightingales do not fear the train. They reverberate through the night, the clear clinking fillipping bubbling through the clay neck of the night. The night is filled to the brim with icy dew.

At the stations children sell lilies of the valley. Everywhere is the odour of lily of the valley. The telegraph pole wavers like a thin spray of lily of the valley. The small moon is white in the green sky, like a little bud of lily of the valley.

We are crossing the Urals.

On the left is the forest; on the right a slope. The slope is covered with brush.

On the left is the compartment; on the right the corridor. This is an international car—a *wagon-lit*. Green scrawls sweep across the windows of the corridor.

The passengers run out into the corridor. The linoleum strikes at the soles of their feet. The floor is elastic, like a spring-board.

In every window is a silhouette.

The passengers have abandoned their pastimes. Their pastimes were various. The Americans were playing poker. A German was transferring some butter from a paper into a cocoa tin. A Soviet engineer was bending near-sightedly over his charts. The correspondent of "Ekonomicheskaya Zhizn," a poet, was reading a stenographic report:

". . . In the history of governments, in the history of countries, in the history of armies, there were occasions when there were present all the possibilities for success, for victory; but they, these possibilities, were frustrated, because the leaders did not notice these possibilities, did not know how to take advantage of them, and the armies suffered defeat.

"Have we the possibilities necessary to carry out the control figures for 1931?

"Yes, we have these possibilities.

"What do these possibilities consist of? What must be done in order that these possibilities may be realised?

"First of all, we must have a sufficiency of natural wealth: iron ore, coal, oil, grain, cotton . . ."

The poet underlined "iron ore" with his finger nail.

". . . Do we have them? We have more of them than any other country. Take, for example, the Urals, which represents a combination of wealth that cannot be found in any other country. Ore, coal, copper, oil, grain—we have everything in the Urals . . ."

We are crossing the Urals.

Flickering across the windows from left to right, swirls the obelisk: "Europe—Asia." It is painted white and the paint is peeling. It is covered with inscriptions, like a provincial address. It is a senseless post. Now it is behind us. Does that mean that we are in Asia? . . . Curious! . . . We are moving toward the east at a terrific speed and we carry the revolution with us. Never again shall we be Asia.

". . . To lower tempos means to fall back, and those who fall back are beaten. But we do not want to be beaten. No, we will not have it! This was the history of old Russia: it was continually beaten because of backwardness. It was beaten by Mongol khans. It was beaten by Turkish beks. It was beaten by Swedish feudal lords. It was beaten by Polish and Lithuanian gentry. It was beaten by English and French capitalists.

"It was beaten by Japanese barons.

"It was beaten because of military backwardness, cultural backwardness, governmental backwardness, industrial backwardness, agricultural backwardness. It was beaten because it was profitable to do so and because the beating went unpunished . . .

"That is why we cannot be backward any more . . ."[1]

The train was flying. Fyenya was timid about leaving the train at the station. She looked out of the window.

The mountains became darker; the air—pungent, mountainous.

A railroad shack or a transformer box! Black and red! It clung to the crag like an ingot of oxidised iron. Above it—the slender, feathered arrows of Ural fir!

Black and red—the colour of attack! The alarming label on the box of a trotilla!

The train leaped like a ramrod from the gun-barrel of the tunnel. It pulled out of the mountain a fetid stream of mineral air. When it was entering the tunnel, the windows had been closed. The glass-panes, transformed by the darkness into mirrors of coal, reflected the lighted electric lamps doubly.

But then how bright the world became after that!

At the station among the mountains, a little girl was selling yellow flowers.

Fyenya looked down at her from the window and cried:

"Come, little girl! Come to me!"

But the girl did not hear. She ran down the length of the cars. With outspread fingers she clutched the flowers against her stomach as if they were ducklings.

"You silly girl!"

From the mail car, compact packages of newspapers, parcels, bags of letters were being thrown out on the flinty soil. Ram-

[1] From an address by Josef Stalin of June 23, 1931.

shackle furniture had been unloaded—an old kitchen table; a wooden bed in parts, back tied to back; a chair; a badly scorched stool.

"They're moving their bedbugs!"

This was said by the girl Lizochka, the train porter, who wore a conductor's uniform, thick grey stockings on her heavy legs, and carried a green, much-faded flag in her hand. She had made friends with Fyenya, was sorry for her, and brought her hot water for tea.

A boy passed under the windows of the international car. He stopped, threw back his head, and read the dusty copper inscription very slowly.

"A sleeping car in a through train," he said, "and they are not sleeping!"

It was daytime.

The astonished boy went along further, flinging stones at the wheels of the cars. Foreigners in hats regarded him through the window. In glasses on the tables before the windows were white and green clusters of lilies of the valley. The glasses stood in silver holders. The zwieback was wrapped in wax paper. The heavy brass ash trays were full of splendid butts!

Fyenya was travelling in a "hard" car from the vicinity of Kiev through Moscow. In Moscow she had had to transfer from the Bryansky to the Kazansky Railroad Station. A tremendous distance!

On the level of her considerably distended stomach, she lifted a bag to the platform of the street car. Elbows shoved her aside. She was helped up, scolded, pitied, pressed. She wiped her smudged yellow nose with the corner of her shawl. As she wiped her nose, she carefully extended her ring finger with its silver ring. In her hot fist she had crumpled a handkerchief with her money tied in it.

The ring she had bought herself. Although she had not registered with Kostya in the local Soviet, when it became evident that she was to give birth to a child she had bought the ring and put it on. She considered herself married all the same, and she was going to the man whom she regarded as her husband. She was taking the journey in order to register.

And as for him, perhaps he did not care to know her any more. He might have already entangled himself with some other girl. Who could tell?

She did not even know his address more than vaguely, but she had grown very lonely, and it seemed a terrible thing to bear a child for the first time.

And so she was going to him.

At the Kazansky Station she alighted from the rear platform painfully. She stepped down back first, stopping the public, hugging the bag, the hot sweat pouring down her body. There she sat on her belongings till evening, eating nothing, afraid that she might be robbed, and faint with nausea.

When it was her turn to board the next train, she moved sidewise, or again backwards, looking wildly about her, hugging the bag like a pavement post, dragging it by the ears, scraping the floor with it, all as if she were dancing a strange polonaise.

Once on the train, Fyenya tried to be sly. She entered the cars where fewer people stood in the doorways, but all of these cars, as if from design, proved to be wrong ones, either cars with reserved seats, or "soft" cars, or service cars, or some sort of international car; it was simply frightful.

And so Fyenya failed to outwit the railroad. She had just wasted her time in dragging her bag through all the wrong cars. At last she had to take her place where the crowds pushed more than elsewhere.

Still she did manage to find a seat; good people made room for her.

So it didn't matter. She may have been crowded, but she had not been slighted.

Fyenya shoved the bag under the seat, curled one foot under so that she might feel the bag with her foot during the journey, threw off her shawl, and made the sign of the cross.

IV

SUPERINTENDENT KORNEYEV wore grey canvas tennis shoes. Shura had advised him to whiten them. Superintendent Korneyev had listened to her. He had acted rashly.

The shoes soiled frightfully. They could very well have been sent to the office of the committee on construction, instead of the daily report. The shoes represented a fairly detailed account of the building materials used at the sector.

Every morning they had to be painted white. This was annoying but unavoidable. The blue uniform (trousers and the single-breasted coat of navy cut) demanded faultlessly white shoes.

In his blue linen coat with its large patch pockets, belted through a severe, double line of thick pleats, Korneyev resembled a ship's mechanic.

He tried very hard to live up to this likeness. He cultivated small side-burns and clipped his moustache in the English fashion. He carried his silver watch on a strap in the outer side-pocket of his coat. His cigarettes he kept in a black leather cigarette case.

The first shift finished at eight.

For Superintendent Korneyev the transition from night to day was indicated by the fact that he could see his shoes again by the light of the sun.

He had not slept for twenty-four hours. He intended to start the second shift and go home. He had not been home since the evening before. It was imperative that he have a talk with Klava.

But then that business with Kharkov again! He had lost track of time. Something had happened at night, but what had it been?

Anything might have happened at night.

It was quite possible that at night she might have been speaking on the telephone with Moscow. It was quite possible that her daughter had fallen ill in Moscow.

At dawn she had telephoned to Korneyev.

He had found it difficult to understand her. He guessed rather than understood. She wept. She swallowed words like tears. She vowed that she could do nothing else. She assured him that she loved him and that she would go mad.

It was embarrassing to speak with her in the presence of strangers. People worked all night long at the nucleus.

Filonov, his ears stopped, his eyes swollen, caught one bit of news after another. All around was pandemonium. Filonov beat the noise away with his large head, as if he were butting it. Out of delicacy and consideration, no one paid any attention to Korneyev; but his ears burned.

He shouted senselessly into the telephone:

"I can't hear anything! I can't hear anything! Talk louder. Oh, the devil . . . Talk louder! What are you saying? I tell you it's noisy here. Talk more distinctly . . . dis-tinct-ly!"

Their connection was continually being broken. Other voices kept interrupting. Strange voices pleaded for the delivery of rubble as soon as possible, swore, demanded the mill-office switchboard, demanded carriers, called superintendents, dictated figures . . .

It was hell.

Korneyev shouted that he could not come right away, begged her not to leave, pleaded with her to wait about buying the ticket. . . .

Korneyev was tortured by a cold. The days were too hot here and the nights too cold. His nose twitched; he sniffed and wheezed; his nose had turned red. Stinging pink tears were burning his eyes.

The sleepless morning glow of the electric lights lost their last lustre in the columns of sunlight.

Tugging at his black satin shirt on his short, broad body, Filonov walked out of the office of the nucleus into the corridor.

Night still held its own in the corridor. The corridor was full of shadows and smoke. People with account books crowded about the window of the bookkeeping department. Cab drivers looking like chauffeurs and chauffeurs looking like cab drivers stopped under the lamps, going over their travelling orders and order slips. Along the plank walls sleepy old Bashkirs sat on their haunches. Women clattered the mug as they drank water from the cistern.

Filonov tore open the plywood door bearing the multicolored inscription:

"Comr! You shd hav some knd of conscnce this is the art shop of the 6th sec please don't come in nd don't bothr us can't u see people ar working?"

The art shop was no larger than a bathing cabin.

Two boys were swaying back to back on a stool. With home-made felt brushes they were writing fire prevention slogans on the reverse side of some wall paper.

On the floor under the window, sideways, sat Shura Soldatova. With her clever russet eyebrows drawn in a frown, she was paint-ing a large wooden graveyard cross with azure oil paint.

Another cross, already completed, stood in a corner. On it could be seen a yellow inscription:

"Here rests Nikolai Sayenko, from the brigade of Ishchenko. Rest in peace, dear toiler of loafing and drunkenness!"

From left to right cars came in empty. From right to left they went out full. Or the other way round. The window flickered like the pages of a book left on the window sill. The edges of the flat-cars were almost scratching the walls of the barracks with their hooks. Light and shadow swirled in the planked room filled with painting materials. All of the free space was occupied by drying sheets of paper.

Shura Soldatova was used to imagining that the barrack was travelling back and forth over the sector. Day and night the bar-rack trembled like a freight car. The floor swayed. The boards creaked. Rays entered through the long slits: in the daytime, sun rays; at night, electric rays.

Filonov, the secretary of the Party collective of the sixth sec-tor, shoved his round simple face into the art shop, a face which

was touched about his shining crimson lips with the angry little
eyebrows of a sprouting young moustache:

"Well now, kids, zip-zip!"

He proffered the piece of paper he held. The boys paid absolutely no attention to him.

In the windowpane, mounds of earth swayed from right to
left, at the level of the window sill.

The barrack rode across the sector, past long stacks of lumber,
past canalisation culverts, black on the outside and red inside,
past steel structures, past red bricks wrapped in straw, past iron
armatures, gunny sacks, cement, rubble, sand, oil, couplers, machinists, connecting rods, pistons, steam.

The barrack stopped, jerked, its brakes screeching, knocked
against the buffer plates, and rode back.

Outside the window, jumping over the railroad ties, Korneyev
ran by in his white cap. On the run, he tapped his pencil against
the windowpane.

Shura dropped the brush into the porcelain cup of the telephone insulator which she used for paint. Shura wiped her hands
against her short woollen skirt, pulled it over her shiny dirty
knees, and rose easily.

Her roughly clipped hair fell across her eyes. She flung it back.
Again it fell; again she flung it back.

Shura grew angry. She was always fighting with herself. She
was now thoroughly sick of it. She was growing up too fast.

Her skirt had become exceedingly tight and short. The blue
football sweater, washed until it was almost white, was tucked
into her skirt and had split under the arms. Her arms were
crawling out of the tight sleeves. The sleeves had to be rolled up.

She was scarcely seventeen, but she appeared to be no less than
twenty. And still she kept on growing.

She was in despair. She did not know what to do with her
hands, which were too large, with her legs, which were too long,
with her blue eyes, which were too beautiful, with her voice,
which was too pleasant. She was embarrassed by her high breasts,
her thin waist, her white throat.

Across the shaggy heads of the boys she took the bit of paper from Filonov.

"What?—Slogans?"

"Text placard."

"How soon?"

"How soon can you have it ready?"

Shura shrugged her shoulders. Filonov quickly wrinkled his nose.

"In half an hour?"

One of the boys glanced darkly at Filonov and squinted as if he were looking at the sun.

"In half an hour! Ho-ho! What's your hurry?"

He shoved two fingers deep into his mouth and whistled piercingly. The other boy immediately shoved his bare elbow into his back.

"Don't shove, you snake!"

"Don't whistle, you bum!"

The boys turned round abruptly, nose to nose. Their noses, bulbous and peeling, were like young potatoes.

"Hey!" cried Shura. "No fighting!"

Filonov came into the room.

"What's the matter?"

"They have a personal competition," Shura said seriously. "To see who will write more letters in eight hours. They have been scribbling since midnight. They have become beastly."

Filonov glanced quickly at the drying placards. He smiled.

"Pretty poor spelling. Quantity at the expense of quality. Not one word is correct. Instead of more—moar. Instead of fire—fier. Instead of down—doun . . . What do you mean by doun?"

"Don't you teach us," said, in a bass voice, the boy who had poked the other boy with his elbow. "You are not very literate yourself. All kinds of people come around here and interrupt brigade work."

"We haven't checked up yet," said the other boy.

Shura took the paper from Filonov. She read it and deliberately lifted her brows.

"Is it really true, Filonov?"

"Certainly."

"Well, good for Kharkov!"

"Well?"

"How many do you want?"

"Two. One in the dining room, the other in the superintendent's office."

Shura thought for a moment and said:

"We need one more. We should hang it in the third shift barrack for Ishchenko's benefit."

"It would do him good," Filonov agreed after a moment of thought. "Go to it."

Shura turned the paper in her hand, placed her feet carefully, heel to heel, and looked at the tongues of her shoes, which were tied across with cord drawn through the white eyelets.

"Say, Filonov, wait."

Filonov returned.

"Well?"

"How about making a picture? I'll do it. You know: an azure blue sky, all sorts of trees around, the sun, and in the middle, in a huge galosh, sit our concrete mixers, while the Kharkov boys are pulling them with a huge rope."

"Hell, no! You have smeared enough pictures all over the place!"

"What's the matter with them? Are they bad pictures?" one of the boys asked roughly—the one who had been pushing. "If you don't like them, draw them yourself. There are too many advisors around here. They come and come here and interfere with our brigade work!"

"You can all go to . . . !"

Filonov covered his ears with his fists and ran out into the corridor.

Korneyev entered. He stood for a moment, twitched his nose, asked that the letters be made larger, and poured a bit of whiting into a small box.

He went behind the barrack, put his foot on a log, and patiently whitened the shoes with an old toothbrush. The shoes turned dark. Then he wiped his dark perspiring face with a wet handkerchief. His face became light.

When he finally reached the crossing, his slippers were dry and had become blindingly white, but his face had turned dark.

Thus the morning began.

. . . She was going away. . . .

V

FROM a distance the plant seemed small and insignificant. At close range it was as huge as, say, a theatre.

The engineers had a bad habit of manœuvring at crossings. The long train rolled slowly forward and backward, holding back the traffic. Like a saw, it cut Korneyev away from the plant. He had to wait. He pulled out the strap and looked at his watch. Twenty minutes past seven!

A hot dusty wind was blowing. People and transport were crowding on both sides of the crossing. The more impatient ones jumped on the slowly moving flat cars. They ran by with their backs or faces to the traffic and jumped down, whirling, on the other side. The girl muckers, the second shift, in coloured blouses and full skirts, linked hands in a chain, sat down in a row on the ground, and kicked off their bast shoes; laughing, they looked up at the running wheels, their shining teeth in brigades.

On the other side, Mosya, the foreman, was hurrying from the plant to the crossing. He was running from the wide gates along planks, dangling his loose arms before him, like a goal-keeper. In appearance, Mosya was something like this: his face— an earthen pitcher with prominent cheek-bones; then a dashing Batoum cap; ears of pottery; the excellent stubby nose of an Indian profile; quick, frantic, thievish eyes.

The flat cars were flashing by between Mosya and Korneyev. Under the lumbering rotation of the wheels, the railroad ties ran by like piano keys. Mosya had noticed Korneyev from a distance.

"Comrade Superintendent!"

Mosya had a raucous, boyish voice, capable of arousing the dead.

Korneyev did not hear. He walked back and forth at the crossing, in deep thought, talking to himself:

". . . finally . . . can it go on like this or not? It cannot. Is it possible to continue to lead a double life? Absolutely impossible. Good. What am I to do then? I must decide. What shall I decide? Something definite. One or the other. . . ."

Korneyev had a very mobile face. He paced back and forth, his nose twitching, making faces.

". . . finally, the girl can be brought here from Moscow. The girl—that's no excuse. Other children live here as well. And nothing untoward happens to them. She's just inventing it. She should write all of this to her husband. She must telegraph. She must send a special telegram. We are not savages. He's a Communist. He cannot help understanding . . ."

"Comrade Superintendent!"

Korneyev did not hear.

Mosya jumped on the buffers, danced on them, turned around, and jumped down on the other side, back first. He was breathless.

"Comrade Korneyev!"

Korneyev recovered.

"Finished?" he asked.

"Yes."

"How many?"

"Ninety cubes!"

Mosya was exultant. He could not suppress the frantic gleam in his eyes. He peered impatiently into Korneyev's face. But Korneyev took the report in silence.

The crossing was cleared. The engine spat some oil on Korneyev's shoes. Three small coffee drops. Almost unnoticeable. But annoying.

"Already!" Korneyev thought with disgust.

From this distance the entrance to the plant seemed no larger than a notebook. Nearby it looked like huge gates. The winding rails of the narrow-gauge railroad entered the darkness of the gates.

In silence Korneyev walked up to the plant, put the report against the gates, and signed it with an indelible pencil.

He merely asked: "Second shift on the job?" And nothing more. Mosya had laid ninety cubes—and Korneyev did not say another word! As if it were just the usual thing!

Mosya placed the report in his cap with an injured manner, and reported officially:

"The second shift is assembling, Comrade Superintendent."

"Good. Margulies there?"

"No."

Korneyev's nose twitched.

"Good."

A multitude of placards had been nailed over the gates:

"Loafers and idlers are strictly forbidden to enter here."

"Smoking is strictly forbidden. Comrade, throw away your cigarette. For violation the fine is 3 rubl. And immediate court action."

"Give us the seventh and eighth batteries by the first of September."

And so forth.

The placards were generously decorated with symbolical drawings in garish colours. Here were: a smoking cigarette the size of a factory chimney; a hellish broom which was sweeping out the loafer; a three-story airplane of amazing construction, with the figures 7 and 8 on its wings; and a snub-nosed tramp in a checkered cap, with the propeller stuck into an altogether unfitting place.

Within, the plant seemed even vaster than without.

At the gate stood a sentry. He did not ask Korneyev or Mosya for their passes. He knew them.

Past the gates, clicking resoundingly and stumbling over the rails of the narrow-guage railroad, a rider of the squadron of the mounted military guard rode by, flashing his orange chevrons, astride a chocolate-coloured horse. He turned sharply, his muscular Kazak face displaying a molten plate of vicious Asiatic teeth.

Within, the plant was huge, like a wharf, like a slip. A transAtlantic steamship could have found ample room there. Surrounded by the light superstructure, the huge space hung like a dirigible at the height of an eight-story house. Heavy strata of dark atmosphere hung overhead by the thin hair of the somnolent sound of one brick striking another brick.

Korneyev cut across the plant in order to shorten the distance. Mosya ran a bit ahead, looking back quickly at Korneyev. Korneyev was silent, biting his lips and moving his eyebrows expressively. Mosya was boiling. It took a great deal of effort to contain himself. And ordinarily he made no attempt to contain himself. He should worry! But now circumstances demanded it of him. Just being a foreman on a world-famous construction was worth something.

"The foreman must be a model of revolutionary discipline and tact." (Mosya caught at this phrase with bitter rapture. This phrase had been invented by himself.)

The superintendent was silent. And so, the foreman would be silent. He should worry! Mosya understood perfectly: neither Korneyev nor Margulies would let the matter rest; they would undoubtedly outdo Kharkov. That much was clear.

But which shift would beat the record and when? There was the rub. Here entered the question of personal self-esteem—of Mosya's self-esteem. If the record was to be beaten by the second or the third shift, that's good. Very good. But suppose it was the first?

The first went on the job at zero hour, and at zero Mosya's watch ended. Of course its foreman might decline to take the shift, but what fool of a foreman would want to yield fame to Mosya?

That meant that if the record was to be established by the first shift, everything would happen without Mosya. That would be terrible. That could not be. But suppose . . .

Mosya could not contain himself:

"Comrade Korneyev . . ."

Mosya even struck the fire extinguisher with his fist as he walked along; on the scale of that plant, it did not seem larger than a tube of toothpaste. All the objects in the plant seemed small, as if observed through the reverse end of an opera glass.

Mosya waved his arms desperately.

"Comrade Korneyev. But in the end . . ."

A large wagonette was moving straight at them. Korneyev and Mosya ran off the rails. The car separated them. On the level of their eyebrows swayed the moulten surface of wet concrete.

Two slick fellows in wide canvas trousers, their backs bare to the belt, their closely cropped hair wet and drooping, pushed against the iron prism of the truck from behind. The muscles on their backs shone like kidney beans.

A spot of concrete fell on the white shoes. Korneyev stopped and carefully wiped it off with his handkerchief. A damp spot still remained. Annoying!

With both hands, Mosya seized his cap as if it were the top of a boiler that was ready to explode from the accumulation of steam.

"Oh!"

A little more and he would accuse Korneyev of being a "Right opportunist in practice." But no! This manner of expression was not suitable for conversation between such a good foreman and such a good superintendent. It must be done some other way.

"Comrade Superintendent," Mosya said tearfully, and at the same time jauntily. "Comrade Superintendent! May I never know happiness again in my life . . . You can strike me if you like . . . Excuse me . . . But—this is a fact! I'll give you three hundred and fifty, and if it should be even one mixture less . . . tear my hat off! The lads guarantee it. Give the order to the second shift, comrade, and you will see!"

Behind them something crashed and clattered: the concrete poured from the wagonette into the opening. They were pouring the flagstone under the oven of the fifth battery.

They walked toward the sixth.

"All right, all right, all right . . ." Korneyev muttered absent-mindedly.

He looked into the distance, hoping to see Margulies, but Margulies was not about. Korneyev began to walk faster.

The scaffolding was being removed from the slab of the sixth battery. The fresh greenish concrete was being revealed. Huge iron hooks were sticking out of it—the ends of the armature. On the scale of the plant they looked like tiny bunches of pins.

VI

THE tortoise waddled on turned-in paws. Its armour was supernatural, high and craggy, like a bowl turned upside down. It had a doleful camel-like face, with whiskers.

The nag walked through the mud, its neck lowered and its bay tail dragging. Its bones stuck out. The lower jaw hung down. From a squinting eye fell a tear, huge, like a wooden spoon.

The bicycle stood on uneven wheels, with an unlikely number of spokes.

The brigade worked in three shifts. Each had its brigadier. That's even how they talked:

"Khanumov's shift."

"Yermakov's shift."

"Ishchenko's shift."

The tortoise, the nag, and the bicycle had a similar landscape for background: fantastically bright ferns, gigantic grass, dwarfish bamboo, a red utopian sun.

Khanumov sat on a tortoise. Yermakov sat backwards on the nag. Ishchenko rode the bicycle.

These pictures of the brigadiers resembled the brigadiers themselves as little as any portrait possibly could. However, Khanumov had a colourful *tyubeteika*;[1] Yermakov, a bright

---

[1] *Tyubeteika*—a Tatar or Tibetan skull-cap.

necktie; and Ishchenko, flagrantly bare feet. And it was this that, like a good epithet, made the resemblance undeniable.

In the midst of this antediluvian landscape, the tortoise and nag looked like symbols of metaphors that had passed anachronistically from Æsop or Krylov[2] into Henri Rousseau's school of new French painting.

But with the bicycle it was different. The bicycle was as antediluvian as a literary detail carried over from a novelette by Paul Morand into a lithograph of an old encyclopædia, representing the flora of the coal period.

These three little pictures, boldly and naïvely colour-washed on bits of cardboard, were nailed with huge carpenter's nails over the entrance to the office of Superintendent Korneyev.

Fresh unplaned boards, which had been quickly knocked together into a small office, stood at a little distance behind the plant. It bore the same relationship to the plant that a launch bears to an ocean steamer.

In the office, the abacus was clicking. The first shift had finished. The second had not yet started. The scaffolders were delaying them. The lads of the first and second shifts sat on the logs calling each other names anent the pictures. Shura's ménage had a reserve of metaphors sufficient to express the most variegated shades of speech.

Shura used them with the disinterested precision of a druggist weighing poison for a prescription. She could have used a snail, an engine, a peasant's cart, an automobile, an airplane—whatever you like. She could resort, moreover, to the negative measure—a crab which crawled backwards,[3] something that, as every one knows, real crabs never do.

However, having conscientiously considered all the indicators for the previous ten days and having compared them with the old, she had chosen the tortoise, the nag and the bicycle.

[2] Ivan Andreyevich Krylov (1768-1844), chiefly famous for his fables, which he began writing in 1805 and which achieved speedy and extensive popularity, is frequently spoken of as the "Russian Æsop."
[3] This is a reference to a fable by Krylov in which a swan, a crab and a pike were competing in a foot race.

This was an absolutely fair estimate. But for eight days now the pictures had offended the eyes of the various shifts. The pictures were changed too rarely, once in ten days. The indicators had changed sharply during the last eight days. Khanumov had marched forward to the extent of one hundred and twenty per cent. Ishchenko was retreating. Yermakov had outstripped Ishchenko and was catching up with Khanumov. Khanumov was already having visions of a metaphorical engine. Yermakov was having visions of at least an automobile.

But the old pictures were still hanging there, deliberately, meting out punishment for the sins of the past. And they would hang there for two days more.

A skinny little chap with an inordinately long nose gazed at the tortoise with hatred. He was from Khanumov's shift.

"Why a tortoise? How could it be a tortoise?" he said, his ribs rising and falling like bellows. "How could it be a tortoise?"

He had already thrown off his canvas overalls, had poured water on himself, but had not yet recovered after work. He sat, his sharp chin resting on his bony knees lifted high, dressed in a pink cotton shirt with open collar and sleeves, his wet hair drooping disconsolately. He spat every minute and licked his thin, pink lips.

"Whoever thought of a tortoise!"

Another one, a gay fellow from Yermakov's shift, in bast shoes and goggles, taunted:

"Those Khanumov boys find it uncomfortable to sit on a tortoise. Rather hard. They are used to automobiles, you see!"

The Khanumov boys interceded for their man:

"And do you find it comfortable to sit on a nag?"

"They have never seen anything but a nag in all their lives!"

"No, that's not true. Last time, they were galloping in a peasant cart!"

"It was you who could not crawl off your snail for twenty days!" the gay fellow retorted. "And everywhere you go, you drag the red banner with you. You are carrying the red banner on a tortoise! Shame on you!"

Others came, crowding around, in bast shoes, barefooted, in overalls, without overalls; in shoes, tow-headed ones, those who had washed themselves; the dirty ones, those covered like millers with the green flour of cement; those with loud voices; the quiet ones; those in light sweaters, in football sweaters, in shirts; Khanumovites, Yermakovites, various ones, but all of them young, all of them with quick shining eyes . . .

"Seriously, how can you talk about a tortoise when we laid ninety cubes in seven hours to-day?"

"But yesterday we laid one hundred and twenty, and the day before ninety-six!"

"Ninety-five!"

"No, no, ninety-six! They lost one cubic foot at the office."

"You spilled it on the way. All the boards are covered, the devil knows how! Concrete costs money."

"You're not paying for it."

"Who is paying for it then?"

"The office pays for it."

"Well, what do you know about that? Did you hear him? That's clever! With such ideas, you'll sit backwards on the nag the rest of your life!"

"Why rub it in about the nag? Get that nag away from here! To hell with it!"

And suddenly:

"If they don't take it away, we won't go to work. Think of it, a nag! While we sat there on the dam in fifty degrees of frost, working with our bare hands!"

And so it went:

"If they don't take it away, we won't go to work!"

"Have you no shame?"

"Enough of that!"

"We won't go!"

"If the rain would only wash away those vile beasts!"

"It never rains here more than twice a year!"

Frowning, Khanumov walked out of the office. He was actually wearing a *tyubeteika*. Exceedingly snub-nosed and exceedingly pock-marked, as if he had been lashed with hail, he was a stocky, red-headed, Arzamass Tatar, yet his eyes were blue. Couldn't tell him from a Russian, except that his cheek bones were a bit more oblique and his legs a bit shorter.

He walked out of the office in new prize-boots, dragging behind him a huge red banner.

Two months previously the Khanumovites had taken by storm the banner that passed from one victorious brigade to another. Since then they had hung on to it with their teeth; they did not take a step without the banner. To work and from work they walked, singing under the banner and, while working, they stuck it into the earth somewhere nearby so that it could be seen. When they went for their pay, the entire shift walked behind the banner. And once they went to the travelling theatre to see "Lyubov' Yarovaya," also under the banner, which had to be placed at the refreshment counter for safe keeping. There it stood throughout the performance, behind a barrel of cranberry kvass.

"So," said Khanumov, in his scarcely discernible Tatar accent, and unfurled the banner. He looked out of the corner of his eye at the tortoise, and struck the black quartz earth with the staff.

"They've licked us twice, and now it's the eighth day that we're sitting on it. And for two more days we'll be a laughing-stock! Very pleasant, I must say!"

His shoulder went up to meet the banner, which he placed there heavily and angrily.

"Fall in, shift!"

The Khanumovites fell in under the banner.

A mechanic ran by, wiping his hands with waste. He was turning the machines over to the Yermakov shift. He threw the waste away, came into the shadow of the banner, and immediately his face became bright pink, like an illumined lampshade.

"Everybody here?"

"Everybody."

"Let's go!"

The shift moved behind Khanumov in a motley crowd.

"Listen, Khanumov. How about Kharkov?" asked a skinny

chap, wiping his forehead with the back of his arm from which
a broad, pink sleeve fell back.

"Don't worry about Kharkov," Khanumov said through his
teeth, without turning. "Kharkov will get what's coming to it!"

At this point, Lusha, a short-legged girl in a full skirt, who
ran a carrier, began to sing with all her might in a clear, piercing
peasant voice:

> "It is good to suffer in spring
> Under a green fir tree."

And the boys joined in with the chorus:

> "You cannot possibly see
> What I have seen.
> You cannot possibly suffer
> As I have suffered."

They returned to the barracks from their work as if they were
marching from the front to the rear. They were lost in the chaos
of black dust, upturned earth, piled materials; suddenly on the
rim of a new hillock they appeared, full-statured, with their song
and their banner.

VII

MARGULIES walked directly from the hotel to the plant.
He squinted against the sun and the dust. The sun smote
the glass of his spectacles. The mirrored reflections flew across
the dusty dry landscape.

Half-way there he met Vasya Vasilyev, a young Communist of
Ishchenko's shift, known as Smetana, and this round, good-
natured quiet chap actually resembled nothing so much as
smetana.[1]

A thin smile touched Margulies's dusty lips. He squinted more

[1] *Smetana*—sour cream.

than ever, and looked inquisitively at Smetana. Behind the thick lenses, Margulies's near-sighted eyes gleamed and stirred like two long, shaggy caterpillars.

"Whither bound, Vasilyev?"

Smetana waved his arm toward the plant.

"Why so early?"

"It's not early," Smetana said evasively.

"When does Ishchenko relieve?" Margulies remarked. "Doesn't he relieve at sixteen?"

"Well, let's say sixteen."

"Isn't it eight now?"

"It's eight."

"Well?"

Once again they looked inquisitively into each other's eyes and smiled. But Margulies's smile was scarcely noticeable on his protuberant mouth, while Smetana smiled so broadly that his ears moved.

"That's a fine how-do-you-do," said Smetana, groaning as he climbed up a hillock.

"Yes, yes," muttered Margulies, stumbling and touching the earth with his fingers as he ascended the incline.

They understood each other perfectly. Margulies understood that the Ishchenkovites already knew about Kharkov and were sending a scout ahead of them to observe developments. Smetana understood that Margulies also knew everything, but had not yet decided, and would say nothing until he had reached a decision.

Every day the appearance of the construction altered sharply. It had changed to such an extent that it was impossible to get anywhere without turning and going in roundabout ways. There were no old roads here. Every day it was necessary to lay new roads as one walked—as if crossing an unexplored region—but the path laid the day before was no good to-day. Where it had climbed a hill yesterday, there was now a hole, and where there had been a hole yesterday, it was cut off to-day by a brick structure.

They ran silently down into the broad trenches, dug during

the night by the excavator. They walked in them as if the trenches were communicating passages, seeing clay around them, the narrow sky above them, and nothing more. Suddenly they stumbled upon deep, dizzying craters. The people on the bottom of these seemed no larger than tacks. And, walking around the top of these craters, they dodged telephone and electric conduits as if they were at the front.

As they walked along the top, Khanumov's shift moved below them with songs and banner.

Smetana looked down on Khanumov's gay *tyubeteika,* on his prize-boots, on the heavy staff of the banner resting upon his lifted shoulder.

"The red-headed devil!" Smetana exclaimed.

Margulies glanced down casually and again his smile was scarcely perceptible. Now everything was clear to him. He knew exactly what Korneyev would tell him and how Mosya would look at him and walk around, swinging his arms . . .

Of course, Semechkin was bound to appear. Nothing could be done without Semechkin.

They had scarcely reached the barbed wire behind Korneyev's office when to the two mirrored reflections that flew in front of Margulies was added a third, reflected from the nickel-plated buckle of a thin brief case. The thin brief case was swinging in the long-veined hand of Semechkin, who had appeared from behind a stack of water pipes.

Semechkin coughed thickly and softly, as if clearing a large Adam's apple, and in severe silence offered his hand to Margulies and Smetana—a cold, clammy hand.

He wore riding breeches and yellow shoes; his shoelaces were tied in a bow; on his thin, pallid face with its scanty growth were large, impenetrably dark, disapproving goggles. Around his lips were scrofulous little pink pimples. A knitted tie in a large brass tie-holder, a grey coat, in the lapel of the coat three badges: the Communist Youth International; the Chemical Aviation Society; and the Sanitary! The back of his cap was cut off, and the visor was as long as the beak of a goose.

They had to make their way across barbed wire which had not been there the day before. Smetana walked along the entanglement, looking for a place to crawl through. Margulies examined one of the posts indecisively. Semechkin stood, feet spread apart, the brief case behind his back, and jerked his knees. He beat himself from behind with the brief case; his knees bobbed up.

Smetana found a suitable place. He pressed the loose lower wire down with his foot, with his hand lifted the next wire and, groaning, crawled through the hole, but caught it with his back and swore as he tore the barbs out of his shirt. Margulies shook the post thoughtfully as if testing its firmness. Semechkin made through his nose a thick noise of dissatisfaction, shrugged his shoulders, ran up, jumped over, tore off the sole of his shoe and, spinning like a top, landed on the other side on all fours. He quickly picked up his brief case and hopped on one foot to the logs.

While he was tying on the sole with a bit of telephone wire, Margulies took hold of the post firmly with his right hand, modestly adjusted his spectacles and his cap with his left hand, and suddenly, without any apparent effort, carried his small broad-backed body across the wire and walked on unhurriedly, clumsily digging up the earth with his sharp toes, to meet Korneyev.

Beside the tortoise, the nag and the bicycle, Shura Soldatava was nailing a new placard with a brick: by a rope, the Kharkovites were pulling a large galosh in which sat Khanumov with his *tyubeteika,* Yermakov with his necktie on, and the bare-footed Ishchenko. The red utopian sun illuminated the antediluvian landscape around the galosh. The galosh had lost its dull significance. The overshoe had become a metaphor.

Under the galosh was written in large blue letters:

"The Kharkovites are towing our concrete men!

"The Kharkovites have set unheard-of tempos. They poured three hundred and six mixtures in one shift, breaking the world's record, while we are sitting in a galosh!

"Shame on you, comrades!"

Shura stood on tiptoe on a stool, biting her lips and nailing the placard with a brick.

Margulies passed her and read the placard in a flash. He smiled. Shura struck her finger with the brick. She blushed deeply, but she did not turn around and she did not stop hammering.

Nearby lay a pile of roofing. The sun burned the roofing and the pine boards of the plant. A bitter burning odour of creosote and turpentine rose from it. The odour of lilacs. Perhaps it was too burning and too strong for real lilac. Perhaps it was too chemical. And still the hot wind blew. It was morning. The dust was flying. Papers were swirling in a carnival at the plant. And it smelled strongly and bitterly, albeit chemically, of lilac.

Margulies went into Korneyev's office for a moment—to examine the accounts.

VIII

KORNEYEV took a mug from the window sill and dipped some water out of the board-covered bucket. He drank avidly. The water tasted of medicated bandage. The water system was temporary. The water was chlorinated. Korneyev had long ago become accustomed to the drug-store taste of chlorinated water. He no longer noticed it. He walked up to Margulies, shoved his cap on the back of his head, revealing a sweaty forehead with a white spot left by the visor.

"Well, what do you think about it?"

"About what?" Margulies asked absent-mindedly.

"About Kharkov."

Without raising his thick eyebrows from the papers, Margulies struck himself anxiously on the side. He took a paper bag from his coat pocket. The lining of the pocket turned out like a calico ear. Earth fell out, and little stones. Without looking up, Margulies proffered the bag to Korneyev.

"Here, try some . . . Candied things . . . Yesterday at the refreshment stand. Taste very good. Melon, I think."

Korneyev tasted and approved.

Margulies put five pieces into his mouth, one after the other.

Mosya was hanging around the door. With an impatience that
approached hatred, he looked at Margulies's long fingers, which
slowly took the candy out of the bag like pincers. Margulies
carefully licked the tips of his fingers.

"I haven't eaten anything yet to-day," he said apologetically.
"Try some, Mosya. Three rubles a pound. Not bad."

Mosya came up politely and looked into the bag with one
eye, like a bird.

"Go on, take some."

He's trying to shut me up with candy, Mosya thought angrily.
But he contained himself. He managed to force a smile on his
broad face with its high cheek bones, a smile as sweet and shining as the candied peel he took out.

"Comrade Margulies . . . I give you my honest,. honourable
word . . . May I never see my own mother again! May I never
see my little brothers and sisters again! Give the order to the
second shift!"

He looked pleadingly at Korneyev.

"Comrade Superintendent, back me up!"

Korneyev walked rapidly twice around the room. The room
was so small that these two rounds appeared to be no more than
two turns of a key.

"Really, David, we must decide. You can see for yourself, the
boys are losing their minds."

"Decidedly so," Mosya corroborated. "The boys are losing
their minds! You can see for yourself, Comrade Margulies. Give
the order to Yermakov!"

Korneyev abruptly pushed a stool under him and sat down
beside Margulies.

"Well, what do you think, David?"

"About what?"

Korneyev wiped his forehead with the palm of his hand.

Margulies's arm hung in mid-air. He forgot to lower it. He was interested exclusively in the accounts. He was being distracted by extraneous questions. The paper bag swayed in his hand.

Mosya ran out of the office. The devil take it, this was too much! He would do it at his own risk, without Margulies! This was a matter of honour, of fame, of prowess, while that fellow stuck his eyebrows into those lousy accounts which had been audited a thousand times, and sat there like a log! No! He would go straight to the boys, straight to Yermakov! You couldn't do anything with a fellow like this Margulies.

Mosya was boiling and he could not contain himself. He was ready to bite.

Mosya had been born in Batoum, a romantic city full of swooning colonial odours: a city of palms, fezzes, bamboo chairs, foreign sailors, smugglers, oil, scarlet shoes, malaria; in the Russian sub-tropics where buffaloes sit in hot mud up to their necks, thrusting forth bearded faces, with dreamy bundles of horns flung across their shoulders; where lacquered Turkish mountains are covered with threadbare rugs of tea plantations; where at night hyenas howl nearby; where through samite groves thunders the shot of the border guard; where the railroad branch leading to a summer resort grows along the sea, suddenly transformed into a banana branch, under which the woman at the station sits on a zinc bucket selling sunflower seeds and tangerines; where the Adjarian sun burns people as a potter burns his pots, giving them colour, sound, hardness. . . .

Mosya had the violent temperament of a southerner, and the not entirely faultless biography of a gamin who had seen all sorts of things in the course of his twenty-three years. He had arrived at the construction three months before, declaring that he had lost his documents on the road. At the office of the construction superintendent, no one had expressed any surprise on this score.

He was sent to the sector.

The first night he spent in a tent on a hill. He looked down from the hill upon sixty-five square kilometres of earth, covered with lights. He began to count them, counted five hundred and forty-six and gave up.

He stood bewitched, like a tramp before the show window of a jewelry store in a strange city at night. The lights were breathing, giving off an aureole, gleaming and flowing like fame. Fame lay on the earth. It was only necessary to stretch forth a hand.

Mosya stretched forth his hand.

For two weeks he rolled a sterling; for two weeks he ran a concrete mixer. He displayed unusual ability. In a month he was made a foreman; he refused to take any days off. His name was never off the red board [1] of the sector. The red board became his fame.

But this was too little. His violent temperament could not be satisfied with such modest fame. Mosya slept, and in his dreams he saw his name printed in "Izvestya." He saw the medal of the Banner of Labor on his breast. With passionate insistence he dreamed of some spectacular deed, of some resounding event, of some exceptional opportunity.

Now he was confronted with this exceptional opportunity: to establish a world's record in pouring concrete. And this—this world record—might be made during the shift of some other foreman. This thought brought him to despair and fury. It seemed to him that time was flying, outstripping itself. Time was making an hour every minute. Every minute threatened the loss of opportunity and of fame.

The evening before, Yermakov had scratched his cheek on an armature wire. The iron was rusty; the wound was festering. His temperature rose; his cheek was swollen.

Yermakov came on duty with a bandaged head. He was very tall. The white bulb of his bandaged head could be seen on the platform. He was examining the drum of the concrete mixer. The shift was surrounding the platform, ready for work. It was eight

---

[1] On the *red* board are inscribed the names of workers who perform unusual feats; on the *black* board, the names of those who disgrace themselves.

o clock. The scaffolders were pounding the final nails. The armature-men were removing the wire.

Mosya's face was shining like a chestnut.

"Well, how's it going?" Yermakov said indistinctly through the bandage that covered his lips. With difficulty he turned his head, swathed in bandages, which resembled a diver's helmet. The bandage covered his eyes. Through the loose texture of the gauze, Yermakov could see the stuffy, fleecy world of a sooty sun and cotton clouds.

"Well, this is what we'll have to do, boys . . ."

Mosya caught his breath.

"Here!"

Quickly and in a business-like way, he thrust forth his hand, raising the large finger like a trigger. There was still time for self-control. But he lacked the strength. The spring flew off the trigger. Mosya was carried away. With his thievish eyes sparkling, he was speaking helter-skelter, licking his lips, terrifying himself by what he was saying:

"Comrades, definitely . . . Kharkov has established a world's record . . . three hundred and six mixtures in one shift . . . it's a fact . . . we must declare definitely and as a matter of principle . . . inasmuch as our management is asleep . . . am I talking sense? We'll beat Kharkov any way we can! I guarantee three hundred and fifty mixtures on my own responsibility! Well, Yermakov, confirm it: will we make three hundred and fifty, or won't we? Even if our noses bleed! Why not? Is there any doubt about it? No use talking . . . I propose a counter-plan . . . Three hundred and fifty and not one mixture less! Those in favour? . . . Opposed? . . ."

Mosya looked around quickly out of the corner of his eye and choked. Korneyev and Margulies were walking rapidly toward the bridge.

They drew near.

Mosya shrank. A wily smile flashed across his face. It grew lop-eared, like the smile of a school-boy caught in the act. He pulled his cap over his eyes with both hands and spun like a top in one place, as if avoiding blows. Nevertheless he had time to shout:

"... inasmuch as the management shuts us up with candy ..."

"What's the matter?" Margulies asked.

Mosya stopped and pulled up his trousers.

"Comrade Margulies," he said in a dashing manner, "inasmuch as Kharkov made three hundred and six, this shift proposes a counter-plan: three hundred and fifty and not one mixture less. Back me up, boys! No use talking about it! Comrade Sector-chief, give the order!"

Margulies listened attentively.

"Is that all?" he asked indifferently.

"That's all."

"So."

Margulies put the paper bag in his pocket, carefully dusted the powdered sugar from his hands, wiping one with the other like a fly, climbed up on the bridge beside Yermakov, and silently began to examine the drum. He examined it long and thoroughly. He took off his spectacles, rolled up his sleeves, and crawled into the drum head first.

"Well, how's your cheek?" he asked Yermakov, after he had finished the inspection.

"It twitches."

"Feverish?"

"It burns."

"You'd better stay home to-day; otherwise ..."

Margulies carefully rolled down his sleeves, jumped lightly down from the bridge, and went into the plant. With the same thoroughness with which he had examined the machine, he now examined the scaffolding. He tested the stability of the arma-ture, tapped the boards with his fist, made a remark to the senior carpenter, and went all the way through the entire plant.

Mosya dragged behind him step by step.

"Comrade Margulies," he whined. "What will we do?"

"Why, what's the matter?"

"About Kharkov. Give us the order."

"Give an order to whom? What order?"

Margulies's eyes were wandering near-sightedly, absent-mindedly.

"Give the order to Yermakov to beat Kharkov."

"Yermakov cannot beat Kharkov."

"What do you mean he can't? Oho, three hundred and fifty mixtures, or tear my hat off!"

"Three hundred and fifty mixtures? How many cubes will that make?"

"Let's say, two hundred and sixty."

"And how many cubes does Yermakov need to fill up the tower?"

"Let's say—eighty."

"Good. Suppose you make eighty cubes, fill up the tower, and then where will you pour the rest of the concrete? On the ground?"

"Then we'll pour the flagstone under the fifth battery."

"And don't you have to move the concrete-mixer to the fifth battery?"

"Well, yes."

"Water, current, planking; how much time will that take?"

"Let's say, two hours, maximum."

"Minimum," Margulies corrected severely. "But granting you are right, how can Yermakov beat Kharkov when he has only six hours' clear work, and he needs eight? Well?"

Mosya flung down his cap and scratched his head.

"What time is it?" Margulies asked.

Korneyev pulled out his watch.

"Ten minutes past eight."

"The second shift is ten minutes late," Margulies said drily.

"Keep it in mind, thirty mixtures an hour and no more," he said with more than his usual indifference, and with a handkerchief he wiped off his shoe on which a new red spot had appeared. "Do you hear, Mosya? No more than thirty mixtures."

Korneyev pronounced the Russian word for mixture—*zamyes*—

as if it were the Spanish surname *Zamess,* with a hard flat *e*—as if referring to some one called Don Diego Z' Am Ess.

"Yes," Mosya called out lustily.

He ran at a trot to the brigade, swinging his arms before him. Fame had moved away for eight hours. Fame was slipping out of his hands. There remained the last hope—Ishchenko.

"David, I don't understand you," said Korneyev when Mosya had disappeared.

Margulies took him by the elbow, tenderly but firmly.

"Come on, let's have some tea. I haven't had anything yet."

IX

ISHCHENKO slept on top of the quilt, face downward, his arms spread out and his small bare feet tucked under him. He slept in the position of a man crawling. Overcome by sleep, his head drooped, yet its shock of hair did not touch the pillow. Illumined by the sun, the red unwrinkled quilt filled the partition of the barrack with a rosy glow.

The brigadier was dressed in new, black, cloth trousers and a new, white Ukrainian shirt, embroidered in cross-stitch. One of his sleeves had fallen back. A bare arm hung from the cot. Its outside was dark, its inside light and fat like the belly of a fish. It revealed a tattoo—the round stamp of a steering wheel. The tattoo was a misty gunpowder blue.

The evening before, quite unexpectedly, Fyenya had come to Ishchenko. As a present she had brought him the shirt and trousers.

The train had arrived at six instead of at two. The nearer it came to the place, the slower it went. Fyenya had entirely lost patience. At every crossing, they stopped to let other trains pass. She had spent four nights in the car. The first night she slept virtually not at all, through worrying. The second and third nights she managed to doze off somehow. On the fourth night she was restless again, overcome with terror. Only God knew where she had come to! To the end of the world! And what was in store for her there?

And yet people were saying that four days from Moscow wasn't so bad, a mere trifle, not so far off. One could ride for ten days and still not come to the end; to get to the end, one must ride twelve days, and where was that end, where was that Vladivostok?

The country was so big it could drive one mad.

At crossings, past the windows rolled trains filled with bluish-rusty ore. Huge rainbow-like bits shook on the flat cars. Just try to push a piece like that! You couldn't budge it. It was pig-iron. The trains coming from the opposite direction were filled with tare—mountains of empty barrels, hoops, sacks, burlap. Other trains overtook them, bearing long piles of red lumber, trucks, auto buses, cisterns: sealed cars with white German inscriptions—long, neat, not like our freight cars that had to return to Stolbtsy, Bigosovo . . .

The new branch went in one direction. That direction was not enough; they began a second.

Along the shaky road-bed lay yellow scraps of freshly-dug virgin soil. Tiny horses stood on the bottom of the broad trenches. Diggers from Chernigov, in lamb-skin hats despite the heat, flung the fresh soil by shovelfuls into wagons. Their robes were piled together and hung over the earthen posts left in the middle of each excavation. The summer before Fyenya had worked with the diggers. She knew that those posts served to measure how much ground had been removed—the measure of artel labour.

She liked those little posts. This is what she thought of them:

There was a steppe. A mound. Grass was growing. Fragrant wild flowers bloomed. For a hundred years and perhaps even longer the mound had stood on the steppe.

But then diggers suddenly arrived, threw off their clothes, spat on the palms of their hands, and as soon as they saw the little mound they removed it! Only one little column of earth remained in the middle of the trench. And this little column would stand

there as an untouched bit of the steppe until the very end of
the work.

On top was grass. A bush of spurge. Above, two cabbage butterflies. The butterflies flitted one round the other as if they were
tied together by a short piece of thread.

The cleft soil glistened with the traces of the shovel that had
been struck into it. From top to bottom it passed from one tone
to another. At first was black soil, black as tar. Then a bit
lighter, brighter, and finally clay as red as the ochre and red
lead with which village ikon painters, under the old régime,
painted in the churches devils and the Patagonian tongues of the
fiery gehenna. Fyenya was travelling to the city. The vague address was written on a soft piece of paper with an indelible pencil: city so-and-so.

But people around her were already beginning to tie up their
belongings, to hurry, to clear the benches, and still she could see
no city. The yellow hillocks were stretching away as before, littered with shovels and gloves. It was as hot and stuffy as ever.
As the strange steppe flitted by, clouds hobbled across it. Far
to one side in the distance a nomad tent swam by, as if it were a
tyubeteika thrown into the feather-grass.

The branches of recently set out birch trees flew by, kilometre
after kilometre, disappearing in the ditch under the hillock, constantly running away. Some of them had not taken root, had
wilted, had dried up. Others had been thrown down by the storm.
Still others had been broken by passing hooligans. (People were
working hard, carting them, transplanting them, irrigating them.
. . . What criminals . . . simply wolves!) And yet neither the
sun nor the storms nor the hooligans could destroy the young
greenness. The little leaves turned with the wind, shining, like
the palms of babes. The thin, white arms and necks stretched far
and tenderly.

Where did Fyenya get this tenderness, this pity, this joy?

Fyenya thrust her head out of the window. The dry wind
fluttered the hair around her comb. Her hair had become very
dusty on the road. She would have to wash it. As soon as she

arrived, the first thing she would do would be to wash it. She thrust her head out the window and with the unbending ring finger lifted the hair from her wet nose. There were tears in her eyes. The steppe swam through the tears, and far ahead of her, far, far away, the hills.

She had not seen them before. Only now did they appear. In the distance they were blue, low, long. Nearby they were sloping, each a special colour, one green, one rusty, one blue. At the foot of the middle one, something stood in the steppe, something like a small cube. They came closer and it was no longer a cube, but a zinc box, placed there on end. At the front, bullets were transported in such boxes.

However, the steppe deceived her eyes. One could not tell immediately whether the thing that stood in the steppe was large or small.

When they came still closer, this zinc box suddenly covered a quarter of the steppe and half the sky. In the growing darkness of the car, it became a huge elevator about eight storys high. The people who walked beneath it were quite tiny.

Beside it stood a tractor on sharp-edged wheels as if on tip-toe, diving over the billowy new road like a toy.

And the tractor was not small, either—a Caterpillar with a chimney and a roof and a van it was dragging behind it, a van the size of a house.

Nearby one could see a large collective farm or a state farm. This picture was familiar to Fyenya: on the grey trampled earth, iron barrels of fuel, fire extinguishers, planed wood, tar, milk cans. (Must be cows here, too.)

Now they had gone further, approaching the very edge of the mountains.

At another car window, his finger clutching the ring of a frame that had been lowered, stood a bony old intellectual in steel-rimmed spectacles and boots. He was a bookkeeper. He had boarded the train at Kazan. He had not left the window throughout the journey. He would thrust his head forward and look out over his spectacles. The wind fluttered his grey hair. The old man kept still most of the time. He would be silent for a spell (and the spell would be very long), looking ahead, and then suddenly he would turn around toward the car, raise his spectacles over his grey eyebrows, and say something.

"Here is a nice 'pull along, grey mare.' " [1]

Or, "This is real Russia! This is peasant Russia—Nekrasov's Russia!"

And then he would laugh in his bass voice.

"Take a long look, ho, ho, ho!"

And through the dirty spectacles, one could see tears in his eyes. And again he would return to the window.

He would see everything there: where a tractor was flung, a new elevator, a new caravan of auto buses, the church where there was a flag instead of a cross, or an automobile being unloaded at a half-way station. What was remarkable about it all? And yet he would look at it as if he were seeing it for the first time. A strange fellow he was, but everybody in the car respected him. He had lost two sons in the Red Army, and the month before a train had run over his wife. He had been left entirely alone, and now he was going to the new construction as an office clerk, to start a new life. The suitcase and a teapot and a pencil in the pocket of his coat represented all his possessions.

Suddenly he turned to Fyenya and cried out:

"Here's the desert for you, and here's Pugachov [2] for you! Eh? Just look at that! That's something!"

The train stopped about four kilometres from the mountain. What was the matter? Nothing. They had arrived.

[1] A quotation from one of Nekrasov's poems.

Nikolai Alexeyevich Nekrasov (1821-1877), one of the first professional literary men of Russia, a poet, critic, and editor of first rank, a courageous radical who staunchly championed the cause of the oppressed peasants in verse that has subsequently gained recognition for high literary excellence.

[2] Emelyan Pugachov, a fugitive Kazak, at the age of thirty organised a wide-spread rebellion of peasants, Kazaks, religious dissenters, nomadic tribesmen and other discontented elements, against the government of Catherine II. The movement spread, principally over Southeastern Russia, from 1773 to 1775, terminating with Pugachov's public execution in Moscow.

The stout doors of the cars were flung open. People stumbled over the high spittoons, dragging their belongings. Dust was columns high.

No station was visible. They had simply stopped along the way. There were six road beds, and back and forth along them trains were moving, clanking. Through the trains one could see the environs: barracks, tents, fences, boxes, horses, lathes, trucks. And the same steppe was to be seen, dry, hot, trampled, without a single blade of grass.

Everybody left the car. Last of all came Fyenya. It was very difficult to get down from the high step directly to the road bed. It was still more difficult to lift the bag from the high step. Her head swirled.

"Where is the station? Comrades, please! Where is the station?"

"What station? This is the station—where you're standing. Where do you expect it to be?"

"Comrade . . ."

He went on. He was in a hurry. He was carrying baggage on his shoulder.

Fyenya turned to another.

"Please, where is the station?"

But the other was also in a hurry. In his hands he was carrying a large plant in a pot. He was afraid of breaking it, and the plant was heavy. It weighed about forty pounds, with large dark green leaves and an unopened bud, the size of a pepper pod.

"There is no station! How could there be a station?"

He did not even look back, but went on.

"Oh, my God, they even bring potted plants with them! Where will he go with it?"

Boxes were being flung out of the baggage car, one, another, a third . . . six boxes.

"Careful with the boxes, you'll spoil the charts! There are charts in those boxes! Take them sideways!"

Fyenya put her bag on the rails. She drew a deep breath. A brakeman passed by. She turned to him.

"Comrade, where is the city, please?"

"Here is the city. Where else could it be?"

Where could the city be? There was nothing around that bore the semblance of a city, neither churches nor stores, nor street cars, nor stone houses! Where was she to go?

But no one answered Fyenya any more. Everybody was running, hurrying, dragging baggage across the rails, calling for transport wagons.

"Look out, auntie, don't stand in the way! Can't you see the train is coming?"

My! What was going on here? She just managed to drag the bag across the rail; otherwise, she would have landed under the wheel. And she sat down in a ditch.

The sun went behind the clouds. The sultriness did not diminish. Evening fell. The wind brought swarms of brown dust. Dirt, papers, earth, flew into one's face. The earth was coarse and acrid, like cheap tobacco.

All around her everything smoked, floated, flickered, tortured her.

X

ON the bit of paper was written: City so-and-so. The office of the new construction. Ask for Brigadier Ishchenko at the masonry. Fyenya had learned this by heart.

It had seemed that nothing could be simpler. However, things didn't turn out so simply.

They had ridden and ridden. Finally they had arrived. They had stopped in the steppe, but there was no city. She peered through the dust, and now there was no steppe either. She couldn't understand it: neither steppe nor city. And she could see no new construction. There was nothing but dust, and in the dust were crooked telephone poles. A huge, stuffy, deserted place. Occasionally, barracks, tents, offices of various sectors, trucks, boxes, cows, wagons. And all this was flung about in all directions, scattered, as if it were wandering helter-skelter over a burned, trampled space of immeasurable and illimitable width.

Now and then things would clear up. Then for a moment she could see a crane, or perhaps a bridge, or something long and very far away, that looked somewhat like reeds. And then it would immediately disappear, buried by the drab cloud of a sandstorm. How could she find Ishchenko there in the midst of the immeasurable, the illimitable that looked like nothing she had ever seen before? Whither should she turn? Whom should she ask? Where could she find out?

She went to offices. There were many offices. Everywhere she inquired on which sector he was working.

What do you mean on which sector? Brigadier Ishchenko, Konstantin Yakovlevich, is pouring concrete. That's very simple.

No, others would say, we have several thousand brigadiers on this construction, and we have perhaps between forty-five and fifty thousand common workers as well.

She walked from one sector to another, and one sector was two or three kilometres from the next. There were all kinds of sectors—sectors of construction and sectors of habitation.

At the construction sectors everything was dug up—rails, ties, posts. Here you couldn't pass; there you couldn't crawl over; or right across the road would be the mound of the terrific drop of an excavation; or she would tear her skirt against the barbed wire; or a sentry would not let her go any further; or a truck, or a train.

At the habitation sectors stood rows of barracks, and not only two or three rows of them, but ten rows—huge, long barracks, all alike; occasionally, tents; occasionally, sod huts—also large and also all alike. She wandered among them like a lost soul.

She would leave her bag with good people, asking them to watch it for her, with tears in her eyes, and then she would go on and could not find anything, and would return breathless, wet, tired, with smudgy nose and eyes, wind-burned until her face was red.

She would take the bag and go to another sector. On the road she would sit down on the bag and weep. Thus she rested.

Evening began. It began, but it somehow stopped. It was neither day nor night. It was neither light nor dark. Only the grey dust swept all around, and through the dust, the moulten ray of the sunset lingered and faded slowly.

Her shoulder felt numb, dead. Her back hurt frightfully. Her neck was so stiff that she could not turn her head, and a terrific weight pulled at her loins.

Oh, if only something would happen soon; if she could fall asleep, if she could find him, if she could go back to the train, if she could have a drink of cold water!

Finally she happened to meet some people from her home town, from Kiev. They came to her rescue.

At night, Ishchenko had returned from the shift to the barracks. Fyenya was sitting on his cot. He saw her at once, but did not recognise her, and did not realise who she was, or why she had come there.

She recognised him at once.

He walked at the head of his lads, wearing a dark soiled shirt that hung over his canvas trousers—a short, stocky fellow, his broad shoulders drooping, walking mincingly over the boards of the floor on tenacious little bare feet.

She sat motionless; the shawl had dropped to her knees, and her arms had dropped to her shawl.

He saw the large bag and the light dusty hair which flew around the steel combs.

She looked at his round head, his bare, dark neck and his tin goggles, pushed back over the shock of hair. She wanted to rise, but could not. She wanted to say something, but her teeth chattered. From the lamp that hung in the middle of the barrack, bright sheaves of light flickered and sputtered in all directions. Fyenya clutched a corner of the shawl with her fingers.

Ishchenko looked at her coarse fingers and the silver ring, at the shawl, and suddenly he remembered its fringe of pink yarn. He understood and sat down carefully on his cot beside Fyenya.

She continued to tremble, shivering frequently. She did not remove her desperate blue eyes from him. He saw very close to him her frightfully emaciated, familiar, and yet unrecognisable face, the hideous yellow blotches and purple streaks of tears. He saw her distended stomach and was horrified.

But immediately a new emotion that he had never experienced before, an emotion of masculine pride, possessed him. This new warm emotion pushed everything else aside.

Across his shoulder, Ishchenko tossed his head to the lads, indicating Fyenya.

"Hello," he said. "Welcome! You found the most appropriate time."

And he smiled at Fyenya crookedly but tenderly. She understood this smile.

"Kostichka," she muttered. "Oi, Kostichka! Oi, Kostichka . . ."

And she could say no more. She grasped his shoulders firmly with her shaking hands, put her wet face on his chest, and, embarrassed by the strangers, wept softly.

The lads were very tired. However, there was nothing to be done. This might happen to anybody. No one went to bed.

While Fyenya wept, while Ishchenko patted her shoulder and asked her questions, while she importantly pulled the present out of her bag, while she washed up and wobbled into the hallway, the lads silently dragged in some planks, some nails, and an electric cord. . . . In an hour or two, Ishchenko was separated from them.

For the time being, Fyenya hung a shawl over the entrance.

All through the night, until the crack of dawn, the lamp burned in this family apartment. Ishchenko and Fyenya spoke in hot, intense whispers so as not to awaken the brigade.

And at seven o'clock in the morning Fyenya was already on her way to the neighbours to borrow a bread-trough.

"You lie down, Kostichka; you lie down, Kostichka, and rest," she whispered, beating up the pillow in its new red cover. "Sleep

and don't worry, Kostichka. Don't think of anything, Kostichka. . . ."

He only mumbled in answer. Sleep overcame him. And thus
he fell asleep, as he was, in his new trousers and shirt which had
been brought as a gift by Fyenya, and the shock of his hair did
not touch the pillow case.

And as for her, she went about as if nothing unusual had happened. She was possessed by a passionate, impatient desire to
rearrange everything as soon as possible, to wash the dirty linen,
to put things in order, to go down to the co-operative store, exchange coupons, scrub the floor, cook the dinner, wash the windows, put a shade over the lamp, find the free market around
here, lay out all the things, place things on the shelf.

She was in high spirits and was only afraid that somehow
she would not have time to rearrange everything, that she might
forget something that was indispensable.

She hurried to the neighbours, quickly, quickly; apologised;
asked for the trough; lit the stove; went to the co-operative store;
walked on tiptoe behind the partition; arranged things on the
table, and with a thread cut the soap. She felt as if she had
lived on this construction, in this barrack, all her life.

She smiled at the neighbours' children, exchanged banter with
a resting brigade; her tired eyes shone. With some old women
she went again to the co-operative, stood in line before the
cashier. And all of this she did quickly, quickly, with desperate
haste, with an insatiable thirst for work, with a secret fear of
something that must inevitably happen to her.

XI

SMETANA looked carefully behind the partition. Ishchenko
was asleep. Smetana did not like to awaken the brigadier.
Smetana entered and sat down on a stool beside the cot. The
brigadier slept. Smetana put his elbows on his knees and with

his hands seized his white head which was as round as a ball and seemed to be covered with plush.

A roasting sun beat through the window. Flies, flying out of the darkness, scratched along the blinding strip, caught fire in it like matches, and immediately went out, flying again into the twilight.

Smetana waited one minute, then another.

"I must wake him. It can't be helped."

He shook Ishchenko's firm shoulder that had become sweaty in sleep.

"Hey, boss!"

Ishchenko groaned.

"Get up!"

The brigadier lay like an oak. Smetana smiled broadly, tickled the soles of his feet. Ishchenko jumped quickly and sat up, curling his feet under him. He looked at Smetana, with sour, uncomprehending eyes in his swollen, pink, childish, capricious face.

"Stop playing the fool, Vasilyev!" he said hoarsely, and with his sleeve wiped his mouth and chin, which were wet with the saliva that had run down.

Vasilyev gave him a mug of water.

"Here, wake up!"

Ishchenko gulped down the water, and instantly came to.

"Hello, Smetana."

He knitted his brows solemnly.

"Well, how are things going? What's the latest news?"

Smetana turned his head.

"A lot of talk."

"Aha, and who talks the most?"

"They all talk the same. They've hung up a poster. We are in a *galosh* and Kharkov is pulling us by a rope."

"That's rather silly. Have you seen Margulies?"

"Yes."

"Well?"

"Margulies is—slippery."

"Does he say anything definite?"

"I'm telling you—he's slippery."

Ishchenko looked with dissatisfaction at the window which was unusually clean. He knew very well all Margulies's ways.

"Did Yermakov take his place?" he asked after a moment of thought.

"He did. They began at eight. They're filling up the last tower."

"Are they pouring fast?"

"As usual. Margulies does not permit more than thirty mixtures an hour."

"Naturally, without preparation. Roughly, how many cubes must they pour into this tower?"

"About eighty cubes."

"And then?"

"Then a new job. They'll put the machine at the fifth battery, and waste about three hours. This and that. And at sixteen o'clock we begin. Well?"

The brigadier inspected the entire partition pensively—the clean tablecloth on the table, the washed dishes, the wavy mirror on the planked wall, the shawl in the doorway, and, smiling, winked at Smetana.

"How do you like this business? I was a bachelor, and suddenly I'm married. I even expect an increase in my family. How do you like that?"

In embarrassment, he wound a shock of his hair on his brown index finger, and then slowly unwound it.

And suddenly, with a quick flash of his brown eyes:

"Have you seen Khanumov?"

"Yes, of course. He marched ahead of his brigade, across the entire construction, under the banner, and in his prize-boots. Looked exactly like an army commander, the red-headed devil!"

"And what do the boys from the other brigade say about him?"

"They're not saying anything. They're sure that it will be nobody else but he who will beat Kharkov."

"Nobody else?"

"Nobody else."

"And so they really think it will be he?"

"That's what they think."

Ishchenko reddened, turned away and senselessly began to look for something on the window sill.

"And Mosya?"

"Mosya is just about ready to dig the ground with his nose."

Ishchenko could not find his goggles. He swore, knocked the stool over with his knees, and ran out into the street.

Shura's boys were already nailing a poster with the *galosh* to the outside of the barrack.

Ishchenko pretended not to see.

"Hey, boss, look here!" the boys cried. "Here! We drew it especially for you! Don't you turn away!"

From under knitted brows the brigadier looked across his shoulder at the poster.

"You can hang it on Khanumov's back," he said quietly. "We have no use for it."

He dropped his head, thrust his neck forward, and walked like a bull, bucking the wind and the dust, walking with mincing bare feet over the hard earth. Smetana caught up with him.

"Where are you going?"

"To the sector, of course."

He stopped.

"Listen, Smetana. In the meanwhile, you find out how the brigade feels about it. Understand?"

"Good."

"Feel them out and find out how things stand."

Smetana instantly turned back.

Near the barracks stood a turnstile. Smetana ran up, leapt quickly, caught a post, rose on his outstretched arms, flung his head back, blinking against the sun, and suddenly, breaking into halves, he quickly whirled over the taut wire. His sandals and his bare, cream-white back flashed.

Out of his pocket, copper coins, buttons, pencils, pens and meal-tickets flew in all directions.

XII

THEY walked across the sector for a long time, looking for
a suitable place. The morning was kindling. Zagirov dragged
himself like a dog after Sayenko. Every minute he would touch
the warm buckle of Sayenko's quilted, sleeveless jacket, and ask
plaintively:

"Listen, Kolya. Why are we going so far? Let's sit down here.
What's the matter?"

Without turning, Sayenko would reply:

"Nothing's the matter. Come on."

The wind changed its direction and quieted down. From the
east, huge swaths of sultry air winnowed the dryness of the
steppes. The closely-grouped clouds streamed in blue wavy
shadows from hilltop to hilltop, from barrack to barrack. Black,
flat, tarred roofs quivered, steaming in the sun, as if ether had
been poured on them.

Behind the plant there were too many flies, horse flies, and
people were passing all the time. Near the road, the brown dust
which stood in a translucent wall from heaven to earth was sultry, too stuffy. Under the railroad bridge was the frequent thunder
of trains. In the mountains, ore was being dynamited, and heavy
chunks flew about.

They might have gone to the lake, but that was too far away,
not less than five kilometres. Zagirov followed Sayenko meekly.

Yesterday, Zagirov had lost all of his savings to Sayenko—one
hundred and fifteen rubles. He had gone to the savings bank
several times with his little book. He had taken almost everything out. Only one ruble remained in the savings bank book.
They had played all day on the mountain, and all night under
the lamp post behind the barrack. They had forgotten to go to
the shift. Zagirov had no more money.

One hundred and fifteen rubles!

Zagirov had been overwhelmed by his bad luck. At first he

had even wept. He had walked away, his head drooping, sat on his haunches against the planked wall and with his fist spread several muggy tears over his cheek bones. Then, suddenly, he had been possessed by senseless anxiety.

He ran over the sector from pillar to post, seeking to borrow a ten-spot. No one would give it to him. Then he went to the barrack and took out his most precious possessions—a pair of large black shoes, new galoshes, two suits of knitted underwear and a cap he had never worn.

He proposed to play for these things. He had entreated. Sayenko agreed unwillingly.

With the articles under his arm, Zagirov dragged after his comrade, trembling with impatience, overwhelmed, beaten, loudly swallowing his saliva. And Sayenko, as if to spite him, kept putting him off. He didn't like *this* place, he didn't like *that* place. Finally he selected a place. It was the graveyard of broken machinery.

The friends crawled through the barbed wire. Everywhere lay the iron skeletons of wrecked machines. Rusty stairs of transports stood on their hind legs, leaning against the hobbled sterlings. An excavator had placed its long beheaded neck on an overturned wagonette. All over were severed wheels, pinions, bolts, the military helmets of projectors, and the chopped torsos of boilers.

They sat down under the wagonette.

"Well, let's go," said Zagirov. "Come on, Kolya, the cards!"

Sayenko lay down on his back, spread apart his feet in their bast shoes, and put his arms under his head. He lazily moved his eyes.

"Shush, there's lots of time. Sit down, Tatar. You'll make it yet."

He took a notebook from inside his shirt. It was wrapped in a grey rag. He unwound it and laid it on his chest. In the notebook was an indelible pencil. Sayenko wetted it. Lilac aniline ran down his large wet mouth.

He lay with his painted mouth as if he had been poisoned, staring dreamily and steadily at the sky with his violet eyes and metallic pupils.

His face was a triangle. Under his ear gleamed the bright red spot of a sore. His thin sharp nose was transparent; the blueness of its cartilage was unhealthy.

For a long time he lay without moving. Suddenly he jumped up, flung himself on his stomach, stuck his shaggy head into the notebook and spread his elbows apart. He carefully drew large scrawls on the grey page graphed with lines of various colours. He puffed, laughed, jumped on all fours, struck his elbows against the earth. Zagirov looked at him in horror. He fell, twitched, the lilac saliva foaming on his lips, as if he were in an epileptic fit.

"Wait, wait!" he cried, breathless. "I'll lose the verse. Go away. Don't stand in my way or I'll kill you!"

Suddenly he quieted down. He rolled up the notebook, and stuck it inside his shirt. He sat down and regarded his companion with his muggy eyes.

"Well, let's see it," he said somnolently.

Zagirov spread the things before him.

Sayenko took the creaking galoshes, measured them against his bast shoes, and laid them aside.

"They don't fit. Too small. Well, all right. Three rubles. What else have you?"

Zagirov wiped the shoes with his sleeves and offered them. Sayenko did not even pick them up. He glanced at them out of the corner of his eye.

"Three rubles."

Zagirov smiled ingratiatingly.

"What are you saying, Kolya! These are very good shoes. I paid twelve seventy-five for them at the co-operative!"

Sayenko looked aside and whistled indifferently.

"Three rubles."

"But they're brand-new! I've never worn them."

"Three rubles."

A fine dew appeared on Zagirov's bumpy forehead. His brown eyes narrowed, slanting more than ever. His lips trembled.

"Are you joking, Kolya? Be human!"

"Well, what do you think I am, a dog? Don't get fresh. I'm not sitting on you. Take your truck and go away. I don't need it. Go back to the brigade. They're getting the fools together for a record. Maybe you'll win some twenty-kopeck prize."

Zagirov knelt and silently gathered the things together.

"Good-bye, you precious creature."

Zagirov stood on his knees, his head drooping. Sayenko turned away. Zagirov touched his sweaty, quilted back.

"How much will you give me for everything all together?" he asked huskily.

"How much?" Sayenko turned his head. "I'll give you nothing. Go back to the brigade. I'll give you nothing."

"Kolya, please be human!"

"For the whole thing, I'll give you this . . ."

Sayenko thought for a moment, unbuttoned his trousers and put his hand through the opening into an inside pocket. He pulled out a large package of currency tied together with a shoestring. He rummaged through it.

Among the flashing papers Zagirov recognised his own new twenty-ruble bills that looked like bits of starched lettuce.

Sayenko laid on the ground three three-ruble notes that were the dirtiest of the lot, and one that was exceedingly old, a shaggy ruble rubbed beyond all semblance of recognition.

"Here you are."

The light went out of Zagirov's eyes. He bared his white, rat-like teeth and swung his head sideways like a trapped beast.

"If you don't want it, you don't have to take it," Sayenko said lazily.

On all sides they were surrounded by the chaos of the piled broken iron. The sun beat against the crossing rails and the rigging. Barred shadows stood around like the crooked walls of a cage.

"Give it here!" Zagirov cried. "Let's have the cards!"

And the game began.

They faced each other on their knees, slapping the thick cards against the earth. They played twenty-one.

Zagirov counted poorly. Every moment he stopped and, drenched in sweat, added the numbers in a whisper: "Twelve . . . eighteen . . . twenty-four . . ." He was unlucky. He was very unlucky. He plucked at his eyebrows and decided that if he plucked out an eyebrow, he would draw a card. If he couldn't pluck an eyebrow, he would not draw a card. Squinting, he sat down on the earth and plucked at his eyebrows with both hands. And then, wheezing for a long time, he looked at his fingers to see whether he had plucked out an eyebrow.

And Sayenko kept doubling the stakes and re-doubling.

Zagirov decided to play carefully and bet a little at a time, but he would lose control of himself. He over-bid the bank, lost, jumped up and pulled at his eyebrows. What could he do with his ten-spot against Sayenko? Sayenko had no less than a half a thousand in money he had won.

In half an hour everything was over. Sayenko put the money away, tied the things in a bundle, and, without looking at his companion, crawled out of the iron débris on all fours.

Zagirov ran after him, begged to be allowed to play on credit. He wept and did not wipe away his tears. He swore that on the very next pay day he would return everything, to the last kopeck. He promised to give Sayenko his dinner tickets and his tickets for produce. He kept thrusting forth the permit that entitled him to manufactured articles.

Sayenko said nothing.

Walking around the barracks, he trudged along, shuffling through the hot dust in his bast shoes, staring at the sky with his blank aniline eyes.

The thin, rare, distant sounds of the construction reached him, carried by the wind. Occasionally he would hear the ring of a hammer, or the rapid fire of a pneumatic motor at the blast furnace, or the scream of a steam whistle, or the puff of an excavator. The heavy sultry air scorched his face with fire, and with the ammoniac odour of the steppe and the horses.

XIII

"STILL, David, I don't understand your policy."

"And I don't understand yours . . ."

Margulies put his arm around Korneyev's waist in a friendly way. With his near-sighted eyes, he looked tenderly into the eyes of his friend and added:

". . . neither yours nor Mosya's."

Korneyev resented this. He was really hurt: Mosya and he! A blush tinted the superintendent's temples. From under the white cap with its straps, his captain's sideburns looked black, like pieces of velvet pasted on. He angrily dropped his eyes and immediately noticed a new spot on his left shoe. A splatter of tar. That was a nice how-do-you-do! Where did the tar come from? He reached for his handkerchief and waved his hand. It didn't make any difference. It wasn't important, the devil take it! His nose twitched nervously.

"David, you simply amaze me. What has Mosya to do with it? How can Mosya and I have any policy in common?"

"And why not? Don't be angry. Let's figure it out. What has actually happened? In a general way . . ." He concentrated and squinted. "Up until now we have been making approximately one hundred and eighty mixtures per shift. Sometimes it has reached two hundred. Once Khanumov even made two hundred and four."

"Two hundred and three."

"Good, two hundred and three. Now, we have received news that Kharkov has set a record of three hundred and six. These are the facts. There are no other facts. What should we do on the basis of these facts?"

Korneyev jerked his shoulder angrily.

"Beat Kharkov!"

Margulies turned his little finger in his long hairy nostril, rosy on the inside. He thought for a moment.

"Quite right. Beat Kharkov."

"That's just what I said!"

"Beat them! That's all there is to it. H'm! That's exactly what your Mosya was saying. Beat them!"

"What has Mosya to do with it?"

"You can see for yourself what he has to do with it. You want to beat them, and Mosya wants to beat them. Beat them, and that's all! But are we ready for it?"

"Of course we are," Korneyev interrupted. "We're no worse off than Kharkov, you may be sure of that. Our machines, thank God, are actually working. And we have excellent brigades. I don't understand why you're hesitating."

"But, you see, I'm not so sure."

"What aren't you sure about?"

"I'm not sure of anything. I'm not sure of the gravel. I'm not sure of the sand. I'm not sure of the transport. I'm not sure of the organisation. I'm not sure of the water. I'm not sure of anything."

Korneyev narrowed his eyes.

"You have no faith?"

"I'm not sure. That doesn't mean that I have no faith." Margulies smiled drily. "First I'll make sure, and then I'll have faith. Don't get hot under the collar. Don't be like Mosya. There's plenty of time."

"Where is the time?" Korneyev shouted, turning red. "What time? You're talking nonsense! Are you joking? As it is, we're behind schedule. We must beat them at once, without delay!"

"Exactly what I said: just like Mosya—exactly! How can you want to beat them at once when you know as well as I do that Yermakov's shift cannot beat them? Can it, now?"

"It cannot."

"There you are!"

"But if Yermakov cannot, Ishchenko can."

"Right. But we have seven hours before Ishchenko begins. Plenty of time. We'll look around and see."

Korneyev stopped. Margulies stopped, too.

"And who told you that I was opposed?"

They looked inquisitively into each other's eyes.

"Does that mean that we will beat them?" Korneyev asked hastily. "Eh, David? Beat them?"

They were standing at the crossing. A long train rolled forward and backward, blocking progress.

"I don't know."

"But who knows, if you don't?"

"It depends on the facts. At any rate, here is what . . ."

Margulies concentrated, drew his long shaggy brows together, and dropped his head.

"Here is what, at any rate. In the first place . . ."

He placed the yellow pencil in the palm of his hand and began to weigh it carefully. He looked admiringly at the shiny facets of this piece of wood.

"In the first place, disposition of forces. In the second place, materials. In the third place, transport. In the fourth place, emergency repair. I wish you would take care of that yourself. Exert pressure on the Komsomol. Make the rounds of the labour front. Take a little walk. And then, here's something else . . ."

He was somewhat embarrassed. He even felt the air with his fingers.

"You see . . . I'd like very much . . ." he lisped. "You understand, yourself . . . Why start a lot of noise ahead of time? I don't like it. There's no point to it. They'll all get excited, raise a commotion . . . We have correspondents here, writers . . . It's a big undertaking, tremendous . . . And to attempt and to fail is the easiest thing in the world. If we make a slight mistake or forget something, we'll fall flat. It can happen to anybody. But they will make a big to-do about it. They'll begin to generalise right away and pull us back. There will be plenty of volunteers for that, don't worry. They'll vulgarise the whole business . . ."

And suddenly he said in a firm voice:

"In a word, less noise."

And unexpectedly, even for himself, he added:

"We are not interested in setting records."

These words came out despite his will. He said them and

knitted his brows. He was repeating some one else's thought. He had heard it somewhere.

But where?

Yes, to-day on the stairway.

The fat man in the Ukrainian shirt! The old gadabout! "This is a construction, not a stunt!" The fat man had said this phrase too rapidly, too carelessly. It was obvious that he was repeating some one else's thought, not his own. It was quite possible that he was repeating the very words of the other person. Of course, this thought had been prepared by some one long ago and was now being skilfully disseminated on the construction.

The idea had sprouted wings. It overcame people, like a drug in the wind. It was in the sultry air. It clung and tormented with its hidden duplicity.

In itself, it was absolutely correct. Then what could one object to? Nevertheless, it roused revulsion in Margulies. It demanded to be repulsed, to be exposed. There was a tiny bit of falsehood in it, the size of a pin-head or of a malaria germ. It affected one subtly, penetrated into the brain, enfeebled one like an attack of malaria. The organism fought against it without premeditation, producing its own antibodies.

Margulies detested it and feared it like the plague.

And suddenly he had discovered its symptoms in himself. As if he had lost his mind suddenly, he had expressed the faultless thought: "A construction is not a stunt!" And immediately he realised that he did not believe in the infallibility of this thought, that he disbelieved it with all of his mind, with all of his blood, with all of his being.

Did it mean then that a construction *is* a stunt?

No! Nonsense! He would have to figure it out. . . . He looked at Korneyev in bewilderment.

"How can you speak of record-setting?" Korneyev boomed angrily. "How can you speak of record-setting when in forty-six days we must begin to set up the ovens? We must work with all our might! That's fairly clear, it seems. But as for making a

noise ahead of time, that's true. On this, I am in complete agreement with you, David."

Korneyev, dropping his eyes, looked at the wheels and the
bands of the flat car that flashed by. It reminded him that something unpleasant had happened recently. Something untoward
had happened that morning. That unpleasant thing had not yet
been disposed of and it would have to be faced.

But he was no longer thinking about it.

The flat car rolled by. The train held up the traffic. People and
transport began to accumulate. But a train now rolled along
the other track. It was another train. And Mosya was waving his
arms.

He remembered something strange and unpleasant. But what?

Yes! Quite right! Klava! She was going away. She had to go
home. Perhaps he could still patch things up.

But how untimely the whole thing was!

Margulies was patiently waiting for the train to pull through.
He put a bit of candy in his mouth, pursed his lips into a tube,
and before biting the candy, sucked it.

He understood.

Korneyev was right. Of course. A construction was not a stunt.
That was clear. But one could say equally well, and with equal
success, that the construction was not a theatre, not a drug store,
not—anything you like. No! There was a subtle slyness here.
Some one had deftly substituted one thought for another—the
main thought—which had been stated by the superintendent so
simply and casually: in forty-six days they must begin to set up
the ovens or the entire schedule would go to pot. So what was
the use of talking about it?

"Yes!" Margulies said decisively.

The train cleared the crossing. They walked ahead quickly,
jumping over impediments. The sun came out behind white, scurrying clouds. The power of the light changed every minute. The
world either disappeared in shadows or struck the very eyes with
all its tremendous, blinding detail. The temperature changed
every minute. The sun hid behind the clouds and the wind be-

came warm, stuffy. The sun came from behind the clouds and the wind became hot, burning, sharp.

"Well, will we beat them?"

"We'll try, but without any noise."

"Of course."

They made their way to the engineers' dining room on the sector. The barrack of the dining room and the barrack of the office stood side by side, door to door. Between them lay a large black shadow through which a hot draught ran. In the window swayed the cook's white cat. A large aluminum pot was being emptied. It was steaming. It contained mashed potatoes. Margulies's mouth watered. They went into the plane-board dining room.

Din of conversation. Crowds. Odours of food. Empty glasses. Empty glass pitchers with the yellow sediment of evaporated water. Dry rings of plates on the oil cloth.

Several men turned toward them. Several glances flashed rapidly. Margulies read in them unmistakably: "A construction is not a stunt."

Under the ceiling swung garlands of paper flags which had faded to white. The little flags resounded with the dry buzzing of flies. Engineers and technicians were waving their multi-coloured ribbons of meal tickets near the cashier. At the refreshment stand were eggs, cutlets, smoked sturgeon, tea, black bread, rolls.

"Wait, Korneyev, one minute." Margulies saw a stand containing books. "You get me something—two eggs and a cutlet and tea, and something else—something that tastes good."

He thrust his long pink ribbon of five-kopeck coupons at Korneyev. The twenty-kopeck coupons were blue. They curled like a wood shaving in the hands of the superintendent.

"I'll be with you in a moment. Perhaps they have Probst here. There are some interesting calculations there. . . . Take my place. Although I doubt if they have Probst."

They also sold technical literature in the dining room. Margulies went to the stand.

"Do you have Probst?"

It was hopeless. He knew perfectly well that there was not a single copy of Professor Probst's book on the construction. And yet, perhaps . . .

With annoyance, the woman clerk raised her eyes from the newspaper, covered and burned with the ashes of cheap tobacco. She adjusted her crooked pince-nez in its black, old-fashioned frame. One lens was cracked.

"The sixth man," she said in a bored voice.

Grey hair stuck out from under her red kerchief. The old woman displayed teeth that were strong, yellow, stained with tobacco. "Take Yeremin's 'Mechanisation and Installation of Cement Work.' I recommend it. The last copy. I sold all of them in an hour. Twelve!"

"Oho!"

Margulies whistled. So they have bought Yeremin! Things are going to happen!

"David, no more eggs left!" Korneyev was shouting, pressed by the crowd at the stand.

"Then grab something else!" Margulies tugged at his nose with two fingers.

"Well, never mind," he said indifferently. "I have Yeremin. I need Probst."

The woman clerk shrugged her shoulders and returned to the paper.

Margulies followed Korneyev with his eyes. The superintendent was fighting his way from the refreshment stand through the crowd. He balanced the tin plates carefully and clutched at a roll with his chin. He could scarcely move.

Nearby was a platform. He climbed up on the stage and walked past a real bench and a back-drop on which a tree in bloom and a hut were painted crudely and vividly. He walked like a juggler or a magician on the stage of an old popular theatre of the epoch of Elizabeth of England, wrapped in the varicoloured ribbons of coupons, the metal plates and knives and forks clanging and thundering.

The cutlets were approaching Margulies. Already he could see them in all their details, and the mound of mashed potatoes covered with brown gravy.

The saleslady took off her pince-nez and tapped the newspaper.

"Comrade Margulies, Kharkov, eh? What do you say?"

Margulies smiled sourly. "Yes, it's possible," he answered non-committally. And he walked away.

Korneyev put the plates on the bench. Margulies climbed up on the stage and thrust his nose toward the mashed potatoes.

"Marvellous cutlets! By the way, what time is it?"

He tugged at the strap of Korneyev's watch.

It was a quarter to nine.

"Is that right?"

"Within five minutes."

Without saying a word, Margulies climbed down from the platform and walked quickly toward the door.

"Where are you going, David?"

Margulies waved his hand. "Later."

"David, wait!"

Margulies turned at the doorway.

"I have a long distance connection at nine."

"But the cutlets!"

"Eat them yourself. I'll have something at the hotel. Maybe I'll grab something on the way. In case anybody wants me, I'll be at the long distance station."

He made his way quickly out of the dining room.

XIV

IT was ten minutes to nine.

Smetana jumped down to the ground. The palms of his hands burned from rubbing against the upright post of the turnstile. His palms had turned yellow. They smelled of rust. Smetana picked up the coppers, pencils, meal-tickets, pens. He wiped his scarlet face with the tail of his shirt.

A high washstand on thin wooden legs stood like a pauper in the middle of the street. Smetana lifted the cover and looked into the zinc box. There was no water.

Very well.

He tucked his shirt into his trousers. In his flaming, crimson face, his eyes, fleeced by his grey eyelashes, shone clearly. He breathed deeply and greedily. It seemed to him that he was blowing flames out of his nostrils.

There was no one in the barrack. He walked quickly over the sector.

Without counting the operator, there were seventeen men in the brigade. (He wondered how many men were in that Kharkov brigade.) Of those: three were Communist Youths; one, Ishchenko, a candidate for the Party; the others were non-partisan; and all of them were young.

First of all he would have to find the other two Young Communists—Olya Tregubova and Nefedov.

The sector was enormous. Time was concentrated. It flew. It interfered. He must tear himself out of it, free himself. He must outdistance it.

Smetana was almost running.

The world of boards and rafters on the sector turned sharply around Smetana. He was all movement, all corners and passages.

Smetana saw:

A corner—a passage—a turnstile—a washstand—a garbage box —and over it, a burning column of flies.

And in reverse order:

Flies—the box—the washstand—the turnstile—the passage— the corner!

The whining noises of black conduits exploded from the telephone pole to the four corners of the world. Radio loud-speakers thundered like grand pianos. With all their might, they were striking, as if on anvils, the chords of Gounod, welded with pieces of "Faust." From pole to pole, from loud-speaker to loud-speaker,

Smetana was caught and led forward by the implacable storm of music.

He ran up to the post office.

Behind the post office, in barrack 104, a troop of amateur actors of the little theatre were rehearsing "Tempos."

The barrack shook.

Bare-footed kids crawled up the walls, stood on bricks and boxes and peeked inside. The windows were open, but there were curtains over them. The wind pulled the curtains outside, twisted them, inflated them, blew them open.

Inside, feet stamped, singers wheezed between notes, shadows flitted across the shining ceiling, a jerky chorus of cries resounded, someone sang.

Smetana pulled the door. It was locked. He knocked. From within somebody sent him to the devil's mother. He drummed his fist on the panel. With a crash and a clang the door was flung open.

On the threshold stood a lad with a red artificial nose, a curly red wig, and a vest over a raspberry-coloured shirt. He pushed his balalaika against Smetana's chest, gritted his teeth, and cried in a tearful, heart-rending voice:

"They won't give us any rest! No rest at all! They come here and come and come! Why can't you let us alone? What do you want? What haven't you seen here? What did you leave behind you here? Can't you see that people are busy with socially useful and indispensable affairs, that you bother them, that you are interrupting a rehearsal? Why do you come and come and come? . . ."

Suddenly his eyes blazed with a wild light and he lifted the balalaika over his fiery head.

"If you don't go away, so help me God, I'll beat you all over the face—all of you in a row! May the true God help me, I'll bash your face in with this balalaika!"

"Sha," Smetana said pacifically. He smiled so broadly and in such a friendly manner that even his cherry-red ears moved.

"Sha, boss, don't get hot. If I come here, it's necessary. Is Olka [1] here?"

"What Olka?" the fellow chanted in his tearful, monotonous voice.

"Olga Tregubova from Ishchenko's brigade."

Without awaiting an answer, Smetana sauntered into the barrack.

"Olka!"

The chap in the vest spat, and banged the door so fiercely that the mug clanged against the barrel of boiled water in the corridor. He slammed the bolt.

At the same moment Smetana ran up and pulled the bolt back. The door swung open. A violent gust blew into the corridor from the street. Dust swirled around. The draught wrought havoc. It tore the wig off the lad's head and ran off with it. A bristly black head emerged from under the wig. The holiday dress of Tregubova blew up like a balloon.

"Where are you going, Tregubova? Where are you going?" the lad cried, running after his wig. "I forbid you! You are breaking up the discipline of the group! You are breaking up the rehearsal! You are defying society!"

He talked too much and said too much.

Tregubova and Smetana went out into the street and quickly turned the corner.

Here was the post office barrack. A log was lying there. They sat down. Smetana began to explain the affair. Tregubova listened attentively. It was not difficult to understand, and she understood everything after the first words. Nevertheless, she knitted her small, round, frank brow assiduously.

Everything on her broad, large, simple face was small. A tiny nose, a tiny chin, a tiny mouth, tiny cheeks. And all of this was grouped so tightly together (like a doll's pink kitchen utensils) under the small, firm, bulging blue eyes that broad fields of her face spread on all sides. She was always in a state of extreme excitement. A moment ago she had been frightfully worried at

[1] Olka, like Olya, is a variant of Olga.

the rehearsal. She was mad about the theatre. The glow of acting
had not yet left her face.

She had been rehearsing the rôle of an energetic peasant girl
who had arrived at a new construction and was bringing a dirty,
forsaken barrack into order. This was an agitation play to stimu-
late attention to sanitary measures. She had run across the stage
with a wet broom, sprinkled the drunkard and the loafer, had
sung songs about bedbugs, and had danced. Her eyes were everywhere, gleaming desperately, shrewdly and even coquettishly.

But this excitement had passed quickly and had given way
to another kind of excitement, intent and business-like.

Smetana pulled the notebook out of his pocket. Here was a list
of the non-party lads of the brigade. She placed her large, rough
hands on Smetana's shoulder and read the names with her eyes,
breathing in a business-like way.

They discussed the technical and personal qualifications of each
one separately and of all of them together.

This was no laughing matter.

They could not afford to make a mistake.

XV

FROM the list before Smetana and Tregubova, each one of the
non-partisan lads of the brigade rose, one after the other, as
if at a roll-call.

There were fourteen of them, fourteen youngsters, and all different. Among them were newcomers, still very "green," who
had come from the village only a month ago. There were "old-
timers" who had been on the construction throughout the winter,
for six months already. There were also the middling ones who
had a production record of two or three months.

Some were still homesick, distraught, nostalgic. Some had become more or less accustomed to the new life: their rough edges
had worn smooth. Others worked with passion and fervour, for-

getting everything else in the world. Even those who were still homesick sang peasant field-songs at night, amassed money and things, and were planning to go back to the village. And those for whom the brigade had already become their family; and those who now recalled the winter they had lived through as they might remember some legendary expedition—the severe Ural winter in the steppes with storms at forty below zero, when they had worked without relief for twenty-four hours at a stretch—who, like fighters remembering their previous battles, were as proud of frozen fingers as of wounds of honour, and returned to the barrack from every shift as from an attack—for these, the construction job was a military front; the brigade, a platoon; Ishchenko, their commander; the barrack, the reserve; the excavation, a trench; the cement-mixer, a field gun. All of them—these and those and the others—were all comrades, brothers, and of one age.

Time flew through them. They changed in time, as in a campaign. New recruits became fighters, fighters became heroes, heroes became leaders.

Smetana and Tregubova sat, their heads bent over the list.

Meantime, a multitude of people walked back and forth over the wooden walk to the post office. The post office was also a barrack. The panelled door, blackened with the imprints of many hands, screeched and banged. People with letters, parcels, newspapers walked up and down. They opened their letters as they walked. They read them, stopping anywhere. They pulled the canvas off their parcels, crouching on the ground beside the planked wall, and leaning against the planks.

A peasant in a sheepskin stood on all fours, his bearded face against the dried earth, as if he were bowing to the ground. The post office was jammed. There had not even been a place where he could put on a stamp. Almost lying down, he put the letter on the ground before him and licked the stamp.

Dignified men of Kostroma with their finely distended nostrils passed by, Tatars from Kazan, Caucasians, Georgians, Chechenians, Bashkirs, Germans, Muscovites, Peterites [1] in coats and high-necked Russian shirts, Ukrainians, Jews, White Russians [2] . . .

Bundles of letters were flung into two-ton trucks. They were rushed to the mail train. The bundles flew, one after the other. Sometimes the string broke and the letters scattered. They were raked into a pile and loaded helter-skelter.

Tens of thousands of letters!

Tens of thousands of addresses clumsily written in purplish ink struck the eyes with their scrawls, mistakes, errors about regions, districts, village soviets, collective farms, cities, post office departments, half-way stations, names, nicknames, surnames . . .

Envelopes—grey, hand-made, checkered blue and red, white, graphed with a ruler, crooked, made of newspaper, yellow, brown, crudely pasted together with soft bread—poured into the truck.

Nefedov had been standing for a long time near Smetana and Tregubova. He had run straight from the second construction sector, from the car of the "Komsomolskaya Pravda," to the barrack to find Smetana. On the way he had met Ishchenko. The brigadier had given him the clue.

Nefedov, quiet and lanky, stood with his arm around a telephone pole. His shadow fell across the list. He was listening to Smetana and watching the letters that were flying into the truck.

They poured endlessly.

And it seemed to him that he could imagine how they would travel, how all these letters would be spread over the entire Soviet Union.

They would wander, return, travel, find no destination, and go on travelling, flickering, falling like fine frost in a snow storm. They would crawl over the transmission lines, and the transmission lines played like a piano, resoundingly, and thundered loudly,

---

[1] Men from Leningrad (from 1915 to 1924 called Petrograd, before then known as St. Petersburg—Peter's city—and popularly referred to as "Peetyer") are called "Peetyertsy"—Peterites.

[2] This refers to the ethnological group, known as *Byelorussy*, and should not be confounded with the political opponents of the Bolshevik régime.

thundered as if a row of hoofs were running over a tightly stretched wire.

They ran and ran and then they stopped as if rooted to the ground. Halt! Then suddenly they struck the strings all together! They started again in various directions, each going his own way, ringing and thundering mightily, as if on an anvil, the chords of Gounod, welded with bits of the march from "Faust."

The telephone pole rumbled within, from the welter of its wooden heart. With the palm of his hand, Nefedov stroked its protuberant roundness, which rang like a ripe watermelon.

The ringing prickled his palm, tickled it, as if ants were swarming over his palm, walking up his arm, enervating his shoulder. He grew slightly dizzy. There was a buzzing in his ears. Nefedov was very fond of music. He listened to it with abandon.

Suddenly he remembered why he was there. He adjusted his goggles. The perforated metal shield flashed in the white sun like a grater.

He bent over Tregubova and Smetana. Deliberately and quietly, he knocked their heads together.

"Hello, bosses! Enough of that. It's all clear and settled. I vote for it. What's the use of talking! As far as I'm concerned, I offer a resolution: If we beat Kharkov, all the non-partisan lads must enter the Komsomol."

XVI

THE Central telephone station was located in a building of the plant office next to the hotel.

The building of the plant office did not differ appreciably from the hotel. It was of brick and glass, five-storeyed, huge. With the hotel, it had a commanding position over the entire locality.

Margulies turned a corner, encased by the wind. Blue lightnings flickered in the lower windows, on the level of his shoulder. The radio station was working. The wind tore the scratched door out of Margulies's hands. Margulies struck it with his boot. The door would not yield. He pushed his shoulder against it. Then the wind suddenly flung open both halves of the door and pushed Margulies onto the stairway. In one breath he ran up to the second storey. The steps were covered with dry black dust. They gritted like emery under the soles of his boots.

Correspondents were crowding around the telegraph window in the corridor. That was to be expected. Margulies pulled his cap over his eyes and walked faster. But they spied him.

"Hey there, boss!"

"Comrade Margulies, one question!"

"Listen, David, wait! All jokes aside . . . what about Kharkov?"

He stopped, surrounded by the journalists. He made as pleasant a face as he could, and spread his hands apart humorously, as if he were being ironic about his own helplessness and inviting his comrades to act similarly.

"You see," he said, "it is a very complex question . . . I, of course, with pleasure . . . but . . . I have a long distance call at nine . . . and now . . ."

"Wait, David, tell us only one thing. Three hundred and six— is it possible or impossible?"

Margulies gently pinched his nose between two fingers and snorted.

"You see . . ."

He realised that he could not get away.

But at that moment the door of the long distance station at the end of the corridor was flung open, and the telephone girl on duty waved a blank sheet of paper.

"David Lvovich! Hurry up, I've connected you. Hurry into the telephone booth."

"You see . . ."

Margulies gestured again, as if to say: they won't even let me talk to people!

"I'll be back in five minutes," he shouted, and ran into the booth.

The electric clock on the table of the telephone girl on duty indicated four minutes past seven. That was Moscow time. Moscow was exactly two hours behind.

Margulies went into the felt-lined booth and shut the door behind him tightly. Immediately he was in utter silence, as if, on shutting the door, he had shut out time. Time became a thick, impenetrable matrix around him.

But no sooner did he apply the special telephone receiver to his ear than, instead of the time that had stopped, space began to speak.

It spoke with the near and distant voices of telephone operators, with the weak rattle of atmospheric devices, with the din of flying kilometres, with the mosquito-like singing of signals, with the calling of cities to each other:

"Chelyaba, Chelyaba" (too—oo—oo, too—oo—oo . . .), "Chelyaba."

"Chelyaba speaking! Perm! Perm!" (too—oo—oo, too—oo—oo, too—oo—oo . . .) "Perm!"

"Perm speaking! Perm speaking! Perm speaking!" (too—oo—oo . . .)

There was a crackling in the receiver. Perhaps a storm was flashing nearby and the path was running through rain, through bright ferns, rainbows, coldness, ozone; and clouds of raven-blue steel were lying like firearms on the Ural mountains . . .

"Moscow speaking! Moscow speaking!" (too—oo—oo, too—oo—oo, too—oo—oo . . .) "Moscow speaking!"

"Hello, I'm listening! Hello, hello! . . . Margulies speaking."

Silence. The noise of space. A microscopic crack. The mosquito-like singing of signals.

Was it possible that Katya was not at home? No, that couldn't be. She must be asleep and could not hear the ringing. The telephone was in the corridor.

It was now seven o'clock in Moscow, five minutes past seven. Two hours ago it had still been night—a bright, northern, May night, almost white, almost not a night at all.

Ah, what a night!

The sky beyond the railroad station would be filled with the green sea water of dawn. Every moment the glowing light flowed more and more swiftly. Rows upon rows of stars of a thousand candlepower each had been attached to the tramway lines.

There was a battle in Moscow, too.

One could hear the roar and the moaning, watery ringing of a tramway rail that was being dragged. People were singing as they strained at their labours:

"Hey there, together! Hey there, heave! Hey there, drop!"

The rail fell with a noise like the discharge of a pistol shot.

And the blue, transparent star of an acetylene torch lay among rails and trusses on a ploughed-up street, blinding and girdled by irradiating shadows of men.

"Hello! Moscow! Margulies speaking."

Silence.

Noise.

And Margulies saw the first street car rattling over the new rails in Moscow. And against a background of the morning clouds, a diver appeared at the "Dynamo" swimming pool.

He mounted the grey-blue steps to the high platform, which resembled a siege gun. He stood on the edge of the springboard that hung over the water. The taut springboard bent easily under the weight of his well-knit body. He spread out his arms as if he wanted to embrace everything that lay stretched before him in this fresh and miraculous morning world of young Moscow— the river, grey-blue, scarcely touched by the glowing flush of the dawn, the pavilions of flowers in the Park of Culture and Rest, the Crimean Bridge, the blue smoke of Sparrow Hills, a little tug and its barge, the wiring of the Shabolov radio station, a cloud, roses, tennis nets, a street car, a building in the process of construction.

He inhaled simply and deeply. He lifted his arms, and, stretching them out, joined them overhead. Now he was no longer a man. He was an arrow. He swayed slightly. Slowly, almost imperceptibly, he lost his balance. Unhurriedly, gracefully moving his arms, he fell.

No, he did not fall . . .

Now he was flying. He was no longer an arrow. He was a swallow. The young sun illuminated every detail of him. His shoulder blades were taut, and down the middle of his back, from his head in its bullet-like helmet to the middle of his waist, was a sharp line.

He was in the air.

His arms quickly joined together overhead. His legs closed like scissors. Again he was an arrow.

An instant—and without a single splash, he disappeared like a key into the molten, astonished water.

XVII

"HELLO! Moscow!"

Stillness.

Roaring.

And suddenly, like a large, sharply illuminated, indifferent face, out of the roar and the darkness came a loud, strange, indifferent voice.

"Are you calling Moscow? Go ahead."

"Hello! Margulies speaking."

A light crackle. Contact. He heard the jingle of the receiver being lifted thousands of kilometres away, and the small, faint, but distinct voice of his sister:

"Hello!"

"Hello, Katyusha.[1] This is Dodya[2] speaking. Can you hear me? Dodya speaking. Hello. I must have awakened you. Were you asleep? Please excuse me."

"What is it? Who is speaking? I don't understand anything!"

"Dodya speaking. Is that you, Katya? *I* am speaking. Excuse me for waking you up. You must have been asleep."

[1] like Katya, a diminutive for Ekaterina
[2] the diminutive for David

"For God's sake, what has happened? What's happened to you? I don't understand anything!"

"Nothing has happened. This is I—Dodya. Is it possible that you hear so badly? I can hear you very well. I was saying, I must have awakened you, that you were asleep."

"What?"

"I said you must have been asleep."

"What has happened?"

"Nothing has happened."

"Is that you, Dodya?"

"Why, yes, it's I."

"What has happened?"

"Nothing has happened. Excuse me for waking you up! Can you hear me?"

"Why, yes, I can hear you. I can't hear everything, but I can hear some."

"Hello, Katya."

"What has happened?"

"Nothing has happened. I said, 'Hello, Katya.' Will you go and look in my basket . . . do you understand? . . . the basket . . . There's a blue notebook there in the basket . . . It's lithographed . . . It's in German . . . in my basket . . . the lectures of Professor Probst. Can you hear me?"

"I can hear you. Have you gone mad? What basket? I thought something had happened. You woke me up. It's seven o'clock now. I'm standing barefoot in the corridor."

"What did you say?"

"I said that I am standing barefoot in the corridor."

"I don't understand anything. Not in the corridor . . . in my basket . . . A kind of blue notebook in German. It's entitled 'The Lectures of Professor Probst.'"

" 'The Lectures of Professor Probst.' I sent them away yesterday to Misha in Kharkov. He sent a special telegram."

"Which telegram? What telegram?"

"Misha Afanasyev. Don't you remember Misha Afanasyev? Volodya's friend. I sent it special delivery to Kharkov."

"Oh, you silly girl! Who told you to do that?"

Margulies was perspiring. He banged his fist against the thick padding of the booth. He was spoiling for a fight. But he was three thousand kilometres away! So he calmed down and gathered his wits.

She was silent.

"Katya, are you still there?"

"Well, what do you want?"

"I say, are you listening?"

"I'm standing barefoot in the corridor."

"Here's what, Katyusha. Please forgive me for awakening you, but be a good girl and go at once to Professor Smolensky. Can you hear me? Write down the address."

"Wait a minute. I'll get a pencil."

Again stillness. Roaring. And out of the roar the very loud, strange, indifferent voice again:

"Citizen, five minutes have passed. Do you wish to talk some more?"

"Yes, I want to talk some more."

"Go ahead."

And out of the roar Katya's voice emerged again:

"Hello! I'm listening. What address?"

"Write this: Molchanovka, House number ten, Apartment fourteen, Professor Smolensky. Did you write it down?"

"Yes, I wrote it down."

He could distinctly hear her yawn.

"Repeat it."

"Professor Smolensky, Molchanovka ten, Apartment fourteen."

"That's right. But wait a minute. Maybe it's the other way around. I think perhaps the house is fourteen, and the apartment number ten. Do you hear me? Or the other way around. In a word, it's either one or the other. Do you understand?"

"I understand. But what shall I say?"

"Tell him that Margulies sends his greetings . . . he knows me . . . and that he asks if he will give him an analytical cal-

culation. He knows. Just tell him that . . . an analytical calculation. Can you hear me?"

"Why, yes, I can hear you. I hear you."

"An analytical calculation. But for God's sake, my darling,
don't forget it. Tell him that it has to do with the record set by
Kharkov. He has read about it, of course. And I want his opinion.
But the main thing is the analytical calculation—the very latest
analytical calculation. Do you understand me?"

"I understand: the very latest analytical calculation and Kharkov."

"That's right. I will call you again at twelve."

"At twelve? What? When? At twelve?"

"Yes, at twelve our time, which is ten Moscow time. Can you
hear me? To-day at ten, Moscow time. Well, how are you getting
along? Have you heard anything from Mamma?"

"Dodya, you're crazy! I am standing barefoot in the corridor.
Did you send Mamma money? Mamma is coming at the end of
June."

"What?"

"I said Mamma is coming at the end of June."

"So. Please don't forget—the analytical calculation. I'll call
you at ten. Well, so long."

"So long."

Margulies hung up the receiver.

Space stood still in its immobile extension.

But as soon as he opened the door of the booth, immobile space
disappeared and free time moved noisily and flung itself upon
him. The control clock indicated a quarter past nine.

Behind a door in the corridor the correspondents were lying in
wait for Margulies. He walked quickly across the telephone department and sneaked through another door which opened onto
a different corridor and a different stairway.

"Comrade Margulies! David Lvovich!"

He shuddered. The telephone operator was running after him.

"David Lvovich! Who is to pay for this conversation? Wait a

moment! Let me have sixteen rubles. Or shall I send the bill to the plant office?"

Margulies was confused.

"Oh, no! For God's sake, what are you saying?" he lisped and put his hand into his pocket. "For God's sake, excuse me! Such absent-mindedness!"

He reached quickly into his side pocket for his wallet. There he found a ten-ruble bill. He rummaged in the pockets of his trousers and found a crumpled five-ruble bill. That was all the money he had. He turned scarlet, and, casting troubled glances at the door behind which the journalists were lying in wait for him, he put the money on the counter.

"That's all right. You'll owe me a ruble. I'll trust you. Do you want a receipt?"

Margulies waved his hand.

"I'll bring you a ruble at twelve o'clock. And will you please get me Moscow again at that time . . . the same number. Will you do that?"

The telephone operator shook her finger at him insinuatingly.

"I wonder why you have suddenly developed a desire to speak to Moscow. Look out, David Lvovich!"

Margulies walked across the corridor, went down the stairway, and came out through another corridor into the vestibule of the plant office.

Here clabbered milk and tarts were being sold. He went up to the stand, but then remembered that he had no more money.

Oh, it doesn't matter, he thought. Maybe I'll get some lunch at the hotel, and then I'll borrow some money from somebody.

He went outside to the semi-circular steps of the entrance.

The hot black dust swirled among the automobiles and woven carts, whistled through the tails of the horses, beat against the face, tore newspapers out of the hand, opened them, carried them away like flying carpets, and noisily thrashed the outspread sheets with its fine, hail-like powder.

XVIII

THE N railroad junction was constantly blocking the routes with machinery and materials. Writing about it had not helped. Telegraphing had not helped. Sending a brigade had not helped. All means had been exhausted. They could not go on like this.

The chief of the construction called up the airdrome. The construction had its own airplane. It was not far to N—only three hundred kilometres. The round trip could be made in five hours.

The construction-chief placed his foot in its russet puttee on the running board of the long automobile. He was completing the mastication of his breakfast. He dropped his goggles over his eyes. The sun blazed sharply on the lenses. The landscape was dry and billowy.

Comrade Seroshevsky was in a hurry. He was afraid that some one might catch him and delay him. He was always in a hurry. He was always being stopped and delayed.

The running board of the automobile was covered with rubber patterned like a waffle. Seroshevsky pressed his foot on it as if it were a stirrup. The chauffeur pressed the foot throttle.

Seroshevsky's wife ran out of the cottage, barefooted. She was in a faded blue dressing gown. She had not finished dressing her hair, and pins and combs were falling out of her wavy tresses. She cried:

"Seroshevsky, wait a minute!" The machine was quivering. "Wait, you fool, you've forgotten this!"

Without turning around, Seroshevsky stretched out both his hands. She placed a brief case and a revolver in them. He flung the brief case into the automobile and thrust the small Colt into the hip pocket of his checkered breeches.

Now he could drive off. The sooner the better.

But he had lost the opportune moment. At the entrance of the restaurant appeared the Americans he had met the day before. There were two of them.

One was a small, elderly, good-natured fellow. His chin, round and suède-like, resembled a purse. Such a chin, such lips constantly chewing a cud, such puffy, shining eyes are only found among Tvenov grandmothers. He wore a dark, light-weight, three-piece suit, a cream-coloured shirt with a large collar, a woven, woollen necktie, and coarse-grained, very expensive shoes made of buffalo hide.

The other was a tall, broad-shouldered young man with a moustache, dressed in a fashionable heliotrope-coloured suit, a light cap and colourful suède sport oxfords.

The older man was Mr. Ray Roupe, a wealthy tourist. The young man was Leonard Darley, the Moscow correspondent of an American news agency and his interpreter. They were guests of the construction.

Seroshevsky had to play the gracious host. This, undoubtedly, was a part of his multitudinous duties. He asked the chauffeur to wait for a minute, and walked quickly to meet the Americans. They shook hands heartily.

Seroshevsky inquired whether they had found their accommodations satisfactory, whether they had spent a comfortable night, hoped that the flies had not bothered them too much.

Oh, they had slept splendidly, quite comfortably, quite like at home! In fact, they confessed, they had not expected to find—in the wild Ural steppes, on the border between Europe and Asia —such a room in such a splendid cottage, and such a palatable breakfast!

Mr. Ray Roupe shook his head benevolently and squinted. Clasping his puffy little hands across his stomach, he would look now at his interpreter and now at Seroshevsky. Then, with a light movement of his head, he would interrupt Mr. Leonard Darley and ask him to translate something, and when that was done, he would laugh shrewdly. He liked Mr. Seroshevsky.

Leonard Darley, smiling respectfully, translated: Mr. Ray Roupe said that he liked vodka very much. Mr. Ray Roupe was not a drinking man—his health would not permit that—but at breakfast he tried a very small glass, and it was so excellent that he was afraid he might become a drunkard here in these Ural steppes.

Mr. Ray Roupe shook his head shrewdly and approvingly.

Comrade Seroshevsky smiled politely. He wanted to pay his respects, but Mr. Roupe was interested in knowing whether Mr. Seroshevsky was fond of vodka.

Mr. Seroshevsky informed him graciously that occasionally he liked to take a few glasses of vodka.

"Oh, yes. At times it is even beneficial. But, of course, not too often."

Mr. Roupe shook his index finger at Mr. Seroshevsky in humorous warning.

Mr. Leonard Darley was interested in knowing:

"Do the workers here drink much vodka?"

Seroshevsky explained that the sale of alcohol was forbidden on the construction. The only exceptions were for foreign specialists, but they had their own restaurant.

"Oh, so you have prohibition here! That's very interesting. And I suppose you already have bootleggers."

Mr. Leonard Darley pulled out his notebook.

"No wonder they say that Soviet Russia is following in the footsteps of the United States. But it is beginning where America is leaving off," Darley muttered, making the note.

Mr. Roupe squinted significantly.

Seroshevsky became nervous.

"However, you must excuse me."

The chauffeur saw that things were in a bad way. With a sharp turn, he brought the machine to his chief's very elbow. Seroshevsky put his hand on the warm body of the automobile.

But Mr. Ray Roupe was evidently not inclined to interrupt a conversation so pleasantly begun. He liked to talk.

Unhurriedly, he made several kindly and witty remarks about the local climate and nature, insofar, of course, as he had happened to notice it since the previous evening. He considered it very practical to have built this habitation sector, consisting of cottages, on the incline of a mountain, somewhat removed from the centre of the construction. There was much less dust and wind here. Remarkably dry and healthful air, as far as he could observe—simply a health resort. By the way, how many metres above sea-level was this? He thought it was three hundred and sixty, or was that an exaggeration?

Comrade Seroshevsky stole a glance at the nickel-plated bars of his wrist watch, which blinded him.

It was a quarter past ten.

Mr. Ray Roupe took Comrade Seroshevsky by the arm. Without hurrying, they walked back and forth, enjoying nature.

The machine followed them softly, at its very lowest speed.

It was an excellent landscape. If it were not for the birches, it might be Alpine.

The birches grew in a canyon.

Their tops could be seen above a steep incline. They were lighted through and through by the sun. They were dry and golden, like sponges. They absorbed into themselves the watery shadows of the clouds. Then they darkened and swelled.

The wind brought the cool odour of lilies of the valley from the canyon.

A heavy cow with the stupid, beautiful face of a Juno walked down the road.

Here opened a splendid view of the Ural range. The mountain chain was drawn across the western horizon with a nervous scribble of blue peaks. Mr. Ray Roupe was enchanted.

"The Ural range, in antiquity, Montes Riphaei, is the meridial range, the border between Asia and Europe . . . The Bolsheviks stand between two worlds, between two cultures. Isn't that so? Isn't that sublime!"

Comrade Seroshevsky shook his head distractedly.

"Yes, it is sublime!"

He was ready to interrupt the conversation at any moment and go away, ready to be rude and tactless in a manner unworthy of a Bolshevik who stood at the border of two worlds.

But Nalbandov came to his rescue.

Nalbandov was descending the mountain sideways, taking huge steps, leaning on a huge orange cane of box-wood.

The Americans looked with curiosity at this colourful Bolshevik, at his black leather cap, his black leather jacket, his narrow jet-black beard.

Nalbandov's abrupt, unceremonious, loose movements were those of a highly qualified specialist who was also a Party member. A rigid nose, with a notch at the tip. A scar. One eye squinted. He did not look; he aimed.

He had just received the new Armstrong drill-lathe. Under his arm he carried a roll of its blueprints and drawings. He was in a hurry.

He had to catch Seroshevsky.

He came up, striding loosely and heavily:

"Listen, Seroshevsky . . ."

Nalbandov began at once, without any introduction, without paying attention to the guests.

"Listen, Seroshevsky. That Ostrovsky of yours must be kicked off the construction at once and sent to the devil's mother with his entire brigade! They're not repair-men, but spoilers. They hurry, mess things up and don't know anything! . . ."

Nalbandov had been wanting to tell Seroshevsky a number of things. He was particularly indignant about Margulies.

Of course, this had no direct connection with Nalbandov, but still he could not allow all sorts of risky experiments. The construction was not a stunt, and the responsible work of pouring cement could not be made an opportunity for the practices of all sorts of dashing careerists . . . Here, of course, there was no question of personalities, but of principles . . .

Seroshevsky let this go in one ear and out the other. (He would investigate when he returned.)

"Permit me to introduce you," he said hurriedly. "The engineer on duty, Nalbandov. He will show you the construction. It seems you are interested . . ." And, turning to Nalbandov: "Georgi Nikolayevich, my dear fellow, take our dear guests for a ride over the sectors and environs. If you please, gentlemen. By the way, you might give me a lift to the airdrome. It's not far from here. And then, if you please, my machine is at your disposal until five o'clock."

Seroshevsky said all of this in one breath, without stopping. He was afraid that he would be interrupted again, and the situation of which he had taken such clever advantage would be ruined. Nalbandov—to the Americans, the Americans—to Nalbandov, while he would take the airplane!

Nalbandov shook hands with the guests in a somewhat affected manner. He was at their service.

Seroshevsky grew solicitous, opened the door, helped Mr. Ray Roupe into the car, yielded his place to Mr. Leonard Darley. He asked Nalbandov to sit with the guests. He took his place in front—with the chauffeur. This was his favourite place.

It was necessary to hurry.

Without changing the expression of his face, set in its beaming good-nature, Mr. Ray Roupe sat down on the firm, comfortable cushions. He felt at home, in his customary atmosphere of comfort and attention. He stretched out in the automobile as if he were in a bathtub. He was very fond of riding fast in a good machine and over new territory. Everywhere he was being solicitously driven in good machines and shown the noteworthy sights, the environs, the landscape . . . Now he would be shown these things again. He dropped his eyelids.

The chauffeur again pressed the foot throttle. The machine started at once. The swiftly moving air rushed against the radiator.

XIX

THE hot breeze tore at the loose-leaf pads, the bits of paper with notations on them, the notebooks and newspapers on the table.

Georgi Vasilyevich, the novelist, carefully weighted every sheet of paper with some object—a mug, a piece of ore, a plate, a nut, an empty inkwell.

Now at last he could work.

The ink had dried in his fountain pen. He took a pencil. He did not like to work with a pencil. He wrote rapidly on a sheet of paper:

"From my window, the world opens like a rebus. I see a multitude of figures—people, horses, woven carts, cables, machines, steam, letters, clouds, mountains, cars, water . . . But I do not understand their interrelationship. But I know that this interrelationship exists. There is some all-powerful interaction. This is absolutely indubitable. I know it. I believe it. But I do not see it. And that is exasperating. To believe and not to see! I am tortured by the thought. I try hard, but I cannot solve the rebus . . ."

He underlined the word "believe" and the word "see" twice.

The rough, warped table was shoved against the wall, right under the window sill. The window sill was too high—one and a half times higher than the table.

The window was in three parts—a Venetian window. Its width considerably exceeded its height.

The hotel room was very small. A table. Three chairs. An unshaded electric bulb. An iron bedstead painted in stripes. The corner of a fibre suitcase projected from under the bed.

Nothing else.

The Celsius thermometer outside indicated twenty degrees in the shade.[1] In the sun it was thirty-four.[2]

The window—the rebus—looked toward the west. The sun was in the eastern half of the sky. It had not yet entered the western half. The hotel room was in the shade. Its temperature was in excess of forty degrees.[3]

The wall opposite the bed was always glowing with heat. It was impossible to touch it. The moulding had cracked. The calcimine

[1] 68.0° Fahrenheit—20° C.
[2] 93.2° Fahrenheit—34° C.
[3] 104.0° Fahrenheit—40° C.

had turned yellow. A stove-pipe from the kitchen passed through the wall. The kitchen was in use almost day and night.

"But I cannot solve the rebus . . ."

Of course not! Not in such heat!

Whatever had made him come to this room? But what could he do about it? Others did not even have this much.

The wind tore the sheet from his hands, flinging handfuls of blue dust as large as poppy seeds through the window.

It was impossible to breathe.

The first night he had slept on the table of the Post Office Department and the State Labour Savings Bank, behind a partition in the vestibule of the hotel. The table was hard and short. The brass scales were in his way. Still, this was better than sleeping on the floor by the door.

No one was allowed to spend the night in the quarters of a state institution. An exception had been made in the case of Georgi Vasilyevich out of respect for his name and profession.

During the day he wandered over the sectors, and, stopping along the way, he made notations in his little book.

Some of his notations:

". . . special planked little barns 'for smoking.' In other places, smoking is strictly forbidden. In the middle is a vat of water. All around along the walls are benches. People sit, smoke, spit, wipe their mouths with their sleeves. Young people, thoughtful ones, who do not at all resemble workers . . ."

"The anarchy of speeds, of rhythms. Lack of co-ordination. I stood at the railroad crossing. A freight train was being switched back and forth. A local-made woven cart was jogging along. A five-ton truck raising dust. A bicycle flickering blindingly. A man walking (by the way, where was he going?). Lean Bashkir [4] cam-

---

[4] The Bashkir nomadic tribes have been around the Ural region for over a thousand years, subjected periodically to Finnish, Tatar and Russian influences. Under Bolshevik leadership they have organised into the Bashkir Autonomous Socialist Soviet Republic, which stretches for six hundred and three kilometres from north to south, and for four hundred and twenty-three kilometres from east to west. It has a population of about three million. The centre of this republic is Ufa, a city founded in 1558 by Muscovite colonisers.

els with long hams dragging logs. A large, three-motor airplane flying. All moving at different speeds. Maddening! We live in an epoch of varying speeds. They must be co-ordinated. But perhaps they have been co-ordinated? But by what?"

"A year and a half ago this was an utter desert—a wild parched steppe. Unpopulated. Dead mountains. Vultures. Eagles. Blizzards. One hundred and fifty kilometres from the nearest railroad. Fifty kilometres from the nearest town . . . But now? Miracles . . ."

"The construction lives through various eras: first, the earth era; then the wood era. Now begins the era of iron, of concrete. Young, greenish, reinforced concrete emerges from the husk of wooden scaffolding. Soon there will be a machine era (montage), then an electric era (CES) . . ."

"Gas drums. Various colours. The oxygen is blue, the acetylene is white, the hydrogen is red. (But how are they used?)"

"The brigade of concrete workers—gun detail—loading, lifting . . . The foreman—the artillery sergeant—is running with a notebook and swearing. The operator is the gunner . . ."

"I saw a Komsomol brigade working without a scaffolding. A new method of laying brick. A blue sky. Frightfully blue! They sang, working on a narrow rib of the brick structure that rose out of the earth. It looked like a factory chimney. They sang, raising the wall brick by brick and raising themselves with it. (The wall and singing people rising to the sky before one's eyes. Youth?)"

And he made notes of many other things.

But what was the connection between these various details?

The next night the manager transferred him to a second-story bathroom, which was not in use. This was somewhat better. But it was still impossible to work.

In the morning, a small corner room on the fourth floor was vacated. It was being vacated regularly every three or four days. Evidently no one could endure it longer.

The old tenants knew this room very well. It had even acquired a special name. It was called the *kauper*.

But what was a *kauper*?

Georgi Vasilyevich was a new man, technically ignorant. He did not know the meaning of the word *kauper*.

He exerted pressure on the manager and received the new room out of turn. And that was quite a room! Georgi Vasilyevich arranged something in the nature of a cooling screen: he placed chairs against the cursed wall and hung a wet sheet over the backs of the chairs. The sheet dried in half an hour.

Georgi Vasilyevich took everything off, opened the door wide, and arranged a draught, but it was not quite the thing to do. The draught blew the curtains into the corridor, leaving the doorway uncovered. The hotel maids passed back and forth. They might see him. With some difficulty, Georgi Vasilyevich caught the curtains, dragged them into the room by main force, and pinned them together. Immediately the pins were twisted and torn out with pieces of the fabric. Only holes remained in the curtains.

He spat in disgust and put on his underdrawers. But it was equally unseemly to be only in underdrawers. He shut the door. In a minute it was again impossible to breathe in the hotel room.

Then Georgi Vasilyevich put a rubber mackintosh over his hot wet body, buttoned it up to the neck, thrust his feet into bedroom slippers, took his binoculars, and went off on a tramp through the hotel.

XX

THEY were returning from the airdrome. Seroshevsky had flown away. Heat poured from the radiator. Ray Roupe was reclining comfortably in the back seat. His chin had sunk into his necktie. His hat had slid down on his nose. The good-natured narrowed eyes were looking everywhere from under the brim of his hat.

The red road was winding and billowy. It bobbed up and down, to the right and to the left, but generally it inclined downward. Going down, the automobile went around the mountain. On the right, the horizon was sharply limited and brought nearer by the diagonal slopes of the wide mountain. On the left, the horizon stretched away in the limitless foggy spaciousness of lowlands.

The mountain was overgrown with coarse, sticky Alpine grass. Heavy, iridescent pieces of crimson ore and round boulders with web-footed imprints of silvery-green lichen were scattered over it. Further on to the right, and higher, burned the sky, almost grey with sultriness. Clouds flew by swiftly. The tips of the brown mountain peaks ran and turned toward the clouds. A long mound stretched against the horizon. Its red top was the colour of dense cinnabar. It emitted flakes of steam. Several seconds later, the whistling of unseen locomotives pierced the clear mountain air.

Nalbandov sat upright, turned slightly toward Mr. Ray Roupe. His large yellowish hands, with their blue-black strips of unclean finger nails, were clasped about the knob of the orange-coloured stick on which he leaned. A bundle of blueprints jogged up and down on the quilted seat between Nalvandov and Ray Roupe.

Their conversation had begun a few minutes before. It had not begun very auspiciously.

Mr. Ray Roupe had asked Mr. Leonard Darley to translate to Comrade Nalbandov this long, gracious, introductory sentence:

"It is very pleasant to meet such an unusual and energetic chief of construction, who flies by airplane for the purpose of personally removing petty difficulties which arise at some junction, when these difficulties could undoubtedly be very easily disposed of by the railroad administration itself."

However, before Mr. Leonard Darley could open his mouth, Nalbandov said quickly and sharply in English:

"Please don't bother. I speak English."

"Oh!" Mr. Ray Roupe exclaimed in delight. "Oh, that is very, very good. That's nice! That being the case, we will no longer have to impose on our dear Leonard, who must be frightfully bored with translating my foolish remarks. Isn't it so, Leonard, old man? Aren't you sick and tired of it?"

With his puffy hand, he good-naturedly thumped the broad shoulder of Mr. Darley, who sat in front of him on the folding seat.

"By the way," Mr. Ray Roupe added, squinting slyly, "by the way, I, too, have learned to speak Russian a bit. I was in Moscow only three days, but on my word of honour, I learned to speak the most indispensable Russian sentence. Isn't that so, Leonard? What is that universal sentence?"

After a brief pause, he bit his lips and tenderly took Nalbandov's hand.

"How is it? Yes . . . this sentence . . ."

He pushed his hat to the back of his head, and humorously distorting the Russian words, pronounced conscientiously and in syllables:

"Yes! . . . 'Who is last? I am next!' . . ."[1]

He was about to laugh gaily. But Nalbandov was severely taciturn. The American coughed, became quiet, and bit his lips.

For several minutes they rode in silence. Then an opportunity presented itself to renew the conversation that had begun so unfortunately: the mountain, the mine, the brown peaks . . .

Nalbandov sharply turned his pitch-black beard. He flung his head back.

"This mountain? Yes. Three hundred million tons of ore."

"Three hundred million?" Mr. Ray Roupe could not find words.

"Three hundred million!" Mr. Darley pulled out his notebook.

"Three hundred million. Yes. Tons."

Nalbandov's eye took long-range aim. Nalbandov was pleased. He loved to give precise, exhaustive, technical explanations, to startle people with figures and dimensions, to spread out a broad statistical picture of the construction. This was his element. Nalbandov was showing off his memory and his knowledge.

Weightily he flung out short, crisp phrases:

"Three hundred million. By incomplete calculation. Further investigation will considerably increase this figure. The quality of this ore makes it one of the richest in the world. Sixty-five to sixty-eight percent of pure iron. The coefficient of ore yield is one ton of pure ore to one ton of waste. The most intense technical

[1] referring to the long queues of people everywhere in Soviet Russia—evidence of chronic shortage of necessities and inefficient management

possibilities of development will provide us a reserve for many decades. Consequently . . ."

Nalbandov jerked his beard to the left several times. There to the left, below, was the tremendous flat stretch of territory covered by the construction.

"Consequently . . . there is nothing surprising in the extensiveness of the construction. I call your attention to this: there is the territory of our construction. You can see it from here as if it were on the palm of your hand . . ."

(As if "on the palm of your hand" . . . No! This was the coarsest, dirtiest palm in the world, extending over forty-five square kilometres, with railroad lines crossing it, with mounds and uneven places, with the fingers of mountain spurs.)

"Here will be eight blast furnaces. The most powerful in the world. The daily melt of each will attain a maximum of 1,200 tons. Beginning with October of next year, we shall have raised the production to 4,100,000 tons. In order to transport this freight out of the mill, we shall need about 6,000 trains. For the transport of raw materials and manufactured articles over the mill territory, we shall have to lay more than five hundred kilometres of railways—that is, approximately the distance between Moscow and Leningrad. Right here, you see blast furnaces No. 1 and No. 2. They are already forty-two percent finished."

And so forth and so forth.

The Americans glanced to the left in bewilderment. From this distance, the two blast furnaces under construction resembled two small miners' lamps. Near by, they must be as large as a twenty-story building.

Mr. Ray Roupe wearily covered his eyes. Too many figures. Too much technique. Too large a scale. No! Positively, humanity had lost its mind! Technique was the greatest evil in the world. Mr. Ray Roupe had long ago come to this conclusion. For a long time he had been nursing the thought of writing a remarkable book about it. Some day he would write it. A book about the destructive influence of technique upon humanity. A venomous diatribe against the machine. Mr. Ray Roupe was engrossed in his favourite meditations.

Nalbandov was speaking, slinging tremendous figures, deftly indicating objects and pointing to the right and to the left with his huge orange stick.

The automobile had already descended the mountain. It was flying in clouds of burning dust, in the midst of chaos, through construction and habitation sectors.

Mr. Ray Roupe opened his eyes. Smiling pleasantly, he asked Mr. Nalbandov whether it was possible to look over the environs. The territory of the construction was too sultry and too dusty. But there in the steppe it was probably very interesting—that limitless Ural steppe where, it was said, nomads still survived.

Nalbandov gave the order to the chauffeur.

The machine raced past the hotel. Around the hotel the ground was strewn with broken glass. The broken glass glittered unendurably in the sun.

"Comrade Nalbandov! Just a minute!"

Out of the hotel and across the path of the machine, ran a small, frightfully black, unshaven and dishevelled man, hatless, with a loose-leaf pad in his hand. He wore boots, mustard-coloured leggings and was dressed in a well-worn leather coat that had once been black. The coat was unbuttoned. It revealed a net undershirt and a chest thickly covered with curly blue-black hair. His gleaming, bright eyes, tinged with yellow, had coal-black pupils.

"Hey, boss! Stop! One minute!" (This to the chauffeur.) The man with the loose-leaf pad jumped onto the running board.

"One question: What is your opinion about the Kharkov record?"

Nalbandov turned sharply. He looked straight at him.

"And who do you happen to be?"

"I am the correspondent of the Russian Telegraphic Agency. We have met before, I think, at the plant office."

"I don't know. I don't remember. There are many correspond-

ents here. Well, what do you want of me, Comrade Correspondent?"

"Your opinion concerning the Kharkov record."

"Are you asking about the celebrated Kharkov mixtures? How
many did they slap together there? Was it three hundred and
six? I don't know. I'm not interested. They may even stand on
their heads if they like."

"So. And what is your opinion about applying the Kharkov experience to our construction?"

Nalbandov abruptly turned away.

"I don't know. Perhaps here, too, we shall find some . . .
lovers of the sensational. At any rate, as far as I'm concerned, I
can tell you only one thing, and I say it with absolute finality: I
regard all of these experiments as utter foolishness and technical
ignorance. This is a construction, not a stunt. My respects!"

"Is this your official opinion?"

"No, it is my private opinion."

"Very well."

The correspondent of the Russian Telegraphic Agency jumped
down from the running board.

"We shall so record it."

XXI

SCRAPING his feet along the floor which was covered with
drifts of dust, Georgi Vasilyevich sauntered past the closed
and the open doors of hotel rooms, past curtains that were motionless, past curtains that quivered, past curtains that flapped,
blown up and stretched out by the wind and straining full length
across the corridor.

He looked into the open, unoccupied rooms.

He saw shining Slavic wardrobes with mirrors; iron beds with
nickel-plated knobs; shaky oval tables; wash-basins; wooden
lamp stands covered with light, round, tautly-stretched, hand-

made, colourful silken lamp shades. All of this hotel furniture had been bought at the market for second-hand goods. It was commonplace, prosaic, incongruous and strange in the midst of this ancient, sultry Pugachov steppe, in the midst of these winds fighting among themselves, these draughts, these blizzards . . .

He walked up and down the stairs, coming close to the huge, square-paned windows at the end of corridors.

He stopped before them, regarding them as if they were magnificent engravings, severe, dark brown, slightly retouched.

The windows looked out to all four sides of the world—the north, the west, the south, the east.

He walked from one corridor to another, from one window to another. Around him turned the distant, segmented panorama of the construction, studded with a multitude of stark, sharply-limned, fine details. Barracks, tents, roads, posts, insulators, thermo-electric plants, cranes, excavators, trenches, mounds, wagons, scaffoldings, mountains, hills, grass, smoke, refuse, horses . . . Tiny human figures—the further away the tinier—and their microscopic shadows scattered sparsely over the tremendous landscape, seemed completely immobile, like a photograph.

He looked through his binoculars.

The binoculars were prismatic, made by Zeiss. They were designed for the field artillery, with lines and markings around the lenses.

Georgi Vasilyevich adjusted the binoculars. The undulating vista flooded toward him, swelling fabulously and flowing out of his circular field of vision in all directions.

The general yielded to the particular. Tiny figures moved stiffly, grew human in size and colour, emerged from their catalepsy. Through the lines and markings (through the pluses and minuses) of the binoculars, they walked, rode, stood, raised their arms, flashed their spectacles.

Who are they, these people, each one separately? thought Georgi Vasilyevich, guiding the binoculars across the panorama and moving them from one plane to another.

Here, for example, half a kilometre away, somewhere—but who

could tell where, now that the general had disintegrated—walked a man.

How distinctly and in what detail could he be seen! Black trousers, white shirt open at the collar, hatless, barefooted. His round head thrust forward, his heavy shoulders bent, he walked on his small, bare, brown feet with mincing little steps. Here he stopped, looked down. What was there? An excavation. He stopped on the edge of the trench, stood for a while, and turned to the right. He walked around the trench, looking for a place to descend. He squatted, jumped down. Now he could no longer be seen. A minute passed. Suddenly he reappeared from underground, on the other side of the trench. He flung a cable over his head. His white shirt flickered. Its back had turned dark, wet.

Where was he going—this small barefooted man in the shirt, the back of which was soaked with sweat? Who was he? What was he looking for? What was his name? What was he doing here on the construction? How was he getting along? What part did he play? What was he thinking about?

Who knew?

Georgi Vasilyevich adjusted the binoculars ninety degrees to the right. He moved them slowly and smoothly. But the objects— the posts, the roofs, the wagons, the uneven surface of the ground, the cars, the culverts—sped by with a purposeful mad speed, daz- zling and flowing together from right to left, merging in the cone of an endless carousel.

Georgi Vasilyevich turned his head slightly to the south and there—in that magic optic world of the binoculars—several striped kilometres of real earthly space flew by.

He stopped moving the binoculars.

Here was an entirely different sector, probably a habitation sec- tor. A wooden porch, steps, banisters. A turnstile. A washstand on high wooden legs. Fifteen or twenty men in various positions. Some sat on steps. Others lay on the ground. Still others stood about. One of them, a tow-headed fellow, seized the post of the turnstile with both hands and pulled himself up on his muscles. Another one embraced the post. All of them were young. Their coloured shirts, yellow and blue football sweaters, kerchiefs, skirts, grey canvas trousers, rope shoes, were bright and distinct.

Why did they come together? What were they doing? Who were they? Were they singing? Were they talking? Were they resting? Had they gathered together to play football? Were they athletes, perhaps? Or excursionists?

Who knew?

Georgi Vasilyevich passed from one corridor to another. He stopped at the windows. He adjusted the binoculars. South, north, west, east were open before him for scores of kilometres. But he understood nothing of what he saw.

He looked to the east. There were hills. The sun was still in the east.

One hill was black and trampled. It stood against the sun above houses that looked like carcasses, above barracks and barns, like a precisely-cut silhouette. On its summit, distinct and black, appeared wooden shaft-bows of horses, shafts, horns of cows, wheels.

What was there?

People were going up and down the hill. Two were going up. The one in front wore wide trousers, walked loose-jointedly; under his arm he held a bundle; his sharp knees rose; he shuffled along in his large bast shoes; the noonday dust smoked. The one behind was thin, doleful; in his gait there was something sinuous, canine; he followed on the heels of the first man. How hot they must be!

Who were they, those two? Where were they going? Why? What did they want on this hill? What relationship did they bear to all of this, for the sake of which Georgi Vasilyevich had come here? And what were they talking about? What were they thinking?

Who knew?

He looked to the west. There was a large, narrow body of water. What was it? A river? A pond? A lake? A column of sturdy telegraph poles stood obliquely up to the waist in this monotonous water which was the nauseatingly bluish-pink colour of lungwort.

Beyond this strip of water was the dusty, lettuce-green strip of the opposite shore. And beyond that was the misty outline of a low Ural mountain range.

The track of a narrow-gauge railway had been laid on this shore along the very edge of the water, amidst splinters and logs. Women walked in single file over the railroad ties. There were about forty of them. On their shoulders they carried boards, saws, sacks. Among them many were pregnant, with high repulsive stomachs.

(For some reason there seemed to be many pregnant women on this construction.)

Here, for example, was one.

In a pink woollen shawl, in a full peasant skirt, scarcely able to walk, she stepped heavily on her heels, swaying under the weight of the boards that bent down like tires on her shoulders. She tried to keep up with the others, but she constantly lost step. She stumbled, afraid to be left behind, wiping her face quickly with the edge of her shawl as she walked.

Her stomach was unusually high and distorted. It was clear that she had only a few days to go, perhaps only a few hours.

Why was she here? What was she thinking? What had she to do with all this?

Who knew?

He passed to another corridor and looked to the north. Over three hills an airplane flew low. It had just risen.

(No, it was not flying. That was not exact. It seemed to ride over the air, rat-tat-ting and diving over the narrow, billowy roadway of the clouds.)

Where did it come from? Where was it going? Who was flying in it? Why?

Who knew?

Georgi Vasilyevich went down the stairs.

A small man in a blue coat too large for him, and large sharp-toed boots, was pushing against the closed door of the hotel restaurant.

Georgi Vasilyevich immediately noted the man's tortoise-rimmed spectacles, camel-like nostrils, the cap that was pulled down low over his head and apparently being split asunder by the bulge of his stiff shock of hair, and the yellow pencil sticking out of his pocket.

"What do you think of this?" the man with the large nose remarked sadly, looking near-sightedly and shyly at Georgi Vasilyevich. "What do you say to this? It's already closed. That's a fine how-do-you-do!"

"There's nothing remarkable about that. It's always closed from nine to one," Georgi Vasilyevich said with some severity. He had already acquainted himself with the customary details and regulations of the construction.

The man with the large nose stood for a moment in thought, tugged at his nose, and, just to make sure, lightly pushed the door again with his foot and went away.

Who was he? Where was he going?

Who knew?

On the plywood bulletin board, near the closed door, hung the kitchen wall-newspaper.

Georgi Vasilyevich pulled out his notebook and copied something from the board. For some reason, he preserved the exact orthography. The note was as follows:

"Our Outrage. Our Comrade Zhukov is a model young man and besides he is a Young Communist. Instead of being an example for everybody on the job, he commits an outrage. After quarrelling with Citizen Molyavina, he threw the innards of some game at her. It got into her eyes, so that it was necessary to send for first aid. But, thanks to the good condition of the water system, the eyes were washed.

"Comrade associates! Do not follow the example of such a comrade! Signed, The Flea."

Under this, in pen and ink, was a childish scrawl of a man in an apron throwing a bit of game at Citizen Molyavina. Sparks flew from the eyes of Citizen Molyavina, and underneath was written: "Pretty strong!"

Georgi Vasilyevich regretted that it was impossible to copy the drawing, but he was quite satisfied with the note.

Squinting against the sun, he walked out the door of the hotel to get some fresh air.

An elephant was being led along the road. Children were running after the elephant. Georgi Vasilyevich was not surprised. Anything might be expected here. He only thought mechanically:

Where did the elephant come from? Where was he being taken? Why?

Who knew?

Meticulously recording the elephant in his notebook, Georgi Vasilyevich returned to his hotel room, sat down at the table with decision, pulled the loose-leaf pad toward him and rapidly wrote the first line of his dispatch:

"A year and a half ago this was a barren steppe."

After writing this line, he grew thoughtful. The cursed wall radiated insufferable heat. He stood on his toes, leaned across the table, and pushed his head through the open window. Unrelated thoughts occurred to him:

Airplane flying . . . Rapacious vultures had infested this region . . . A shaggy-haired youth with a loose-leaf pad jumped on the running board of an automobile . . . A barefooted man walking . . . Pregnant women carrying boards . . . An elephant being led . . . Comrade Zhukov threw innards at Citizen Molyavina . . . But why do I need all this? What is the connection between them? No, there's something wrong here, something wrong!

In disgust, he ripped off the first page of the pad and tore it into tiny pieces.

"Creeping empiricism!" he muttered.

XXII

KATYA dressed hurriedly.

"Oh, these everlasting tricks of David's!"

She ran noisily across the corridor. Excited tenants looked out into the corridor. Her sleepy face was angry, her large lips swollen. She tore her little hat from the rack. The door slammed. The echo resounded along the stairway, rolled down and crashed to bits, as if a cupboard had been thrown down the four flights of stairs. As she ran down, Katya put on her knitted béret.

She had the same sort of hair as her brother—coarse, fluffy, curly. She pulled her crimson hat over it with difficulty. The hat immediately puffed out and became large and fluffy.

The front windows were wide open. Beyond were the bright diagonals luminous between the slanting shadows of a summer morning. Beyond that, long moving strips of construction. A new building was going up in the yard. In a window, she caught a glimpse of the city's roofs. Below lay the armoured torso of a boiler. A workman passed by and struck the riveting with an instrument. A watery sound rolled down the length of the boiler, but it was immediately cleft by the light crash of a falling beam. From surrounding attics grew the crooked, double-jointed webs of antennæ.

Ten years ago Katya had come from the provinces to live with her brother. She had been sixteen then, and he twenty-five.

She had come to Moscow with a small osier basket, fastened with a pencil instead of a lock. She had worn a man's ragged overcoat and a cotton-lined cavalry cap with a blue star. The slight, frail girl had looked about her with wide frightened eyes.

Winter was ending.

Katya had looked down from the fourth story of the unfamiliar house in the unfamiliar city.

Below lay a pile of firewood. The dull snow, soiled with soot, flowed into the pile of wood. There had been no antennæ over the attics. There had seemed to be many more churches, and actually there had been many more of them then. The seventeenth century of churches was still resisting the eighteenth century of private residences and gabled roofs. History had painted its apiary in miraculous indigo, ochre, and cinnabar. It had solidly gilded the turnip-like cupolas and had whitened the columns.

Like a feudal lord, it still exercised its indivisible, self-assumed authority over the Red Square, throughout the entire tremendous

length and breadth of the painstakingly set cobble-stones between the Kremlin wall and the monument to Minin and Pozharsky,[1] from the round stone platter which is the place of the Forehead,[2] and from St. Basil the Blessed [3] with cupolas and walls
representing a miraculous mixture of pineapples and Scheherazade
melons, and the tunic and chin strap of a fairy-tale drummer, to
the low arch of the Iberian gates.[4]

Every quarter of an hour, day and night, it spoke the chro-
matic language of chiming bells.

Like a boyar in a high sable hat, it walked the length of the
Kremlin wall, amidst patriotic decorations.

Perhaps its morocco boot had touched the very spot, where—
years hence (and Katya would remember this for the rest of her
life) in that fierce frost when birds were to fall dead on the wing
and the smoky pinkish sun was to be scarcely marked on the
hoary sky—pyroxylin would rend the flinty ground . . .

But how Moscow had changed since those vanished days!

Katya ran quickly from Zaryadye to the street car stop at the
Moscow River bridge.

She muttered:

"He's absolutely crazy! He woke up the entire house. He ought
to be locked up! He ought to! Here I'm running at breakneck

[1] Tradition regarded Minin (a meat and fish merchant, prominent citizen
of Novgorod, subsequently an advisor to the first Tsar of the Romanov
dynasty, Michael Feodorvich) and Prince Pozharsky (a military leader,
courtier and public administrator) as patriots who had saved Russia from a
Polish conquest in 1612. The monument erected to them was more massive
than beautiful.

[2] Place of the Forehead—*Lobnoye Myesto*—constructed presumably early
in the sixteenth century, had been subjected to considerable alterations from
time to time. Since its first mention in history, in connection with Tsar Ivan
IV's promise to rule his subjects justly (1550), it had been a tribunal of the
Tsars, an historic rallying point and a witness of public executions.

[3] St. Basil's Cathedral, built in 1555-61 by order of Tsar Ivan IV, has
had such a hectic career of fires, repairs, and reconstructions that nothing
of its original architecture has remained on the inside, and only restoration
work carried on since the Bolshevik Revolution has partially uncovered the
characteristic features of sixteenth century architecture on the outside

[4] These gates derive their name from a chapel built at the Voskresensky
Gates to house the miraculous Iberian ikon of the Holy Virgin, which was
brought to Moscow from an Athenian monastery in 1648. The ikon was
removed to Vladimir in 1812. The chapel no longer exists.

speed to Molchanovka, looking for Professor Smolensky. That's a fine how-do-you-do!"

Of course, she was angry. That was natural. But, at the same time, she was delighted with her brother. She hurried to carry out with precision and accuracy his strange, hurried, and apparently very important commission.

She kept repeating to herself:

"The very latest analytical calculation. The very latest analytical calculation. No, so help me, my brother is mad! House No. 10, Apartment 14. 10, 14. Or the other way around—14, 10. The very latest analytical calculation. Professor Smolensky. Professor Smolensky. Kharkov, Kharkov, Kharkov . . ."

Blazing cauldrons of tar. They belched heat, stung the eye. The repair work had made a purgatory of Moscow. Street car routes changed daily.

Katya was waiting for "A." It did not come. Instead of "A," altogether unsuitable, fantastic letters and numbers passed along the steamy, mirror-like river. It was something like a confused game of lotto. Katya was unlucky. Out of the sack shaken up by the repair work of the quay, fate was pulling little barrels of wild street car numerals. They did not correspond in the least to the numerals placed on the chequered chart at the street car stop. The street car clock indicated twenty minutes past eight. There was no taxi. There was no cab.

Katya ran back across the Red Square.

(In ten minutes I can run along Mokhovaya and Volkhonka to the Prechistensky Gates, and from there in five minutes through the side streets to Molchanovka, and that's that . . . The very latest analytical calculation. The very latest analytical calculation . . .)

The new, smooth pavement of the enormous square gleamed like a polished floor.

Minin and Pozharsky were enmeshed in heavy chains. Minin and Pozharsky were being lifted and shaken loose by a crane. The monument had turned somewhat askew.

In front of the mausoleum grew roses. Fully reflected in the black marble and rosy granite mirrors of its façade, floated St. Basil the Blessed, pedestrians, automobiles, clouds.

Over the Iberian Gates stood columns of plaster dust. The famous gate was being torn down. At the corner of Tverskaya, Okhotny Ryad was being wrecked. At the Prechistensky Gates, idlers were crowding. A cupola of the Cathedral of Christ the Saviour was being taken apart. It was being taken apart in narrow golden segments. They disclosed a complex azure carcass, through which, like through the lattices of a summer house, gleamed the greyish-blue summer sky which suddenly appeared strangely empty. Small cupolas of the belfry were also being stripped. They resembled wire cages. People were scurrying in the cages, like birds.

Quite recently Katya had been at the Prechistensky Gates, but the appearance of the cathedral which was suddenly being taken apart did not surprise her in the least. She merely glanced at it. She was in a great hurry.

At that moment they were pulling down one of the bells. It was pulled down simply and easily: it was held by steel rigging which was being wound steadily.

Katya saw the cage of the bell lifted high over the tower. It croaked and, suddenly turning slowly in the air, flew down.

Peaceful Molchanovka glistened with greenery, breathed shadows, resounded with the thunder claps of grand pianos. May rolled the green cart of a red-shirted iceman along Molchanovka. Katya quickly found the house and the apartment.

Professor Smolensky opened the door himself. In his hand he held a glass in a silver holder. He was sipping tea with milk. The spoon threatened to jab not merely his eyebrow, but his eye.

Breathing rapidly, hot, licking her lips, Katya conveyed her brother's message while still in the doorway and before she even thought of entering.

"Ah!" said the Professor. "Ah! Margulies. Of course, David Lvovich. Of course, of course, I know him very well. A student of mine. Delighted. I understand. Won't you please come into my study? As you see, this is my study and it is also the dining room and even the music room. I rely on your indulgence."

Ganon's études were running through the depths of the apartment.

Katya pulled off her béret and, fanning her flaming cheeks with it, followed the professor.

"As Chekhov has it," he murmured in his deep bass, "here is the police department, and the justice department and the militia department, all in one, quite like an institute for young ladies."

They entered an old room crowded with all sorts of furniture and full of green light: thick maples massed against the windows.

"And as for you, ma belle Ta-ti-a-na,[5] may we trouble you to discontinue your divine tones for the time being?"

An unattractive girl with very long and very black eyelashes immediately closed the piano and walked noiselessly out of the room, carefully adjusting her cotton blouse with her small thin hands.

"Oh, really, I am so sorry!" said Katya.

"Don't be disturbed. According to our private family constitution, there is mutual non-aggression in the affairs of others. Well, now! Please sit down."

Katya sat down at an oaken writing table which was carved elaborately and in bad taste.

"Well, now! As far as I understand it, David Lvovich seems to be interested in the entire complex of problems connected with Kharkov's last experiment in increasing the number of mixtures on cement-mixers of various types. Is that not so?"

Katya blushed.

"Yes . . . Various constructions . . . Rather . . ."

"That's so. An exceedingly interesting problem. Its solution opens the broadest industrial perspectives. We at the Institute of Construction had an unusually interesting conference night before last. Yes. We formulated a series of regulations. To-day these were printed in 'Za Industrializatsiu.' "

---

[5] Current Soviet platitude characterises the older intelligentsia as admirers of Chekhov and of Tschaikovsky's opera *"Eugene Onyegin."*

Professor Smolensky spread his elbows on the table. He gathered his thoughts.

"How can I explain it to you in a general way? If you will be so kind, note that there have developed here two sharply antagonistic lines of thought, and this is extremely curious. Excuse me, I hope that you are more or less familiar with the subject?"

She looked at him pleadingly with upturned eyes.

"Dodya asked for an analytical calculation," she said timidly. "You know: the very latest analytical calculation. And it's about Kharkov . . . Moreover, I must be home by ten o'clock. He will call me at ten. At ten Moscow time and at twelve according to their time."

Smolensky smiled benevolently into his moustache.

"So," he said, bending low his beautiful head with its broad brow. "So. I understand."

He was somewhat corpulent and ample. He wore a light cream-coloured shirt tied around the waist with a blue-tasselled cord.

His wet, iron-grey hair was parted and still bore traces of the stiff brush. His large red neck was washed clean, and had apparently been well rubbed with a rough towel.

XXIII

DECIDEDLY, Semechkin was irritated.
        In the first place—the shoe.

That sole—the devil take it! The telephone wire was cutting his instep. It was painful to walk. Small stones and splinters were filling the shoe. They were irritating, torturing him. He had to walk on his heel. He had to hop too much. But the main thing was the kind of people before whom he had to be at his best. Smetana? Margulies? A fine lot of people! A fine lot of workers!

In the second place—the Kharkov record. It was a very interesting fact, of course, but what conclusions had been drawn from this fact? Actually, none.

Semechkin had purposely risen earlier than usual. He had put the newspaper containing the dispatch from Kharkov into his brief case and had gone immediately to the sector.

He planned to be the first, to take the initiative, to take matters into his own hands—as became a special correspondent of a large regional newspaper.

But instead, everything was going wrong. Already everybody was running over the sector. Some one had hung up the placard about besting Kharkov. In every corner people were whispering. And nobody would tell him anything he really wanted to know.

And where was the organisation? Where was public opinion? Where was the press? They weren't worth a damn! Semechkin went to Margulies.

Margulies mumbled vaguely, lisped, offered him some candy: "Try it, it's very good." He ran hither and thither and nothing happened. Where was Margulies? There was no Margulies! There was no trace of him! He went to Korneyev.

Korneyev heard nothing, said, "Yes, yes, yes," while his eyes gleamed insanely and his nose twitched. Korneyev ran up and down with a piece of paper and a pencil in his hand, counting his paces, measuring . . . That admiral of the Swiss navy!

As for Smetana, there was no use talking to him. That handshaker of a Smetana merely smiled from ear to ear, slapped Semechkin's back and soothed: "Don't you worry, Semechkin, don't worry." He was a fool and a dummy, and that was all there was to it.

Mosya was decidedly of the careerist type. All he wanted was to get into the newspaper and he cared nothing about anything else. All he did was to run around, his eyes sparkling, swearing softly through his teeth.

(By the way—a significant fact: certain foremen on the construction swear. They should be swept clean off the job. A special dispatch should be written about that. One might even start a campaign, rouse large sections of public opinion, attract the attention of the trade union.)

And as soon as he turned away, all of them—Margulies and

Korneyev and Mosya—immediately began to whisper behind his back, conferring, carrying on secret diplomacy. Disgraceful treatment of a special correspondent of a regional newspaper! Clearly, under such conditions there could not even be any talk of establishing records. Moreover, was it timely to be concerned about establishing records, when all around was chaos, swearing, lagging behind, opportunism, indifference, mismanagement?

He must go to Filonov, bring this to his attention. Of course, Filonov was a fairly reliable fellow, and yet, somehow, he could not manage things. To be quite frank—he simply could not manage. It was absolutely necessary to speak plainly to him—in dead earnest. He would have to pose the question in all its aspects and on the basis of fundamental principles. Semechkin went to see Filonov.

The sector was aflame, almost imprisoned by noonday sultriness. The nickel-plated lock of the brief case twinkled like a star. Its reflection swirled and jumped around Semechkin, running far away and bouncing back as if it were on a rubber band.

Peering everywhere through his impenetrably black goggles, Semechkin hobbled across the sector. In the black lenses, the world was reflected minutely and elaborately. But, somehow, it was reflected ominously, disapprovingly. The tones changed insidiously. The sun appeared too white; the sky too smoky; the earth, an incredible olive-green; the planked walls of the offices and sentry-boxes were a photographic lilac; the faces and hands of men were the colour of straw.

Semechkin would appear suddenly, now here, now there—bobbing up everywhere. Along his way, he would approach people, stop beside various machines, peer into excavations, feel the stacked materials with his long fingers. Throughout this inspection trip, he mooed vaguely in his bass voice. He would clasp his hands behind his back, droop his head, and stand thus in profound thought, slapping his brief case against the back of his knees. His knees would jerk in reflex action.

Semechkin writhed in troubled thought. He was overwhelmed by the gigantic complexity of the problems presented by this scintillating world in construction. He could not comprehend this world, could not penetrate it, could not learn to love it. Semechkin and this world were irreconcilable. Between them stood an invisible but insurmountable barrier.

Semechkin was energetically calculating how to take this world in hand, how to set everything in the world right, how to arrange everything, to organise it, and, by means of the regional newspaper, connect it with the largest sections of public opinion—in a word, to do everything that a clever, exemplary, militant special correspondent should do.

But this world would not give in. This world was all sharp corners. It slipped out of his hands. It was managed and ruled by others—by Margulies, Korneyev, Smetana. Even Mosya ruled this world . . .

Clever, venomous, disapproving, Semechkin was hostile to this world. And thus it had been ever, everywhere. Semechkin had not been able to get along at the regional centre. He had then gone to a collective farm—and could not get along there, either. Then he had come here. He sought deeds of fame and of sweeping dimensions. At first it had seemed to him that he had found them here. But although the deeds soon proved petty, his hands could not encompass their dimensions.

Semechkin had come to hate this world. Semechkin went in to see Filonov.

Filonov was completely hoarse. He no longer shouted or even spoke. He merely opened wide his red mouth which was topped by the black, shining eyebrows of a virgin moustache, and with his fist he diagonally cut the air, grey with cheap tobacco.

From the table he snatched documents and graphs, striking them with his husky palm, which was crossed by sharp black lines. In his fervour, he savagely flung the papers back on the table. He resorted incessantly to the stub of indelible pencil behind his ear.

Various people walked in and out endlessly. The door never stopped slamming. An old typewriter clattered and tinkled in a staccato patter, like a racing motorcycle. Dusty bars of light that glistened like sugar, and sharp cages of shadow black as coal swirled, broke, and crashed in the small room of the Party nucleus.

The telephone rang every minute. It jangled. Impassioned voices shouted into the bulky transmitter. The telephone was large, old-fashioned, oaken. It hung on the wall, occupying a huge space. In order to call some one, it was necessary to crank long and tediously the metallic handle, which shot a tingling current of electricity into the palm of the hand.

Semechkin's eyes sought a place where he might sit down. There were three stools in the room, but they were all occupied. He walked up to Filonov and leaned against the wall behind him.

For a while he looked over Filonov's shoulder at the papers. He looked down, bending his head like a goose. He sneered malevolently: the papers were all trivial, as if deliberately petty and frivolous:

"Re: issue of two pair of boots and one canvas bucket to muckers of Vasyutin's brigade."

"Notice. Categorical and final. By Sanitary Inspector Raisa Rubinchik. Re: the disgraceful condition of the shower baths and garbage boxes at the sixth habitation sector."

"Investigation of the stupid waste of eight and one-half kilograms of badly needed nails."

"Workers' proposal to substitute rubberised cord boots for the costly leather footwear now used, thus effecting a saving for the sector."

Trifles, trifles, trifles . . .

And the people who crowded around Filonov clamoured likewise for trifles. Smudgy-nosed carters grumbled about hay. An old Bashkir with the jasper-brown face of an idol muttered something utterly incomprehensible and showed everybody a greasy account book, poking at it with his saffron finger nail. A woman in canvas gloves splattered with dabs of concrete pertly demanded in a shrill voice some information for the village soviet. A boy with a peeling nose desperately cursed a certain comrade Nedobed, who was interfering with socially useful and indispensable work by refusing to give the art shop blue paint.

Semechkin was profoundly disgusted and bored by all of this. He cleared his throat impressively. Filonov paid no attention. Then Semechkin slapped his shoulder with a sweeping gesture.

"Hello, boss!"

Filonov raised his swollen eyes. Semechkin placed his long grey fingers in the broad palm of Filonov's hand.

"Well, how's business, boss? Is it getting on?"

"Eh," Filonov responded indifferently in a hoarse voice. "Hello. What do you want?"

Semechkin cleared his throat significantly: H'm, h'm.

"I want to talk to you."

"Come on, come on. Make it short."

Semechkin bounced the brief case up with his knee, rummaged in it unhurriedly and placed a newspaper on the table.

"Read this, Filonych." [1]

"What is there to read! I have no time to read. You tell me what it's about."

"Kharkov."

"Well, I know, I know. What about it?"

Semechkin looked around. He thrust his malevolent spectacles at Filonov's nose and lowered his voice considerably:

"Bear this in mind, Filonych, I have just walked all through the sector. H'm, h'm. I have observed unhealthy attitudes toward the Kharkov record. Here and there people are going to extremes. Margulies . . . Korneyev . . . Extremists are at it again. That's a fact. In the first place—absence of organisation. In the second place—public opinion is asleep. In the third place—the press is being suppressed. In the fourth place—the foremen are swearing."

Filonov knitted his brows painfully. He tried to understand and to grasp Semechkin's main thought while Semechkin's dull bass continued to pile sentence upon sentence. He stirred up so much confusion that he soon stopped understanding himself; having

[1] One of the many possible variants of Filonov, expressing affection or familiarity.

ceased to understand himself, he grew angry, and although he had begun with wishes for a long life, he ended up with a prayer for the departed soul.

He had begun apparently with a demand to beat Kharkov immediately. Then he had complained of disorder and carelessness. Finally, he had delivered himself of the expression about the stunt, which he had picked up somewhere, and to it he had added another that was equally quotable: "Conceived as if by Napoleon and executed as if by Vanka the Dauber."

Twice he repeated this last sentence about Napoleon and Vanka the Dauber with particular delight, stopped, was silent, and repeated it a third time. Anger choked him.

"Wait, my friend," said Filonov, turning red. "Wait. I don't quite understand . . ."

A forked vein swelled on his forehead. Suddenly, with all his might, he thrust his fist against the table and lifted himself from the stool.

"Did you come here especially to gossip, to cast gloom over a bright day? Talk straight: what do you want? And if you don't know yourself . . . if you don't know yourself . . ."

Filonov rubbed his face with the palms of his hands, squinted, cooled off, sat down. His voice gave out completely. He opened his mouth wide and spread out his arms.

"Here," he whispered in a voice barely audible. "Here, if you like . . . pipes . . . they're not giving us any pipes for the showers . . ."

He thrust a piece of paper at Semechkin.

"Factual material . . . Grab these fellows by the seat of their pants! Shake them hard. Expose them in your newspaper. As for this business—leave it alone . . . Listen, Semechkin, drop it . . ."

He waved his arm in disgust and annoyance.

With dignity, unhurriedly, Semechkin replaced the newspaper in the brief case. He smiled wryly. His lips trembled. He was deathly pale.

"Very well," he said in a thick, low voice.
He walked out.

XXIV

"SAY, I'm very glad that I met you. How are you, Georgi Vasilyevich? You're just in time. I want to talk to you about something."

Georgi Vasilyevich smiled genially and in bewilderment.

"Ah—ah—ah!" he sang out. "Ah—ah—ah! My respects. Of course, of course . . . As you see, I have been walking around the hotel . . . Frightfully hot . . . Yes . . . Have you noticed how much broken glass there is around this hotel? Simply frightful . . . It's like walking on snow crust . . . And it's all because of the draughts . . ."

Georgi Vasilyevich painfully tried to recollect where he had seen this young man and who he was. He must have met him somewhere quite recently. Those clumsy boots, grey with dust, those mustard-coloured leggings, that frightfully unshaven, thin, young face with eyes like coals.

Georgi Vasilyevich pressed the narrow delicate hand tenderly and held it for a long time. He was trying to gain time. He uttered various exclamations of greeting, and all the time he kept thinking to himself: Was it at the factory office? I think not. On the train? No. A student doing practice work? No. Is he in charge of the dining room? No. This is terrible! It's so embarrassing! And he even knows my name and patronymic. A worker-correspondent? No. There's such a lot of people here! It's impossible to remember them all!

"Here . . . That's it . . . Yes . . . Hot . . . Well, now . . . And how are you? Forgive me . . . But you know, I have a frightful memory for names and surnames. I remember your face perfectly, but as for the name and surname . . . And where we met . . . That's my weak point."

The young man smiled solicitously.

"I'm the correspondent of the Russian Telegraphic Agency. I even greeted you at the railroad station when you arrived. My name is Vinkich."

"Yes, yes! Quite right. Oh, yes! Comrade Vinkich. For God's sake, forgive me! Vinkich, of course!"

"A Serbian surname. My father is of Serbian descent. So you see, Georgi Vasilyevich, I'm glad that I met you here. But excuse me, perhaps you are busy? Are you thinking things over? Are you observing?"

"Thinking matters over? Yes. In a way, I'm thinking things over and observing, but, generally speaking, I'm not busy. On the contrary. I'm at your service. You know, to tell you the truth, I'm absolutely lost here. The newspaper expects a sketch from me, and literally I don't know where and how to begin."

"Yes, it's almost impossible to grasp everything all at once."

"And how long have you been around here?"

"A year and a half. I haven't been away once."

"Oho! Phew—phew!" Georgi Vasilyevich whistled. "I call that smart. But tell me, is it really true that a year and a half ago there was actually a bare steppe here?"

"An absolutely bare steppe. An empty place. People lived in tents."

"I must confess that I was contemplating some such beginning. Like this: 'A year and a half ago this was a bare steppe. People lived in tents.'"

Vinkich modestly lowered his blue eyes.

"You see, Georgi Vasilyevich, we have had a number of literary men here (of course, not men of your calibre). And all of them invariably began thus: 'A year and a half ago this was a bare steppe.' This . . . is the path of least resistance."

"Yes, what a pity!"

"However, Georgi Vasilyevich, I have something to tell you."

The correspondent of the Russian Telegraphic Agency pulled a loose-leaf pad from the side pocket of his well-worn leather jacket, revealing the grey baize lining of his coat.

"What is your attitude toward the Kharkov record?"

"Was there a record set by Kharkov? That's very interesting."

"Of course. It was in the newspapers yesterday. Haven't you read it? A world record."

"A world record? You don't say! Of course I read about it, but apparently I paid no attention to it. But you must admit that Kharkov . . . While for the present I'm interested principally in so-called local material . . ."

Georgi Vasilyevich fingered the air cautiously. The solemn Vinkich stood before him with bowed head.

"You see, Georgi Vasilyevich," he said indulgently, "that being the case, I shall explain it to you in two words."

And with precision, brevity, and respect, he explained the history and significance of the Kharkov record to Georgi Vasilyevich.

"So that," he added, "our construction, Georgi Vasilyevich, is confronted by the very serious problem of utilising the Kharkov experience, and by the opportunity to proceed further along this path. Hence I am very eager to find out your personal opinion: should we enter into competition with Kharkov and establish a new world's record or should we not?"

"Naturally we should!" Georgi Vasilyevich exclaimed. "What else can we do! As I see it, this calls for competition with Kharkov. And the significance of socialist competition is tremendous. That is a generally known fact. If they do three hundred and six, then we must do three hundred and seven . . . If they do three hundred and seven, then we must do three hundred and eight . . . And so on. Naturally."

Vinkich shook his head.

"So you are for it?"

"What a strange fellow you are! Can there be any doubt about it?"

"There are doubts about it."

"In other words . . ."

"Public opinion is sharply divided. There are very ardent partisans of the record. There are no less ardent opponents. I'm very glad that you are among the partisans. Without a doubt we shall have to fight vigorously."

"One moment . . . I don't quite . . . What do you mean—fight? My opinion is—purely subjective . . . As you know perfectly well, I am not an authority on concrete . . . I am, so to speak, an objective observer and no more . . . So, you see, I cannot assume any responsibility, and particularly, I cannot, as you expressed it, 'fight' about it. And besides, why is it necessary to fight? Whom do you propose to fight?"

Vinkich lifted his pale face to Georgi Vasilyevich. His eyes were black, shining and calm.

"You see, Georgi Vasilyevich," he said softly, "our situation on this construction is such that every question, even the most trivial, assumes a tremendous significance as a matter of principle. One cannot be neutral. Of necessity, one must choose definitely either one or another point of view and fight for it to the last drop of blood. I, for example, have been fighting day in and day out for a year and a half."

"One moment, my dear comrade. What has all this to do with the Kharkov record? It seems to me that the problem is perfectly clear."

"It's clear; and yet, it is not quite clear. And that is the point. We don't have to go very far. Take Comrade Nalbandov, for example. I have just talked to him. Do you know Comrade Nalbandov?"

"Nalbandov? . . . Yes, yes . . . The name is familiar. Nalbandov, Nalbandov . . . Say, is he the man in the black leather coat with the huge orange stick and the jet-black beard? . . . Of course, of course . . . He has taken me around the construction. Engineer Nalbandov. A remarkable engineer! He knows his business. A good man!"

Georgi Vasilyevich pronounced the words "a good man" with special pleasure. He had heard the words recently and had noted them in his little book as an example of folk lore.

"Yes . . . Comrade Nalbandov," he said with emphasis. "A *good* man. Very *good*."

Vinkich smiled subtly, but he smiled only with his lips. His eyes remained black, calm, and even a trifle sad.

"Well, you see, Georgi Vasilyevich, I must warn you that Engineer Nalbandov is categorically opposed to all such experiments."

"What did you say? How strange! But why?"

"Engineer Nalbandov considers all such record-setting as evidence of ignorance of technology."

"One moment . . . And Kharkov? What about Kharkov? I don't understand."

"I cannot tell you anything about that."

"But there must be some reasons."

"Nalbandov seems to have only one reason . . . The point is that every concrete-mixer is provided with a set of instructions by the firm that manufactures it and in this is indicated the precise norm of manufacturing wet concrete. Well, according to the set of instructions, no less than two minutes should be allotted to each mixture. Consequently the maximum per hour is thirty mixtures, and in an eight-hour shift, two hundred and forty and no more."

"And you say that Kharkov made three hundred and six? How on earth did they do it?"

"Nalbandov thinks that this strains the machine, that it's a technical trick, a sleight of hand, a stunt . . . If we go on in this way, we shall soon wear out all our machinery. For example, a concrete-mixer will last only six or seven years instead of ten."

"On second thought . . . Do you know . . . Nalbandov is right. What do you think?"

"Are you changing your point of view?"

"But you can see for yourself. This is a new angle. It alters the case fundamentally . . . After all, we cannot accord barbaric treatment to expensive, imported tools . . ."

"And Kharkov?" Vinkich asked briefly. "Before they decided to set the record there, they must have had similar doubts in Kharkov. Nevertheless they went ahead and set the record, didn't they? After all, the fellows over there are not fools."

"Mm—yes . . . Quite a problem . . . And of course, they have good people there, too . . . not fools . . ."

"Well, how about it, Georgi Vasilyevich? What is your opinion?"

"I'm afraid you're too direct. On the one hand, of course, there is competition, increase of tempos. But on the other hand, my dear fellow, we cannot wear out our machinery. You yourself say that it'll last six years instead of ten."

"Well, what about it?"

"What about what?"

"Georgi Vasilyevich, judge for yourself which is the more important: to finish the Five-Year Plan in four years or to save the machinery for an additional four years? The sooner we develop our industry, the less significance will amortisation have for us: we'll make new machinery of our own. Isn't that so?"

"Well . . . You know . . . That's a good reason . . . Perhaps you're right. What do you think?"

"You are changing your point of view again."

"Well, yes . . . But that's quite natural. Here is a new concept . . . It fundamentally alters the aspect of the case. After all, we have machines for socialism, and not socialism for the machine . . ."

"In other words, you are—for? Will you give us your signature?"

Georgi Vasilyevich glanced at Vinkich in bewilderment.

"Upon my word, you're a strange fellow! How can I . . . suddenly . . . give you my signature? But suppose there is something wrong about this business . . . some new circumstance . . . I'm no expert . . . And why do you want my signature?"

"We need it, Georgi Vasilyevich. We need it very much. You can't even imagine what a fight we'll have on our hands. We shall be sending telegrams to the metropolitan newspapers, and your name carries a good deal of weight!"

Georgi Vasilyevich was flattered. He smiled modestly.

"What are you talking about! What are you talking about! What weight can it possibly carry? Perhaps in literature . . .

some sort of a protest . . . a letter to Romain Rolland . . . but as for concrete . . ."

"In all fields of endeavour!" Vinkich said quickly and ingratiatingly. "In any case, we shall depend on your support. Now I must go to the sector. I must see some people. By the way, wouldn't you like to come with me? Perhaps as you observe the work, the matter will become clearer to you."

"Perhaps. But you see, I'm not an expert . . . Will you please initiate me into the swing of things? Be my cicerone. It's simply impossible to stay in my hotel room, anyway. The heat is insufferable. Upon my word of honour! It's a real Sahara!"

XXV

MARGULIES had a very clear image of the cutlets. The cutlets were large, black, covered with brown gravy. He again went to the sector. The dining room there might still be open.

He walked, carefully avoiding all acquaintances. What was the use? An unnecessary encounter and more conversation. Until he had the latest analytical calculation in his hands, all discussion was futile. The calculation would alter matters. By twelve, everything would be clear.

The crux of the matter was: would Katya find Smolensky.

Margulies was in torment. He avoided groups of people, machinery, crossings. He tried to go the lower way, through trenches and excavations. He ran from corner to corner, from turn to turn, bending his head as if avoiding bullets. By roundabout ways he reached the dining room. It was closed.

"So. Good-bye, cutlets!" he exclaimed. "Well, all right. We'll wait for dinner. Anyway, I have to see Yermakov for a minute. I wonder how he's getting on."

He made his way to the plant. He walked around it on the right, on the western, the shady side.

Here was a stuffy, noisy world of brick and straw. Very expensive, imported fire-brick covered with fragrant straw was being carefully unloaded from a freight car.

There were ten or fifteen cars there—a whole train. And yet they were almost unnoticeable in the clearly-limned, gigantic shadow of the plant.

Wooden wheelbarrows wobbled along, their wheels screeching.

"Look out!"

In single file, boys and girls rolled narrow long-handled barrows along a footway one board wide. From right to left, the barrows rolled empty. From left to right, they were neatly piled with fire-brick. Markers with yellow folding rules in their side pockets walked among the high narrow stacks of materials, piled with severe neatness.

This innovation roused Margulies's interest. He stopped to examine what was going on. Previously, the brick had been unloaded helter-skelter. It would block the side entrances and the fire exit of the plant. A lot of time had been wasted every day. It had been necessary to cart the materials in a roundabout way, making a detour of almost a kilometre. Unneeded brands blocked the needed ones. They had to be moved from place to place all the time. And there was a constant shortage of labour. The confusion was disgraceful.

Margulies noticed that now the brick was being sorted and piled outside the plant in accordance with a strict plan: in stacks which corresponded to the quantity and the brands for the battery ovens, but piled in reverse order. The brick for the upper row was on the bottom and that for the lower row was on top. Thus in laying the ovens, there was not a moment of delay in the handling of the materials.

Margulies forthwith appraised this innovation: Reverse order! The idea was: to handle the materials in reverse order.

Interesting!

He was pensive for a moment. Why not utilise this idea for rationalising the process of handling and pouring wet concrete?

"Hello, boss! Good day! Good health to you!"

Margulies turned around irritably, but immediately his face grew pleasant.

"Ah! Foma Yegorovich!"

The American engineer, Mr. Thomas George Bixby, called in Russian Foma Yegorovich, for short, was waddling toward him.

This was the fifth year that Foma Yegorovich had been working in the Soviet Union. He had been at Dnieprostroi, at the Stalingrad Tractor Plant, and at the Rostov Agricultural Machinery Construction Plant. He had not only learned to speak Russian fluently, but he also knew a number of proverbs and quips. He had grown a long Ukrainian moustache, and when he drank vodka, he grunted Russian-style and wiped his lips with a sweep of his sleeve.

He came up to Margulies, and with a broad Russian gesture, offered his dry, muscular hand. He wore a blue woollen overall fastened with a zipper. He was bare-headed. He wore a hat only on Sundays. His hair was bleached by the sun. His bleached eyebrows and moustache seemed considerably lighter than his face. In his tanned, well-shaped American face with its Poltavian [1] moustache, shone clear steady deep-set American eyes set close together.

They greeted each other.

"How do you like this?" asked Foma Yegorovich, pointing to the straight, neat stacks of brick. "Quite a different tune."

"Very curious," Margulies remarked.

Foma Yegorovich stroked his moustache in a self-satisfied manner. He understood perfectly well that Margulies had immediately and fully appreciated his innovation. He smiled quietly and radiantly. Tiny brown wrinkles rippled about his eyes. If it were not for these wrinkles, one would not take him for more than thirty-four. But the wrinkles betrayed his real age—forty-seven.

"Comrade Margulies, do you understand what it's all about?"

"Of course, of course! I understand it very well."

"It cost me exactly forty-eight hours of sleeplessness. It's laughable and sinful! Stop! Where are you going?" he suddenly

[1] a long, drooping moustache—like that of Taras Bulba

shouted in a voice that did not seem his own, and ran off. He caught a marker by the shoulder.

"Stop! Where are you putting that? Oh, a plague on your soul! What people! You should do it like this . . . Like this! . . . Like this! . . ."

Foma Yegorovich began to show him. When he returned, Margulies was standing in the same place, turning a newspaper in his hands.

"By the way, Foma Yegorovich, what's your opinion of this?"

Margulies passed the newspaper to the American and indicated the place with the tip of his pencil:

"Kharkov made three hundred and six mixtures."

Foma Yegorovich took the newspaper and brought it close to his eyes. Aloud and distinctly, he read the news dispatch with evident relish. He took the greatest delight in reading Russian aloud. After each sentence he would stop and look at Margulies with his clear, steady, shining eyes, as if to say, "See how well I read Russian!"

"What do you think?" asked Margulies.

"Good!" the American exclaimed. "Bravo! *Bis!* Now you must go beyond that."

"We're thinking of trying it. What do you say?"

"Beat Kharkov? Without fail. You must. As the saying goes: 'One that's been beaten is worth two that haven't been beaten.' "

Margulies repressed a smile.

"You are an enthusiast, Foma Yegorovich."

"I an enthusiast? No, I am an American. Beat them!"

"But is it technically possible?"

"Technically, everything is possible. Where there's a will, there's a way. I'll tell you in confidence of a certain instance: in the year 1919, I was laying a concrete highway in the state of Montana, and on one occasion we laid five hundred cubes in one day. That cost us not going to bed for twenty-four hours."

"And did the machine hold out?"

"We got the machine from a contractor. We rented it. We took more out of the machine than it could give. But then we had no notion of brigades. There were no shock brigades, but we were interested in the percentage."

"Wait a moment. The machine has a set of instructions—the manufacturer's official set of instructions."

"Official sets of instructions are written by sinners like you and me."

Margulies quickly pulled a piece of candy from his pocket and threw it in his mouth. He could hardly contain his excitement.

"And did that actually happen?"

"As I live and breathe! Five hundred cubes. As God is my witness!"

Margulies unbuttoned his coat and immediately buttoned it up again.

This changed everything. New possibilities were opening up. He swiftly offered his hand to Foma Yegorovich.

"Well, so long. Many thanks. I'm in a hurry."

"You must never hurry," the American remarked. "The slower you ride, the further you'll get."

Margulies smiled.

"From the place to which you are going," he added quickly.

"Well, Comrade Boss, you are riding to such a place that it doesn't much matter whether you ever get there. Better not get there too soon."

Margulies shook the paper at him:

"You are a notorious bourgeois and counter-revolutionary, Foma Yegorovich."

"Counter-revolutionary? No, God preserve me! A bourgeois? No, not by any means. I am an honest non-partisan specialist. I work by voluntary agreement with your government, and I even do more than I should. Sometimes it costs me forty-eight hours of not going to bed. My labour against your money. We are quits. And as for socialism—we shall see what we shall see."

Margulies placed his hands lightly on Foma Yegorovich's hips and squeezed him.

"And how many little dollars have you got in the bank, my dear Foma Yegorovich? Confess!"

Yes, he was saving money. Ten years ago he had left the States to make money. He had left an unattractive wife and children at home. It had been difficult to find work in America. He had been frightfully poor. He had left five hundred dollars with his family. He was a fairly good engineer. He had made up his mind not to return until he had twenty thousand dollars to his account. With this money, he would begin life. He would open up a construction office, start business, lay the foundation stone of future wealth. Twenty thousand dollars added to his many years of experience and his determination—that would be sufficient. In ten years he would have a hundred thousand.

So he had started on his wanderings. He did not decline any conditions or any contracts. He had worked in China, in India, in Portugal, in the Soviet Union. It made no difference to him where or for whom he worked, as long as he got his money on time. He divided his salary in two parts. One half he put to his account in the bank, the other half he sent to his family, after deducting only a very small portion for his living expenses. He denied himself the most necessary things, but this in no way affected his temper. On the contrary, he was always and everywhere gay, courageous, life-loving, healthy. Before him was the gleaming perspective of wealth and prosperity. With every month this perspective grew closer and more tangible. This was the promised land of joy.

The American's face shone with pleasure. Smiling slyly, he took out of his pocket a small aluminum notebook, which was also a pocket slide-rule. Margulies looked at it enviously. He had been dreaming of having such a thing for a long time. It was amazingly convenient. On the spur of the moment, one could make the most complex calculations, including even logarithms. It was indispensable. Such was American technique!

Meanwhile, without hurrying, Foma Yegorovich opened his little book, gazed with pleasure at the figures for some time, and then, closing it, said:

"Exactly eighteen thousand, four hundred and twenty-seven dollars and forty cents. Patience! A few more dollars, and you will have a new American bourgeois here, Comrade Margulies. Then please come to see me in Chicago. I am formally offering you the job of senior engineer in the construction office of Mr. Bixby and Company. Well?"

"We have enough work here."

Foma Yegorovich squinted slyly.

"A good salary, Comrade Margulies. What? Think it over. You will have a pleasant boss, what? Perhaps you don't care to have anything to do with the bourgeois that you haven't killed yet? But I don't care about your political views." The American laughed loudly.

"You're a fine fellow, Foma Yegorovich," Margulies said heartily. "Stay here with us. We will elect you to the city soviet. How would you like that?"

"And we'll elect you to Congress. How would you like that?"

"No, thank you. I can manage without it."

"And I think I can manage over there just as well."

They stood for a little while side by side, laughing and nudging each other.

"Well, I'm off," Margulies said suddenly.

"So long, so long," said Foma Yegorovich. "Can you leave me the newspaper? I'd like to read the news. You don't need it, do you?"

"With pleasure. You may have it."

Foma Yegorovich took the newspaper and shoved it in his pocket. Did he know that this was to bring about his end?

Margulies went to Yermakov's brigade. But along the road he became interested in a new section of the labour front.

XXVI

ISHCHENKO hurried to the sector, pulling up his *sharovary* [1] as he walked. He moved rapidly, his brows firmly knitted. However, at times it seemed to him that he was going too slowly. He began to run. He ran at a trot for some time, thinking of nothing. Then thoughts returned, and he again increased his speed. He perspired. The back of his new shirt grew wet and black with dust. A multitude of thoughts disturbed him.

Needless to say, the brigades of Khanumov and Yermakov were stronger and more experienced. They had been formed five or six months before. Ishchenko's brigade had been in existence only two months. Nevertheless, Ishchenko struggled against Khanumov and Yermakov. He fought against them with all the stubbornness and deep passion of an Ukrainian.

At first, when Khanumov had been proudly speeding along on the motorcycle, and Yermakov had been cavorting on the horse, Ishchenko had stayed on the snail or at best in the peasant cart.

However, he had not despaired. He had done everything to beat Khanumov and Yermakov.

Once he had been successful. He had been put on the bicycle, while Khanumov had landed on the snail and Yermakov on the nag. At the end of the next ten days, he had been cruelly flung back again. That had been just the other day. The indicators had not yet been hung up, but Ishchenko was already anticipating the new picture in gloomy disgust.

It would not be so bad if Shura were to place him on a nag or a snail. But suppose she placed him on a crab—on a long, red crab with a mouse-like head and whiskers as long as the tail of a mouse. And that would be the very time that Khanumov would be looking out of the oval window of a locomotive flying along on a diagonal, while Yermakov would be lolling back in an automobile!

[1] a kind of loose Turkish or Kazak trousers

Still, he might stand that. But to surrender such a thing as a world's record to Khanumov—no, my dear friends, that was impossible! He would not leave the sector until he had received the order to beat Kharkov!

As he walked, he calculated in his mind and on his fingers what more than a score of people on the construction were calculating: he divided the three hundred and six Kharkov mixtures by the eight hours of the shift. He divided them approximately and got in round numbers, forty.

He would have to make forty mixtures an hour!

He stopped suddenly in the middle of the road, picked up a splinter, and with great concentration wrote the figures sixty and forty on the thick crust of dust. He was attempting to divide sixty minutes by forty mixtures. He had only learned division recently, and now, in his haste and excitement, he could not divide for anything in the world. He only felt that the answer was a little over a minute. That meant that he would have to make one mixture in approximately one minute.

That was no joke!

Passing Yermakov's brigade, which was at work, Ishchenko stopped. For the first time, he regarded from the sidelines the work which was performed every day by his own brigade. From the sidelines, the work of Yermakov's brigade seemed to him disgustingly slow and clumsy. It went forward in spurts and dashes, stopping every moment or so, as if marking time.

The heavy barrows in which sand, gravel, and cement were brought to the concrete-mixer were constantly riding off the narrow boards, which were laid across the refuse of the construction to the scoop of the mixer. To lift them and to place them back on the boards involved much time and effort. The barrow was wheeled by one man, but it took two to lift it. Every minute some one had to abandon his own work and assist some one else.

The cement was in barrels. It had to be shovelled out into the barrows. The gravel had been dumped too far away. The barrows would collide, lock wheels, graze each other's sides. The lads would get tired. . . .

Sometimes five or six barrows would gather around the mixer waiting for the scoop, while at other times, there would not be a single barrow there, and, awaiting its load, the drum would revolve empty.

How much time did it take Yermakov to make one mixture? Ishchenko had no watch.

He waited until the drum poured out a portion of concrete. Then, in a whisper, trying not to hurry, he began to count seconds:

"One, two, three, four, five, six, seven . . ."

In order not to lose count, he bent back a finger after each ten numbers. When he had bent back all ten fingers and two more, the drum turned over.

One hundred and twenty seconds! Two minutes!

From the sidelines, this time seemed too long to the brigadier. However, it indicated that the Yermakovites were making thirty mixtures an hour; that is, they were making two hundred and forty per shift. Up until now, no one on the construction had made two hundred and forty, while Ishchenko's brigade had not exceeded one hundred and eighty.

Well, thought Ishchenko, if it is possible to make two hundred and forty with all this playing around, then may I see no good in the world if my boys cannot slap at least four hundred together to-day!

"Ah! Are you here already? Are you figuring? Hello, Boss!"

Korneyev appeared before Ishchenko. Ishchenko regarded the superintendent with quizzical persistence.

"How's everything?"

Korneyev squinted slightly. His cheek twitched.

"How are things going?"

He turned aside, placed the palm of his hand to the peak of his cap indifferently and gazed into the distance like a seaman.

The distance was spacious, black and billowy. The forty-five-metre pipe of the scrubber was being lifted obliquely. Winches were chirruping.

"The office writes that affairs are progressing."

Ishchenko understood that everything was in order and that it was useless to ask more questions. His heart felt lighter.

"And how are your lads getting on?" Korneyev remarked casually.

"Don't you worry about my lads," Ishchenko answered maliciously. "You may worry about some of the other lads, but not about mine."

They walked to the fifth battery in silence. The concrete mixer would soon have to be transferred here.

Here, Margulies was already busy. He was engaged in doing a number of things, lightly, unnoticeably, as if by the way. He was trying not to attract any unnecessary attention to himself.

Making it appear that he was just taking a walk, he was pacing off the platform. At the same time, he was giving apparently unimportant orders to the carpenters who were nailing the planking and to the plumbers who were connecting the pipes. He would appear outside or, climbing up the trap-ladder, would disappear into the tremendous twilight of the plant.

Passing Ishchenko, he asked, "Your wife has arrived?"

Ishchenko wiped the palms of his hands on the sides of his trousers. They shook hands.

"Yes . . . She's in a bad way."

Brusque tenderness touched the swollen lips of the brigadier. "I hear that you are expecting an addition to your family?"

Ishchenko struck the back of his knees with his hands and sat down on a log. (Yes, an addition to my family!) He grew thoughtful. He was silent as he rested. His brown eyes gazed as if they were peering through a fog.

"How is Yermakov getting along?" Margulies asked Korneyev.

"Yermakov is just finishing up. There are about twenty cubes left."

"Good."

"David," said Korneyev, "I must go home. What do you think? At least for twenty minutes."

"What time is it now?"

Korneyev pulled at the strap of his watch.

"It is ten minutes of twelve."

"Good Lord!" Margulies exclaimed. "I have a long distance connection at twelve o'clock."

"Another long distance call?"

"Yes. You see, I have not yet been able to get hold of a certain thing. And without that, you see . . . In a word, I'll be back in half an hour. Please, Korneyev. I understand, but you can't leave the sector alone. If you don't keep your eye on them, they'll make all sorts of fine blunders!"

Margulies grasped a small post and jumped over the barbed wire.

XXVII

THE superintendent sat down beside the brigadier on the log and looked at his shoes. They were disgracefully spotted. It would be useless to try to clean them up. He would have to paint them again. That was the only thing to do.

But what was Klava going to do? Would she really leave? If he could only go home for a quarter of an hour, or even for ten minutes! And what a way for this affair to come to a head! And at what a time!

"That's how it goes, Ishchenko," he said, putting his arm across the brigadier's shoulder.

But at that moment he jumped up and ran over to the carpenters.

"Hey! Wait! Don't nail it!" he cried in an unnatural voice. "Where are you nailing it? Pull it off! Is that a metre and a half?"

Ishchenko sat alone, staring steadily at one spot. That spot was the bandaged head of Yermakov which showed white in the distance above the planking, where the drum of the concrete mixer turned smoothly, thundered, and emptied.

Wheels and shirts flickered there. Shouts came from there, and the rough rustle of concrete as it was poured and as it crawled down the wooden trough.

The Yermakovites were pouring the last cubes. Immediately the mixer would be transferred here to the fifth battery. At sixteen o'clock, Ishchenko's brigade would take its place—to beat Kharkov!

Then—hang on!

But Brigadier Ishchenko was not thinking about that. For the first time, he was thinking about himself and his life, about Fyenya and their future child.

Until now, his life had been swift and smooth and thoughtless. Like a river, time carried life to the right or to the left, turning and swirling it smoothly. Time flowed like a river, and, like a river when you swim in the middle of it, it appeared to be closed in and without direction.

Time was like the Dnieper: from Kiev to Ekaterinoslav and from Ekaterinoslav to Kiev! A steamer moved along, and on all sides it was surrounded and closed in by the shore. It seemed that the steamer was sailing on a lake and that there was no way out for it. But suddenly there was a turn, and the lake spread out in breadth and in length. Where there had seemed to be no way out, appeared a bend. The bend passed into another bend. The lake flowed into another lake. The steamer followed the bend. The bend led to a new lake. The lake flowed into another lake, and this was the river and this was the Dnieper, and this was the steamer.

His brother had worked on a steamer. He had been a sailor. He stood on a barge with a striped pole. He measured the depth. His name was Terenty.

Ishchenko was still a little boy, a very small boy—about seven. Little Kostya would go with his big brother Terenty on the steamer.

The steamer beat the water with its red paws. They sailed. They drank tea, biting into the lumps of sugar. With it they ate *bubliki.*[1] Then his brother had been taken away. They had sent him to the German front.

And again life had gone on in the village and in the peasant hut where his grandfather sat on the oven and coughed, and his mother swore, and the straw glowed in the hot opening.

At first the fire was golden, unbearable. Then it calmed down. It glowed redly. The horny shadow of the oven fork flew around the hut like the devil. The red straw became sharp black ash.

He herded cows. He shot out his long whip. The cows rustled among the bushes. The bushes were dry and hot. It was warm, and it smelled strongly of the twisted brown leaves of oak trees seared by the sun.

Then the year 'seventeen had crashed. His brother returned. He sewed a crimson ribbon across his tall fur hat. The children wove crimson ribbons into the manes of the horses. Then, after a while, the same brother Terenty became a sailor of the river flotilla.

Came the winter of a certain year. The red star Mars burned in the leaden sky. The wind blew on it. It glowed over the steppe which was merged and fused like cast iron by the keen frost.

Spring came. Three-inch guns thundered and pounded. The cornices of the Pecherían[2] bell towers were shattered by shells and crashed to the ground. The gods were being gutted. There in their midst was cotton, all sorts of trash, and chicken bones.

Steamers passed: from the left, white; from the right, dingy yellow. From the left, General Denikin, from the right, Ataman Tschaikovsky. Grenades whistled. Terenty lay on the deck, clinging to his machine gun. The machine gun jerked like a frog caught by its legs.

The ship was struck in the very middle. A black column rose where the stack had been. A red column was reflected in the Dnieper. Bullets poured into the water. By sheer strength, in the midst of the bullets, he managed to swim to the shore and hide in the reeds.

[1] a crusty, doughnut-shaped pretzel
[2] the Pecher monastery of Kiev is famous for its catacombs

And life flowed and flowed like the Dnieper, twisting to the left and to the right, and it seemed that there was no way out. But the way out was right there, straight ahead. The river was a chain of lakes. Every lake seemed a motionless, immovable mirror, from which there was no escape.

His older brother Terenty had perished. Perished. . . .

The younger Ishchenko, Konstantin, took his brother's place at the steering wheel, which his hands grasped and held tenaciously. But, later, he succumbed to a longing for the village and went home. There was no one there. There had been a typhus epidemic. Mother had died. Grandfather had died. He was alone. He became a farm drudge. He grew. He grew up.

He became a mucker, a seasonal worker. He enrolled in a collective farm. There he had met Fyenya.

The night was warm and splendid. The cook was scrubbing some pots with a brush. . . . The stove was glowing right in the middle of the yard. The wind blew at the stars and could not blow them out. The thin moon had dropped very low. It no longer glowed. Its light was almost gone. The moon lay on the steppe, a yellow sickle, and the thin, cold silver of dew glistened on watermelon rinds.

And then he had gone to the Urals. He had enlisted. And why not? He had to live, he had to save money, he had to line the nest. He started on the journey. He reached the end of the journey. Time flew by. In time life changed.

He came there to be a seasonal worker, a mucker, and to save money. At first he was homesick. Here, too, was a steppe, but it was an alien steppe. Here were stars, but they were strange. Here were songs, but they were unfamiliar. But the work was tremendous. Little by little, he became adjusted. He began to discriminate. He became a brigadier. Just how he had become a brigadier he could never remember. It seemed that he had been a brigadier all his life, that he had been born a brigadier.

Ishchenko forgot everything in the world. He had come to get one thing and had found something else. He even forgot about

Fyenya. And Fyenya? Here she was, this Fyenya. Suddenly—just like that! And now there would be a child. There would be a son. Perhaps a daughter. A child.

And all this life—all that had been, and that was, and that was still to come—would not be in vain. All this was for him, for this little one who was not yet even in the world, but who would be. To-day or to-morrow, "he" was bound to be here. And "he" would be of his blood, of his tenderness, of his flesh, of his past life, of his present, of his future.

Here carpenters were nailing the planking together. That was for "him."

Here a train passed; frequently and for long moments, the shadows of the cars flickered like a cage across the plant. And that, too, was for "him."

Here, on every side, clouds rose, breathing heat, and that, too, like everything else, was for "him."

There would be a flagstone under the fifth battery. On the flagstone sixty-nine coke ovens would be erected. Blast furnaces need coke. The blast furnaces were being put together. The mountain would be blown up. The ore would be extracted. The ore would go into the blast furnaces. The coke would be lighted. Molten iron would flow. The molten iron would be boiled into steel. They would make rails, wagons, saws, axes, ploughs, machines.

And all this would be for the needs, for the happiness of "him."

To make life happy, it was not enough to say good words. It was not enough. One needed steel, steel, steel! With steel, there will be a new, happy life, a life that has never been before, a life that has never been seen before!

And all this was for "him." And "he"—that is I. And "he" and I—are we. And we—that is life!

Until now, life had gone by like a river, from backwater to backwater, from lake to lake. Time was life. Life flowed as it wished. When it wished, it flowed slowly. When it wished, it flowed swiftly.

Now Ishchenko opened his eyes, and, for the first time in his life, looked down the entire length of time. It flowed too slowly. But it flowed for him. The past flowed for the future.

And it lay securely in his hands.

Oh, how good life was, after all!

XXVIII

SHE was only a few minutes late.

But even as she went up the stairs, she heard from above the frequent, insistent, importunate ringing of the telephone.

Breathless, she leaped up two steps at a time. Red spots glowed on her face.

A woman neighbour stood in the open doorway of the apartment.

"Ekaterina Lvovna!" she cried, leaning over the bannister. "Hurry! It must be your crazy brother again. This is the second time. My head aches from this mad ringing!"

Katya burst into the front hall.

With one hand, she clutched the bundle of papers and newspapers to her breast, and with the other, she snatched the telephone receiver. It began to fall out of her hand. She caught it with her knee. She flung it against her ear, pressed it to her shoulder with her cheek, and at the same time tore off her béret and fanned herself with it.

It was David.

"Well? Did you find Smolensky?"

"I found him! I found him! I did everything! Wait, I'll tell you everything right away. Wait. . . . Have you a piece of paper and a pencil? Wait. . . . The newspapers are falling. . . . I'll dictate it to you."

"I have, I have. Go ahead. I'll write it down. Dictate!"

"Right away, right away!"

She hastily unrolled the package, clutching it with her chin, which made her look as if she were harnessed with a bit. Finally she opened the paper.

In the dim light of a weak, fly-specked electric-lamp, which seemed darker and yellower than ever after the blinding sunlight of the summer morning, Katya could hardly make out the blurred print of the newspaper. She brought the clippings right up to her nose. Gasping and perspiring, she read paragraphs that were barely comprehensible to her.

Now and then he would ask her to repeat. She would repeat. He would shout:

"Wait, wait!"

He was writing it down, and apparently it was as difficult for him to write as it was for her to dictate.

"Good! Very good! Thanks. Go on, go on," he would say at times. "You're a fine fellow, Kat'ka!"

And gladdened and encouraged, even proud, she continued to read the newspaper article rapidly into the telephone.

Five times a coarse, dispassionate voice severed them, reminding them that their time was up. And five times David's irritable voice insisted that they be not interrupted. They spoke on double rates, then on triple rates.

At times he would ask her to wait a bit. He was evidently sharpening a pencil or turning over a piece of paper. Then she would shout various bits of Moscow news to him.

"They are wrecking the Cathedral of Christ the Saviour! They are wrecking the Okhotny! They have just moved the monument of Minin and Pozharsky!

"Do you understand?" she would shout quickly. "Can you hear me? Do you understand? On my way there, Minin and Pozharsky were in their place. When I came back, there was only an empty pavement. What do you think of that?"

"Good!"

"And the cupola of Christ the Saviour . . . do you hear me? I am saying that the cupola of Christ the Saviour. . . . Half of it has been taken apart. I never realised that it was so enormous. . . ."

"Good," Margulies muttered.

"Every part of the cupola was several feet wide. And by the way, from the distance, it looked like the rind of a melon. . . . Do you hear me?"

"Good!" Margulies roared. "Go on, go on!"

And so, on this splendid summer morning, at ten o'clock Moscow time, and at twelve o'clock by the other time, at a distance of several thousand kilometres from each other, a brother and a sister talked to each other, and their voices flew from Europe to Asia, and from Asia to Europe, drowning the stubborn roar of time that lagged too far behind, and of space that was too cumbersome.

XXIX

KATYA dictated to Margulies the essence of an article by a group of engineers of the State Institute of Construction. It had just appeared in the newspaper "Za Industrializatsiu":

SPEED UP THE PREPARATION AND PRODUCTION OF HIGH-GRADE CONCRETE

The successes attained by several workers' brigades on constructions in those regions where machines have been best utilised, are phenomena of great social and economic importance. These successes controvert all previous conservative ideas in regard to this problem.

The overwhelming majority of construction organisations, working along so-called daily experience norms, base their work on exceedingly low estimates of machine-productivity.

These organisations place the norm of productivity of concrete-mixers at 15 or 20 mixtures per hour, despite evidence from the Institute of Construction indicating that it is possible not only to raise the productivity of concrete-mixers to no less than 30 to 35 mixtures per hour on the average, and, with proper organisation of work, to eliminate both obvious and as yet unsuspected loss of time, but also, with mechanised loading (from silos through gauges), to attain even 37 or 40 mixtures per hour, assuming that the time of mixing is not less than one minute.

What then should be regarded as the actually attainable and permissible maximum productivity of concrete-mixers?

The time allotted to the work-cycle of the concrete-mixer is composed basically of: loading the scoop, lifting the scoop, loading the drum, time of mixing, and unloading. Some of these items can be accomplished simultaneously; for example, the loading and lifting of the scoop occur during the period of mixing. The normative data of the Institute of Construction concerning the details of the work-cycle of the concrete-mixer, which were sent to construction organisations, pointed out that the loading and the unloading of the drum (for Jaeger and Kaiser) should consume from 31 to 40 seconds with one machinist.

The fundamental variable which influences the number of mixtures is the time of mixing.

It is easy to calculate that, with complete rationalisation during 6 hours of uninterrupted work, it is possible to produce the following maximum number of mixtures:

Time of mixing (in seconds)	Number of mixtures during mixing time	
	of 30 seconds	of 20 seconds
15	640	820
20	576	720
30	480	516
45	384	443
1 min.	320	360

What mixing time should be accepted in practice?

According to the norms that we have followed so far, the minimum mixing time has been calculated as 1 minute. Norms abroad, and likewise the data of the German experiments of Professors Graff and Garbotz, demand a similar or even longer period.

This was determined by the fact that the consistency and firmness of the concrete increases to a certain extent with an increase in mixing time.

It is likewise necessary to consider that the plasticity of the concrete diminishes with less mixing, and, therefore, it is more difficult to handle.

True, the necessary plasticity may be obtained by adding water, but as is well known, this considerably lowers the durability of the concrete (the addition of 10 percent of water lowers the durability of the concrete, on the average, 10 percent).

Mixing for 15 seconds instead of 1 minute decreases the durability of the concrete by 20 percent and more, and for 30 seconds—by 10 percent and more.

This data is for 28-day concrete. Over a longer period, this difference is somewhat less.

Our norm establishes a minimum durability of concrete which gives a reserve of construction durability of no more than 1.5 to 2.5 times, instead of the reserve of 3 to 4 times accepted abroad and at one time accepted by us. In order not to lower even this minimum durability of concrete while lowering the mixing time, it is necessary to use a heavier composition of concrete; that is, to use more cement per cubic metre of concrete.

One may calculate an average of from 200 to 300 kilograms of cement for each cubic metre of reinforced concrete.

An analytical calculation indicates that in order to restore the durability of the concrete which is diminished by accelerated mixing, it is necessary to use the following increased quantity of cement for each cubic metre of concrete:

In mixing in the course of:
15 seconds instead of 1 minute ....35 kilograms
30   "   "   " "   "   ....15 to 20 kilograms
45   "   "   " "   "   ....an   inconsiderable
quantity of cement

Thus, to raise the number of mixtures, it is necessary to increase the amount of cement from 15 to 35 kilograms per cubic metre of concrete.

When there is a shortage of cement, this is hardly permissible.

We suppose that in an extreme case it is possible to accept the

following norm: mixing the concrete with the addition of cement
—no less than 30 seconds; without the addition of cement—45
seconds. This yields from 480 to 576 mixtures per shift with the
addition of cement, and from 384 to 443 mixtures without the
addition of cement.

It is necessary to emphasise especially that this quantity of
concrete mixtures may be obtained only under conditions of complete rationalisation, proper organisation of labour and place of
work, and correct disposition of the personnel.

In case these conditions are not present, concrete of a lower
quality will be obtained and this may reflect negatively on the
construction.

Taking this into consideration, special attention should be
called to cases in which the number of mixtures has been increased
to 135 and even to 150 per hour.

In these cases, the figures indicate that there was almost no
mixing at all.

If 27 to 28 seconds were allotted for the entire work-cycle of
the concrete-mixer, then, considering that the loading of the drum
consumed 5 seconds, and its unloading 10 seconds (the minimum
time required for carrying out the operations with a large number of extra workers), we can only conclude that only 11 to 12
seconds were allotted to the mixing. In case the loading and
unloading consume even as little as 5 seconds more than the above
estimate, then not more than 10 seconds can be left for the mixing.

This means, approximately, only 3 turns for each mixture,
which is obviously insufficient.

Here quantity is manifestly being increased at the expense of
quality.

However, in case of extreme need, such an increase in the number of mixtures may be permitted, in cementing parts of construction of less import, such as floors, massive foundations, etc.,
and especially those that involve the repeated pouring of concrete.
But for reinforced concrete constructions, and also for concrete
that is intended for vital construction, such a quantity of mixtures

is not permissible. It cannot assure the homogeneity of the entire mass of concrete, or, therefore, the necessary durability of the entire construction.

Socialist competition and shock-brigading in work that employs concrete-mixers must aim not only to produce a maximum quantity of mixtures, but also to maintain the required quality. We therefore recommend that the indicators of socialist competition and shock-brigading be not the quantity of mixtures per shift, which may lead to quite undesirable results, but rather the following indicators:

1. Reduce time-waste during the shift to a minimum (as near as possible to zero).

Judging by the data we now have, this has not yet been done by a single brigade.

Despite exceedingly high quantity of mixtures per hour, hence per shift, we still have not been able to obtain the elimination of time-waste. Therefore, per each labor shift, the actual work is not eight hours, but considerably less.

2. The general and equable increase in the number of mixtures over a considerable period of time—ten days, months, etc.—is determined by the proper organisation of work.

A record-setting quantity of mixtures in one shift, without a general and equable increase of mixtures over a considerable period of concrete-laying, bears witness to the fact that the successes realised are not sustained throughout that period.

3. Reduce to a minimum (no lower than the norms of the State Institute of Construction) the time of separate items of the cycle. In each instance, the time spent on mixing should depend on the composition of the concrete and on its ultimate use. For reinforced concrete, it should not be less than 45 seconds; for less vital uses, the time should be determined by the field laboratory and based on a minimum of 20 to 30 seconds.

4. The next indicator should be the quantity of cubic metres of concrete produced by the machine by each worker of the brigade during one shift, which serves the given machine or aggregate with contiguous processes.

This opens up tremendous possibilities.

The data published in the article by Comrade M. Tsagurya indicate that on our constructions machines are very imperfectly utilised. It is sufficient to state that in six construction trusts the utilisation of the power of concrete-mixers varies between 3.3 percent and 27.3 percent; mortar mixers, 23.3 percent to 52 percent; rock crushers, 5 percent to 25 percent; hoists, 2.7 percent to 32 percent. The time indicators of the utilisation of the same machines vary from 6.7 percent to 64 percent.

This small co-efficient of machine-utilisation clearly indicates that in these cases we are faced with the absence of personal responsibility for machinery. Hence, as the fifth indicator it is necessary to eliminate the absence of personal responsibility for machinery and to place it upon responsible individuals.

Certain data from constructions concerning the durability of concrete obtained from different quantities of mixtures per hour, which have been published, do not give the real answer to the question posed.

Experiments carried on under conditions of construction are invariably conducted very unscientifically (no precise proportioning; the quantity of materials varies) and are concerned with isolated, accidental facts. During the current year, the Institute of Construction has been conducting extensive, scientifically conditioned investigations concerning the problem of the utilisation of concrete-mixers, the mixing time of various kinds of concrete, the quality of the resulting concrete, etc. Shock-brigading, supported by scientific investigation, will make it possible to equal and exceed the world's record for the preparation of concrete without sacrificing quality.

At the same time it must be borne in mind that further increase of production by our concrete-mixers meets an obstacle in the structural defects of the usual type of standard concrete-mixers.

By altering the existing concrete-mixers (speeding up the lifting of the scoop and the unloading, automatisation of operation), it is possible to attain only a relatively slight increase of tempos.

With our tremendous tempos and the magnitude of our construction, we shall inevitably have to employ new types of machines —mixers of uninterrupted activity.

And in order to eliminate time-waste that lowers concrete-laying and is caused by the length of the transport and the scaffolding of the inner construction, we must obtain the wide use of concrete pumps, which bring the concrete in pipes to the places of pouring it, and a high quality of cement which will make possible an increase in the repeated utilisation of scaffolding.

XXX

VINKICH had been trying to find Margulies since eight o'clock and had not succeeded. That morning Margulies was not to be found. Vinkich understood that there must be a good reason for this. Therefore it was all the more necessary to get hold of Margulies.

Now Vinkich had found an ally in Georgi Vasilyevich. After ten minutes' conversation, they had felt sympathetic toward each other. They realised that they needed each other, that they complemented each other. For Georgi Vasilyevich, Vinkich was the key to the rebus. For Vinkich, Georgi Vasilyevich was a name, a trademark. Where a correspondent of the Russian Telegraphic Agency might have been ignored, all manner of respect and co-operation was accorded to a famous author.

In half an hour, Georgi Vasilyevich learned more than during the three days he had lived here. For him, the construction was no longer merely a Construction with a capital C; people were no longer merely people; the steppe no longer merely a steppe; the mountains no longer merely mountains; the machines no longer merely machines. Things and people acquired a tangible, mutual connection. They ceased being nameless and voiceless. Vinkich invested them generously with names and characteristics.

And once it had received a name, the thing or the man suddenly

began to speak, to act consciously, to exist consciously in the
world which, to the eyes of Georgi Vasilyevich, had lost the irritating splendour of a rebus.

Now the people he met were brigadiers, superintendents, foremen, shock-brigaders, loafers, enthusiasts, senior and junior engineers, business managers, bookkeepers, secretaries of nuclei,
machinists, chauffeurs, rakers, concrete men, repair men, geo-
deticians. Now the machines, scattered over the entire space of
the construction, could be distinguished from each other by func-
tions, noises, signals, smoke, names.

Here were steam shovels, the so-called excavators. They stood
at the bottom of holes they themselves had dug. A small sentry
box turned on its tooth-like axis with a rattling noise. The chain
clanked. The iron arrow swooped down. The tooth-like box of the
scoop scraped up the surface beneath, leaving deep white traces
of its teeth in the bright red clay. The scoop was filled with earth.
The arrow pulled it up. The sentry box turned around. The scoop
hung over the flat car. The hinged cover crashed open. It fell like
a broken iron jaw, swinging helplessly from the ponderous hooks.
At the same time, the freed earth poured out, falling like black
smoke to the flat car. Then, suddenly, the dead jaw monstrously
came to life and clamped shut with tremendous strength. The
sentry box swung around again, and again, with a crash, the
arrow fell.

Ten times the scoop opened over each flat car. Then the excavator blew a siren. Immediately it was echoed by the thin
whistle of the donkey engine of the train. The machines were talking to each other. The excavator demanded that the next flat car
be brought up. The little steam engine replied: "Good! Wait!
Right away!" The train jerked. The buffer plates knocked noisily,
tapping signals to each other. The train moved up one flat car.
"Stop!" cried the excavator. "Here!" replied the little steam
engine.

"Look!" Georgi Vasilyevich exclaimed admiringly. "I am already beginning to understand the bird language of the machines!"

"I have been speaking it for a year and a half," Vinkich replied.

He gave Georgi Vasilyevich his arm and pulled him up the mound. He supported him. And when the novelist, clumsily scraping his shoes and raising clouds of dust, jumped down into the excavation, Vinkich would catch him at the bottom.

There were steam excavators. Over them gathered smoke so thick and black that it looked as if it had been painted on a wet blue field with China ink.

There were electric excavators. They did not smoke. They moved on wheels and caterpillars. There was a Marion and a Busaires.

There were excavators that worked on a cost accounting basis, and excavators that had not yet been placed on a cost accounting system.

And from above, the train which carried out the earth dug up by the excavators reminded one of the gigantic spine of some antediluvian animal discovered by a scientific expedition at the bottom of a long-dried-up river buried beneath paleontological layers.

There were machines that resembled excavators. They were called grippers. They raised their folded scoops to a dizzy height, their claws tightly clutching the earth they had dug out. They stopped above a truck. The claws opened wide. The earth fell into the truck like a black sheep. The rapacious shadow of a double-headed eagle flew over the scarred surface.

There were concrete-pouring towers, transportable bellows, electric locomotives, tractors, cement-mixers, screens, sieves for gravel and cinders. . . . Vinkich searched the entire sector. He did not leave a single nook or corner uninvestigated. Margulies was nowhere to be found.

Finally they met him.

He was striding along a high mound, his nose buried in a piece of paper. He stumbled. He might have fallen at any moment. He was completely absorbed by what he was reading. In a trice, Vinkich flew up the mound and appeared in front of Margulies.

"Hello, Boss!" he cried in a gay, ominous voice.

Margulies stopped. He saw Vinkich. "Well, what can I do about it?" his smile said. "It can't be helped. He has caught me."

They greeted each other. Georgi Vasilyevich was toiling up the mound.

And right then Vinkich used Georgi Vasilyevich as his trump. He assumed an impenetrably official manner and said coldly:

"I want you to meet some one, David. . . . I'd like you to meet some one, Georgi Vasilyevich. This is Engineer Margulies, the chief of the sector. I don't have to tell you who this is, David. That is obvious. At the moment, Georgi Vasilyevich is interested in a certain matter. Couldn't you explain it to us?"

"If you please," said Georgi Vasilyevich, brushing the earth from his knees.

"Georgi Vasilyevich would like to know," said Vinkich with angelic tenderness, "your opinion concerning the Kharkov record. And furthermore, Georgi Vasilyevich wants to know whether you intend to start anything on your part. . . . That is, does your sector intend to? In general, what conclusions have you reached based on the Kharkov record?"

"Yes, yes! Is it possible . . . that is . . . that Kharkov. . . . Is it possible?" Georgi Vasilyevich interposed timidly.

Margulies concentrated, knitted his brows, squinted and dropped his head.

"You see," he said quite positively, "I consider the Kharkov indicators in no way supernatural. They should have been expected. When such an experiment is placed on a strictly scientific basis, it is always possible to attain more or less high . . . h'm . . . tempos. But as far as we are concerned, and particularly my sector—what shall I say? . . . There are many circumstances of various kinds here. . . . Personally, I believe that of course we might try. . . . Why not try? . . . Perhaps we might succeed. But I want to emphasise that, based upon a strictly scientifically regulated experiment, we might possibly succeed in raising the quantity of mixtures to, let us say . . ."

He grew thoughtful, as if weighing again to himself all the data and reasons.

"Well?" asked Vinkich, taking out his notebook.

Margulies's face wrinkled slightly. "Well, let us say that we might try to raise the quantity of mixtures to three hundred and ten, or three hundred and twenty. . . . Perhaps even to three hundred and thirty. But, of course, I repeat, we must prepare thoroughly."

"Tell me!" exclaimed Georgi Vasilyevich. "There is a fellow here—Engineer Nalbandov—who is also, you know, quite a good man. . . ."

Vinkich pulled covertly at his mackintosh. Georgi Vasilyevich stopped. But it was too late. Margulies's face changed. He suddenly became impenetrable and unpleasant. Vinkich swore under his breath: the devil himself must have prompted Georgi Vasilyevich to pronounce that name in front of Margulies!

"Well, how about it, David?" asked Vinkich. "When will you beat Kharkov? Will it be to-day? Who is on your third shift? I think it's Ishchenko. Well, why not? Ishchenko is a good man. What?"

"I don't know," Margulies said indifferently. "I don't think it will be to-day."

Oh, yes, you do think so, you sly dog! Vinkich thought to himself.

"I don't think it will be to-day. We'll have to look around and get things ready. . . . Perhaps to-morrow. Perhaps even the day after. . . ."

He grew thoughtful.

"You know what, Comrades?" he said. "Suppose you come to the sector to-morrow at sixteen o'clock. Perhaps we shall try to-morrow. . . . You might find it very interesting . . . especially you, Georgi Vasilyevich. . . . And in the meanwhile, please excuse me. . . ."

Margulies touched his cap and offered his hand to the novelist. He went away.

"Well?" asked Georgi Vasilyevich.

"I am up to his tricks," muttered Vinkich. "And so, Georgi Vasilyevich, here is the situation: what do we have?"

"We have two opinions: Nalbandov says that it cannot be done; Margulies, that it might be done."

"And that it *ought* to be done," added Vinkich. "I know that sly dog very well. He thinks that it ought to be done. I am willing to swear to you by anything you like that it will actually be to-day, and not to-morrow or the day after to-morrow, that he will beat Kharkov. It will actually be to-day. Well, we still have time. What a careful fellow he is, the devil take him! . . ."

"And so," said Georgi Vasilyevich, "Nalbandov thinks that it is absolutely impossible. Margulies thinks that it is possible to make three hundred and thirty. Very interesting."

They went straight to the plant. Vinkich went up to Korneyev.

"Well, Korneyich, and what do you say?"

"Four hundred mixtures. That's a fact," Korneyev responded quickly, understanding at once what was meant.

And he pronounced the word mixture—*zamyes*—not as if it were a Russian word, but the Spanish surname—Zamess.

"Interesting," said Georgi Vasilyevich.

"You may be sure of that," muttered Vinkich. And then, noticing Ishchenko, he walked up to him.

"Well, and what do you think, Boss?"

Ishchenko also understood immediately.

"What do I think?" he said angrily. "I think not less than four hundred and fifty!"

"Five hundred!" cried Mosya, who had just run up.

The screen-like arrow of the seventy-metre cement-pouring tower disappeared high in the heavens. To see its top, it was necessary to crane one's neck, and then it seemed to be flying slantwise across the blue sky filled with swift, hot clouds.

The scoop and the man on it rose like the mercury in a thermometer.

XXXI

M R. RAY ROUPE'S request coincided perfectly with Nalbandov's secret desire. Nevertheless, he felt constrained to shrug his shoulders dispassionately and formally.

"And so you wish to see the environs? Splendid!"

It was really too dusty and sultry here. Everything here annoyed Nalbandov especially to-day. And he might have found any number of reasons for his irritation. Seroshevsky was altogether too easy-going. The repairmen were badly trained. There was a shortage of labour. The work of the transport was disgraceful. . . . And that was not all. Finally—these Americans. All they did was to waste people's time.

On this point, however, Nalbandov was not altogether honest with himself. Secretly, he found it extremely pleasant to ride and to talk in English with these polite, cultivated people, who could appreciate his excellent pronunciation, his sharp, pointed wit, his first rate technical education; in short, the remarkable, confidence-inspiring, though somewhat coarse, personality of a Bolshevik which overlaid a brilliant European education, refinement and culture.

He made a vivid and pleasant impression on Mr. Ray Roupe. He knew it. He sensed it. Secretly he was flattered by it, and he continued, not without satisfaction, to play the double rôle of outward coarseness and inner subtlety. This play somewhat tempered his irritability. Still, it could not efface it.

To-day, of course, it did not rise particularly from the unsatisfactory work of the transport or the poor training of the repairmen. The secret causes of Nalbandov's irritability were Margulies and yesterday's Kharkov record. To-day Margulies would try to beat Kharkov. There was no doubt of that. It was in the air. Nalbandov could foresee it in countless, minute symptoms. He had felt it since even the evening before. To-day it was being confirmed. There were placards, conversations, hints, smiles. . . .

He detested Margulies. He could not forgive him his reputation as the best sector-chief, as the idol of the workers, as the favourite on the construction. For, after all, who was Margulies in comparison with Nalbandov? A rough, practical man, a quickly ripened engineer, a demagogue and careerist, who ignored theory for the sake of attaining inflated production effects!

Yes, so far Margulies had been lucky. Every one of his victories enraged Nalbandov. He could scarcely contain himself.

But this could not go on forever. Sometime or other, of course, Margulies would break his neck. And one would not have to wait very long for it now. It was sheer madness to try to beat Kharkov. To beat Kharkov meant to go against all traditions, to violate the elementary demands of technique, to commit crude violence to the machinery. Machinery would not forgive violence.

"The construction is not a stunt!" It was only yesterday evening that Nalbandov had put this thought into circulation over the construction. It was caught up. For a time it had possessed the minds of the people.

Nalbandov had suppressed his triumph.

But to-day a new thought had appeared and was flying around the construction: "In the epoch of Reconstruction, tempos decide everything!"

Two ideas, "The construction is not a stunt!" and "In the epoch of Reconstruction, tempos decide everything!" engaged in a combat with each other, and evidences of this struggle, which had already begun, harassed Nalbandov at every turn. They tortured him, raised his bile.

The windshield of the automobile was broken up by a cluster of white, winding cracks that glided over the unrolling landscape like an excellent drawing of forked lightning.

The extent of the construction was tremendous.

Before the automobile had dashed across its borders into the steppe, Mr. Ray Roupe and Nalbandov had come to understand each other completely. Between them a certain definite relationship was established. This relationship was that mutual understanding and inner agreement of men of one culture who formally professed different, mutually exclusive religions.

But neither of them forgot his rôle. With soft courtesy, Mr. Ray Roupe asked questions. With exaggerated precision and deference, Nalbandov answered them. Mr. Ray Roupe made interesting remarks. Appreciating their subtlety, Nalbandov accepted or rejected them. It was understood that Mr. Ray Roupe was primarily interested in and amazed by the scale of the construction. Nalbandov nodded his head.

The white drawing of lightning glided over roofs and clouds. Here were gathered approximately one hundred and twenty or one hundred and thirty thousand workers, clerks, engineers, their families, and visitors. He did not have more precise information. Statistics could not keep up with life. Time left behind rows of dead figures.

But what was this? A village? Of course not. A city? No. A camp? Workers' quarters? A station? No. Officially this huge populated place was called a city. But was it a city? Hardly! At any rate, it lacked that intangible something without which it is impossible to have the sense of a city.

It lacked tradition. It had grown too rapidly. It had appeared with a speed that had upset the conception of time necessary for the creation of such a large city. History had not yet had time to place its brand upon it. It had no monuments, no customs, no style, no age-old national atmosphere. Furthermore—and this was the principal thing that struck the eye—it did not have a single characteristic indicative of religion.

In his time, Mr. Ray Roupe had visited a multitude of cities.

Among them were cities that had been founded thousands of years ago, and had continued to live until this day.

There were city-states, city-corpses with eyes that had turned glassy, resplendent witnesses of ancient culture, of brilliant eras— cruel monuments of inimitable architectural styles created by the hands of slaves.

There were cities that had grown to fame, and cities that had reached their bloom long ago and now were slowly fading.

And finally, there were cities that had grown up in some ten or fifteen years—new American cities, industrial centres. With all the lack of ceremony of a *nouveau riche,* convinced that his money can buy all the culture of the past, but actually receiving only more or less successful imitations, devoid of soul and sense, these cities used the styles of all epochs and all peoples for their palaces, churches, hotels, and libraries.

But in all these cities, even in the newest and most recently arisen, triumphed the old tradition of religion, of artisanship, of production, of consumption, of nationality, of social order.

XXXII

THEY rode along broad streets. These streets were both high-ways and dirt roads. They passed homes, stores, cinemas, banks, schools, newspaper offices, printing establishments, technical schools, and even a morgue.

There was also a circus tent.

But the houses had no style. The houses were standard wooden constructions, tents, barracks, sod-huts. The stores resembled the barns of fire stations. The banks and schools looked like side-shows. The cinemas were empty, fenced-off spaces with rows of benches planted in the ground. Everywhere were railroad crossings, semaphores, turnpikes, hissing, and steam.

It was a preliminary sketch for a city. But in this rough preliminary sketch one could already sense a certain division into regions. The character of these regions could be guessed. The outlines of daily life had already appeared.

Everything on the right-hand side of the main railroad line was the production-centre. The panorama of the monstrous lath-like figures of objects in aggregate was like a charcoal drawing. All that was on the left-hand side was the consumption-centre, but a productive colouration predominated even in this consumption centre.

Surveyors were everywhere, setting up their striped poles. They pulled the ribbon of their measuring tape along the length of the road. Its mirror-like screw gleamed in the sun like a brace and bit.

There were entire streets of cooper shops. Here were knocked together the huge wooden vats needed for water towers that worked by pressure, for launderies and bathhouses. The air resounded with the oaken boom of mallets.

There were enormous courtyards entirely filled with huge piles of ironware: iron beds, washstands, washbowls, spittoons, buckets.

But there were also yards where black and reddish shrubs set close together in narrow flower beds grew feebly—pathetic twigs, covered sparsely with little wilted leaves. They drooped under the unbearable rays of the sun, oppressed by the thick layer of stifling, corrosive dust.

Bright book covers faded in the show windows of book stores. At the one and only barber shop stood a long line of people.

Automobiles, woven carts, autobuses, bicycles, tractors, motorcycles, and pedestrians moved to meet each other in the crooked colonnades and portals of dust. The wind carried the dust away to the side. The colonnades crashed, swirled. The dust stretched itself over the trampled steppe, settling in a grey veil.

Mr. Ray Roupe wiped his nostrils with a clean cambric handkerchief. Black wax-like smears remained on the handkerchief.

"There's a great deal of all kinds of noise here," said Mr. Ray Roupe, smiling weakly. "A great deal of all kinds of noise. But there is no 'noise of time.' Do you understand me, Comrade Nalbandov?"

Nalbandov shut his eyes and shook his head.

Yes, of course. There was no "noise of time" here.

The so-called "noise of time" preceded and accompanied the growth, life, and especially the death of "those" miraculous foreign cities. It enraptured historians, travellers, and poets. "There" history spoke in a stone language of portals, quays, stairways, chapels, basilicas. A thousand copper echoes filled "those" cities with legends and conjectures. "Those" cities! How sweetly sounded that "those" "here"!

But "here" history was only beginning.

"Here" there were no legends, no conjectures. "Here" were cities without the "noise of time," without the copper language of history. This seemed incredible. This disillusioned—even affronted one.

He is right, Nalbandov thought to himself, but he said:

"You are mistaken, Mr. Ray Roupe. I do not agree with you." He squinted narrowly. "What is the 'noise of time'? Here, an airplane flies over the city. At first we hear the noise. Note that: the noise."

"Yes, yes. At first we hear the noise. My dear Leonard, listen. What he is saying is very interesting. I see what you're driving at. But go on, go on. And so, first the noise."

"At first, the noise. After the noise, we see an airplane appear over the housetops."

"Well, yes. The noise precedes and accompanies its flight. Isn't that right? But what do you see in this?"

"The speed of the sound competes with the speed of the flight. Technique is struggling with time."

"Oh, technique . . ." Mr. Ray Roupe's face wrinkled. "Yes, technique . . ."

Nalbandov laid both hands on the head of his cane. His hands were covered with such a thick layer of dust that they seemed gloved in suède. He looked straight before him with misty, narrowed eyes. He continued:

"But sound makes a thousand kilometres an hour, while the airplane only makes six hundred. Sound conquers. Sound precedes the flight."

"Eh, Leonard? That's right. Nature conquers technique. That's what I think."

"But will it always be thus?" Nalbandov continued. "What is incredible in the thought that the airplane may some day make a thousand and more kilometres an hour, instead of six hundred. That will happen in a year. In half a year. Perhaps even now . . . And then the machine will attain the speed of sound."

"That is very interesting. Hear, hear! The machine will reach the speed of sound."

"And then," Nalbandov said loudly and sharply, "we shall see a miracle. An airplane will appear soundlessly, with miraculous speed but in miraculous silence. It will pass over us. And only after a certain interval will tremendous noise reach us in its wake. The furious noise of time conquered by technique . . ."

"Oh, technique! . . . But the laws of nature . . ."

"The laws of nature are immutable," Nalbandov cut him short. "They are inert and conservative. They are closed within themselves. They cannot emerge from their own confinement. But human genius is limitless."

"You are a poet," said Mr. Ray Roupe, smiling.

"No, I am an engineer—a Bolshevik," Nalbandov replied roughly. "We shall attain the speed of light and we shall become immortal!"

"If your poor, earthly human heart can bear it," Mr. Ray Roupe said with a religious sigh, clasping his hands on his stomach and glancing covertly at Nalbandov.

He is right, Nalbandov thought to himself, but he said:

"It will bear it. You may be sure of that."

XXXIII

THE green Pullman train with a rosette of the Order of Lenin was sidetracked in the very middle of the blast furnace department.

It had been brought there about two months before, uncoupled from the train, and its path blocked with ties.

Within, electricity and a telephone had been immediately installed. The car became a house, an office, and the permanent appurtenance of the sector. This was the transient editorial office of the newspaper "Komsomolskaya Pravda." This was the field staff advanced to the firing line. Here it remained.

But although it had stopped in space, the car continued to move in time.

Time flew, changing the appearance of the space around it from minute to minute.

There was no sense of immobility. Opposite the window of the car rose red mountains of clay, gaping craters yawned, distant water gleamed; bridges transported on flat cars and portable cranes flickered by; as if they were stations, booths, barns, posts, barrels appeared and suddenly disappeared and appeared again . . . Day and night the panes trembled from the ceaseless clatter of passing tractors, electric locomotives, trucks, from the fractional knocking of pneumatic hammers and perforators.

Time rushed along, increasing its speed with each succeeding day; and in time, the green Pullman car with Lenin's profile rushed along, as if it were still breathing the iron smoke of Zlatoust,[1] the ferns of Miass,[2] the anthracite of Karaganda,[3] the glitter of Chelyaba,[4] all the freshness and power of the Great Urals, all its route traversed in space and time.

In the door of the car stood a lad in a blue cotton shirt, with a wet, dark-red head of hair, smoothed back and glistening like a mirror. He was knocking the old tea leaves out of a soldier's copper teapot. This was the make-up man.

The car step was too high above the track. Margulies had to lift his leg very high.

[1] The first iron and copper smelters of Zlatoust were erected by the Tula merchant Maslov in 1754. Twenty years later the rebel armies of Pugachov took possession of them for three days, and in the course of battle the plants were wrecked. Iron mining and smelting was resumed in Zlatoust in 1776, became the property of the Imperial Ministry of Finance in 1811 and subsequently a centre of metal industries and munition manufacture.

[2] Miass (or Meeyas)—a river and a gold-prospecting settlement.

[3] Katayev's reference to Karaganda anthracite is an unhappy one, for Karaganda coal is reputed to be of very poor quality.

[4] Chelyabinsk (located on both banks of the Miass River and starting point of the Trans-Siberian railroad) developed into a provincial and industrial centre from the Tatar village Selyaba (Chelyaba). In 1746 it became a fortress populated by Kazaks; in 1774 it withstood the attacks of Pugachov's rebel armies; in 1893, with the opening of the Trans-Siberian railroad, it became a transfer point through which passed multitudes of colonists bound for Siberia.

The make-up man stretched forth his strong arm. Holding it, Margulies swung lightly and buoyantly up to the platform.

"You haven't dropped in to have tea with us for a long time, Comrade Margulies."

"Here I am."

"You are most welcome."

"Are the folks at home?"

"Indeed they are. They're sitting around."

Lightly opening the thick, well-made, massive and noiseless doors, Margulies entered the car.

Its yellow, carved, lacquered interior had been adapted to the needs of the newspaper.

The first two compartments and that part of the corridor which belonged to them had been transformed into a fairly spacious printing establishment. Here stood two printing stands, a zinc table for the make-up man, and a hand printing press—American, with a thick black disk.

The sun, which had long ago passed the zenith, filtered through windows caked with dust. It burned the walls, intensified the print-shop odour of kerosene and zinc until it was as stifling as smoke.

Traces of fluid gleamed on the floor in shiny purple figure eights. Drops of glistening water rolled and curled up in the dust, like pills.

In the adjoining compartment, a voice could be heard shouting into the telephone. It was really there that the editorial office was located. Out of it rolled thick clouds of lilac tobacco smoke.

Margulies entered.

The managing editor, Vl. Kutaisov, lay face downward on a bench, which was covered with a grey woollen blanket. His head buried in a scrawny pillow, he was talking over the telephone. He held the receiver with both of his hands, at the same time trying somehow to close the other ear as best he could. It was too noisy in the compartment. People disturbed him.

Beating the toes of his unbuttoned sandals against the floor, twisting his back, pulling down his coat, flinging his dishevelled yellow hair from side to side, he shouted roughly and insistently into the telephone:

". . . But I tell you once again, my dear Comrade, that you cannot get away with it! You cannot get away with it, my dear Comrade! I tell you definitely: it won't do! It won't do! No, no! You'd better not tell me anything. It won't do. Do you understand? That's all. It won't do!"

Without looking up, Kutaisov reached back his hand, caught Margulies by the sleeve and pulled him down.

"How are you, David? Sit down. I'll be through in a minute. We have already made certain plans . . . No, never mind. I'm not talking to you," he continued, laughing, into the telephone. "It's all over with you, my friend. What? Whatever you do, don't you try to frighten us. That's the main thing. Suit yourself. You can complain even to the Politbureau [5] if you want to. It won't do. Well, that's all. Good-bye. That's all, that's all. It won't do. Go to—you know where! . . ."

Under the window, on a squeaking basket locked by a splinter of wood, sat the very small, neat secretary of the editorial office— Triger. He was almost a boy.

He wore a grey duster with black, diamond-shaped checks, and sandals, but his were neatly buttoned.

On his knees he held a copy book. His bulging, somewhat swollen Jewish eyes drooping, he was writing assiduously. But at the same time, he was listening to what Kutaisov was saying over the telephone; and to what the third and last member of the editorial staff, the poet Slobodkin, was saying.

Ishchenko sat on another bench, which was also covered, not with a blanket, but with a raspberry-coloured quilt.

He sat with his bare feet twisted under the bench, winding and unwinding a lock of hair on his finger, and occasionally interrupting Slobodkin in a surly manner.

Slobodkin, tall and youthful, with a milk-blue, freshly shaven head, a brown face and spectacles—not dust goggles, but ordinary, small, steel-rimmed magnifying glasses—placed his large porous

[5] The Political Bureau is the highest authority of the Communist Party.

hand on Ishchenko's shoulder and stooped over him. He spoke thickly and slowly in a Volga dialect:

"Here is what I'll tell you, my friend Ishchenko. Don't get excited. Don't worry. We had the same thing in Chelyaba. A fellow like you, also a brigadier, also a concrete man, came to our car, and he declared . . ."

Ishchenko stared stubbornly at the floor without listening.

"But I want to tell you one thing, Slobodkin. Your Khanumov won't laugh at us forever! That will never be!"

"You're a queer fellow . . . What has Khanumov to do with it?"

"Anyway, that will never be."

Margulies sat down on the raspberry-coloured quilt beside the brigadier.

"You are here already, Ishchenko. You don't waste any time. You're here ahead of time."

"Anyway, that will never be," Ishchenko muttered again.

Kutaisov hung up the receiver.

"What do you say, David?"

"And what do you say?"

"What news have you?"

"And you, what news?"

They regarded each other shrewdly and quizzically.

Margulies was unrecognisable. Gone was his flabbiness, his indecisiveness, his lisping. He was gay, sociable, light and precise in his movements—but all in a subdued manner. He was an entirely different person.

He slapped his pocket, pulled out the sheets covered with pencil scrawls, and laid them out on the bench.

"Well, my dear Comrades! Ten minutes of your attention! Put this in your pipe! A small article entitled 'Speed Up the Preparation and Production of High-Grade Concrete' from *to-day's* issue of 'Za Industrializatsiu.' "

He emphasised the word *"to-day's,"* and his spectacles glistened triumphantly.

"How on earth did you get *today's?*"

"The Holy Ghost got it for me. I have a special correspondent in Moscow. My kid sister. By telephone."

"You dog!" Slobodkin exclaimed in sheer admiration. "What a low dog you turned out to be!"

"Do you want me to read it to you?" Margulies covered the sheets with the palm of his hand. "Or isn't it worth while?"

"Read it. We've lost too much time as it is," Triger said solemnly, closing his copy book.

"Here goes," said Margulies. He began to read rapidly, stuttering at times, and bringing the pages of illegibly written or abbreviated sentences close to his spectacles.

While he was reading, several people entered the compartment.

First appeared the face of Mosya, excited, with shining, hysterical eyes. Mosya had been looking everywhere for Margulies. Apparently he had some very pressing business. He spotted Margulies and had started to open his mouth, when Kutaisov shook his fist at him. Mosya bent over like a hook, winced, and struck his thick lips with his hand. He pulled his cap down to his nose, folded his legs under him, and silently dropped to the floor right in the doorway.

After Mosya appeared the disapproving figure of Semechkin, the blue football sweater of Shura Soldatova, the blue aprons of the type-setters.

Margulies finished reading.

"What conclusion can we draw from this?" he said without pausing. "The conclusion is that we may try to beat Kharkov."

"Right!" cried Mosya.

"Wait. Don't yell," Kutaisov said.

"But not Khanumov!" Ishchenko cried ominously and tensely. "Still harping on it . . ."

"That will never be," the brigadier said even more ominously and intensely.

He gritted his teeth until lumps stood out near his cheek bones like tumours.

Mosya looked piteously at Margulies.

"David Lvovich! My word of honour! Give the order to Ishchenko! Let the comrades of the editorial staff be the witnesses. It is the very best shift! They are already transferring the machine, and in an hour it will be in place."

"I also think that we should make way for the youngsters," Kutaisov chuckled. He spread his feet apart in their unbuttoned sandals, and placing his hands behind his head, shook his long hair.

Margulies glanced earnestly over his shoulder at Mosya. He smiled vaguely. Still, he said drily, as if to no one in particular:

"I have already told the superintendent."

Ishchenko swung around quickly.

"Who is it: Khanumov or I?"

"Is your shift next?"

"Mine."

"Then it will be you."

Ishchenko and Mosya exchanged lightning glances.

"But no wagging of tongues!" Margulies warned.

"Ay, ay, Captain!" Mosya cried exultantly.

He sprang to his feet, snapped to attention, and saluted.

"What do you say, Comrade Editors?"

"We approve."

"Not enough! Not enough! . . ."

Slobodkin laughed affectedly in a deep voice:

"Ho, ho, ho! He's not satisfied with the approval of such an authoritative press on wheels. What else do you want from us?"

Slobodkin winked at little Triger:

"Go to him with all your complaints."

Margulies rubbed his hands briskly.

"In the first place, dear Comrades," he said, "the carriers. In the second place, the transport. In the third place, the water supply. In the fourth place, the electric power. Will that be enough for you?"

"That will do."

"Korneyev and I will be responsible for the rest."

Little Triger opened his copy book, checked over what was written there, and lifted serious, bulging eyes to Margulies.

"Carriers, transport, water supply, electric power. And nothing else? Don't you need machine repair?"

"Quite right!" said Margulies. "Machine repair. It's indispensable."

Everybody laughed. Margulies laughed louder than anybody else. How could he have forgotten it? How could he have overlooked such an important thing as machine repair? He, the engineer, the chief of the sector! While the quiet little Triger, the secretary of the editorial staff, had not overlooked it.

"Don't get funny with our little Triger," said Kutaisov. "He's experienced! He ate a dog in this business and had a pup for dessert!"

"And washed it down with kerosene!" Slobodkin added.

Although Triger half smiled, he blushed like a little girl. He had actually learned the concrete business fairly well. Wherever the car happened to be, he had watched the work of the concrete men on the new constructions attentively and persistently. He had read everything on the subject that was available in the Russian language.

To the knowledge derived from books, he had added his own theory of tempos.

It consisted of this: increase of the productivity of one machine automatically entails the increase of the productivity of others indirectly connected with it. And since all machines in the Soviet Union are connected with each other to a greater or lesser degree, and together represent a complex interlocking system, the raising of tempos at any given point in this system inevitably carries with it the unavoidable—however minute—raising of tempos of the entire system as a whole, thus, to a certain extent, bringing the time of socialism closer.

He had selected that point. He had specialised in concrete. He was convinced that accelerating the work of even one concrete-mixer would lead to accelerating the tempos of work of all the machines indirectly connected with the production of concrete.

And indirectly connected were: the water system, which supplied the water; the railroad, which brought up the cement, the sand and the gravel; and the electric station, which produced the power. So the daily requirements of sand, cement, and gravel would be increased. Hence, the work of the sand and stone carriers must be accelerated, and likewise that of stone-crushers, and sieves, and the output of the cement plant.

Since, in order to strengthen the work of the water system, the electric station, the stone-crushers, and so forth, it was indispensable to accelerate not only the work of all the machines connected with it, but also the work of all the machines connected with these machines, then it became absolutely clear that with the small, and at first glance, minor matter of raising the productivity of one concrete-mixer was connected all the tremendous, complex, important, interacting system of the Five-Year Plan.

In a drop of water, Triger saw a garden. He thoroughly studied this drop. He devised a scheme. He drew it. It was the blueprint of a garden.

It was a five-ray star, in the centre of which was a concrete-mixer. From the concrete-mixer radiated lines. Two of these lines connected the centre with sand and rock carriers, one of them with the cement storehouse, the two others with the electric station and the water system. The first three lines were transport; the other two, the electric carriers and the water system.

This was a crude depiction of the nervous and alimentary systems on which the efficient and uninterrupted work of the concrete-mixer depended.

In addition, close to the centre was placed a dot—the machine-repair. This point might have been omitted, but Triger knew well the condition of hand carts, barrows, and sterlings which were on the sector. They were few and they were well-worn. Every moment the need for rapid repair work might arise.

This was the scheme of the mechanical interaction of power points and lines.

But without the ardent human will, without live, quick thought, without creative imagination, without the sharp human eye, without sensitive awareness, without a centre where all the human qualities could unite, of what use was this scheme, drawn precisely to a minute scale?

Without all this, it would have been vapid and dead.

So, little Triger had painstakingly and thoughtfully populated it with people.

He had selected them, weighing their attributes and faults, evaluating them, thus and so, and had placed them along the dots and the lines. All over his scheme were written the names of these people. The names of the people stood side by side with the figures, investing them with soul and sense. At all points—on both carriers, on the water system and the electric station, at the cement storehouse, in the dispatching office, at the portable machine repair—sat dependable loyal lads.

But even that was not enough.

One had to create, and precisely dispose according to duties, a central emergency staff, ready on the first demand to send a member to a given place, so that he might remove a possible delay on the spot.

Into this staff went the entire editorial office. Slobodkin was assigned to the electric station, Kutaisov to cement, Triger assumed the responsibility for both carriers. A suitable man for the water system was lacking. This was one of the most dependable sectors. It could be attended to without worry. Still, it could not be left without supervision.

Triger screwed up his eyes as if they pained him.

"Semechkin, will you attend to the water system?"

Triger did not trust Semechkin, but in case of emergency even Semechkin could be useful.

Semechkin cleared his throat importantly and profoundly. He was flattered by Triger's unexpected offer. It meant that, after all, some one did appreciate Semechkin. It meant that Semechkin might still be of some use to some one.

Semechkin walked from beyond the door into the compartment. He even turned slightly pink. Of course, this was not at all what he had figured on that morning, but it was not bad either. At any rate, it brought the record closer.

"Why not?" he said. "I might do it. Why not?"

Under the dot of the water system, Triger wrote into his scheme: "Semechkin."

Margulies put his arms around Ishchenko's shoulders. He looked closely into his eyes.

"Well, Army Commander, are you satisfied now? Have you calmed down?"

Ishchenko wanted to glower, yet against his own will, his cheeks spread out into a smile. But he immediately controlled himself and said severely:

"Don't worry about me. I'll answer for my boys."

The telephone bell spluttered. Kutaisov raised his arm and lazily caught the receiver.

"Yes. The car of the 'Komsomolka.' I'm listening. What's the matter?"

He buried himself and the receiver in the pillow (shush, lads!).

"Well, what's the matter? I'm listening."

For some time he lay quietly with his nose in the pillow and the receiver at his ear. Then he said:

"Brigadier Ishchenko? He's here. I'll connect you with him right away." And turning to Ishchenko: "Take the receiver. They want you."

"Me?"

Ishchenko looked around in alarm. Never before had anybody called him to the telephone.

"You, you! From the office. Take the receiver."

Awkwardly, with rough carefulness, the brigadier took the receiver, turned it, and placed it neatly to his ear.

"Hello, hello!" he cried in an exaggeratedly loud voice. "Brigadier Ishchenko at the telephone. What do you want?"

As if they had a premonition of something unusual, all grew silent.

The blow of the short, trigger-like turn of the pneumatic hammer at the blast furnace broke against the window.

Ishchenko stood tensely, the receiver at his temple, and listened. He turned pale. Then, without saying a word, he placed the receiver on the cot.

"What's the matter?"

Ishchenko looked around in bewilderment.

"She found the most appropriate time," he said lugubriously.

"What's the matter?"

"My woman . . . She's in a bad way . . ."

Helplessly, sweetly, with embarrassment, and gregariously, he smiled.

"Imagine! Her labour pains have begun! What do you think of that!"

For a short time, he stood in the centre of the compartment, not knowing what to do. Sweat glistened on his dark brow.

"Have to take her there."

Everybody made way for him.

He walked out.

XXXIV

ON this special day no one went far from the barrack. Soon the entire brigade had gathered.

"That's how it is," said Smetana, sitting down on the ground.

He clasped his knees in his hands, put his head on his knees, and rocked back and forth.

From the windows of the barrack were heard low cries at regular intervals:

"Ah-ah-ah . . . ah-ah-ah-ah . . . oo-oo-oo . . ."

It was Fyenya moaning.

Since early morning she had been on her feet and had not once sat down. By ten o'clock she had managed to accomplish everything. There was nothing more to be done, and the day was only beginning.

Fyenya was bored and did not know what to do with herself. She kept feeling that she had failed to do something, that something was not arranged or finished, that she had to hurry, and yet there was no place to hurry to.

Then she attached herself to some women at a meeting of women-activists. From there the women went on their *subbotnik* [1] to build a public nursery. Fyenya joined the activist group and went with them. They tried to talk her out of it. She paid no attention to them.

"When *this* is going to happen!" she continually exclaimed.

And she went.

Among them were many pregnant women. She did not want to lag behind them. In this, there was not so much stubbornness involved as shrewdness and simple economic calculation.

Since morning Fyenya had decided to remain with her husband forever. She liked it here. The products were good, and there was a brigadier's food card, and even some manufactured articles would occasionally appear. But, while she proposed to stay here, she did not propose to stay without working. No, she would work.

There was plenty of work. She might go to the mines as a carter. She might get a job as a waitress in the restaurant. Or she might do some mucking with the diggers. But to sit at home as a housewife, with nothing to do, was shameful and boresome. Then also, while one shock-brigade card was good, two were better.

But there was going to be a child . . .

What would she do with it? The public nurseries were full. But if the women-activists of the sector were building their own public nursery, then, if she herself helped to build this public nursery and was herself a woman-activist, her child would get the first turn. That was certain.

And so, walking heavily on the soles of her feet, stumbling, drenched with sweat, she went to work, and pulled at the boards, and wiped off her sweat, and busied herself, and gave orders, and signed some sort of a declaration and sang songs . . .

But Fyenya had not calculated her strength. It suddenly gave

---

[1] *Subbotnik*—literally the Sabbath—a day of volunteer labour contributed without pay to the Soviet State. The precedent was set by Lenin himself during the Civil War.

out. She became sick. They could scarcely assist her to the barrack. It was two kilometres of walking, dust, sultriness, stuffiness.
The wind had died down.

They ran after Ishchenko. Ishchenko was nowhere to be found.
They ran to the office of the sector. From there they telephoned
to the "Komsomolka." There they located him and told him.

And meanwhile, Fyenya lay on the cot and moaned:

"Ai-ai-ai, Kostichka . . . oo-oo-oo, Kostichka! . . ."

Neighbours wet her head with a towel and gave her water. The
brigade was making a noise under the window.

"That's how it is," said Smetana. "I went to the sector. Margulies is quiet and so far says nothing. He is waiting, taking his
time. Korneyev is not opposed. Mosya, of course, is digging the
ground with his nose. Well, it's clear. Ishchenko will come right
away. He will report. So, you see, everything is in order. Yes . . ."

"Now I have the floor, Comrade!" Olga Tregubova suddenly
cried in a piercing voice, such as is used at a public meeting, rolling her small blue eyes, which were bulgy enough as it was.

"Shush!" cried Smetana. "Shut up! I didn't give you the floor."

He sprang up, caught Tregubova by her leg as quick as lightning and pulled her down. She gasped, swung down with a crash,
and landed sitting on the step.

She bit her tongue.

"Hey, you!"

"So this is the picture," Smetana continued quietly. "Now, as
Comrade Tregubova correctly remarked, it's up to us . . ."

He stopped suddenly.

Galloping across the street, a small woven cart rolled up. While
it was still moving, Ishchenko began to crawl out of it. He was
tangled up in the straw. He pulled his legs out of the straw.
Finally, he straightened out and jumped down. The cart stopped.

His trouser legs rolled up, covered with straw chaff, Ishchenko
went up to the porch. The lads made way for him. Banging open
the door with his knee, he went into the hall.

It was frightfully hot.

Leaving the car of the "Komsomolskaya Pravda," the brigadier had immediately started running for home, but half way there, he turned back. He realised that he would have to have a wagon.

The driver, whom he did not know, did not want to give him a horse. He demanded a hospital order. Ishchenko begged. He swore. Finally he overcame the driver's resistance.

Now there was something else—another difficulty: the drivers were dining. With a note in his hand, Ishchenko ran into the dining room tent to the driver. Here he begged and swore again.

It seemed to him that if he did not leave at once—that very minute—something horrible would happen to Fyenya. She would die. She would choke. And he could imagine her choking to death. He imagined it so clearly that he choked himself.

But the driver refused to go until he had dined.

So he waited. He walked around the table. The waiters pushed him away with their bare elbows. Smiling idiotically, he sat down on the edge of the bench. But immediately he jumped up and walked around the table again, drooping his strong head and angrily compressing his lips.

He detested the stuffy, yellow, even light—like that of a show booth—which came into the tent through the hot homespun walls yellow against the sun, and the ceiling raised aloft on high poles. He was nauseated by the grey salt crystals in white china jars on the table. He was nauseated by the bread, the flies, and the water pitcher. But more than all, he hated and was exasperated by the drivers, who, despite the heat, were dressed in dark, heavy, dirty cotton overcoats.

"Just like swine!" he muttered through his teeth. "There, a woman is choking to death. And here, like pigs, they eat deliberately, slowly!"

He finally got a pretty bad horse and a driver who was somewhat crazy. Thinking to gain time, the driver, smacking his lips, drove straight through the construction sector, and brought them to a place out of which they could scarcely make their way. They had to unharness the horse, and roll the cart by hand out of an excavation.

They drove back and lost their way again. In a word, they made a detour of at least five kilometres and finally drove up to the barrack from the opposite side.

There was a pounding and knocking in Ishchenko's ears, as if thundering water had poured into them.

He expected to see something unusual at home, something extraordinary, terrible, unknown. He prepared himself for it. But he had no sooner gone behind the partition, than he was astounded by the peaceful simplicity and the homely regularity of what he saw. There was nothing unusual here.

On her back, on the cot, lay Fyenya. She was moaning softly, but her face was shining and alive. A neighbour was tying up her things. Fyenya saw Ishchenko and stopped moaning.

Smiling quickly and nervously, she lightly rose to her feet unaided, and began to pull a shawl over her head, pushing her hair under it with her stiff index finger.

"Well?" said Ishchenko, somewhat disappointed. "What's the matter?"

Fyenya regarded him guiltily with her lively blue eyes, but did not reply.

"Take the things," said the neighbour woman, putting the bundle in the brigadier's arms. "Did you get a wagon?"

Ishchenko automatically pressed the things to his breast and looked severely at Fyenya.

"Will you make it?"

She made an effort not to moan, bit her lower lip with her fine, pearly teeth, and nodded.

"I'll make it," she said with an effort, and again a convulsion seized her.

Ishchenko offered her his shoulder. She put her arm around his neck and they went out.

While the neighbour woman was helping the heavy Fyenya into the small cart—which was narrow for two people and a basket— and while she was putting straw under Fyenya's back, Ishchenko walked up to the lads.

Curiously and respectfully, they looked at the brigadier, at his dark, careworn face, at the bundle in his hands. They waited to hear what he would say.

The sight of the brigade gathered here, immediately brought back Ishchenko's interest in the world from which he had been so abruptly pulled away.

"Well, how are things going?" he asked, looking around and mentally counting the number of lads.

"The boys don't object."

"Is everybody here?"

"Everybody."

Ishchenko frowned.

"What do you mean, everybody? And where is Zagirov? Sayenko?"

Zagirov and Sayenko were not there. They had disappeared. They had missed the previous shift as well. Zagirov had been seen early in the morning. He had been running among the lads, seeking to borrow a ten-spot. Sayenko, however, had not appeared since the previous day.

"What's the matter with those sons of bitches?" Ishchenko cried out. "Do they want to cut our throats? Couldn't they find another day? We've got such important things to do . . . that . . . that . . ."

Words failed him. He struck the ground with his bare earthy foot.

In the cart, Fyenya began to moan. Ishchenko ran to her. And when he was already seated beside her, his right foot hanging out, and supporting his wife with his left arm around her back, he cried out:

"Everybody—to the last man—must be in his place or we won't be able to look people straight in the eye!"

The cart started. Smetana ran after it.

"Wait! Stop, Ishchenko, stop! What was decided?"

"We decided to beat them. Lead the brigade to the sector . . . Everybody . . . to a man . . . I'll be there right away . . ."

He indicated Fyenya with his eyes and smiled.

"You can see for yourself the kind of music this is . . . A fine how-do-you-do . . ."

Fyenya curled against her husband's shoulder.

"Oi, Kostichka . . . It's so annoying . . . Oi, Kostichka, I won't make it!"

"Hurry up, you, the devil take you!" Ishchenko bellowed in a terrible voice, poking the driver.

There was no more wind. But neither was there any sun. The sun hid behind a low, smothering, blinding white cloud.

The air was steaming and immobile, as in a bathhouse . . .

XXXV

IT was the end of May—the beginning of an intense and beneficent Ural summer—a bit of primitive nature untouched yet by people and uncomplicated by planning.

Here, the narrow edge of the tarnished sky seemed the only intermediary between sun, wind, clouds and grass.

Here grass grew over the round side of the hillock. It had not yet been entirely trampled. It was dry, fine, hot, full of dust, but grass that was still pungent, fragrant. The market was above. It stood with its shaft-bows and shafts thrust into the sky and supporting it with its tents, its stalls—with all its nondescript gypsy encampment of trade.

The two comrades sat down on the edge of a ditch and began to play.

But this time, Sayenko soon took away Zagirov's permit to purchase drygoods, as well as his ration card and meal tickets.

They rose from the ground and went to the market. Zagirov wept no more. His eyes shone feverishly, like those of a sick man. His face was sunken and earthy. He no longer begged for anything, no longer said anything. It was difficult for him to unglue his parched lips. Crushed and desolate, he dragged after Sayenko, senselessly trying to place his feet in the other's footprints. He smiled with an effort. His smile was stiff and ingratiating.

The crest of the hill, trampled by the crowd until it was black, smoked on all sides as if some one had set fire to it.

Olya Tregubova had been sent to fetch Sayenko and Zagirov. She looked for them everywhere. She dared not return to the brigade without them. She found them in the market place.

The market place was jammed with hobbled horses, with wicker carts crowded together, barrels of *kvass,* dismembered rubbery carcasses of sheep side by side with poisonously green sheaves of reeds, oily spotted fingers, large bottles of *koumiss* wrapped in hay, messy lumps of Bashkir butter.

Here on felt blankets, in fox-fur hats, sat grey-bearded Bashkirs whose large faces gleamed like bowls of pottery decorated with somnolent traces of Asiatic smiles. Here walked gypsy women who scattered glances heedlessly like small coins. Ragamuffins were pushing wobbling bicycles. From hand to hand passed old pulverisers, cartridge belts, packages of cheap tobacco, watches, shoes, boots, cheap cotton shirts covered with suspicious little nubs of badly combed cotton . . .

Ural Kazaks came here with their entire families from near and distant Kazak villages and collective farms to look at the miraculously rising city. They gazed around in dumb astonishment. From everywhere—from the west, the east, the south, the north—the hill was crowded with machines, pipes, cranes, houses, towers, such as they had never seen before.

Like an invincible encampment, all these things surrounded the besieged redoubt of the market place. They stormed it with companies of barracks, with line-battalions of plants, with artillery regiments of sectors, with mortars of construction machinery, with machine guns of pneumatic drills.

But the market place held its own.

At night the wagons creaked. At dawn, mysteriously passing through the enemy encampment, they entered the besieged redoubt.

The Kazaks came here with food and went away with manufactured goods.

That is how the market place appeared. That is how trade
began.

Everything characteristic of Asia was here, except colourful-
ness. There were no rugs, no fruits, no aniline-dyed weavings, no
copper utensils. Here black and grey predominated—the dull colours of a Central Russian market place—more nearly resembling
a newspaper than a Persian rug.

Sayenko felt quite at home here. With jaunty agility, he untied
the things he had won. The tapes of the underwear slapped against
the wind.

"All right, come on! Grab it! Buy it!"

He threw out the galoshes. They turned over heavily in the
air, their beet-red lining flashing. The sun blazed stickily on their
soles, patterned like pressed caviar.

"Who wants rubbers? They're very good. A fool lost them for
a three-spot. Come on, boys! Don't be stingy with your ten-
spots!"

He ran through the crowd, pushing his way with his elbows.
The market place intoxicated him. His eyes became languid, purplish, drunken. Saliva trickled down his pimply chin. His voice
was hoarse, strained, demoniac.

"And here is a fine cap—strong enough to slap. Who wants a
cap that's slick, for a head that's healthy, from one that's sick!
It sells for a five-spot, but was bought for a hundred. Back me
up, Comrades, for I'm a shock-brigading enthusiast!"

And out of the corner of his mouth, he would say rapidly and
complainingly:

"So help me God, Citizens, we have nothing to eat! We're dying
of hunger, my kid brother and I! We haven't eaten for three
days. By the true Cross!"

He startled all with the new shoes, slapped them together, sole
against sole, caught them by the shoelaces and swung them before
him intently.

"Leningrad shoes to chase away blues! Take a poke—strong

as an oak! Come on, lads, they're cheap at twenty! And here is underwear, made by Arishka—not a single patch, and a ten-spot apiece."

He was surrounded by peasant men and women. Jesting and punning, looking sly and foolish, he soon sold the things. He caught the customers by their coats. He spat on the palm of his hand. He clapped his hands. Walked away. Returned. Stamped his bast shoes. Winked. Sang.

Zagirov could scarcely keep up with him. Terrified, he saw his own precious things passing forever into strange hands. Sayenko had given him a ten-spot for them, but he was getting fifty in return.

Zagirov wanted to say something, but he could not open his mouth. He could not part his tightly clenched teeth. He wanted to eat and drink. He should have liked some *kvass*, some *koumiss* . . .

He saw that Sayenko, turning away from the crowd, would stealthily and quickly put the new money inside a roll of old currency, shoving it through the fly of his trousers into some deep, secret, inner pocket.

Olya Tregubova pounced on them noisily. She stopped short, placed her arms akimbo.

"Comrades," she began in an unusually high, almost screaming, female voice. "All the lads are in their places. You are the only ones not on the job. That will never do, Comrades! As class-conscious shock-brigaders, you should be ashamed, especially before this important record-breaking shift . . ."

Sayenko regarded her with boredom—her holiday dress, her flounces, her buttons.

He winked at Zagirov, whistled, turned around slowly, and walked away from the market place in silence.

She ran around him and again confronted him.

"Yesterday you missed your shift! Are you trying to miss it again to-day?"

She fluttered before them in the wind like a banner. Her eyes gleamed enticingly and stubbornly.

"Do you hear me? Are you trying to miss it again? What's the matter with you? Have you lost your senses? All the boys are at the production conference, and here you are on the market place! What is there here that you haven't seen before? Haven't you seen this trash? And you are supposed to be shock-brigaders! That's a fine way to act!"

Sayenko regarded her shamelessly from head to foot, and smiled tenderly.

"Do you know what I would advise you to do?" he said caressingly. "Kiss me. Do you know where?"

And without hurrying, he lifted his leg; without hurrying, he bent down; and without hurrying, he slapped his buttocks, which were as broad as a box.

"Kiss me right here, my dear Olyechka."

She turned crimson, but contained herself.

"That's very silly," she remarked, carelessly shrugging her shoulders. "Just plain hooliganism."

And suddenly she attacked Zagirov.

"And what's the matter with you? Haven't you a head of your own? He leads you, and you follow him as if he had you on a string!"

"Well, now, why are you insulting my little comrade?" Sayenko said piteously. "My precious little playmate! I warn you, I'll knock the wind out of any one who insults my little friend. You see, he hasn't won back yet what he has lost. Isn't that right, Zagirov?"

She knitted her bulging little brow.

"Look out, Sayenko!"

"I'm looking. What's next?"

"We'll make an issue of it. Bear that in mind. We know you!"

"I haven't any time to waste on you. Do you understand?"

"Comrades, be class-conscious . . ."

Olya Tregubova drew a deep breath. Ugh, how she detested Sayenko!

She gathered all her strength, so as not to say anything amiss. She realised that she had to outwit him. A careless word would spoil everything. And every man was especially needed to-day. Perhaps the whole business might depend on one man.

Sayenko looked at her with squinting, crafty eyes. He saw right through her. He realised his own power.

"Comrades," she said soberly, "be class-conscious. Since we have discipline, we must maintain it. Once we decide to do something, we must do it—like Bolsheviks. Is that clear? Zagirov, how about you? You can't leave the boys in the lurch!"

Zagirov stood silent, as if he had lost his wits. Sayenko put his arms around him.

"Well, how about it, my dear little playmate? By the way, I'm not holding you back. Go ahead, go ahead! Otherwise they'll frame up some case against you because of me."

He looked closely into his eyes.

"Or perhaps you'd rather go with me, my little brother?"

He nodded his head toward Olya.

"Come on, let's show them what famous enthusiasts we are."

His voice became more insidious and more honeyed, and his mouth more poisonous. Sayenko dripped with hatred. Olya sensed it. She knew that to-day something untoward would happen, but she pretended not to notice it.

"That's right!" she cried in a ringing voice. "That's right, boys! Clear yourselves of yesterday's disgrace!"

"Disgrace?" Sayenko asked suspiciously. "What do you mean, yesterday's disgrace? What disgrace? Look out, Olya, don't you go too far! How dare you shame us before every one? What right have you? Get away from here! Go to the devil's own mother!"

Olya let the insult go past her ears.

"Well, how about it, boys? You won't fail us! You won't fall down on us!"

"Scoot!" Sayenko cried in an unnatural voice. "Scoot, for God's sake! And don't stand between me and the sun. We told you we'd come. That means we'll come. That's all!"

She pretended to believe. But she did not go away. She followed them at a distance.

They descended the smoking hill, Sayenko in front, Zagirov behind.

She thought that Sayenko would deceive her, but she was mistaken. Sayenko and Zagirov were walking toward the sector.

"Sha, listen to me. In the first place, listen to me, and try to understand. You'll win it back. If I tell you so, that means that you'll win it back. You'll get a chance. You can take the half a thousand away from me. That's a fact. Wait, but the main thing is to listen to me."

XXXVI

FINALLY the machine tore itself out of the hell. They stopped at the edge of the lake.

The lake covered fourteen square kilometres. It was quite new, made only five months before.

Previously, a skimpy steppe river had flowed here. The future factory needed a tremendous quantity of water for industrial purposes. The river could not satisfy this need. So it had been banked by a high dam a kilometre in length. In the spring, the river thawed, flowed, overflowed, and began to fill up the artificially created basin.

The river became a lake.

Having flooded fourteen square kilometres of the steppe, the water immediately acquired the topographical delimitations of the basin's rim. Still, it did not quite become a natural lake. One bank, one shore made by the dam, cut it off too sharply, too much like a fence. It appeared as if a long oval lake had been cut across in the middle, and one half placed in the steppe.

Mr. Ray Roupe shook his head approvingly and pensively. Yes, of course, this confirmed his ideas. It was a brilliant example for his future book.

"Don't you think," he asked, "that this is a crude invasion of nature by man?"

The artificial lake lay in the grass like a pier-glass which had been carried out of the house into the yard. Accustomed to reflect walls and faces, now it was compelled to reflect sky and clouds. And in this lay the unnaturalness of its half-fainting condition.

The play continued.

Nalbandov looked somewhat ironically at the American.

"The invasion of nature by man—that is too metaphysical a definition. We say: the invasion of geography by geometry."

Ray Roupe smiled subtly.

"But geometry failed. Geometry did not pass the examination to become a god. You wanted to make a whole lake, and you have made only half a lake."

"No, we did not want to make a lake. We needed merely a basin of water for industrial purposes. We took from geography what it could give us, and we built it. Do you know what it cost us?"

Mr. Leonard Darley pulled out his notebook. He noted a multitude of the most interesting facts.

The building of the dam had been started in the latter half of winter. It had to be finished by spring. If it were not finished before the breaking of the ice, all of the work would be swept away. The concrete work had been done at forty degrees below zero, with unendurable winds. The water for the concrete had been heated. People froze their hands and feet. The work was beyond human power. Nevertheless, it did not stop. It was a battle of man against nature, and man won. On the seventy-fifth day, the last cubic metre of concrete was laid into the dam.

Nalbandov talked. Ray Roupe shook his hat approvingly.

Of course, all this confirmed his ideas again and again. Frozen fingers, people falling from fatigue and cold, the mad duel of man with God. And the result—a kilometre of dam and half a lake! It seemed to man that he had conquered nature. Man exulted.

But why did man need all this? Water for industry. Excellent! But for what was industry needed? For the production of things. Excellent! But what were things needed for? Surely, they were not needed for happiness? Youth and health were the only things needed for happiness.

Was the ancient patriarchal state of man less happy than now? Oh, there had been much more happiness on earth then than now! There was a wise, contemplative existence under the eternal sky—now terrible, now merciful. There was proximity to God. There was submission to Him—now terrible, now merciful. There was a complete and beatific fusion with the world. It was a warm, primeval paradise.

And people had abandoned this paradise. People had entered into a struggle with nature, with God. The devil of pride and technique had possessed humanity.

Yes, indeed. It should be a remarkable book.

"Look, Comrade Nalbandov," he said. "We have driven only eight kilometres out of this hell, and how miraculously everything around us has changed! Nature is breathing such joyous warmth. How clear and fragrant is the wind! What a soothing primeval quietness! We have barely left technique behind, and yet we have already come closer to God . . ."

"Yes . . . We have come closer . . . in a 1930 Packard!"

Nalbandov looked biliously along the top of the dam and the entire length of the lake. Here everything reminded him of Margulies. Margulies had built the dam. At forty degrees below zero, he had risked laying heated concrete.

At that time, Nalbandov had regarded it as technically unwise. It went counter to the academic traditions of laying concrete. Margulies had dared to violate those traditions. Nalbandov had referred to science. Margulies had insisted that science be regarded dialectically. What was a scientific hypothesis yesterday became an academic fact to-day; what was an academic fact to-day became an anachronism to-morrow—a stage passed by.

There had been a terrific battle at the office of the plant. The engineers had divided into camps. But the youth had been behind Margulies. Margulies had insisted on his point of view. He had been granted permission to try the experiment. Nalbandov had been convinced that Margulies would break his neck. He desired it passionately. But Margulies had conquered. The dam had been built.

Nalbandov did not surrender. He still clung to his opinions. He was sure that the concrete would prove insufficiently strong. He predicted that the dam would not endure the pressure of water. In the spring he would go to the dam and watch the river overflowing its banks. The lake was slowly filling up with water. Chunks of ice that could find no outlet swirled senselessly like flocks of paraffin geese, and collided with each other. The concave span of the dam stood in the water like a stack of gigantic horseshoes, one on top of the other, and each a kilometre in size. Every day the water covered more and more of them. But the dam held. Now the water covered it to the brim. The thinnest sheet of water flowed over the fence-like edge along the entire kilometre-long vista of the dam. Sweeping past, the wind tore at it, sprayed it, carried it away in a fresh damp cloud. The trees which grew in the valley of the banked and dried-up river were covered with a thin silver spray of moisture. They stood in silvery-blue clusters, in bright nests of white-limbed birches, blue lambskin mounds of brush.

"What else does humanity need, I ask you?" said Mr. Ray Roupe, removing his hat with the respectable gesture of a civilised Christian upon entering a church.

Nalbandov did not reply. He gazed intently and passionately at the outward surfaces of the oblique, deeply curved, lofty span of the dam. It reminded him of the outer wall of a bathtub filled to the brim.

It seemed to Nalbandov that if he were to strike it with his huge cane, the entire lake would resound with the ringing of church bells. He sought some evidence of a crack. Sometimes it seemed to him that the water was seeping through the dam, but it was an optical illusion. The water flowed over the dam, but it could not seep through the concrete that had been laid by Margulies.

Yes, Margulies had won. But it had been an accidental victory.

One could still hope that Margulies would break his neck with to-day's record.

They left the machine and climbed up the dam on an iron ladder.

Here, at its beginning, on an ordinary concrete plinth, stood a small black figure of Lenin. Lenin stood, surrounded by a light iron barrier on which hung a lifebelt, in the modest pose of a captain on the bridge of a battleship of concrete.

Here the lake broadened out to make a deep, round bay. Behind it, a double-humped mountain rose sharply. It hid the construction. Two geological survey tents, decked with red flags, were on its side.

On the other side of the mountain ran a road. It smoked, dense and black. From the rising, floating clouds of dust one could guess the heavy traffic along the road.

"Look," Ray Roupe remarked. "Have you noted this phenomenon—a Neapolitan bay? Man has competed with nature and has reproduced in miniature the Bay of Naples with smoking Vesuvius behind it. Comrade Nalbandov, have you ever been in Sorrento?"

"Yes."

"Don't you think there is a remarkable resemblance?"

"Really, I had never noticed it before. There *is* a resemblance."

"And these white tents on the incline . . . They are spread like two cities of antiquity. To the left is Herculaneum, to the right, Pompeii."

Nalbandov smiled.

"Those are the tents of the geological survey—the Herculaneum and the Pompeii of the technique you so detest."

Mr. Ray Roupe's eyes sparkled.

"Oh, excellent, excellent!" he exclaimed gaily. "Bravo! Let us pursue the analogy. Do you remember the fate of Herculaneum and Pompeii? Excellent! At times nature loses patience. Then she floods her intransigeant children with moulten lava . . ."

Ray Roupe stopped. His cultivated tact told him that in a little more he would transgress the limits permissible in jesting with a man he scarcely knew. With what firmness his age permitted, he took Nalbandov's arm above the elbow and shook it.

"Anyway," he said quickly, "let's leave philosophy alone. We shall never understand each other. You are a young dialectician. I am an old, and perhaps an obsolete, scholastic. But really, I like this modest monument to Lenin very much. What a splendid position! Lenin against the background of Naples! Especially since it quite corresponds to historical truth."

Mr. Ray Roupe looked at Nalbandov directly and good-naturedly.

"I'm very familiar with the biography of this remarkable man. Lenin really had a most unusual mind. I'm only giving him his due when I say that, although on many points I do not agree with him. But I know that Maxim Gorky had a Marxist Academy at Capri, and occasionally your great leader Lenin was his guest. It is quite possible, and even probable, that he may have very frequently looked appreciatively from there to the Bay of Naples and Vesuvius. And then, perhaps, looking at Naples, that great monument of the culture of the past, he had thought of his country and of the future of Russia . . . And perhaps he visioned the Naples of the future and the Bay of Naples, made by the hands of free Russian workers . . ."

And with these pleasant words to Nalbandov, Mr. Ray Roupe, his blue eyes gleaming modestly, returned to his place in the automobile.

XXXVII

THE time was twenty minutes past fifteen o'clock.
Korneyev was reading a note:

"Cannot reach you by phone. You are mad. I have a ticket. Had to take the international car. For God's sake, come immediately! I haven't a single minute, absolutely! The train leaves at 17:10. Don't curse me! I will explain everything! I love you! I am going mad! Klava."

"Comrade Superintendent!"

It was—Mosya.

Korneyev thrust the note into his outside pocket.

"Yes! What's the matter?"

Mosya was self-controlled and severe in an official manner. He was frightfully quiet. This calmness cost him tremendous effort. He could scarcely conceal his wild boyish joy. Only with difficulty could he restrain his arms, so that they would not dangle, and his feet so that they would not run but walk. But he could do nothing with his eyes. His eyes would not obey him. They exulted. They sparkled thievishly. They blazed.

"Comrade Superintendent, the electric transmission is laid. You may test the machinery."

"Good."

They walked up to the machine.

The cement-mixer was standing on a new high platform at the very wall of the plant, directly opposite the fifth battery.

At that place, the wall of the plant had been taken apart. One could see a tremendous, gaping, shadowy inside. There, through this opening, the concrete would be brought up.

Korneyev walked up the bending trap to the platform. The motorist was wiping the pinion with waste.

From the outside, the mechanism of the cement-mixer looked like a siege gun. A Howitzer. A mortar. It stood on small cast-iron wheels.

The revolving drum was the short barrel of the gun. The scoop was a box with bombs. The directing rail along which the scoop rose was the guide-rod. The entire machine was painted a protective green, military colour.

The work of the mechanism was very simple. Into the scoop were poured the necessary quantities of cement, gravel and sand. The scoop was lifted along the rail to the mechanism and turned over automatically into the revolving drum. Also automatically, a portion of water was poured into the drum. After some time of mixing, the mass of concrete was ready.

Then, continuing to revolve on its vertical axis, the drum

turned over to the other side and poured out the mass of concrete into an inclined wooden trough, whence it slid down into
iron barrows—the so-called sterlings—and was carted off to
where it was needed. At the same time, the lowered scoop was
again loaded with barrows of sand, gravel, and cement.

While the emptied but still revolving drum was assuming its
former position, the scoop was crawling up. The drum bent down.
The scoop again automatically dumped the dry mixture into it.
Again water poured in. And, without stopping, everything began
again from the beginning.

"Come on. Turn it on," said Korneyev. The motorist turned the
lever.

The drum started with a soft, oily clatter.

"Good! Turn it!"

Continuing to revolve on its vertical axis, the drum bent down
to the trough. Korneyev looked into its throat, like a doctor.

"Good! Turn it back! That's right! Let's have the scoop!"

Clanging and crashing, the scoop crawled up the rail, turned
over the smoothly revolving drum and slid down.

"Good."

Mosya could not contain himself.

"You may rest easy, Comrade Commander."

Korneyev's nose twitched.

"Water," he said curtly.

There was no water.

"Water!"

In one breath, Mosya flew up the trap to the platform. He was
terrible.

"Water, . . . your mother!" he cried in an incredible voice,
tearing his cap off his head. He struck the barrier with it with
such force that a cloud of dust flew from his cap. And right then,
noticing Vinkich and Georgi Vasilyevich below, he smiled pleasantly, and remarked:

"Of course, I apologise for such an uncultured expression, Comrade Journalists."

He had great respect for journalists. He flattered them and

was pleasant to them. His most passionate dream was to get his name in the newspaper. But at the same time, he flaunted his crude emotions before them in strong language. This he deemed quite excusable in an atmosphere of battle.

Nevertheless, there was no water.

"Water?" Korneyev asked, turning pink.

"The water men are holding things up, Comrade Superintendent."

Korneyev pulled the watch from his pocket. With the watch, the note flew out. It fell down. He did not pick it up.

"Half past three—and no water!"

He ran to the water men. They were screwing in the last knee of the pipes. He stepped on a can of red lead. One of his shoes turned red.

At the same time, below, in front of the planking, the carpenters were laying a platform of boards. This was an innovation invented and developed by Margulies and Triger. The innovation was really extremely simple.

Until now the materials had been delivered to the scoop of the cement-mixer on barrows along specially laid narrow boards. The barrows constantly fell off or collided. That delayed the loading, created confusion, broke the rhythm. Would it not be simpler to make a complete planking? Of course, this simple thought had been in the air. But simple thoughts are difficult and seldom found because of their simplicity and obviousness.

Margulies and Triger had arrived at the idea of complete planking in different ways.

Margulies: by strange association after observing the delivery of fire brick and thinking of Foma Yegorovich's innovation of disposing his materials in an order inverse to the order of using it.

Triger: purely by mental observation—noting in his copy book all imaginary and possible causes of retarded tempos of laying concrete, and then eliminating every delay by imaginary but possible methods.

Their projects coincided.

Immediately Margulies called out the carpenter-brigade on

duty. While they were working, Triger did not move a single step from them. With a pocket tape measure, he measured and checked the surface of the planking. He handed them nails, sawed boards, hurried them, urged them on, pleaded with them, demanded, swore. It was difficult to put him off. Little Triger was persistent and tenacious, especially in those cases when it was necessary to put into practice what he had arrived at theoretically.

The planking was ready. With delight, Triger ran over it, leaving dusty traces of his sandals on the fresh lemon-golden grain.

The brigade was changing its clothes in the superintendent's office. The first to come out was Smetana. He was dressed in coarse, canvas overalls that stuck out stiffly. His large, stiff, canvas mitts made his hands look like lasts. Smetana examined the planking exultantly.

"That's fine!"

He seized a barrow, started it with his knees, flung it on the planking and, with a crashing noise, rolled it diagonally along the hard unbending wooden platform.

"That's what I like! Beautiful!"

He turned the barrow sharply and ran it in the opposite direction. He delighted in the lightness of its movement and in the solidity of the floor. Playing and trying his strength, he ran with a screaming barrow in all directions on the planking, leaving behind him traces of wheels and feet. He left spots all over the platform.

Little Triger stood on the side, lovingly observing the lightness and the play of the barrow.

"Hey there, Smetana! Wait. We'll try a couple of them."

Triger took another barrow and ran it up to meet Smetana.

"Keep to the right."

Each swayed their barrows deftly to the right, and passed deftly, like automobiles on a narrow road.

"It works magnificently!"

From the superintendent's office the overalled boys ran out in single file.

All of them were in hard, stiff canvas. Clumsily waving their last-like mitts, they ran up the planking, stamping their boots and shoes, leaving spots and heavy tracks on the grain, gambolling and passing each other, and testing their strength as if before an athletic contest.

XXXVIII

THEY drove around the lake.

On the way, they stopped on the other side, opposite the middle of the construction.

From here it spread out beyond the lake, even more sweeping and grandiose. In smoke and water spouts, in running spots of light and shadow, in wooden towers and walls, like ancient Troy, it floated and smoked and dimmed, in a floating, moving, and, at the same time, immobile, mute panorama.

They left the machine and strolled along the shore over the green steppe, which came up to the very edge of the water.

A clumsy boat floated on the lake. In the boat, some one was singing. The balsam air of the steppe turned one's head.

Not far from the shore, boys were swimming.

In the water, the swimmers grew green frog-legs.

Nalbandov stood, his elbow on the hot radiator of the automobile. He stared intently at the panorama of the construction. He was seeking the coke-chemical plant where now they were preparing to set the record. He found it. From here, the plant seemed a small yellow strip.

"Babylon, Babylon," Mr. Ray Roupe remarked with a sigh, answering his own thoughts aloud. "Is it possible that the world is not beautiful? What is it that people lack?"

"Here, on this place where we are now standing, there will be a socialist city a year from now," Nalbandov remarked significantly.

Mr. Ray Roupe looked mechanically at the place where he was standing and saw a strange object on the grass. He turned it over with his cane, poked it, and lifted it. It was an old, trampled, dried-up bast shoe.

Mr. Ray Roupe regarded it with intense curiosity and said finally:

"Oh, yes, I understand. This is a species of Russian national footwear. Very interesting. But I have forgotten its name, Leonard."

"In Russian, it is called *lapot'*," said Leonard Darley.

"Yes, yes. I remember now. *Lapot'* in Russian," Mr. Ray Roupe repeated. "A peasant *lapot'*. On the one hand Babylon, and on the other *lapot'*. That *is* a paradox."

Nalbandov repeated stubbornly:

"Here will be a socialist city for a hundred and fifty thousand workers and service men."

"Yes, but will humanity be any happier because of that? And is this presupposed happiness worthy of such effort?"

He is right, Nalbandov thought.

"You are wrong," he said, looking coldly at the American. "You lack imagination. We shall conquer nature, and we shall bring back its lost paradise to humanity. We shall surround the continents with warm streams. We shall compel the Arctic Oceans to produce billions of kilowatts of electricity. And we shall grow pine trees there—a kilometre in height . . ."

XXXIX

"OH, Kostichka! I'll never get there!"

"You'll make it."

She bit her lips in pain and fear. He bit his lips in impatience.

They drove too slowly. The maternity hospital was at the other end of the construction.

Fyenya laid her head on her husband's shoulder, tickling his ear with her hair.

She put her arms around his back, and he felt on himself the warm, living weight of her body.

Occasionally the pain would leave her. Then she would become lively and talkative. In a hot, rapid whisper, she would tell Ishchenko all her impressions of the day:

"Do you know, Kostichka, there on the third sector—right opposite the fire brigade—they are building a circus. There is a whole zoo there, so help me God! . . . They are already putting the roof on. They have brought an elephant . . . so help me God! . . . He's chained there; they have hitched him by the leg to a little post, as if he were a convict. He chews hay, so help me God! He just picks the hay right up with his snoot, as if it were a hand, and lifts up a whole bundle . . . He waves it and waves it, and then shoves it into his mouth . . . And his mouth is so small . . . it's simply tiny—like a little pitcher. There seems to be no place for it. And there's such a crowd around! And the monkeys! And a wolf in a cage! And a parrot! Oi, Kostichka, what parrots! Red, and blue, and green, and pinky, pinky ones. They scream and flap their wings, and their beaks are so silly—just like pincers. They caught one boy by the finger, and, so help me God, they bit it right to the bone!"

"He shouldn't shove his finger at them."

She looked into his eyes trustingly and tenderly.

"But, Kostichka, why do they build a zoo on such an important construction?"

Ishchenko snorted importantly.

"What do you mean, why? It's very simple why. For cultured entertainment. Instead of gambling, it is much better for them to become interested in animals."

She sighed.

"That's right."

"That's very clear."

"And it is interesting for the children to see. Isn't that right, Kostichka?"

"Very clear. Our Party and the working class are first of all interested in children."

"Children . . ." said Fyenya. And suddenly she turned a deep red, and coyly laid her face on his chest.

And then another labour pain gripped her.

"Okh, okh, I'll never make it!"

"You'll make it!"

But as soon as the pain left her, she began to chatter again.

"Okh, Kostichka, do you know what the latest fashion is among the women on the construction? Just imagine: well, all the women wear at least twenty or thirty buttons in a row on their dresses, in front and in back, so there is no place left. And would you believe it, it looks very beautiful and very dressy! Do you know, Kostichka, the buttons are of various colours— green and blue and red . . . Okh! . . ."

Another labour pain gripped her.

"Okh, I'll never make it!"

"You'll make it. You *must* make it."

And again she began to chatter.

He listened to her hot whisper and bit his lips with impatience. If he could only get there, get rid of her, get her off his hands, and get back to the sector!

When the labour pains gripped Fyenya, all his sympathy was with her. But when they freed her, his mind immediately flew to the sector.

Under no circumstances could he be late. More than that: it was absolutely indispensable for him to come at least half an hour ahead of time.

Watching the work of Yermakov's brigade to-day, he had noticed the confusion that occurred when the barrels frequently rolled off the planks. Now a simple thought occurred to him: it might be a good idea to board over the entire space along which the materials were being carted to the machine. If he were to hurry up the carpenters and himself pitch in with the entire brigade, it could be done in half an hour. He saw clearly how this would lighten and speed up the work.

The thought that he might come late, and that there would not be time to build a complete planking without him, brought him to a state of extreme agitation, and even of anger against Fyenya. She certainly found the most appropriate time, he thought.

How long they seemed to be riding! How slowly the striped semaphores rose before him at the crossing! How stupidly the driver drove! Having made one mistake, he now tried to extricate himself. In order to drive straight there, he assiduously drove off to the side, making a frightful detour. And, despite his good intentions, he drove into blind alleys and holes which had not been there at all an hour before.

With Fyenya, however, it was quite the opposite: whenever the pains gripped her, all her emotion concentrated on him. She loved him so much! What a shame that she was taking him from his work! She was even sorry. But as soon as the pain passed, her thoughts scattered, her eyes darted to all sides.

She noticed everything around her, jerkily and in detail, but without any sense of participation in it.

A fat boy with a large head was walking along, scraping his bare feet. In one hand he held a piece of bread, and in the other, he held a wire that dragged along the ground, raising the dust.

Somewhere a machine screeched, as if a suckling pig were having its throat cut.

Muckers were digging a large excavation. A bearded peasant in bast shoes and a pink shirt was walking along the embankment. He splashed some water out of a cup. The water ran down for a long time, gleaming in the sun like a silver rope.

Fyenya saw all this with remarkable precision of detail, but she forgot it immediately.

Finally they arrived.

This street was distinguished from the others by its length and width. Here the barracks were stuccoed and white. Here all the medical establishments of the construction were concentrated:

"Pharmacy."

"Maternity Home."

"Infirmary."

"Hospital."

"Surgical Department."

"Contagious Diseases."

All these terrible words, written on sign boards, merged with the odour of iodoform and with people in dressing gowns sitting on benches and stoops.

Women with white hospital aprons tied around them were hastily crossing the road. The sick were being brought in carts and wagons. A man was walking, holding up one arm with the other. The arm was bandaged and looked like a clapper.

Fyenya's head was in a whirl. She turned pale and haggard. Bright yellow spots appeared on her bloodless face. Ishchenko pushed her with difficulty into the hallway. In a large bowl on the floor, a huge piece of ice glowed in a dusty ray of the sun.

An angry, middle-aged woman in a hospital apron came out into the hallway.

"Another one! How do you do! The tenth one! How do you manage it? Well now, tell me—where will I put her?"

She glanced at Fyenya.

"Well, little mother! You're a fine one, needless to say! You waited until the last minute!"

She took Fyenya under the arm and led her to the door. Ishchenko followed them.

"You can't come. You sit here for a while."

Something half-white, half-blue and oily flashed through the open door, and then the door closed.

Not knowing what to do, the brigadier sat down on a bench. The bundle lay in his arms. All around him was quiet. The quietness horrified him.

Five minutes later, the woman came out again and silently handed the brigadier Fyenya's belongings—her goat-skin shoes, her skirt, her shawl with its rosy fringe.

Ishchenko turned pale.

"And where is Fyenya?" he asked timidly, expecting to hear something terrible.

He took the things mechanically. They had her odour, were

still warm with her warmth, but, at the same time, they were somehow already frightfully and incomprehensibly estranged from her.

"Where is Fyenya?"

"Now, where do you think she is?" the woman asked ironically. "Don't worry. Your Fyenya won't get lost."

"I haven't said good-bye . . . Perhaps she needs something . . ."

"She needs nothing."

The woman took a piece of chalk and, under a long row of names, wrote: Ishchenko. Then she went away.

Ishchenko sat down.

The clock on the wall indicated ten minutes to three. Then it indicated ten minutes past three. The ice melted in the bowl. The ticking led a life separate from the clock itself. It ran on the little steel legs of seconds, limping along the hallway.

The woman came out again.

"Well, what are you waiting here for?"

Ishchenko rose, hemmed and hawed.

"Is there nothing else?" he asked timidly.

"Nothing else."

The brigadier tied the things together clumsily.

"And when shall I come back?"

The woman smiled.

"Oh, come around sometime."

Ishchenko hesitated; then, indecisively, and for some reason, on tiptoe, went out into the street.

The wicker cart was gone. The silly driver had driven away. Where was he to go now?

And suddenly, with returning sobriety and clarity, he saw before him a clock that indicated thirteen minutes past three. And it was five kilometres to the sector!

He ran down the street, clutching to his breast the bundle of things that kept falling apart. An automobile appeared. Ishchenko ran into the middle of the road.

"Stop! Hey, Boss, give me a lift!"

The automobile careened past, covering him with a black cloud of dust, and disappeared from view.

Ishchenko managed to distinguish only a heliotrope-coloured suit. He spat and ran on.

XL

"COMRADES!"

Mosya could not manage his voice. He should have begun with reserve and importance, but suddenly he shouted exultantly and his voice broke. He was transported with joy. Unable to find words, he jerkily slashed the air in front of him with his fist.

Twenty-two barrels smoked in the wind. The wind pulled at them tenaciously. It lifted a greenish-grey cloud of cement from the barrels. Mingling with the hot, artificial odour of lilac, it floated and swirled in colourful dust. The grey powder settled on the eyebrows and eyelashes of the brigade.

Ishchenko was missing. But this evoked no apprehension. He would come.

Mosya faced the brigade. There were no intermediaries between them. He had argued with Korneyev and Margulies themselves for this honourable militant privilege. The foreman had been given a task and he would carry it out. He had guaranteed it. That was sufficient. No intermediaries. No interference. That was all. He would answer for the rest. Tensely and passionately, he had awaited this moment. He had prepared a speech. Now the moment had arrived.

And words failed him.

Mosya walked back and forth in front of the brigade. He walked over the new planking as if on a stage, his head sunk in profound thought, gaining time. Odds and ends of unsuitable newspaper slogans occurred to him:

"The country is waiting for cheap vegetables." . . . No! No! "The system of the state bank is a powerful lever of cost accounting." . . . That wasn't it! "The main thing now is . . . rabbit breeding." . . . No! No! . . .

Mosya stealthily cast frantic glances from side to side. People and materials crowded about him. He saw attentive eyes turned toward him. He recognised them.

The blue eyes of Smetana, and the brown eyes of Nefedov, the aniline misty eyes of Sayenko (oh, Sayenko came!). Here were the black, serious, tender eyes of Vinkich, and the round, sharp eyes of Georgi Vasilycvich. They embarrassed him more than any of the others and deprived him of his last shreds of calmness.

He saw the handles of the turned-up barrows, the smoking barrels, the smoking mound of sand. He saw the repairmen pulling a telephone cable to the superintendent's office. And he saw little Triger dogging their footsteps.

The steam engine whistled. Couplings clashed. Hooks dropped. The sides of flat cars were flung back with a roar. Gravel poured out. Korneyev with his velvety sideburns ran by. The high round cap of Margulies would appear and disappear in the twilight of the plant.

Two girls who were passing by, stopped. In each hand, they held a canvas mitten full of water. Evidently they were bringing it for some one to drink. The gleaming water dripped to the earth in long earrings. The girls looked at Mosya with shining eyes and half-opened mouths.

Low, heavy clouds ran past.

And still he could not say a word. It was scandalous. It was terrible. It was like a nightmare . . .

Time flew with such speed that it seemed static. It swirled in a spiral like a steel spring. It whirled and grew numb, ready to rear up at each instant, to ring out and unfurl with a whistle, carrying the elongated and dimly smoking panorama of the sectors behind it in a whirl.

Mosya was failing disgracefully.

He gathered all his strength. He flashed his eyes in the direction of the journalists.

"Comrades!" Mosya cried out, almost piteously. "Dear Comrades! All of us, as rank and file fighters, as shock-brigaders and enthusiasts of our authoritative, second cost-accounting section of the sixth sector . . . And let the comrades from the Central newspapers be witnesses . . . We give our firm, inviolate, Stalinist word . . ."

He faltered.

On tiptoe, Smetana approached Mosya from the rear.

"Finish the meeting," he said, winking at the lads. "That's enough."

In a friendly way, he took Mosya by the shoulders and lightly kicked him with his knee.

Mosya swore frightfully and lewdly, made a beastly face, but immediately flung a sly, apologetic smile toward the journalists.

"Of course, I am very sorry for these expressions."

Ishchenko was walking across logs and pipes. His new trousers were covered to the knee by velvety, rusty leggings of dust. His bare feet were torn and bloody. His shirt was black with sweat. His wet hair gleamed on his forehead, like feathers pasted together. His chest heaved broadly and powerfully.

Without stopping, he had run five kilometres along the ploughed-up, rocky earth of four sectors. He was urged on by a burning, insistent thought: the wooden planking! However, a miracle had occurred! Without his knowledge and participation, his idea had been realised: the labour front was covered with a neat new floor.

The brigadier noticed it at once.

So he had not thought of a miracle. His idea had been thought of and carried out by others. That was as it should be. He accepted it, if not as something that had to happen, at any rate, as something quite natural.

He stopped and drew his breath.

But at that instant he was pierced by a new thought, a new burning alarm: the gravel! On which side of the railroad track was it being unloaded?

It should have been unloaded to the right, directly at the

planking. But they might have failed to realise that. They might have begun to unload it on the left. Then the railroad track would be between the gravel and the concrete mixer, and it would be necessary to carry the gravel across the rails in barrows.

He ran forward.

The gravel thundered minutely as it was being flung down. He saw that it was being unloaded on the left. He turned crimson. He wanted to cry out with all his might. But at that instant he understood the reason.

The right side was covered with materials, with lumber and armatures. They could not be taken away. There was simply no other place for them.

XLI

WITH the experienced eye of a manager, the brigadier took in the picture of the labour front at once in all its details.

The brigade was in its place. All sixteen of the lads were on hand. Zagirov and Sayenko had been found. That was good. Mosya was digging the earth with his nose. That was good.

The cement was in open barrels. Bad. It would have been better in a special box.

The sand was conveniently located. Good.

The gravel was to the left of the track. Bad.

The wind was not strong. Good.

He had left his working clothes in the barrack. Bad.

He had arrived on time. Good.

Korneyev was pacing the sides of the front with large strides, walking mechanically around the planking, as if he did not wish to cross the line of demarcation of the field, in which, by agreement, all power had already passed to the foreman.

Ishchenko quickly passed him, exuding the hot odour of a healthy, sweaty, excited body.

"What time is it?"

"Fourteen minutes to," said Korneyev, without stopping and without looking at his watch.

"Come on, lads . . ."

Ishchenko stopped and cast a quick, quizzical glance at Smetana.

"Did you tell every one what he's to do?" he asked quickly.

Smetana nodded.

"Come on, lads," said Ishchenko slowly, but lifting his voice inexorably to the vibrating heights of a cavalry command. "Listen to me! To barr-r-r-o-w-s! To your pla-aces!"

And this "To barr-r-r-o-w-s!" he shouted as if it were "To horse!"

It worked as it had not worked even once on such occasions with the terrifying brigadier, Khanumov.

Ishchenko was the first to reach his barrow. The lads followed him. In a flash they scattered along the labour front, and each one, with a spade or with a barrow, took the place previously assigned to him.

Ishchenko attentively surveyed the disposition, calculating to himself in a whisper the number of lads at each point.

"The operator—one. Two on the sand—and two on the barrows. Two on cement—two on barrows. Two on gravel—and two on barrows." He muttered it to himself.

"Stop!" he cried. "Stop!"

The gravel situation altered matters. Two men on the gravel were not enough. This point had to be strengthened.

Quickly the brigadier recalculated in his mind. He had to have two extra lads on the gravel. There were no extra ones, but he could weaken another, more favourable point.

The same thought had simultaneously struck the others.

"Not enough on the gravel!" cried Smetana.

Little Triger was hurrying the repairmen. At the same time, he was observing the disposition of the brigade.

"Two on the gravel!" he said quickly.

Ishchenko knitted his brow. His decision was precise and explicit.

"One from the sand, one from the trough! Sayenko, Zagirov, to the gravel as extras!"

Korneyev walked past, muttering tensely out of the corner of his mouth:

"Get a move on, get a move on, get a move on . . ."

With a challenging, enticing flash of her eyes, Olya Tregubova turned.

"Come on, Sayenko! Zagirov!" she shouted in the voice of a woman swearing. "Come on. Show us what shock-brigaders you are! Take the blot off your names!"

Sayenko and Zagirov did not move from the spot.

Korneyev walked back still more tensely. His nose twitched nervously. He was tugging at the strap of his watch.

"Come on, lads, come on, lads, come on, lads . . ."

Sayenko, somnolent, stood with drooping shoulders, his feet in their wide trousers spread widely apart. He looked impudently at the brigadier. He smiled contemptuously and deliberately. Zagirov glanced from side to side like a hunted animal. There was a ten-spot in his pocket which Sayenko had lent him on the way.

Ishchenko looked darkly at his comrades.

"Sayenko! Zagirov! To the gravel as extras," he repeated without hurrying.

They were silent.

Ishchenko looked about him. Curious observers were gathering around. He noticed nearby the golden *tyubeteika* of Khanumov. His features darkened. A sharp oblique line disfigured his face like a scar.

"Come on," he said evenly.

Sayenko looked past him into the distance with contempt.

"Why are you hurrying us? What do you think we are—horses? Did you buy us? Or did you hire us?"

"Do you refuse to work?"

"And did you give us special shoes? Do you expect us to tear up our last bast shoes on the gravel?"

"What?"

"You heard me!"

"You may talk about special shoes after the shift."

Ishchenko was stupendously calm. He could scarcely contain himself, but his fists were bound by ropes of swollen veins.

Sayenko's shoulders played freely.

"You give us special shoes."

"Speak for yourself."

"How can I speak for myself alone?" cried Sayenko in an irate voice, and beat his breast. "How can I speak for myself alone, when perhaps my comrade is walking naked and barefooted, and is too bashful to ask? Isn't that right, Zagirov?"

Zagirov stood, grey-faced. His saffron fingers twitched nervously.

"Can't you see? His conscience won't let him. He's embarrassed. Zagirov, show them your holes!"

"How can I get you shoes now?" Almost crying with rage and from the necessity of restraining this rage, Ishchenko articulated with difficulty: "Take your places at the gravel, both of you! We'll talk about the shoes after the shift. You refuse?"

"We won't do it!"

"Sayenko, you'd better speak only for yourself."

"I speak for both of us. He will do what I do. Isn't that right, Zagirov?"

Zagirov, benumbed, was silent.

"So, in front of the entire brigade, you refuse to take your places?"

"Give us the shoes!"

Mosya rushed toward Sayenko.

"Stop!"

Ishchenko caught Mosya's arm on the fly and squeezed it so that Mosya turned a somersault and landed on his haunches. He gritted his teeth.

"Let go . . . let go . . . May I never see the light of day again . . . Let me at this whore . . ."

"They sold their shoes at the junk market!" Olya Tregubova

cried out in a desperate voice and turned red to the roots of her hair.

Korneyev passed by faster than ever, looking sideways.

"Hurry, hurry . . . hurry . . ."

"You refuse to take your places?" Ishchenko asked with super-human calmness.

He regarded Sayenko with bloodshot eyes, and at the same time he saw Khanumov smile and wave his arms, and then turn and walk off carelessly, his golden *tyubeteika* gleaming.

There was a strained smile on Sayenko's face.

"What I do, he will do. We will not take our places without shoes. That's final."

Ishchenko was choking.

"What do you want to do—disgrace us before all the construction workers? Do you want to make us so ridiculous that we will never be able to look people in the eye? Do you want to do it now, on the most important shift of all? Have you a vestige of conscience, Comrades?"

He was on the verge of tears.

But Sayenko continued to stand there, his shoulders drooping like sacks, and impudently licking his lips soiled with aniline.

"You can throw salt on our tails! . . ."

"Shut up!" Nefedov shouted.

He quickly sat down on the floor and began to tear the laces of his shoes.

"Stop it, Sasha," Triger said quietly, calmly.

He quickly walked right up to Sayenko. Without looking at him, and biting his lips until the blood came, he tore the shovel out of his hands, slapped his sandals firmly against the planking, walked up to the gravel, and with a resounding clatter, thrust his shovel into the pile.

"Right!" said Smetana.

Ishchenko looked at the lads.

"Well?"

Mosya tore off his cap and flung it to the floor with all his might.

"Let them go to . . . mother!"

"Who is opposed?" asked Ishchenko.

Not one hand was lifted.

"Get out!" said Ishchenko in a terrible voice. "To-morrow we'll talk about the shoes."

Sayenko made a foolish face. Loosely shrugging his shoulders and scraping his bast shoes, he walked off the planking. Zagirov looked around in fright. All eyes looked past him. Quivering, he followed in Sayenko's footsteps.

For several seconds all were silent. Only Ishchenko breathed noisily and with difficulty. Unable to quiet himself at once, he turned his head away and rubbed his fists against his cheeks. His chest rose and fell broadly and powerfully. His thick neck was black and taut.

Then Mosya picked up his cap, slapped it against his knee, and put it on neatly, pulling it down to the tips of his sharp clay-like ears.

He smiled thievishly. The yellow whites of his hysterical eyes gleamed in the direction of the journalists, and suddenly a three-barrelled policeman's whistle appeared between his lips.

"Get ready! Begin!" he shouted in a reckless, boyish voice, rushing to the scoop of the machine. "Let's go!!!"

He gave three, short, disjointed, shattering whistles.

And everything rushed from its place. Everything began to move.

The shovel struck the gravel resoundingly. A high cloud of colourful dust rose over the cement barrows. Sand scratched. The wheels of the barrows screamed. The motor crashed. The drum started smoothly. The scoop thundered out and climbed up. The water dashed in noisily.

"What time is it?" asked Margulies, brushing the dust off his elbows.

Korneyev pulled out the strap of his watch.

"Sixteen eight."

"Good."

XLII

"**K** LAVA . . . What's the matter?"
　　　　"My God, see what you look like!"

"What has happened?"

"Look at your feet! You've painted your grey shoes white! It's a nightmare! . . ."

"Why all the hurry? . . ."

"I can hardly stand up . . . My knees are shaking. Wait . . . I've been on my feet since seven o'clock. I haven't sat down once."

"Why are you going away? . . ."

"Oh, for God's sake, don't ask! I don't understand it myself. It seems I've lost my mind. How hot it is!"

"Klavdya, stay here!"

"I shall return soon. Very soon."

"Why are you going away?"

"In August. Or in September. In the middle of September. What time is it?"

"Five minutes to five by my watch."

"I still have a quarter of an hour. Fifteen minutes."

"Stay here! Klava!"

"Help me, my darling, to put the suitcase above. Don't talk nonsense. Lord, how stuffy it is in here! That's right. Thank you. That's all. There's nothing to breathe."

"Naturally. The car has been roasting in the sun all day long. The roof is red hot. Shall I open the window?"

"No, no! Look how dusty it is there. I would rather ask the conductor later. When we are in the steppe. If it would only rain a little!"

"Stay here."

"I will write you from every station. I will telephone you from Moscow. Do you want me to call you up every day? Sit down.

I will sit down, too. Well now, let me have one good look at
you."

Seated beside him, she seized his head firmly in both her hands.
She had short, powerful hands.

So far, there was nobody else in the compartment.

She held his face before her and looked into it as if into a
mirror. His cap fell on the worn cushions of moth-eaten blue velvet.

He saw her weeping and laughing face, dirty, with a smudged
nose, not too young any longer but still childishly plump, covered with golden down, amiable and perturbed. Tears made her
blue eyes slant. He began to stroke her head, her bobbed hair,
which was smooth, shiny, like an acorn . . .

"I beg you . . . explain to me. I plead with you, Klavochka!"

He was in despair. He understood nothing. Really, in the
depths of his heart, he had always had forebodings that it would
end just like this. But he would not believe it because he could
not explain it. After all, she loved him.

What was it that had happened?

It was doubtful if she herself understood. The decision to go
away had somehow grown gradually, by itself. At any rate, so
it seemed to her. There was as much of the unconscious as of
the conscious in it. Like him, she, too, was in despair.

Time passed.

Outside, beyond the windows of the compartment, clouds of
dust flitted by spasmodically. They advanced in rows and lifted
themselves, one ahead of the other, in impenetrable blinds. At
times the gusts of wind diminished. The blinds of dust fell. Then,
quite close, a temporary station emerged from the dust—two
broken-down, green cars with a brass bell and rusty sides and
a strip of a red flag, faded until it was white, on a stick that
had been mowed down by a snow storm.

All around were the same wicker carts and shaft-bows, horses'
tails, obliquely standing trucks, boxes of potted meat, bast shoes,
knitted boots, dark goggles, the trunks of the seasonal workers,
women, dark, dirty worn clothes, grey silhouettes of people run-

ning to trains, the snapping canvas of tents, the black, billowy horizon, and the scattered companies of telephone poles—crooked, massive, wandering against the wind and the dust.

But here, inside the international sleeping car, everything was clean, comfortable, elegant. The slate-grey linoleum of the corridor was as yielding as springs under the feet. It had just been scrubbed with brushes, boiling water and soap. Everywhere was the odour of pine extract.

At the end of the corridor—narrow and shiny like a pencil case, with a perspective of milky tulips of lamps and the open doors of compartments—in a corner lined with brightly polished brass, the burnished samovar was already steaming on a special table. The porter was washing the glasses in a large, brass, brightly polished slop basin.

Dusty, grimy people were entering the car—Russian and foreign engineers—dragging in substantial but dirty suitcases. They carelessly spotted the linoleum. They immediately began to wash and to shave, to put on cool pyjamas and slippers, stuffing their impossible boots under the seats.

Korneyev asked in despair:

"But what is it all about? What?"

Akh, she herself did not know!

The tears rolled down her smudgy nose, but nevertheless she attempted to smile. The tears fell one after the other, like little buttons, on her yellow leather coat, which was split and well-worn at the elbows.

His cheek twitched nervously.

"Husband?"

She firmly bit her lips and began to shake her head vigorously.

"Are you bored here? Do you dislike it?"

"No, no!"

"Well, if you like, I'll arrange it so that you can live in the American section—in a cottage. There you'll have birches, cows . . . Would you like me to? Miraculous, marvellous air . . ."

"No, no! . . ."

"Daughter?"

She suddenly turned away, and her head fell on the arm-rest of the seat.

"Klavochka! Klavdyushka! On my word of honour, it's so wild! If you like, we will write and have Verochka come here. It will be so simple. What is the matter? I don't understand."

She shook her head hysterically and bit the arm-rest.

A new passenger entered.

"Excuse me. I'm sorry. Which is your place? Thirteen? Mine is fourteen, the upper."

He was a military man. He had three rhomboids.[1] The neat, dusty boot stepped carefully on the cushion. The corner of a fibre suitcase flashed by as it was flung up.

"That is all. I beg your pardon."

The distinct imprint of the grey sole was left on the blue velvet. The military man carefully brushed it off with a newspaper.

She quickly wiped her face with the sleeve of her leather coat. Her eyes burned, dry and animated. She was ashamed of weeping and indulging in explanations before strangers.

The military man laid pamphlets and cigarettes on the table in front of the window.

"Well . . . And how are things going with you on the sector?" she asked quickly in a business-like way. "Are things moving?"

"We are fighting. It's a regular battle. During the first half hour, we made twenty-five mixtures." (Again he pronounced the Russian word *zamyes* as if it were the Spanish surname *Zamess*.)

"And what does that mean, my darling?"

"If it keeps on like this, Kharkov will shed tears! Four hundred mixtures per shift! Only things worked out badly with the gravel . . ."

"Why, what happened?" she asked, frightened.

"We had to dump it on the other side of the railroad track, and the trains are moving back and forth there. It's inconvenient and dangerous, but I think we'll manage without any accidents."

"Ah!"

---

[1] Three rhomboids indicate the rank of a commander of an army corps, equivalent to the rank of major-general.

She grew quieter.

"Well, praise God! I'm very glad. Can you imagine? At our plant office nobody has any confidence in it yet. They're laughing. They say that it is technically impossible. I've almost fought with everybody for you there."

Korneyev pulled at his nose and raised his eyebrows.

"Who is it? Who doesn't believe?"

"There are people like that. And, of course, they are attacking Margulies. They are convinced that he'll break his neck on it. By the way, how is David Lvovich? I haven't seen him for a thousand years. He is always at the sector."

"David is flourishing. David is flourishing. He sends you his regards. Well . . . How will it be, Klavdyusha?"

He lowered his voice. She looked at him pleadingly and indicated the stranger with her eyes.

The military man considerately went into the corridor and lighted a cigarette.

"I detest military men!" she whispered emphatically, referring to her husband.

He took her hand.

"Well, how will it be then, Klavdyusha?"

She again dropped her head on the hard square arm-rest in its faded blue cover.

"Well, upon my word of honour! This is simply wild! Klavdyusha! We'll bring the girl here, and that will end the matter."

"No, no! For God's sake! You must have lost your mind. How can we bring the child here? Dust, dirt . . . God knows what kind of water . . . dysentery . . ."

"Yes, but other children live here, and there's nothing wrong with them. On the contrary, they are healthy, chubby children. Look at the local children! Malsky has a child, Seroshevsky has a child . . ."

She quickly straightened up. Her face became vicious, pitiless, beastly.

"You don't understand the meaning of one's *own* child!" she said quickly and jerkily.

"And our brigadier Ishchenko . . . His pregnant wife has arrived, for example . . . Came here especially to bear the child. And nothing happened . . . No tragedy. What's the matter?"

Her eyes gleamed and her cheeks became hard and uneven.

"A strong, healthy, peasant woman! . . . How can you make such a comparison? And her child will be strong and healthy. But Verochka is frail and sickly! How could she possibly endure this crazy climate?"

"There is nothing crazy about it. It is the usual continental climate."

"Don't talk nonsense! She shouldn't come here. She should go to the beach. Vasily Nikolayevich telegraphed that he has travelling orders to Anapa.[2] I must take her to Anapa."

Oh, so that's it: Anapa! Korneyev thought bitterly.

She caught the fleeting expression on his face. She caught it and understood.

"And finally, I . . ." she muttered, "I myself . . . See what I look like now? If I don't get a rest . . . You can see perfectly well for yourself . . . And besides, it would be simply mad to let such an exceptional opportunity slip by . . . I will soon return. I swear by whatever you like. By the middle of September. At the latest, in October . . ."

She embraced him tenderly and placed her wet smeared cheek on his chest.

He realised that everything had come to an end. He knew her too well. Yes, she loved him, but not him only. Everything else here was foreign to her. And there was Anapa, the sea, illusions of some new unparalleled happiness.

Fyenya had come here to her own, to something that was part and parcel of her. It had been easy for her. She had not even suspected that it might be difficult . . . No, there was nothing to be done about it. He sighed heavily.

The bell struck. He began to look for his cap. His heart was torn with love, and with pity for her and for himself. She wiped

[2] a health resort in the Crimea on the Black Sea

her face. They walked out into the corridor. Here, strange people stood at the windows.

"Well . . ."

She put her arms around his neck convulsively, and casting dry, feverish glances about her, laughing and crying, she muttered:

"No, no, don't! So help me God! We are saying good-bye as if we were in the theatre . . . just as on the stage!"

The bell struck twice.

They embraced, no longer embarrassed by the strangers. He fervently kissed her mouth which was full of tears, her eyes which were full of tears, her cheeks, her chin, her forehead, her ears—all drenched in tears.

The train started. He rushed out of the car like a madman.

He stood alone on the deserted track and held his cap in his uplifted hand. The wind blew clouds of cement dust through the open gates of the warehouse.

He remembered that, with such tempos, there was only enough cement to last for three or four hours of work, and that he must run to the warehouse to expedite the delivery. After all, that was the only justification for his absence from the job.

And meanwhile, drenched in tears, she was tugging at the brass latches of the window, leaning against the glass heated by the sun, hurrying the porter.

The window was opened for her. A hot draught rushed in. But she could see nothing behind the train, only the long, dark, swimming dust.

And ahead, from behind the zinc box of the elevator, the whirlwind outlines of the advancing rainstorm grew swiftly out of the slate-grey, almost purple steppe.

XLIII

"LOOK, Tatar. Haven't you ever seen one before? Parrots. Look at the carrion! The convicts sit on their staffs as if they were generals."

Sayenko was right. The parrots actually resembled generals.

They sat on the staffs in bright, multicoloured uniforms. Drooping their long, straight tails, narrow and bright, like the striped breeches of generals, sticking out their thick chests decorated with orders and ribbons, the parrots wickedly clicked their aristocratic hooked beaks and looked around somnolently from beneath bulging, aristocratic, suède eyelids.

With scaly claws they clung to the perch to which they were fastened by a little chain.

From time to time, they would emit short, sharp, burring cries— as if they were biting through a steel wire.

And they actually looked like conceited generals, like a mournful session of a military council, like the last exhibit of military frock coats, trouser stripes, epaulettes, tufts, dolmans, spurs, and black beards à la Boulanger.

They might have been the staff of interventionists captured in battle after they had made their way too far into a strange enemy country, which they had studied very poorly, and so were doomed to perish.

Here were the yellow trouser stripes of the Ural hangmen,[1] mixing tremulously with tri-coloured republican *sultans* and the blue military overcoats of the cadets of Saint-Cyr.

Here Roumanian *kepi* and the pseudo-military confederates of Rzecza Pospolita [2] were gloomily living side by side with the scarlet pelisses of His Imperial Majesty's Hussars.

But they were doomed and chained. Around them, as far as the

[1] referring to the military commanders of the White armies who fought against the Red Army on the Ural fronts during the Civil War (1917-21)
[2] Rzecza Pospolita is the Polish Republic.

eye could see, arose silhouettes of redoubts, fortresses, fortifications, siege guns, surrounding them in a ring . . .

Zagirov regarded these strange foreign birds with the docile, insensate curiosity and stupid despair of a boy sold into slavery.

How could it have happened? How had it begun?

He could neither understand nor realise, just as a man who has lost his footing and slid down a mountain cannot understand or realise what has happened: why was he lying face upward on the ground, looking at the clouds? when did it happen? and how did it happen?

They had played again and Zagirov had lost to Sayenko the ten rubles he had borrowed from him.

Everything was over. Zagirov no longer wept, nor pleaded, nor said anything. He silently walked before his master, hungry, tortured by burning thirst, desolate . . .

He looked into his master's eyes with dry, shining canine eyes.

"Now you will be my flunky," said Sayenko. "Do you know what a flunky is?"

Zagirov was silent. He did not know what a flunky was. He only sensed that it was something extremely shameful. But he submitted. It was all the same to him now.

Sayenko swaggered. He dragged Zagirov with him to various places.

On the way, they dropped into "The Little Shanghai." That was the name of a distant habitation sector where, in small sod-huts, the refuse of the construction led a dark and isolated existence: bootleggers, sharpers, fugitive thieves, buyers of stolen goods, prostitutes—all so horrible that they never left their lairs, but sat there in the darkness on their rags, gathering in greasy three-spots and five-spots with swollen potato-like fingers.

Sayenko entered one of these earthen houses, but came out very quickly.

"There's nothing there. They've drunk up everything, the dirty riffraff! There's only one thing to do: go to the Kazak settlement."

Then they went on, avoiding meeting people, and avoiding the construction sector.

They walked in the region of the market near the cosmetic stalls where blue boxes of tooth powder gleamed behind dusty windows, and multicoloured soap swam amidst glowing bottles of *eau de cologne*. They walked into the co-operative and the cool barns of the stores of the Uraltorg.

But Sayenko bought nothing. He was merely shopping around greedily. He pushed around in the queues. He was stingy and calculating.

Behind the large barrack, the only itinerant photographer had established himself. On the wall of the barrack hung the backdrop: a smoothly but coarsely drawn canvas—a large enticing picture. They stood before it for a long time, enchanted. The wind blew it up like a sail. The sail swam away, lured them.

Everything was there at the same time: the earth, the water and the sky; houses, balustrades, flower pots, trees, benches, clouds, flowers, birds; boats, steamers, dirigibles, airplanes, life-preservers, life belts, and lanterns; mountains, canyons, waterfalls; planets, luminaries, and stars.

In two square metres, the surface of the canvas completely encompassed all humanity's dreams of human harmony, comfort and happiness. This was a dream carried to ideal manifestness and tangibility. There was nothing utopian here, nothing unreal, nothing supernatural.

The semi-naval steamer stood at anchor in a canal as straight as a corridor. The steamer was called "Komintern."[3] On it were six brick smoke stacks. Out of them poured cast-iron smoke that spread over a jade sky.

On the deck stood ideal sailors with black moustaches and sailor hats with ribbons. A red sun was sinking into the canal.

A Moorish castle with striped awnings entwined with ivy and roses descended step by step to the very water. And above the castle stood a round Spanish moon.

A fat, seamed dirigible with the inscription "Enthusiast"

[3] Comintern—Communist International.

floated overhead. And overhead flew an airplane of unusual construction with a multitude of motors, six-winged like a seraph,
and with the inscription "Shock-Brigader." Cypresses of mala-
chite, entirely covered with large pale flowers, disappeared into
the distance in a faultless palisade down the length of the ideal
canal. And over all this shone the stars.

Around thick marble benches of confectionary whiteness and
sumptuousness, stood tall lilies like plaster of Paris vases, and
plaster of Paris urns grew miraculous roses of Sharon. Here
everything was for beatitude.

They stood before this picture that had been meticulously
drawn by the diligent brush of a master who had not spared the
brightest and the best of his paints, but who, nevertheless, had
abused the white and the black.

It lured them, led them into its cool fairy-tale world of rest
and satisfied desire.

Sayenko wanted to have his picture taken. He bargained with
the photographer for a long time. Finally they agreed on a price.
Sayenko sat down on a chair in front of the canvas.

The photographer—a man in bast shoes and black dust goggles—worked fussily for a long time to get the right pose. Idlers
gathered around. But when everything was ready, Sayenko
changed his mind. No, two rubles was too much. He rose lan-
guidly from his chair, whistled to Zagirov, and they went on their
way.

Near the bus stop, the circus was being put up. They crawled
under the canvas where carpenters were still hacking fresh logs
with axes. They feasted their eyes on the parrots, and stood before the elephant who, his front leg bent at the knee, was heavily
fanning himself with his thick wrinkled ears.

But the magic picture continued to haunt Sayenko's imagination. He leaned on Zagirov's strong shoulder and whispered:

"Listen, Tatar, don't let me down. We'll have everything.
Wait! To the devil with that sort of thing! Have we been hired
by him, really? Ekh, my little Comrade, what woods there are
in the Urals! What forest thickets! There are bears here. We'll

roll along . . . And then we'll throw some salt on their tails. I'm telling you the truth . . . Listen to me!"

When he heard these words, Zagirov's heart fainted and turned cold with fright.

The autobus came. It was only called an autobus, for in reality it was an old, open, five-ton truck, and benches had been nailed inside of it.

The conductor was a plain, smudge-nosed woman, barefooted but wearing dust goggles and carrying a bag.

The crowd rushed to the first step. Commotion. Crush.

"Make way for shock-brigaders and enthusiasts!" cried Sayenko.

They squeezed their way into the autobus. There were no places to sit. The autobus started. They stood swaying in the crowd like nine-pins.

An hour later, having driven past the kilometre-long dam, they arrived at the Kazak settlement.

The Kazak settlement was overgrown with greenery.

XLIV

AN engineer without a watch!

He was not careless or absent-minded. On the contrary, Margulies was precise, neat, well-organised, had an excellent memory.

Still, he never had a watch. Somehow, he could not keep a watch. He would buy one now and then, and he would always either lose it or break it. Finally, he had become accustomed to getting along without a watch of his own. He did not miss it.

He could count time by a multitude of the most minute indications scattered around him in this gigantic, mobile world of the new construction.

For him, time was not an abstract concept. Time was the number of turns of the drum and of the driving pulley; the lifting of the scoop; the end of one shift and the beginning of another; the firmness of the concrete; the whistle of the machine; the opening door of the dining room; the knitted brow of the time-keeper; the shadow of the plant, passing from west to east and already reaching the railroad track. . . .

There was no real disagreement between him and time. They moved without getting behind or ahead of each other, knee to knee, like two runners, or like the runner and his shadow, rec-ognising seconds by eyes and palms of hands that flitted past.

The girl walked up the ladder and sat down on the barrier opposite the drum that had started smoothly.

With school-girl neatness, she adjusted the short skirt across her lap. Her feet in socks that had slipped down did not reach the floor. She tightened the knot of her white kerchief on the back of her head, so that her hair would not flap too much. Her hands gleamed, yellow from the sun. On her wrist was the black ribbon of her watch. She was the time-keeper from the construc-tion committee.

The first portion of concrete thundered out and crawled noisily along the trough. The girl put the paper on her lap and, with a pencil, made the first check.

Ten minutes past four, Margulies thought at once, mechani-cally.

He walked around the labour front, not wishing to interfere with the lads or to embarrass Mosya. However, from the dis-tance, with apparent casualness, but very carefully and very thoroughly, he again examined the allocation of the men and the disposition of the materials, the action of the machine—all of the well-planned and efficient arrangement that had been put in mo-tion by the agitated whistle of Mosya.

Everything was in its place. Everything was in order. Every-thing moved in a strong, fresh rhythm. But the gravel continued to be an annoyance. Margulies walked up to the pile.

With a stony, stubborn face, little Triger was loading Olya Tregubova's barrow too fast.

Olya Tregubova had not had time to put on her overalls. She

was still in her best skirt, which billowed around her. Gloveless, the palms of her hands had already been rubbed until they were red. They did not hurt her yet, but they were beginning to burn slightly.

Spreading her fingers apart, she flipped her hands back and forth, cooling them. The wind blew about her multicoloured combs, her unbobbed hair, arranged in an old-fashioned manner. Now and then she would glance alertly down the length of the rails whence any minute a train might appear. Her barrow was not yet full, but Smetana was already on her heels, pushing his empty barrow across the rails.

"Come on, come on! Get a move on!"

His face, scarlet, hot, covered with greenish dust, resembled a peach.

"Getting on?" Margulies asked.

"Getting on," Triger grunted and threw the last shovelful of gravel into Olya's barrow.

"Roll on! Next!"

With a ringing sound, he thrust the shovel into the pile.

Olya caught the barrow by the handles, strained, pushed at it, turned deep red, and, with thunder and clanging, rolled the heavily grunting barrow across the rails.

That's bad, Margulies thought to himself. Such bad luck! We should have at least two more at this point.

But there was no way to help this.

"Are you steamed up?" he asked Smetana.

"We'll steam up some more. Wait, Boss. Not all at once. Pile it up!"

Margulies took several small stones from the pile and brought them up to his spectacles. He examined them attentively on all sides—as if he were looking at them through a magnifying glass.

"Good gravel, the devil take them!" he said, lisping. And with satisfaction, he threw the little stones back into the pile. "They have learned—at last."

He stood for a while, silently watching Triger loading Sme-

tana's barrow with a stubborn, implacable face. He was thoughtful for a moment.

"Let me give you one bit of advice, lads," he said. "Don't strain
too much. Take it easy. Save your strength. Steady, steady. The
main thing is not to give out toward the end. Everything depends on your strength at the finish."

Triger deftly flung the last shovelful into Smetana's barrow.

"Roll on! Next!"

Smetana jauntily clapped his huge canvas gloves which resembled lasts. He seized the barrow.

"Ekh! If it were not for that trash! . . ." he growled, straining angrily. "If it were not for those two carrion! . . ."

Mosya ran up.

"David Lvovich!"

He pounced down like a bird of prey, like the devil, like a
storm.

"Comrade Chief of the Sector! . . ."

He was yelling for all he was worth, until he was hoarse.

"Word of honour! Comrade Margulies! If you don't go away,
I will simply swear at everybody! You yourself promised not to
interfere. And the comrades from the Central newspapers are
witnesses! For God's sake, don't interfere with my shock-brigade
work! Go away from the front! Don't interfere with my lads!
Otherwise . . . my honest honourable word, I won't guarantee
anything!"

Margulies smiled good-naturedly.

"Hey! All right, all right. I'm going. But you calm down."

But Mosya persisted.

"It's one of two things," he cried, hearing nothing except his
own voice. "Either I'm the foreman or I'm not the foreman! Who
is responsible for the shift? I am responsible for the shift. Who
will be disgraced? I will be disgraced. Really, now! . . ."

And suddenly turning to Triger, hewing the air with his fist:

"Speed it up! Get a move on! Don't stop! All this talk! Faster,
faster!"

A second portion of concrete thundered out and crept down.

Margulies adjusted the shafts of his glasses behind his ears, and went around the labour front at a fine trot. The girl made a second check on the paper.

Twelve minutes past four, Margulies mechanically noted in his mind. He went toward the raised platform.

But Mosya was already flying diagonally across the planking at break-neck speed, swinging his loose arms before him like a goal-keeper.

"David Lvovich!" he cried furiously. "One or the other! . . . Go and have your dinner! The devil take you! . . ."

Margulies waved his arm and turned back.

Behind him the third portion thundered out. Restraining a smile, and looking attentively under his feet so as not to step on a nail, he went away.

XLV

THE business was arranged and under way. For the time being he was not needed. Really, he might just as well go to the dining room and have some dinner.

But to go there now was beyond his powers. The dinner would not run away. He could stand here for half an hour. In half an hour, certain things would have become clearer. Then he could go and eat in peace. It would not hurt to have something to eat . . .

He sat down on the edge of the scaffolding. He adjusted himself so as not to interfere with the laying of the concrete, but, at the same time, so that he could see the work of the brigade through the space where the wall of the plant had been removed.

Here was tremendous darkness, permeated with a complicated system of winds and draughts. He took off his cap and passed the palm of his hand over his high, luxuriant, marcelled shock of hair.

Past him from right to left, in single file, the boys were rolling heavy sterlings filled to the very brim. The concrete thundered wetly as it was dumped into the open trap of the scaffolding.

From the left to the right, the sterlings returned empty and light, like baby carriages on high light wheels with innumerable thin spokes. The mud scrunched under the wheels. The movement of wheels and people meeting each other filled the narrow quadrangle of the wall that had been taken apart. It covered it with a fine, drizzling flicker, through which the planked platform flooded with the dim sunlight and coloured by the swiftly moving shadows of the working brigade flickered and drizzled.

Time flickered and drizzled in seconds, and Margulies had to see the work in all this detail in order to know just how it was progressing.

He determined all its phases by a multitude of the tiniest sounds which reached him distinctly from the outside.

The ringing blow of the shovel. The stamping of bast shoes on the planking. The sinuous screech of the wheels. The clanging of the scoop. The rush of water. The leaping clatter of the barrow across the rails. The sound of the spilling drum and of the pouring, crawling concrete. A voice. A cry. A word.

All this spoke to him of time and rhythm.

He listened to the sounds. He counted them, as if they were a pulse. The pulse was even, somewhat accelerated, fresh, and full of vigour.

Half closing his eyes and bending his head, he listened to the sounds. He revelled in them. They cradled him, lulled him. But this was not sleep. This was a sharp, strained, half-slumber—a trauma—ready at every instant to snap and to pass into activity.

Time passed and he with time, knee to knee. They walked, he and time, like two runners, like the runner and his shadow, recognising seconds by the flickering and drizzling sounds from the outside.

The main sound was the sound of the spilling drum. This sound signified a mixture. It was repeated with ever-increasing frequency. Margulies noted it subconsciously twenty-five times.

Korneyev appeared.

"David? How do you like it? Ishchenko made twenty-five mixtures in thirty-one minutes. What do you think of that?"

That meant approximately fifty an hour, four hundred a shift. If one were to discount possible delays and loss of rhythm, it would mean no less than three hundred and fifty. That exceeded the boldest calculations.

Eat now? No, any time but now. In another half hour. If the tempos had not fallen in a half hour, then he could go to eat calmly.

"Good."

Korneyev lingered for a moment, and then disappeared. Thirty-eight minutes past four, Margulies noted mentally.

He continued to sit without changing his position, and listened to the sounds of the work. They came with increasing frequency. Time approached six o'clock.

Margulies made his way out of the place and carefully walked edgewise around the platform. Mosya was running along the planking, his eyes flashing hysterically. The platform was surrounded by curious people.

Margulies sat down at a distance on a little post. His arms dropped between his knees. He rubbed the palms of his hands together. He could not take his eyes from the moving barrows.

"Hello, Boss! Good health to you again! Good evening!" Margulies did not hear.

Smiling good-naturedly through his Poltavian, corn-coloured moustaches, his hard, spectacled American eyes gleaming amiably, Foma Yegorovich walked up from behind and placed his firm arms around Margulies's shoulder.

"He sits and looks. He sees and hears nothing around him. Comrade Margulies, do you know what I shall tell you? In just this way did our American miracle-maker, Thomas Alva Edison, sit when he and his students were constructing the incandescent electric lamp with a metal thread in the middle. The lamp glowed, and they sat around and looked and watched it glow. It glowed, and they could not go to sleep. They had to see how long it would last. For sixty-two hours they sat in front of the table in the laboratory."

Margulies smiled faintly.

"You are a poet, Foma Yegorovich."

"No, I'm an American engineer, no more, no less. The lamp glowed. And they sat in the laboratory as if they had been tied to the table. I'm telling you that. That is history. You, Comrade Margulies, are just like our little Edison, Thomas Alva Edison. How would it be in our language—in Russian? Foma Alexeyevich Edison. You are Foma Alexeyevich Edison." He laughed gaily.

"How do you like this?" asked Margulies, indicating with his eyes the new planking in front of the machine. "Quite a different tune, isn't it?"

"Very interesting," said Foma Yegorovich. "Simply remarkable!"

Margulies stroked his knees with self-satisfaction. He knew perfectly well that the American was quick to recognise the innovation for all it was worth.

"However, Foma Alexeyevich Edison Margulies, there's a time for everything. You've looked at your lamp long enough. Come, let's eat, or they will close the dining room before we get there. It never hurts to eat well, and your lamp won't go out without you. It glows well—that lamp of yours. It is the lamp of Ilyich.[1] You may believe me. You have lighted it very well. Very well. I can see that already."

"Perhaps . . . for about twenty minutes . . ."

"Come on, come on. You'll see later on whether it will be for twenty minutes or not. One should eat well. It is bad to hurry when you eat."

Margulies hesitated. There was no one with whom he could leave the sector. Korneyev had disappeared.

He glanced from side to side indecisively.

"Go on and eat, David Lvovich! We can get along without you!" Mosya cried in an exultant voice as he passed by, and

---

[1] Lenin is spoken of affectionately thus by his patronymic.

throwing lightning glances at the American, suddenly yelled hoarsely: "Hurry, hurry, hurry! Faster! Stop talking!"

Foma Yegorovich and Margulies went quickly toward the dining room. The American pulled out of his pocket a roll of illustrated American magazines.

"I received them to-day by mail from the States. We'll read them at dinner-time. This is a remarkable magazine. It was founded by Benjamin Franklin himself. For one hundred and fifty years, it has appeared on time every week—not like Soviet magazines. Look at this advertisement! Anything your heart desires! All the American firms! We'll look it over."

They were at the crossing.

Across their path, striding clumsily, came Nalbandov. He was striking the rails with his cane. They greeted each other. Nalbandov threw back his head, and squinting cannily, looked off into the distance as if he were aiming.

"*Your* sector?"

"Mine."

"One minute, Mr. Bixby . . ."

Nalbandov and Margulies walked off to one side.

The wind blew in short, hot gusts. There was no sun. The low sky moved heavily, laden with thick, slate-coloured clouds. Margulies sensed the hot odour of Nalbandov's black coat—an odour of leather and wax. But it seemed to him that this was the odour of his beard and forehead.

"What is happening here, David Lvovich?" Nalbandov asked casually.

"You see . . ." Margulies began.

Nalbandov interrupted him.

"I'm sorry. Perhaps we had better go to your office?"

"If you like . . . Foma Yegorovich!" Margulies shouted. "You go to the dining room in the meanwhile . . . Go on, go on! . . . Get something for me, too. I'll be there in ten minutes."

Margulies let Nalbandov precede him, since the latter was his superior and in charge of the construction.

They entered the office.

XLVI

AT five o'clock Nalbandov assumed charge of the construction. Until five, he had been showing the Americans around. He enjoyed their cultured society. He relaxed.

Mr. Ray Roupe revealed remarkable erudition in the field of Russian history. It was extremely pleasant to converse with him, to exchange short, pointed observations.

They had covered about a hundred kilometres.

Mr. Ray Roupe faultlessly placed a small, wooden weather-beaten church in one of the distant Kazak settlements as belonging toward the beginning of the eighteenth century.

Smiling subtly and good-naturedly, he expressed the supposition that in this small, ancient church made of fir-logs, which seemed to beg to be placed on the stage of Stanislavsky's Art Theatre—in this same graceful chapel with green pillows of moss on its black planked roof—perhaps the legendary revolutionary hero, the Yaeek Kazak, Emelyan Pugachov, had once been married.

He remarked that this wild steppe-landscape might have been brought here straight from the pages of "The Captain's Daughter," an entrancing tale by Alexander Pushkin. The only thing that was lacking was snow, winter, snow storms and troikas.

He remarked that certain of Pushkin's poems had a kinship with the stories of Edgar Poe, which, of course, was somewhat paradoxical, but quite explicable. He complimented Nalbandov subtly. When still a youth, Edgar Poe had visited Petersburg on a boat. They say that in one of the taverns he had met Pushkin. They talked all night over a bottle of wine, and the great American poet made a gift to the great Russian poet of the plot of his remarkable poem "The Bronze Horseman."

Nalbandov dined with them in the American dining room.

At five o'clock, not without some regret, he bade the Americans good-bye.

Seroshevsky had not yet returned. His office was still closed. Annoying! It was necessary to have it out with him, to say everything he had to say.

At the plant office, his colleagues were running down stairways grey with dust. The working day had come to an end. Offices were being locked. Maids in aprons were sweeping the red xylonite floors. Under the green hanging lamps in the empty draughting room, crooked-legged draughting tables and boards carefully covered by faded newspapers stood like desolate orphans.

After the automobile, the free, healthful air, the open steppe, after the company of sophisticated, cultured people, all this dull world of a Soviet office seemed disgusting to Nalbandov, repulsive.

The walls covered with the smears of dirty fingers. The nicked corners of the corridors. The broken windows. The hooks ripped out of the frames. The torn scraps of paper. The gawky wall-newspapers—yard-wide rolls of wall-paper—with their semi-literate remarks and clamorous, insistent, exhorting slogans, with this constant pretension to technical superiority over Europe and America . . .

He slouched disgustedly along the corridors and stairways, striking his cane against the steps, bannisters and wall. By the way, the bannisters were iron, for they had never found the time to attach their wooden handrails. They had a pathetic, ragamuffin appearance. Americans!

This was typical, native, ineradicable, Russian slovenliness!

Here in the steppe they had built a five-story building of brick and glass, the last word in European technique. They had invested a million. And yet they did not know how to take care of it. In three months it had come to look like the devil knew what!

Was it feasible to construct such buildings here? Dust, sand storms, cyclones, air-currents . . .

Was it worth while to go to all this trouble, so that—in the middle of the devil only knew how wild a Ural steppe, at the crossing of four raging winds, under the most impossible, utterly outlandish conditions—this grey, dull, stupid Soviet institution might be organised?

"Asia, the devil take it!" Nalbandov muttered. "World records! Demagogy!"

People met each other, greeted each other. A fat man in an unbuttoned Ukrainian shirt, with newspapers under his arm, ran by.

"To Georgi Nikolayevich! Where have you been? Did you show the Americans around? If you only knew what's going on here! It's simply the devil knows what! On the sixth sector, Margulies is wringing such figures out of the Jaeger concrete-mixer . . ."

Nalbandov passed by in silence.

"This is not a construction, but a stunt!" the fat man shouted after his disappearing figure, and laughed aloud.

Nalbandov snarled viciously into his beard.

On the third-story landing stood a group of engineers. One of them, a young, red-headed, freckled fellow with a long red neck emerging from an unbuttoned military uniform worn over a net-like undershirt, shouted joyously:

"Nalbandov, have you heard what's going on at the sixth sector? Have you heard about Margulies? He's beating Kharkov! You may regard him as a cavalier of the Red Banner."

"I've heard, I've heard . . ."

Without turning around, Nalbandov walked quickly to the fourth story. Flinging doors open with his cane, he passed to the office of the chief engineer on duty at the construction. It was a large, dull, deserted room. Without taking off his coat and cap, he sat down at the table and placed his cane over the papers.

"Let him break his neck! To hell with him! We'll see!"

Across a huge, square-paned window, dark, slate-coloured, vicious clouds swept threateningly. A wall of yellowish, charred dust was advancing. The open wicket shuddered and snapped on its hook. It shed black grains of dust.

Nalbandov walked up to the window.

Large posts wandered obliquely against the wind in clouds of dust. Roofs, roads, lanes, trenches, mountains smoked. Under the red walls of the hotel, broken window-glass and shards of plates gleamed dimly. Cavalcades of torn bits of paper swirled in nooks and corners.

In the distance, beyond the long plant of the Coke-Chemical Combine, four huge pipes of the new scrubbers rode against the dust. That morning there had been only three.

Nalbandov shrugged his shoulders.

"A scrubber a day. I can imagine!"

He put his hands behind his back and turned from the window.

On the Swedish oaken desk stood a six-sided inkwell with a seamed, knobbed cover, all made of green glass and obviously second-hand. In proportion to the size of the room, it occupied as much space as, in proportion to the extent of the construction, was occupied by blast furnace Number One, which was already eight storys high.

The telephone sputtered.

"Hello! Engineer on duty."

With the careless curtness and assurance of a senior surgeon, Nalbandov accepted reports and gave orders. His decisions and measures were as quick as they were traditional. They revealed him as a brilliant engineer and executive of academic tradition. His quickness and decisiveness were grounded in the precise and faultless knowledge of laws whose immutability and sacredness he never doubted himself and permitted no one else to doubt.

To-day he was more curt and ruthless than usual. He was irritated, and he could not calm down. Laws were being revised at the sixth sector altogether too boldly and too irreverently. They were invading the fields of mechanics too brutally. They were subjecting the affirmations of foreign authorities to doubt too impudently. They were shaking traditions.

An inkwell is an inkwell and a blast furnace is a blast furnace. That was all there was to it.

But to-day, in Nalbandov's eyes, all things had begun to lose their allotted places and dimensions.

As he ruminated, he caught himself thinking that the inkwell in front of him had suddenly grown to the dimensions of a blast furnace, and that he was about to take the blast furnace off the sector, put it on his writing desk, and dip his pen into it.

It was almost six o'clock.

What was happening on Margulies's sector? He was determined not to interfere, to let Margulies break his own neck. But he could not overcome the temptation. Besides, after all, he was the chief construction engineer on duty and was taking the place of Seroshevsky.

He went downstairs and, with his cane, poked the chauffeur who had fallen asleep on the ground beside the machine.

XLVII

"WHAT'S going on here?"

Nalbandov laid his hand firmly on the head of his huge orange cane. He was sitting sideways on a low stool in front of Margulies's table. The ends of his leather coat lay on the unpainted planks of the barrack floor.

In profile, Margulies saw his narrow, pitch-black beard, and his rigid nose with its scar.

Squinting, Nalbandov looked now at the window and now at the corner. At any rate, he looked somewhat past Margulies.

He shook his head curtly and carelessly and remarked:

"I am in charge of the construction."

He seemed to have placed this remark in parenthesis, so that it would not be necessary to refer to it again and in order to define their relationship precisely.

Margulies put his elbows on the shaky, plywood table covered with faded blue sheets of old draughts.

"At your service, Georgi Nikolayevich!"

"What is going on here?"

In the corner of this small room, which looked more like the cabin of a bathhouse than the office of the chief of the sector, a tin plate with remains of food stood on a stool. These remains seemed to be something between a crooked lamb-bone and a crust of black bread.

Margulies took off his glasses and peered at the plate near-sightedly, trying to determine what it was, after all—a bone or a crust.

Nalbandov glared at him with revulsion.

"Well?"

Margulies put on his glasses and mechanically pulled out of his side pocket a yellow pencil which had been sharpened with amazing accuracy.

He placed it on the palm of his hand and lightly played with it, delighted by its shiny sides.

"What is it that you are interested in?" he asked timidly, lisping, and without looking at Nalbandov.

"The condition of the sector. In general."

Nalbandov emphasised the words "in general," and again directed his gaze carelessly into the space between Margulies and the window in which the light and shadow of a passing train flickered like pages in a book being turned.

The light and shadow flickered from the right to the left. The train was passing from the left to the right.

On the planked wall behind Margulies twinkled graphs, diagrams, printed placards in colours—sanitary instructions for first aid to the wounded; the rescue of the drowned; what to do in case of gas attack; various coloured drums—blue for oxygen, white for acetylene, red for hydrogen; a lithograph portrait of Karl Marx.

Marx's beard was yellowish-white; his moustache had a dash of black. His elegant frock coat was cut low and revealed a starched white shirt, and something round hung from his neck on a ribbon.

Is it a monocle, really? Nalbandov thought, lightly shrugging his shoulders.

"In general . . ." said Margulies and tugged at his nose with concentration, "in general, the picture that the Coke-Chemical Combine presents to-day is . . ."

"Well . . . well . . ."

Margulies's eyes almost met in his intense concentration.

"At the eighth battery, we have laid eighty and seven-tenths percent of the quota. At the seventh battery, sixty and nine-tenths. The excavation on the silos' foundation was approximately one hundred and twenty percent of the quota. On the stockades . . ."

"That I know," Nalbandov cut him short. "Further, what about the concrete laying?"

"As to concrete laying, we have the following picture: The shoe is finished. The grate under the fifth battery is finished. At sixteen eight we began to pour the fifth."

It looks like a monocle, Nalbandov thought. That's incredible. He turned abruptly on the stool.

"Excuse me. You began to pour at sixteen eight. Now it is . . ."

Without hurrying, Nalbandov unbuttoned his overcoat, opened it like the door of a safe, and took out his gold watch.

"Now it is eighteen fifty-two."

The dining room will close, thought Margulies.

Nalbandov snapped the cover of the watch and replaced it.

"How many mixtures?" he asked with exaggerated indifference.

Margulies bent over the table and cautiously touched the paper with the point of his pencil, as sharp and long as a needle.

"I cannot tell you exactly. But approximately—between one hundred thirty and one hundred fifty."

"So. Fifty mixtures per hour. H'm!"

He croaked sarcastically and, unable to contain himself any longer, jumped from the stool and walked up to the portrait of Marx.

He began to examine it closely.

(It actually is a monocle! Curious!)

He put his arms behind his back and turned toward Margulies. "Interesting."

"Yes, it is very interesting," said Margulies simply.

"You think so?"

Nalbandov reseated himself at the table. Margulies rose and walked across the room. Passing the tin plate, he bent down a little. No, it was not a bone. It was a crust. And beside it was a bit of dry *kasha*.

He sat down at his place again.

Nalbandov found a bitten-up indelible pencil on the table, and placed it disgustedly on the palm of his hand.

Now they sat facing each other, weighing pencils in the palms of their hands held over the table, as if they wanted to determine their weight in the most meticulous manner.

"I hope that it is not necessary for me to remind you," said Nalbandov without raising his voice, and altogether too calmly, "that less than two minutes for each mixture is against the rules. That is a-b-c. You may find it in any textbook." He emphasised the word "textbook." "Nevertheless, in your sector, you are permitting mixtures to be made at the rate of one every one and two-tenths minutes."

"For us, information contained in any textbook is not compulsory. Every year, textbooks come out in corrected and supplemented editions."

Margulies said it quietly, lispingly, almost in a whisper. He was apparently concentrating his attention upon the pencil.

"That's all very well. But during the *current* year, it is recommended that you be guided by the textbooks of the *current* year. Is that not so?"

"Why shouldn't we take advantage of next year's corrections, if we happen to discover them now?"

"Oh, so you want to get ahead of time?"

"We want to finish carrying out the industrial-financial plan."

"It is not timely."

"To go ahead is always timely!"

"By the way, it seems to me that we have passed into the realm of philosophy. Let us go back. If I'm not mistaken, you are doing your work on the Jaeger cement-mixer?"

"Yes."

"I hope you are aware that the instructions on this machine has it printed in black and white that the time of each mixture cannot be less than one and five-tenths minutes."

"I am aware of that."

"Nevertheless, you are so bold, so to speak, as to doubt their competence, the competence of those who have composed these instructions, to doubt the official instructions of a world-famous firm?"

"Official instructions are written by sinners like you and me."

Margulies smiled faintly; it occurred to him that he was repeating the words of Foma Yegorovich.

Nalbandov frowned and turned red.

"It seems to me that your jests are somewhat out of place," he said loudly. "Of course, every one entertains himself to the best of his ability, and . . . and . . . as he has been taught . . . But please spare me these jests. I am sufficiently literate in technique. I regard your treatment of an expensive imported machine as, to say the least . . . risky. If you will excuse me, I do not want to employ another adjective, although at the present it is extremely fashionable."

Margulies's lips trembled slightly. He turned pale.

"You have in mind . . ."

"I say, that with such exploitation the machine is amortised too rapidly."

"In five or six years."

"But, according to the official instructions, it should work, under normal conditions, from ten to twelve years. You are doing violence to a machine."

"Whether it is five or ten years does not matter. Under normal conditions, as you express it, the kind of combine we are building here should take eight years to build, and yet, as you are perfectly well aware, we shall build it in three years."

"You may keep your demagogy to yourself. I am calling your attention to the fact that you are contributing to the exceedingly rapid amortisation of imported machinery which has been paid for in *valuta,* and that we do not happen to have dollars scattered on the ground."

"By the time this machine is amortised, we shall no longer have any need of dollars."

"Are you quite sure of that?"

"We shall be building our own cement-mixers. But I must tell you that, in spite of that, we are doing no special violence to the machine."

"But your barbarous speed!"

"It is composed of several elements which have no direct connection with the exploitation of the machine."

"So!" Nalbandov exclaimed derisively. "That's curious. Will you share it with us, if it is not a secret?"

Containing himself, Margulies drew a thin straight line across the paper with the sharp point of his pencil.

"It is composed of a rationalisation of the process of bringing up the inert materials. That's one. Of the correct disposition of men. That's two. And finally, of . . ."

It was very difficult for him to pronounce the word, but he nevertheless pronounced it without hesitation.

". . . and finally, of the enthusiasm of the brigade."

He pronounced this too emotional and newspaperish word "enthusiasm" with serious and businesslike simplicity, as if he were talking of improving the feeding of the workers, or arranging for piecework. When he spoke this word, he turned red to the roots of his hair. It was very difficult for him to say it before a man who would undoubtedly interpret Margulies in the wrong way.

Nevertheless, he pronounced this word because, when he reported to the chief construction engineer on duty (disregarding the fact that this engineer on duty was Nalbandov), he felt that it was his duty to express precisely all of his ideas on a technical question.

The concept of enthusiasm was one of the elements of his understanding of technique.

Nalbandov clutched his beard in his fist and squinted venomously past Margulies.

"Enthusiasm—that is very beautiful perhaps, but not very scientific," he said carelessly. "By the way, speaking of the rationalisation—as you express it—of the process of delivering inert materials: you have in mind, no doubt, your complete wooden planking before the machine. I have seen it, by the way. I must tell you that I regard it as utterly uncalled for to waste such a mad quantity of lumber, of which we have a shortage, on experiments of such dubious nature. Why don't you make a hardwood floor? That would make it even easier for your enthusiasts to work. Why don't you put a piano there? Then it will be just like a dancing class."

"If music can lighten our work," said Margulies calmly, "and help us to carry out the industrial-financial plan on time, we shall place a piano there."

Nalbandov snorted viciously.

"That's it, that's it! That's just what I was saying! This is not a construction, but a stunt!"

He leaned back and began to laugh with sonorous contempt.

Oh, so that's where it came from! Margulies thought to himself.

"We used the lumber that was left from the scaffolding," he said.

"Of course, of course!"

XLVIII

NALBANDOV continued to laugh viciously and demonstratively.

"Fine cost accounting! Fine economy! Your records are going to cost us a pretty penny, Comrade Margulies."

Margulies shrugged his shoulders. They were speaking two different languages.

"Excuse me," he said.

But at that instant the door was flung open and Mosya ran in. "David Lvovich!"

His face was glistening and excited.

"One hundred fifty-four mixtures in three hours! May I

never see my father and mother again!" he cried from the door sill. He noticed Nalbandov, and checked himself.

"Excuse me."

He walked up to Margulies and bent over him closely. Sweat ran down his dark, inflamed face, gathered on his chin and dripped in dirty drops to the floor.

"David Lvovich," said Mosya, breathing heavily, and coming so close that Marguiles could feel the heat of his body. "David Lvovich, at these tempos, this cement cannot last more than half an hour!"

He screwed up his eyes and stole a glance at Nalbandov.

"There you are," said Nalbandov viciously. "See for yourself."

Margulies frowned, waved his arm.

"Go, Mosya, go. I'll be there right away. You see, we are busy."

"I beg to be excused, of course."

Mosya tiptoed out of the room, but he stopped in the doorway and looked at Margulies with wild, excited eyes. He indicated his throat with the palm of his hand, as if to indicate the last extremity, and pulled his cap over his ears.

"Go, go."

Mosya dashed out.

"See for yourself!" cried Nalbandov. "You are already short of materials. What should last an entire shift, you squander in three hours."

He emphasised the word "squander."

"We are not squandering it," Margulies remarked emphatically. "We are pouring a flagstone."

He was furious, but he controlled himself splendidly. Tact and discipline did not permit him to raise his voice. He rose decisively and pulled at the yellow-spotted blue coat all too large for him.

"Excuse me, I must go."

"To get cement?"

"Yes."

"You are violating the plan of daily provisioning, and you will disorganise the transport."

"Every plan has another plan—a counter-plan."

Nalbandov rose.

"Then you will need more gravel than the plan permits, more sand than in the plan, and the devil only knows what else above the plan! You will demand that the sand and stone carriers work at a mad, break-neck speed, and the same of rock-crushers, and so on, and so on!"

"We shall require a certain acceleration in the operation of carriers and rock-crushers."

"Oh, so you have pretensions to influence the raising of tempos over the entire construction! Forgive me, I did not know, I did not know."

"Our pretensions are to carry out and to exceed the industrial-financial plan."

"The Kharkov record will not let you rest in peace. You have all lost your minds to-day. This is the most common, garden variety of vanity and thirst for notoriety."

"What of it? If vanity and thirst for notoriety can help the success of construction, I am not against it . . . I am not opposed to instances of vanity in my sector . . ."

Margulies glanced at the window with alarm. The landscape was dimming and seemed to be disappearing out of sight. The room was quickly growing darker.

"What else are you interested in, Georgi Nikolayevich?"

Nalbandov's irritation had reached its limit. However, it did not exceed that limit. Nalbandov was sorely tempted to strike Margulies down with the strongest and most irrefutable reason.

But he controlled himself. He kept this reason in reserve. The time would come, and then he would pronounce the word that would destroy Margulies.

That word was—"quality."

Preoccupied with quantity, Margulies was evidently failing to consider quality. That being the case, let him break his neck.

No, he would not pronounce this word even if it were necessary to break up the entire flagstone and begin pouring it over again from the beginning. Let him! That would destroy Margulies for good. There was no reason why he should be Margulies's wet-nurse. Margulies would be personally responsible for his technical ignorance and vanity, and he would receive his just deserts.

"You are not interested in anything else, Georgi Nikolaye-vich?"

Margulies was already standing at the door, politely awaiting the end of the conversation. He was prepared for Nalbandov's final argument: quality.

For that, he had in his pocket the article transmitted to him by Katya from Moscow over the telephone. So far as quality was concerned, everything was in order. Speeding up quantity, he had so far maintained the necessary level of quality.

Here he rested firmly on his own experience, on the experience of American contractors, and on the norms recently worked out in Moscow by the group of engineers of the State Institute of Construction.

But Nalbandov did not bring up this question.

"At any rate," Nalbandov said, dryly and carelessly, as if drawing the conclusion and the sum total of the entire conversation, "it is my opinion that work of this kind can bring to the construction nothing but harm."

"Are you saying this in your capacity as chief construction engineer on duty?"

"I am saying it in my capacity as assistant chief of construction," Nalbandov replied irritably.

Margulies glanced gloomily at Nalbandov's cane.

"Then—you forbid it?"

"I do not forbid it."

"Does that mean that you permit it?"

Nalbandov shrugged his shoulders irritably. "I neither forbid it nor permit it . . ."

"In that case, will you be so kind as to tell me how I am to understand you?" Margulies smiled faintly with his parched lips.

"You may understand it as . . . as the counsel of an older comrade."

Margulies was tactlessly silent. Nalbandov pushed open the plywood door with his cane.

"Good health to you!"

Margulies let him pass out first. Nalbandov stooped so as not to strike the top of the doorway with his head, and went out into the corridor.

As in the morning, so now, the corridor was full of shadows and smoke. Grimy people crowded the bookkeeper's window with account books.

Shura Soldatova looked out of the doors of the art shop. Carefully brushing back her hair with her hand, which held a paint brush full of paint, she walked up to Margulies. Her face was alarmed, solicitous.

"What? What, David?" she asked in a whisper.

She was slightly taller than Margulies. She put her hand on his shoulder tenderly and walked several paces in step with him.

"Nothing, Shura. Everything is all right. I'll tell you later."

She dropped back.

From the dark corridor, a door led outside. It was open. With the speed of bicycle spokes, rain flickered across the bright quadrangle. Margulies escorted Nalbandov to the plant through the fine, warm rain.

The work was going on. From a distance, Margulies already noted the somewhat slackened, more cumbersome rhythm.

Rain . . . bad, he thought, and hearing the crash of pouring concrete, he mentally approximated: one hundred and sixty-seven.

The wooden planking shone dimly like lead under the rain. The spilled cement had been turned into a thin, slippery mud. It completely covered the planking. It was very difficult to work. The men slipped; their legs slid apart.

"The devil take those bast shoes!" Margulies muttered.

Faces, red, dirty, drenched in sweat and rain, trousers and shirts darkened with sweat and rain—these testified that things were moving with difficulty.

It was too slippery! Some of the lads had put sacks over their heads. Others, on the contrary, had thrown off their shirts and bast shoes. Naked to the waist, shining like seals, bare-footed, and with uncovered wet heads, they pushed on the barrows, slipping every minute and falling to their knees.

As he passed, Nalbandov cast an oblique, careless glance at them. It seemed to Margulies that he shrugged his shoulders contemptuously. Margulies unerringly read the expression of Nalbandov's back and shoulders. He awaited a new attack, but Nalbandov was silent. This was irksome.

Only when Nalbandov reached the automobile and put his hand on the door, did he say over his shoulder, revealing his profile:

"Your rationalised process of bringing up inert materials . . ."

He emphasised the word "process."

". . . is a dance."

And to the chauffeur:

"Back to the plant office!"

The fine, sharp rain beat against his face, his forehead, his beard, and the white strokes of forked lightning slid and jumped before the chauffeur across the slaty strip of the horizon.

XLIX

THE rain did not cease, but neither did it increase in strength. Unfortunately, it was not sufficiently strong to wash the slippery slush off the planking.

Wash off the slush, Margulies thought mechanically. Yes.

He ran to the superintendent's office. "The fire hose!" he cried. "The fire hose!"

But others were already ahead of him. Here ideas were never born in isolation. Vinkich and Georgi Vasilyevich were dragging the fire hose out of the superintendent's office. Vinkich looked quizzically at Margulies. He seemed to be begging to be excused for overstepping the bounds of discipline.

"Right!" said Margulies.

"This was Georgi Vasilyevich's idea," Vinkich said fondly.

"Oh, no! Together! Together!" Georgi Vasilyevich cried with

exaggerated gusto. "We thought of it together. Wash it off! Wash it off! Sprinkle it! Sprinkle it!"

Croaking, he dragged the heavy, flat canvas hose. His round eyes darted from side to side with astonishment and daring. His wet mackintosh spread open. His white underdrawers were showing. The binoculars were dangling heavily and striking against his knees. His shoes were slapping against the mud.

"That's all right, that's all right," croaked Georgi Vasilyevich. "That's the way. Sprinkle it, sprinkle it! Sprinkle it, and that's all. Both of us, both of us! Both of us thought of it. We arrived at it empirically, purely empirically, you know."

Margulies entered the office.

Kutaisov lay face down on the table in the midst of reports and news. He was talking on the telephone. Beating the board wall with his unfastened sandals, he was shouting:

"And I tell you once more, dear comrade, that you can't get away with it! Don't worry, don't worry, you'll find some. If you look for it, you'll find it. Use the name of the travelling edition of the 'Komsomolskaya Pravda.' Yes. The chief of the repair staff—Kutaisov. If you please, write that down. What? Don't you try to frighten me, because I'll frighten you. I'll frighten you in the newspaper . . . What? Sit down, David. What? Go on, I wasn't talking to you," he laughed into the telephone. "Your turn will come."

"Cement," said Margulies.

Kutaisov swung around and looked at Margulies with his red face turned up.

"What? Cement? You'll have it right away."

And into the telephone:

"Well, how about it? Did you hear me? Forty barrels and at once. Do you understand? Oh, you understand? Well, praise God! Is Korneyev there? Very good. So much the better. He can write the order right on the spot. Be good, be good! Well, thank you, friend. What? The dispatch department? They won't give you a train? Ho, ho, you'll get a train right away! Be good. So long."

He replaced the receiver and wiped his wet, steaming face with his sleeve.

His yellow hair had turned dark, tangled, was crawling into his eyes.

"Oof, it's hot!"

He again tore the receiver off the hook.

"Hello! Central! Give me the dispatch department! Wait, David, you'll have everything right away. Hello! Dispatch department? Who is speaking? Hello, young fellow . . . The travelling edition of 'Komsomolskaya Pravda.' Well, this is what I want, friend . . ."

Margulies went out of the office.

With his underdrawers turned up and his mackintosh tucked around him like a janitor, the novelist was watering the planking. The water crackled. The stream beat at the planking, broke, and scattered fanwise like a palm branch. The palm branch swept and chased the mud. The yellow board emerged in all its cleanliness and neatness.

The lads ceased slipping and falling. Some tried to get under the stream. Crashing, the stream beat against the hot young bodies and broke, flying into a palm branch. The bodies, cleansed of dirt and sweat, began to gleam with muscles bulging and shining like beans.

Margulies went up to the machine.

In the rain, the time-keeper still sat in her place opposite the revolving drum. She was neatly tallying on the wet paper.

Her tidy white kerchief had turned dark and had slipped to the back of her head. The wet hair stuck to the round, stubborn forehead. She was covered with spots of concrete. Dark-green rivulets ran down her cheeks and nose, her ears, and her bare childish feet over which the socks had rolled.

"How many?" Margulies asked.

She looked carefully at her hand, around the wrist of which was the black ribbon of her watch.

"Twenty-three minutes past eight—one hundred seventy-two mixtures."

The drum crashed as it turned over.

She quickly adjusted her hair with the back of her hand, and neatly made a notation.

From all sides and from all the other sectors, lads were running. New ones kept coming up. They crowded around. In bast shoes, barefooted, in overalls, without overalls, in shoes, tow-headed ones, clean ones, or covered with greenish cement mud or smeared with black earth like water-carriers, noisy ones, quiet ones, in light sweaters, in football sweaters, in shirts, the Khanumovites, the Yermakovites, engineers, superintendents, foremen, brigadiers, but all of them young, all of them with quick, shining eyes . . .

"One hundred seventy-three . . . one hundred seventy-four . . ." passed from one to the other in the crowd. "One hundred seventy-five . . ."

"Get back. Don't push!" Mosya cried, his eyes gleaming. "The price of admission is two kopecks. Ladies half-price."

In the meanwhile, Nalbandov, in his wet overcoat, was pacing the office of the chief engineer on duty, striking the walls with his cane. The telephone rang. He did not lift the receiver. Occasionally he would walk up to the window.

"Fame . . . He wants fame."

Everything had been blotted out by the swimming smoke of the rain mixed with the dust. It was steaming. From here, on the fourth floor, one could see far into the environs—for thirty kilometres. And low over the fleecy horizon, on all sides, hung deep black, stormy tongues of clouds.

To meet them, Asiatic towers and fortresses of the rainstorm rose as if from underground and reared themselves. They were ready to fall at any moment on the construction platform.

The room turned dark. Nalbandov shut the wicket and turned the switch. Under the ceiling, a very weak red globe burned stingily. It gave almost no light, emphasising more than ever the blackness of the rainstorm in its formidable flight.

L

SAYENKO was enjoying himself thoroughly.

Maples, poplars, elders, lilacs swayed and rustled throughout the Kazak settlement. The settlement rocked in the valley of the Yaeek as in a crib. The wind swept across the dam and carried off the watery dust. The rain spattered into the oilcloth leaves of lindens. The leaves babbled in the wind, swished, tossed in huge shining mounds, scattered over the dusty grass like fine beads.

A rooster stood motionless in the rain, as if he had been embroidered on the prim towel of the road.

This place was only ten kilometres from the construction. And yet, how quiet, how forsaken it seemed! Green fences, palisades, the wheels of wells. Neat Kazak houses under iron roofs, under osiers, under scaly shingles black with time, under moss spread out in velvet pillows. And front porches on four thin little posts.

Here, the traces of the old traditions of religion, handicraft trades, usages, social conditions lay over everything.

A tall, drab, Kazak settlement church, straight and neat as a blind soldier, swam and swayed among the low, threatening clouds. In the green churchyard, narrow pathways ran in all directions. But deadly nightshade grew out of the wooden steps, out of the porch.

At some of the small gateways stood large, well-preserved iron signboards. Attached with rusty wire, they turned and screeched like weather-vanes.

Crudely but conscientiously painted emblems of handicraft workers and tradesmen were useless and melancholy, like the orders and regalias carried on the green velvet pillow before the grave of a distinguished nobleman. The scissors and flatirons of tailors, the teapots and rolls of innkeepers, the coffins of coffinmakers, the shoes of shoemakers, the watches of watchmakers.

A multitude of watches—large, curious ones, like signboards, with hands stopped forever at two o'clock by the will of the nameless painter. And who could tell whether it was night or day?

Sayenko was enjoying himself thoroughly.

Under the dark window of the barn ran a high, thick row of hemp. The blue brushes swayed and struck against the glass. The yard around the barn was overgrown with weeds, burdock, nettles.

Inside the barn, new pine coffins stood at the door, placed one on top of the other and piled against the wall. On the other side of the door, red banners decorated with tassels and galloons stood against the wall.

It seemed that the master of this place was a jack-of-all-trades. Biblical piles of wood shavings lay under the joiner's bench.

On the shavings, with shavings in his hair, sat Sayenko, his arms around his knees.

He swayed somnolently, his purplish eyes staring at the window. Near him on the shavings lay the copy book he had taken out of his rags.

Weeping and moaning, he was reciting from memory:

> "They have buried my dear old mother,
> My father fell for no good reason . . .
> Give me, give me a large cup, Brother!
> Let me drown my sorrow in season!"

His face twitched hysterically. Foam trembled on his lips, dark with aniline.

He put his arms around Zagirov's neck, squeezed him convulsively, and dragged him closer. The Tatar's face was strained. His eyes were popping. The veins on his forehead were swollen. He was choking.

"Let go, Kolya! Let go!"

Zagirov tried to free himself, and struck his back against the leg of the joiner's bench. The joiner's bench swayed. A bottle of vodka fell down. The master caught it.

Bootless, clad in an old pair of Kazak riding breeches with yellow Ural stripes, a blue cotton shirt, and vest, he caught the vodka bottle on the fly, with the strong, agile movement of an

old man's dark, porous, cork-like hand. He smirked benevolently
into his little silver beard.

"Go easy, boys. Have a good time, but take it easy."

The dark light of the window was reflected vividly in his brown,
apostolic bald spot, surrounded by an old man's yellowish-white
hair. The one good eye he had left looked roundly and penetrat-
ingly to the side, like the eye of a rooster. The other eye was
blind, with a white, dim blind spot.

"One eye at us, the other at Arzamas,"[1] Sayenko laughed,
straining with all his might.

He was pulling Zagirov's head toward him. He mauled it, embraced it, stroked it, pulled at the hair.

Turning aside, Sayenko had gone into his secret pocket three
times, and three times the master had gone somewhere across the
yard, knee-deep in the storm, and had returned with yellow dill
pickles in his hands and with a bulging pocket.

"Listen to me, my darling. Listen to me, you Tatar mug!"
Sayenko cried, shoving his wet mouth into Zagirov's ear. "Understand me!"

And he began to wail again:

> "Ekh, I was a boy with blue-black locks.
> I landed on a construction job.
> A homeless orphan, on the rocks
> For no good reason—that's my lot!"

"Let go, Kolya, let go! . . ."
"Take it easy, lads, take it easy."
The glasses fell off the wet joiner's bench.
Sayenko cried:

> "The little cut-glass glasses
> Are falling off the table! . . ."

Sayenko drank. The master drank religiously. Zagirov did not
drink at first, refused, looked greedily at the dill pickles.

"Drink, Tatar. Drink, my darling. Have a good time. Don't be

[1] a popular quip

bashful. Don't insult me. Anybody can hurt my feelings. It's my treat. Maybe I'm throwing away my future!"

He was shoving the glass between Zagirov's teeth.

Outside the window tossed the hemp, blue to the point of blackness.

Clenching his teeth, Zagirov took the glass. He dipped his fingers into it and threw several drops to one side. He closed his eyes. He drank. He reached for the pickles.

"Feed your face, feed your face, you son of a so-and-so!" laughed Sayenko.

The vodka went to Zagirov's head. Again he dropped his fingers into the glass, flicked some drops on the shavings, and drank.

He was imitating the old Tatars. Allah forbade the drinking of vodka. According to the old men, the Koran said that the devil sat in a drop of vodka. But they were sly, those old men. They dipped their saffron fingers into the glass and threw a drop to the floor—the very drop in which the devil was sitting—so the rest could be drunk without danger.

Zagirov was drinking on an empty stomach and grew drunk quickly. He wanted to tell his friend about the sly old men, about the drop, about the devil, about the Koran.

"Listen, Kolya," he confided, opening his mouth from ear to ear—those pointed, clay-like, moving ears. "Listen, Kolya, to what I tell you. Whenever our old men drink, they always throw off a drop. You see, they actually throw it off with their fingers, because the power of darkness is bound to be in that drop. That is, the devil is always in that drop. Our old men are very smart. And we have a book. It's called the Koran. Do you understand, Kolya? . . . It's called the Koran. The old men say . . ."

Sayenko laughed viciously.

"Oh, you Tatar mug! I have your number. You're trying to fool your God."

"You can't fool God. You can't fool God," muttered the master, making the sign of the cross toward the dark corner. "You can't fool Him."

"Your God is a fool, an idiot! He won't let people drink. But our God gives you anything you like—as much as you like. You can eat as much as you like. Isn't that right, Boss?"

Zagirov, lover of peace, smiled ingratiatingly.

"Why do you talk like that, Kolya? *Our* God, *your* God, the Tatar God, the Orthodox Catholic God—there's one God for all people. There's one good God for all people."

With joyous incoherence, he muttered these words which he had heard many times in his childhood from various people.

He smiled broadly, tenderly, and timidly.

LI

THE master put on his spectacles. He pulled from the shelf a small thick book in a black shagreen binding, with the words "Religious Songs" stamped in gold.

He opened it and made the sign of the cross.

"Blessed are the people whose Lord is God," he whispered, closing his eyes beatifically.

And suddenly he sang out instructively in a high, unbending, dolorous voice:

> "Our native country—great and dear—
> It is a knight in strength.
> From end to end, a hemisphere
> It is in breadth and length.
>
> "With goodness make our country great—
> As great as it is large—
> With early Christian truth elate,
> With Christ's each holy charge.
>
> "Far above the highest steeple
> Let the Word, the Holy Ghost
> Lift the thoughts of Russia's people—
> Lift our Russia to the Host."

The master lifted his good eye to the dark ceiling and repeated in the profound manner of an instructor:

> "Lift the thoughts of Russia's people—
> Lift our Russia to the Host."

"And you say your God, our God!" cried Sayenko. "This is what our God is like. Ekh, you Tatar mug!"

"Why are you swearing, Kolya?" Zagirov asked plaintively. "Oh, that's not good! Oh, that's bad! What if I were to say that to you?"

Looking severely at the comrades, the master continued:

> "The idol of the flesh must die—
> The material ideal!
> Every righteous soul must sigh
> For the heavenly ideal."

With all its might, the door banged shut and opened again. The wind, the dust and the rain swept into the barn. The wood shavings rose and swirled in a dry cloud. A tin of nails fell off the shelf. The pages of the book flickered and swirled like a wounded dove.

Across the yard flew a branch torn off the tree. The sombre towers of the rainstorm belaboured the settlement. It grew dark.

The master rushed to the door. The coffins crashed down. The cherry-coloured cloth of the banners flapped and snapped. The master pulled at the rope on the open door as if it were a stubborn horse. Finally it slammed shut.

The hemp had turned completely black.

"It must be bad, pretty bad for the lads on the sector," muttered Zagirov.

"Drink, you Tatar mug!" Sayenko cried, having entirely lost his mind. "Have you heard: the idol of the flesh must die, the material ideal! . . . Go on. Keep going! Let the storm pull it out of the earth and take it to the devil's own grandmother! Let it sweep everything clean!"

The towers of the rainstorm flew over the settlement, over the dam, over the lake—to the construction.

"Hey, Boss, my good man! Sit by me and listen to what I'll tell you. Look here!"

Sayenko turned aside and, rolling over, quickly began to dig into his secret pocket. He pulled out a piece of paper, worn until it had holes in it, and covered with scribblings in indelible pencil.

"Look here, look here, Boss! It's a letter from my own dear father. I got it three months ago. They have taken him away, my own dear father, my own father! They said he was a *kulak* when they took him away . . . And a letter came from there. Stop, don't grab it! Don't grab with your hands! The precious words of my own dear father! Don't stand in the light! Don't stand in the light or I'll kill you!"

Sayenko's head fell on the shoulder of the master.

"Do you hear what my father writes from there? He writes: 'Don't stand in the way,' he writes. Do you see? 'Don't,' he writes, 'stand in the way. And if some one has some of our cattle, make a note of it. Make a mental note of it. And freeze the bees. Let the bees die, rather than go to them.' Do you understand me, Boss?"

Tears rolled down Sayenko's face.

"So, so, so," the master shook his head and whispered. "That's right: let them freeze rather . . . He writes sense, sense."

"Stop, there's more. Look further. 'Don't go into the collective yet, but if you care to, go ahead.' Do you understand this, Boss? 'But if you care to, do as you like, do as you like.'"

Sayenko fell head first into the shavings, and then suddenly jumped up.

"Drink, Tatar! Drink, parasite! They have taken my own dear father away, and you don't want to drink!"

In his ferocity, he caught the Tatar by the head and began to pour the vodka out of the bottle straight into his mouth. The vodka ran along his chin, flowed behind his collar.

"Why do you torture me?" Zagirov whispered, tearing himself away. "What do you mean by calling me a parasite?"

His teeth were tightly clenched. He was trembling. The vodka had gone to his head. His head was whirling. The window swam before his eyes.

"Shut up, you mug, shut up! Are you sorry for the lads at the sector? Aren't you sorry for my own dear father? Drink, you Tatar snout!"

"Don't swear." Zagirov turned frightfully pale. "I don't call you a Russian mug. All people are equal."

"You're lying, you son of a bitch. You're lying. You and I are not equal. I have bought and sold you. I bought you for a tenspot, and all your Tatar trash. Now you are my flunky. Hey, flunky, pull off my boots. Mug! Flunky!"

Zagirov turned crimson. His brown eyes were filled with blood and they looked like ripe cherries.

"Dog! You dog! You are worse than a dog!"

Trembling feverishly, Zagirov stuffed his index fingers into Sayenko's mouth, and began to tear at the lips painted with aniline, and to turn them inside out.

"I will kill you! I will kill you! I have your number! I know who you are," he rattled hoarsely. "I'll drag you to the *gehpeh-oo!* [1] Let them kill you! You are worse than a mad dog. You are a *kulak's* son. You are a *kulak* cur!"

Growling like a dog, he kept repeating with obvious pleasure:

"You are a *kulak* cur! You are a *kulak* cur! *They* are people, but you are a *kulak* cur! You should be shot! You're a crook!"

With distended fingers, Sayenko leaned against the hot face of the Tatar. Bloody slobber ran out of the corners of his mouth like reins.

"Guests, guests, take it easy," the master muttered. "Guests!"

They rolled on the floor.

The master managed to strike Zagirov's back with his foot. Zagirov jumped to his feet, and, stumbling over the things that had fallen down, over the coffins and the stools, floundering among

[1] a variant of O G P U—the United State Political Administration—the secret police

the banners, he rushed to the door. He tore it open and ran into the yard.

He did not have to run. The storm caught him, flung him and rolled him like a barrel over the burdocks flattened to the earth.

The wicket flew off its hinges. A signboard thundered down.

Turning in the air, the rooster flew along fences, like embroidery torn off the towel.

The painted hands of the clocks swirled madly.

Ahead stood the black wall of the rainstorm fleeing over the willows.

LII

NALBANDOV took the receiver off abruptly. The hook clicked.

"Hello! Central! Hello!"

He was impatient. At any moment, the rainstorm might crash and damage the telephone service.

Nalbandov stood in his coat and cap, with his cane under his arm, and the receiver at his cheek, his head bent sideways.

"Give me the socialist city."

The receiver lay against his cheek like a sideburn.

"Central laboratory? Thank you. The engineer in charge of construction speaking. Yes—Nalbandov. How do you do, Ilyushchenko! This is what I want . . ."

Nalbandov squinted, aimed at the window. Outside was unimaginable chaos. In the half-light, Nalbandov's face assumed the earthy colour of a potato.

"Here's what, Ilyushchenko: send some one immediately to the sixth sector. Margulies is up to his usual stunts there. Yes, yes. Kharkov, of course. They have lost their minds. Quite right. Tell them to take samples of the concrete for testing its resistance, but along the entire form, of course. Officially. Commissions, representatives of public opinion, the press—everything as it should be. After every fifteen or twenty mixtures, a sample. And have them send the little cubes to the laboratory. We'll see, we'll see. You will go yourself? So much the better. I will go also. What? The rainstorm? It isn't here yet. How is it where you are? Pulling the tents down? All right. Good-bye. I will send the repair brigade."

Without taking the receiver from his cheek, Nalbandov pressed the telephone hook with his index finger. The short click of disconnection.

The lamp went out slowly, but this did not make the room any darker. The same, even, grey, insidious light, neither day nor night. Objects were visible, but details were indistinguishable.

The window panes shuddered. The inkwell, dimensionless, stood in the desert of the room like a mosque.

Nalbandov took his finger off the telephone hook and spoke calmly into the receiver:

"Repair."

The towers of the rainstorm crashed over the construction. People ran in all directions, with the wind and against the wind.

With the wind, they were carried, swirled, turned over. They were almost flying, their clothes sticking to them. Against the wind, they fought their way with their chests, their heads, their shoulders, their bodies. The wind knocked them off their feet, but they did not fall. The wind held up their weight. They seemed to be reclining on the oblique wall of air, and they lay there obliquely, making swimming motions with their hands and feet.

The wind tore at their clothes and waved them like tattered banners. Their faces were lacerated until blood appeared, lashed with dust, as sharp and harsh as emery.

The storm rushed at the hotel.

The window frames slammed on all five floors of the hotel. Broken glass rang out. The pieces flew down, and, with them, shaving tackle, glasses, lamps, pieces of wood with hooks and latches. The storm pulled the curtains out of the windows and balcony doors. They blew up, snapped, slapped back and forth madly like grey tongues of pennants, tore off, flew away. From top to bottom, the entire hotel was permeated with an insidious system of cross-winds which battled in the desolate and echoing muzzles of corridors.

The circus posts, which had been torn out of the ground, toppled and fell. Crushed by the logs, the parrots were screaming. The canvas roof, inflated, flew through the air, caught against the wires. Multicoloured feathers were flying—red, yellow, blue.

The elephant stood, his huge forehead defying the storm. He spread his ears into fans, lifted his trunk. The wind blew up his ears like sails. The elephant fought off the dust with his trunk. His eyes were beastly, mad.

The wind compelled him to retreat. He lurched back. He was entirely surrounded by the black whirlwind of dust. He smoked. He wanted to run, but the chain would not let him go. He emitted a terrifying, devastating, elemental shriek. It was like the whistle of a ship of horror. The chain grew taut. He tore at the clanking chain. The ring bit into his leg. He pulled the stake from all sides, but the stake would not yield.

The storm came to the aid of the elephant. It leaned against him. Its whole horrible wall fell on him. It pulled the stake out of the ground.

The elephant ran, dragging behind him the stake that bobbed up and down at the end of the chain. He ran boldly with a smooth, sweeping, elephantine gait, breaking fences, tearing tennis nets, flinging down sentry boxes, felling telephone poles and football goal posts, maddened and blinded, like a convict chained thunderously to a ball.

The storm stalked over objects like a giant in seven-league boots.

The storm rushed down the sixth sector.

Scaffoldings and steel constructions swayed and shook. The latticed masts of cement-pouring towers, cranes, bridges, coverings swayed and shook. The plant swayed and shook like a cardboard box. Smoking, the empty cement barrels rolled, one after the other, along the planking, flying at the barrows and knocking people off their feet.

With one hand, the operator clung to the barrier. With the

other, he moved the levers. The storm tore the barrier out of his hand, but his fingers clutched the wood tightly again. The storm again tore it away. He again caught it.

The time-keeper sat on the floor, her head buried in her knees, her eyes squinting frantically, clutching the flapping papers with both of her hands. The storm tore off her kerchief and carried it away like a bird. Her hair blustered. But she sat motionless, pressing the papers between her knees.

The concrete thundered. She looked at her watch, covered with mud, and adroitly made a note on the paper with her pencil.

Eight o'clock thirty-two minutes, Margulies remarked mechanically to himself. Two hundred twenty-four mixtures.

Two hundred twenty-four mixtures in four hours and twenty-four minutes!

The wind chased Margulies into the plant. Here it was somewhat quieter. He figured rapidly in his mind:

Four times sixty—two hundred forty. Plus twenty-four—two hundred sixty-four. Two hundred sixty-four divided by two hundred twenty-four—one and approximately two-tenths of a minute. That is, on an average, one mixture is made in approximately one minute and ten seconds. A new record on the construction is established. But we have not yet attained Kharkov's.

But is it not *too* fast?

Coats, hats, boards, tins, were flying in the wind.

Steel tackle was groaning.

Quality!

Margulies made his way to the trough. The drum spilled thunderously. The greyish-green, stony mass crawled, rustling, along the trough.

Margulies dipped his hand into it. He brought a fistful of the fresh concrete close to his spectacles. In the twilight of the plant, he examined this plastic mass as if he were looking at it through a microscope.

He examined each little rock separately, each grain of dust. He rubbed the sticky mass between the palms of his hands. He stuck and unstuck his fingers. He was ready to smell it and to taste it.

The concrete seemed excellent to him. But he knew perfectly well that its quality could not be determined either by its colour, its texture, or its weight.

Its quality could only be determined later, in the laboratory, no sooner than seven days after taking a sample.

Nevertheless, he mauled the concrete, rubbed it, examined it, could not part with it.

His hands were covered with concrete, and splashes of concrete were on his large nose, on the lenses of his spectacles, on his coat, on his cap, on his boots.

"The devil take this technique!" he muttered. "It is so far behind, so far behind. They haven't yet invented a method for determining the quality of fresh concrete! What are they doing there in their scientific research institutes? It's a shame!"

He walked away from the trough and listened. Now he had to listen attentively and intently in order to catch the rhythm of the work. The whistling and roaring of the storm swallowed the smaller sounds by which he could gauge the tempo.

Nevertheless, he found them. He found them as small household objects are found in the ruins of a city destroyed by an earthquake.

The rhythm was breaking. The drum was turning over less frequently.

Margulies broke his way through the wall of the storm to the labour front.

Barrels were rolling. Olya Tregubova's holiday dress was torn to rags. It swirled madly around her in dirty trappings.

The wind tore columns of cement and sand out of the barrels. The gravel flew out of the barrows like bits of an exploded bomb. This was the front. These were the explosions. This was the roar of a charge and the smoke of a gas attack. The storm forced Margulies back into the plant.

"David Lvovich!"

Thundering over the boards, Mosya jumped into the plant as an artillery sergeant burned by an explosion might run into a blindage. He was yelling at the top of his voice, but because of the tornado-fire of the storm he could scarcely be heard.

"David Lvovich!" Mosya cried. "There is no cement! The last barrel! Comrade Chief, this is no way to work! There is no cement! To the devil's mother with all of you!"

He waved his arms hysterically. Blood mixed with dirty sweat was running over his slit cheek.

"What's the matter with you?"

"One barrel! One barrel! May the devil's grandmother take you! Is that the way to work? The last barrel of cement!"

"Right away!" Margulies cried.

They were two paces from each other.

"What? Wha-a-a-at?"

"Right away!" Margulies cried in an unnatural voice.

He ran to the gangway and again fought his way through the wall of the storm. The wind attempted to tear off his cap, but it was pulled tightly and tautly over his stiff coarse hair.

Margulies made his way to the superintendent's office. He tore at the door. The door was closed by the wind. It was impossible to open it. Suddenly the wind changed. It was flung open.

Margulies rushed into the office.

"Cement!"

Kutaisov was lying face downward on the table and shouting into the telephone:

"Hello! Hello! Warehouse! Hello, station? Hello, station!"

He flung the receiver against the wall.

"It won't work. The connection is broken! May they go to all the swine! The connection is broken! Korneyev and Slobodkin are at the other end."

For a moment he stared at Margulies with dim, unseeing, wide-open eyes, and then suddenly seized the receiver again.

"Hello, station! Hello! Hello!"

He struck the apparatus with his fist.

"Repair! Repair! Hello, repair!"

LIII

SLOBODKIN—the electric station and transport. Kutaisov—cement. Triger—both carriers, sand and rock. Semechkin—the water system.

Such was the disposition of forces of the central repair staff of the "Komsomolskaya Pravda."

However, from the very first minutes of work this disposition had been violated.

An unforeseen circumstance had occurred. Two members of the brigade—Sayenko and Zagirov—had refused to work. The weakest and the most dangerous point on the front—the gravel—was left exposed.

Then the reorganisation had occurred on the spur of the moment. It had occurred elementally. Little Triger had torn the shovel out of Sayenko's hands and had taken his place on the rails at the gravel. He, alone, had to replace two men for eight hours. This seemed almost impossible, but there was no other way out.

Time did not wait. Time raced. It had to be outdistanced.

For this reason, the two carriers—sand and rock—remained unattended.

But—there was Vinkich.

"Let me have the carriers," he said to Kutaisov. "Georgi Vasilyevich, what do you say? Georgi Vasilyevich and I will take the carriers."

There was no other way out because every man was worth his weight in gold.

Time raced.

The storm swept from the west to the east. It swept down inexorably, crashing upon the sectors, one by one, shaking the scaffoldings and the steel structures. It swept from the west to the east, and then changed its direction.

The storm reorganised itself on the spur of the moment. It turned from the west to the south. It went from the south to the north, and again turned. It whirled back from the east to the west, crashing again upon the sectors which it had just subjected to destruction.

Four whirlwinds—from the west, the north, the south, and the east—clashed, lost their footing, whirled in the black rows of winds.

The four whirlwinds were like four armies.

The whirlwinds carried thick clouds of choking, pistachio cement dust out of the open gates of the warehouse. The cement dust sifted through the cracks in the board walls. The walls were smoking. One might have thought that the warehouse was on fire.

For two hours Korneyev had argued with the chief of the warehouse, demanding forty barrels of Volsky cement of the Three Zeroes brand.

For two hours the chief of the warehouse would not yield. Forty barrels of Volsky Three Zeroes! Korneyev demanded the impossible. The chief of the warehouse himself had no right wilfully to increase the norms set for twenty-four hours. A plan was a plan. That is why it was a plan, in order that it might be carried out with precision.

Korneyev shouted about a counter-plan. The chief referred to his instructions. Korneyev talked about increasing productivity, about tempos. The chief talked about a stunt.

They spoke different languages. They raised their voices until they were shouting, and lowered them until they were whispering hoarsely. They stood facing each other, covered from head to foot, like two millers, in cement flour, with pale, excited, dirty faces, and glittering eyes. But the eyes of the chief were cold, glassy, while Korneyev's eyes were alive, brown, red-rimmed, and somewhat swollen.

For two hours the chief of the warehouse fought off Korneyev. But Kutaisov stormed over the telephone, and the chief surrendered.

"Forty barrels. Sign the receipt. Have you got a train?"

There was no train.

Kutaisov promised by telephone that the train would be there immediately. But it did not come.

Every moment Korneyev ran out of the warehouse and looked down the track. The wind almost swept him off his feet. The wind beat his face with sand and earth.

Korneyev's nose twitched nervously. He coughed. Stinging tears stood in his bloodshot eyes. He could not hold them back. They ran down his cheeks, carrying the dirt with them. He licked his chapped lips and tasted their saltiness with his tongue.

Desolate iron blinds of the storm rose and fell clangorously.

The two broken green cars with rusty sides and shaky wooden stepladder, which were the familiar, pathetic station, flashed in and out of the storm. The storm tore the once-red, bleached bit of rag to tatters, shook the stick. The storm swung the bell. The bell rang out frequently and irregularly, beating like an alarum.

But the road in front of the station was deserted. The rails were frightfully and hopelessly clear.

The train came up slowly, overcoming the pressure of the wind with tremendous difficulty. Slobodkin jumped down from the engine while it was still moving.

"What's the matter with you? What's the matter with you?" Korneyev cried. "Why do you procrastinate? Give it here."

"What people! The devil take them!" Slobodkin said.

Outwardly he was quite calm.

"I simply had to tear it out of their throats—the whole train! The dogs!"

Outwardly he was quite calm.

He breathed heavily, with difficulty. His milky-blue shaven head and his brown face were covered with streams of sweat. His spectacles were wet and dirty. One lens was cracked.

"Some splinter broke it, damn it all!"

"Give it here, give it here, give it here!"

The loading brigade rolled the smoking barrels, already splitting in places, out of the warehouse.

The storm quickly changed direction and ran back—from east to west—along the miraculous tracks of its seven-league boots.

Now it blew madly at the tail of the train. It urged the train forward, hurrying the engine. The train rolled as if it were going down hill.

But the smoke torn out of the stack in a whirl was still ahead of the engine. The engine could not catch up with the smoke. Turned inside out, the smoke was pulling the train after it, shrouding the path.

Korneyev and Slobodkin swayed as they sat on a barrel.

Semaphores, sentry boxes, barracks, scaffolding, flickered past them. Horses reared at crossings. Noodles crawled out of a badly fastened thermos box: a hot supper was being carried to some one at the sector.

Men in dark goggles were running about. The sectors right-about-faced, formed companies of sheds, doubled their rows, scattered into a chain, lay down, rose, fell, ran in all directions under the tornado-fire, in the smoke of the storm's gas attack.

Loping along with light, firm, long steps, the elephant flew past in a black cloud with the stake chained to his foot. The stake leapt over piles, over mounds, over stacks of materials.

At the crossing, the elephant stopped as if rooted to the ground. The engine covered him with smoke, steam, whistles, hot metallic soot.

The startled elephant ran to the side into a hole and stumbled onto an excavator.

A Marion 6, wrapped entirely in brown smoke, stood with its drooping arrow and scoop bitten into the ground.

The elephant stood stock-still, up to his knees in the soft clay. His ears stood out, and he lifted his trunk. The excavator clanged its chain and lifted its arrow high. The elephant trumpeted. The excavator whistled.

Thus they stood facing each other with lifted trunks—two elephants, one alive, the other mechanical—and neither would yield the road to the other.

The ears, spread out by the wind, trembled. The wildly gleaming, bloodshot eyes of the living elephant moved madly, like mice.

The train ran past quickly.

"It seems that they have been leading the elephant along this street as a side show," Slobodkin said in his impressive basso through the wind.

And he began to laugh.

Korneyev put his arm around his shoulder:

"Have you written anything good, Slobodkin? What can you show us? Have you written a new poem? When can I read it?"

Slobodkin waved his arm.

"How can I write poems, brother, when I have to swear and argue for two solid hours with that viper in the dispatching department? He doesn't understand any language except the swearing language. And so it goes, every day. And you talk about a poem!"

They became silent.

"And how are things with you, Korneyich?"

"My affairs, brother . . ."

Korneyev pulled the strap of his watch.

"Twenty minutes to nine," he said, and his nose twitched. "We are late. We are late."

He turned away. Stinging tears were in his eyes.

The storm swirled on with inexhaustible power and persistence.

On the crossing near the plant, people and transport crowded. Margulies ran up to the train, clutching his spectacles, clumsily digging the earth with the toes of his boots.

"What's the matter with you, you devils? We've lost twenty minutes because of you! You'll ruin everything!"

Mosya rushed up.

"Give it here! Give it here! Give it here! Gi-v-e it—here! May God curse your mother's soul!"

He was irresponsible. His face was beastly, distorted, flaming, dirty, and out of it blazed white, hot eyes.

Ishchenko jumped up on the still-moving flat car and seized a barrel.

"St-o-o-p!"

The train stopped. But not at once.

Under the pressure of the wind, it went a bit too far and

stopped right opposite the planking, cutting off the gravel from the cement-mixer.

"Ba-a-c-k! B-a-c-k!"

"Stop, stop! Where the devil are you backing?"

They could not back because the armature was piled there. It would be impossible to unload.

"Uncouple the train!" Ishchenko cried. "Uncouple!"

It was the only way out—uncouple the train, take it apart, and while the cement was being unloaded, roll gravel in the opening between two flat cars.

Korneyev jumped down to the ground.

"How many, David?"

"Two hundred ninety-two. That's what a mere planking has done."

"I told you so. Too bad for Kharkov, too bad . . ."

"Where the devil have you been? I've missed my dinner because of you. Well, it doesn't matter."

Korneyev angrily tugged at his nose.

"Two hours solid . . . Do you understand, David? For two solid hours I argued with that idiot at the warehouse. He didn't want to give in. He was bull-headed. You couldn't budge him. People are trash!"

"Yes . . ."

Margulies examined his boots thoroughly.

"Did she go away?" he asked, gently taking Korneyev by the arm.

Korneyev looked absent-mindedly into the distance.

"Don't worry, she'll be back soon," said Margulies.

Korneyev again looked at his watch.

"How is the gravel?" he asked, knitting his brows.

"Tough."

"Are they getting winded?"

"Yes."

"Well, all right. You go and have your supper, David. You haven't had anything to eat since morning."

"Yes . . . It wouldn't hurt me to have something to eat. They say that for supper to-day there is a remarkable loaf of macaroni and meat."

He narrowed his eyes with delight and, opening his jaw widely, repeated lusciously:

"With meat!"

He suddenly turned around and listened.

Through the din of the wind and the thunder of the storm, his ear caught the weak sound of the machine that had started again, and of the tumbling drum.

"They've started. They've begun!" he cried excitedly. And he immediately noted mentally: two ninety-three.

He walked to the planking.

LIV

TWO hundred ninety-three. Two hundred ninety-four. Two hundred ninety-five.

. . . six . . .

. . . seven . . .

. . . eight . . .

Forty barrels with their tops knocked off were rising in thick clouds of smoke in the wind.

One after the other, the smoking barrows rode up and spilled into the scoop.

A barrow of gravel.

A barrow of cement.

A barrow of sand.

"Scoop!"

The operator moved one lever. The scoop began to rise. He moved another. The water began to pour.

The water retarded the drum. The water poured while the scoop was rising. The water poured while the scoop was spilling into the drum. The water poured while the drum was turning.

Khanumov did not budge from the machine. The storm had

scattered the curious. They had taken shelter in the plant, in the barn, in the office.

But Khanumov did not budge. With tightly clenched teeth, with jaws like boulders, with little, narrow, blue eyes in a very freckled, stubby-nosed face, he waddled around the platform, stuck his nose into everything, touched everything with his hands, scribbled in his little book.

"What are you doing, Khanumov? Spying?" Ishchenko cried gaily, running past Khanumov in the course of his work. "Are you spying on me? Scribble away, scribble away! Copy my plans! They might come in handy."

"Don't worry about me," Khanumov muttered through his teeth. "I can take care of myself."

He was irritated. He was particularly angered by the planking. Why hadn't he been able to think of such a simple thing? It was the planking that had turned the trick. Ishchenko was showing class. Ishchenko was setting a world's record. Khanumov could not consider it with equanimity.

"Don't you worry about me. I can take care of myself," he muttered. "I can take care of myself, you may be sure of that."

There was no doubt that Kharkov was already beaten. Another ten mixtures—about fifteen minutes of work—and it would be the end of Kharkov.

Besides, Ishchenko had still three hours more on his shift. True, the lads were tired. But he could do a lot in three more hours.

Ishchenko was sure of an engine. That was certain. But Khanumov's shift came next, and then Ishchenko would get a good run for his money.

Khanumov had noted one or two things.

In the first place, the gravel. First of all, Khanumov and his lads would clear a good space to the right of the railroad track so that the barrows would not have to be wheeled across the rails. That would lighten the work considerably.

And in the second place, there was a small error in the construction of the cement-mixer. With one movement of his arm, the operator lifted the scoop. With the other, he poured the water. Between the first and the second movements, five seconds elapsed. Thus, the time of each mixture was burdened with five extra seconds because of the water.

And in this work, five extra seconds was no small matter.

Khanumov examined the levers of the machine very carefully. He realised that it was possible to connect both levers very simply with the most ordinary piece of wire. Then the water would start at the same time as the scoop.

Time would be gained.

Khanumov would keep this discovery to himself until the very last moment. And then how he would show off! How he would triumph! Khanumov foretasted this moment with secret delight.

The storm almost swept him off his feet, beat at him, turned him around, flung earth into his eyes. But he was seeing himself in an airplane. He would not budge.

One after the other Ishchenko's barrows were spilling into the scoop.

A barrow of gravel.

A barrow of cement.

A barrow of sand.

"Scoop!"

The clanking of the scoop, the noise of the mixer, the water, and the wet thunder of spilling concrete.

Two hundred ninety-nine. Three hundred. Three hundred one. Three hundred two.

. . . three . . .

. . . four . . .

. . . five . . .

. . . six . . .

"Hur-r-a-h!"

Mosya threw up his cap hysterically. The whirlwind snatched it up and carried it away like a rocket, high into the black sky. Tiny as a sparrow, it soared on the level of the concrete-pouring tower. It was lost in a cloud of dust.

The drum clattered.

Korneyev looked at his watch. Margulies looked over his shoulder.

Nine o'clock, seven minutes. Three hundred six mixtures. Kharkov's total had been attained. The world's record was broken. And there yet remained two hours and fifty-three minutes of work.

Little Triger slumped down on the pile of gravel. The shovel fell from his hand. His palms were covered with blisters and were bleeding.

Smetana sat down on the rail between the two uncoupled flat cars. The barrow stood beside him, its wheel against the ties. Olya Tregubova sat down opposite Smetana. Sweat ran down their faces. Their eyes shone happily. They were silent. They thought they might rest for one minute.

For one minute the work died down.

Margulies ran across the planking into the midst of the lads who had stopped working. They had frozen in the very positions in which the three hundred and seventh mixture had found them. They stood motionless, facing the machine.

"Boys! My dear boys!" Margulies muttered. "Get a move on! Hurry! Don't lower the tempos. We'll all rest afterwards."

Mosya ran up.

"David Lvovich, don't make me swear! Who is responsible for the record? Go and have your supper! Get the hell out of here, and go to the devil!"

Ishchenko stood leaning on the shovel and looking at Khanumov. Khanumov passed by quickly without looking at Ishchenko.

"Get off the engine!" the brigadier shouted at him as he disappeared.

The scoop crawled slowly up.

Shura Soldatova ran across the plant. The cross-winds tore the roll of paper out of her hands. She clutched it to her breast. She ran, tightly knitting her brows that were like yellow ears of wheat. Her roughly cut hair slapped her painfully across the eyes. She shook her head, flinging it back. Again it slapped her. Again she flung it back. Again it slapped her. Shura bit her full rosy lips. She was angry.

Both boys ran after her. One of them carried nails, the other a hammer.

She climbed up on the platform, examined a wall of the plant. Beside the machine was a likely place.

Shura Soldatova jumped up on the barrier. She put the rolled paper against the boards. The wind buffeted her, almost knocked her off her feet.

"Vaska, the nails! Kolya, the hammer!"

She balanced herself with the hammer. The hammer served her as a counter-weight. Carefully and firmly, she nailed the upper edge of the roll to the wall with four nails. She unwound the paper slowly, rolling it down.

The large blue letters of the first line appeared:

THE BRIGADE OF CONCRETE MIXERS

Shura Soldatova nailed the unwound part neatly on each side. The wind blew up the paper but it could not tear it off.

The letters of the second line appeared. They were large green letters:

OF KUZNETSKSTROI

The hammer pounded, and the next, a yellow line, appeared:

TO-DAY ESTABLISHED HITHERTO UNKNOWN
TEMPOS

And further down in huge red letters:

402 MIXTURES IN ONE SHIFT
THUS BEATING KHARKOV'S WORLD RECORD

And below, in tiny brown letters:

SHAME ON YOU, COMRADES, TO SIT IN
THE GALOSH ALL THIS TIME!

The drum crashed.

"Too late!" Ishchenko said through his teeth.

He spat and flung the shovel away. But he picked it up again immediately.

"David Lvovich . . ." Mosya swung his loose arms pathetically. "David Lvovich . . . What has happened? Can't you see that we are too late? I told you so!"

And suddenly, in a voice that was not his own:

"Get off the platform! Anybody who doesn't belong here get away from the front! David Lvovich! Comrade Chief! Who is responsible for the shift? For God's sake, go and have your supper, David Lvovich!"

Margulies repressed a gay, indulgent smile.

"All right, all right!"

He carefully searched his pocket and tossed into his mouth the last piece of candy.

"Lads, my dear lads," he said, lisping. "Get a move on, get a move on! We still have three hours. Don't drift!"

"David Lvovich!"

"I'm going, I'm going."

"Get behind it! Get a move on! Don't stop! No talk! . . . Tempos, tempos!"

Everything moved from its place. Everything started. Little Triger jumped to his feet. With all his might he dug the shovel under the gravel.

"Roll on!"

Olya caught the barrow. The palms of her hands were on fire. She strained, pushed, turned deep red to the roots of her hair, and, with a crash and a clang, rolled the heavily jumping barrow across the rails between the two uncoupled flat cars.

"Next!"

Smetana immediately took her place.

"Come on, load it! Come on, load it! Hurry!"

His face was wet and flaming, like a split watermelon. His eyes shone clearly under their downy, greenish-grey eyelashes.

The storm suddenly changed its direction.

The storm flew again from the east to the west in its own tracks, crashing over the sectors in reverse order, like a tornado-fire. It struck, bore down upon the tail of the uncoupled train. One after the other, the crashing couplings thundered out. Smetana lifted the barrow and rushed it onto the railroad track.

The flat cars rolled.

"Look out!"

The couplings of the uncoupled flat cars struck against each other.

Smetana cried out:

"My hand! My hand!"

His face instantly changed colour. From flaming crimson, it became as white as rice. The barrow had been smashed to bits.

Smetana stood on the railroad track between the two couplings that had been knocked together. The canvas glove dangled from his left arm like a rag. It was rapidly getting wet, turning dark.

Smetana bent over, staggered off the railroad track and sat down on the ground. People were running toward him. With his right hand, he pulled the mitten from his left. He saw his shattered, bloody, yellowish-red wrist, and quivering, began to weep.

The pain did not begin until some time later.

LV

ZAGIROV ran as if he had lost his mind.

He understood nothing. He did not know what road he was running down. He did not recognise the locality, disfigured by the storm.

He ran along the tracks of the storm.

He stumbled over broken fences. He made his way through barbed wire, leaving tatters of his shirt on it. He drank water from the churning lake, choking on it. He drank and drank and drank, until his stomach was heavy to the point of nausea, and still he could not drink enough. He could not quench his immeasurable thirst.

Zagirov climbed up the mountain, sliding on the quartz stones, falling, tearing his face, and crawling again, helping himself with his arms like a monkey. He threw away his boots, ripped to shreds. He walked barefooted. He lurched from side to side.

Between the earth and the sky, black, oblique columns of dust moved ahead of him, chasing each other and collapsing.

They led him on. He comprehended neither what was happening to him nor what was happening around him. Despair and fear urged him on and on, further and further from the Kazak settlement, from Sayenko, from the dark barn and the running blue hemp.

It seemed to him that Sayenko would follow in his footsteps, was following his footsteps, even as he was following in the tracks of the storm.

Remembering nothing, Zagirov ran toward the brigade.

He came to. His memory returned. He looked around and saw that he was walking across some sort of field. There was something familiar here. But such stillness, such heat, such an unbearably strong, clear light!

He recognised his surroundings. This was the sector on the primeval steppe, untouched as yet by planning. It was on the west side of the plant. Here there were still flowers and grass.

The air was fetid, dead. The storm had come to an end.

A huge, low, dry cloud, as black as charcoal, hung motionless over his head. It stretched from horizon to horizon, from the west to the east. In the east it merged with the slaty earth. But in the west it did not reach the earth—the billowy outlines of the Ural range.

Over the western horizon, it broke abruptly. Its wavy edges, bordered in deep mourning, contrasted sharply with the clear sky.

The sun had already touched the horizon, but had not yet lost its steppe-like ferocity and power. It was as blinding and full of rays as at noon, only it was somewhat yellower. Its blinding, horizontal rays beat along the amber-yellow lacquered earth.

The panorama of the construction was drawn in minutest detail on the black horizon lighted by the fireworks of the sunset. From the tiniest mote, shadows stretched across the steppe for scores of metres.

Zagirov walked toward the plant, and ahead of him over the bright earth swayed his gaunt shadow, so huge and long that he seemed to be walking on stilts.

He was approaching the labour front from the west.

Shadows of people and wheels moved across the entire height of the eight-story walls of the plant.

Shura Soldatova led Smetana to a woven cart. Lanky and solicitous, she supported him carefully by his shoulder.

He walked in his wet shirt, his round white head drooping, squinting against the sun, weeping and biting his lips. He limped, and supported his left arm with his right. His left arm was large and bandaged like a clapper. He carried it carefully, pressing it to his chest as if it were a child. Across Shura Soldatova's shoulder hung a first-aid bag with a red cross.

They met.

Smetana lifted his head and looked at Zagirov. Neither surprise nor anger were reflected in his broad, pale face.

"Did you see? Here . . ."

He indicated his arm with his eyes. A piteous smile twisted his ashen lips.

"Here . . . See? . . . There was a hand . . ."

"Does it hurt?" Zagirov asked.

Smetana clenched his teeth and shook his head.

The shadows of the giants ran back and forth along the wall of the plant.

Shura Soldatova patiently flung the hair off her forehead.

"Go."

Zagirov walked up to the planking. Mosya was running with a barrow. Zagirov was surprised. This was a violation of the order. Usually the foreman never worked himself. He only supervised the work. But now he was working.

Little Triger was ferociously loading Olya Tregubova's barrow.

"Move on! Move on! Tempos! Tempos!" Ishchenko was crying.

His shock of hair, wet until it was black, crawled into his eyes. The brigadier did not have the time to push it away.

People ran to the labour front from all sides.

The drum turned over with a crash.

"Three hundred twenty-nine, three hundred thirty, three hundred thirty-one . . ." the crowd whispered.

The figures passed from man to man.

Khanumov stood beside the machine, his small intent eyes constantly on the operator.

"Come on, come on!" he muttered, twisting and breaking a splinter in his hand.

At times he forgot that it was not his brigade but some one else's.

Korneyev ran by in spotted shoes. On the run, he tugged at the strap of his watch.

"Thirty-two minutes past nine! Boys, boys, boys! . . ."

Brief spasms twisted his face. His nose twitched. He coughed, clutched at his empty cigarette case.

Zagirov came still closer. He looked around him indecisively. All about him was a multitude of eyes, but everybody looked past him. He edged his way to the crossing.

With glazed eyes, Triger was plunging his shovel time and again into the gravel.

"Roll on! Next!"

Zagirov hesitated for some time in silence. Then he pulled up his trousers in his customary manner, spat, and said:

"Let's go."

Triger looked at him over his shoulder and flung back his head.

"Over . . . there . . ." he said, choking. "Shovel . . . the other one . . ."

Zagirov lifted the shovel from the ground, spat on the palms of his hands, and took his place beside Triger.

He looked irresolutely at Mosya. Mosya turned away. He

looked at Ishchenko. Ishchenko looked past him into the distance. Zagirov grunted and thrust the shovel under the gravel.

"Next!"

LVI

FOMA YEGOROVICH wiped his russet Poltavian moustaches with his large white handkerchief bordered in colours. He hid the kerchief in the breast pocket of his blue jumper.

He had just finished a good supper, had washed his face with soap and had combed his hair. For supper he had had a very palatable loaf of macaroni and meat. Now he could rest.

He was slowly walking home to the hotel. There he would smoke and read. He was putting off this happy moment.

"Well, how are our affairs, Comrade Edison?" Foma Yegorovich asked, passing Margulies. "Did you put it over on Kharkov?"

Margulies silently nodded toward the poster.

" 'The brigade of concrete mixers,' " Foma Yegorovich read aloud unhurriedly and with pleasure, " 'of Kuznetskstroi to-day established hitherto unknown tempos. 402 mixtures in one shift, thus beating Kharkov's world record. Shame on you, comrades, to sit in the galosh all this time!' "

He began to laugh gaily.

"Good!" he exclaimed, his hard bright eyes gleaming. "Bravo! Bis! They got there first. Now they must be well beaten, so they won't be too proud. Beat them!"

He took Margulies by the arm.

"I waited for you in the dining room for dinner. You did not come. I waited for you for supper. The same thing. Evidently, Comrade Edison, you can go without eating for a whole week, like a camel. Come with me. I will show you a very interesting American magazine, the latest issue."

A new portion of concrete crashed.

"Three forty-two," Margulies said automatically.

He stopped and began to listen. He wanted to determine by

sound the length of a mixture. He counted slowly under his breath:

"One, two, three, four, five, six . . ."

"Come on, Comrade Margulies. You cannot work for twenty-four hours without resting. They'll beat Kuznetsk without you, you may be sure of that. I can see that they're already working like little demons. Let's go. There's a time for business, and there's a time for play, as they say. I have a little bottle of cognac for you."

Margulies did not hear.

"Seven, eight, nine, ten, eleven . . ."

Now, in order to beat Kuznetsk, they had to make each mixture in not less than one minute and ten seconds.

Foma Yegorovich put his hand to his eyes and watched the brigade. Before he knew it, he was delighting in the rhythm and precision of the work. One after the other, at equal intervals, the large-wheeled sterlings rolled, barrows rushed past each other, shovels flew up, cement smoked.

And all this fresh, strong, youthful movement on an incredibly large scale was projected on the gigantic wall of the plant as on a golden screen.

It was a splendid Chinese theatre of shadows.

The shadows of giants moved on the screen of the plant, split and broken by the unevennesses of its boards and the hollows of windows. Gigantic coolies rolled their rickshaws, one by one. The turning wheels were as high as a five-story house.

The shadows of the wheels flashed with the close-spaced spokes of a Chinese umbrella. One wheel rolled against the next. The wheels merged and parted. In the fresh, strong rhythm, the spokes crossed and recrossed each other.

Margulies counted slowly to seventy. The drum did not turn over.

He counted to eighty. There was no noise of the spilling concrete.

He counted to eighty-five.

Stop!

The machine had stopped!

"Water!" some one cried in a voice that broke.

"Excuse me, Foma Yegorovich. One minute."

Margulies ran to the machine.

"What's the matter?"

"Water!" the operator cried hoarsely. "Water!"

Foma Yegorovich went to one side, sat down on the boards and pulled the magazine out of his pocket. He slowly unrolled the thick, heavy folio of glossy, chalk-white paper, which had been rolled into a cylinder, and spread it on his knee.

Advertisements took up three-quarters of the magazine. Foma Yegorovich's favourite occupation was to read and examine these advertisements. Slowly, pleasantly, he sank, page by page, into the luxurious world of ideal things, materials, and products. Here was everything that was necessary for full and complete satisfaction of man's needs, wishes, and passions.

The muse of distant travel offered round-the-world tours. It showed trans-Atlantic steamers crossing oceans. Delicate smoke rose from four shining stacks. An immobile wave stood sharply along the immeasurably high bow, with the turned-out eye of its anchor hatchway. Luxurious cabins tempted one with the cleanliness of their luxuriant beds, with the comforts of fireplaces and leather armchairs.

And, as a matter of fact, all of it was not so expensive. It was available, evident, tangible, possible, desirable.

Camel cigarettes poured out of a yellow package. Their thick oval segments revealed tufts of ideal, golden tobacco which spoke of the sweetness of dates and the aroma of honey.

Elegant wrist watches and the latest cigarette lighters. Stylish furniture. Bronzes. Pictures. Rugs. Gobelins. The most fragile Copenhagen china. Toys. Economical gas ranges. Books. Shoes. Suits. Neckties. Fine cloth. Flowers. Dogs. Cottages. Perfume. Extracts. Fruit. Medicine. Automobiles.

Foma Yegorovich looked at these objects with delight, found pleasure in them, or criticised them indulgently. Any of them, separately, were available to him. But he wanted them all to belong to him, at once.

Eighteen thousand dollars! This world of things was almost in his hands. In one year, twenty thousand! And in ten years, two hundred thousand!

Then all the things would belong to him. With the exception, of course, of the most expensive ones. But why would he need a motor yacht?

He loved to select automobiles, to compare makes and models. He knew all their attributes and defects.

But the sweetest, the most precious to him, was on the last page.

A perfected, patented refrigerator!

It was a coloured drawing, an entire picture covering a whole page. A small, elegant cupboard stood on porcelain legs. The cupboard was open. And inside of it, on its shelves, in strict order, food was spread out. Rosy ham, firm and luxuriant vegetables, a loaf of bread, canned goods, lard, cream, pickles, eggs, a pullet, jam; and all this was of ideal freshness, and in the most delicate and natural colours.

And bending over this cupboard, stood a dazzling woman. She was a young, pink-cheeked, blue-eyed, honey-haired, pleasant, gay Maggie. She smiled joyously. Her little, cherry-red mouth was open, like a jewel-case containing a necklace of tiny pearls. She looked at Foma Yegorovich as if to say: "Come, kiss your pretty little sweetheart. Come on."

And convenient Lares and Penates were scattered around her like bouquets—forms for jelly, copper pots, irons, fire tongs, meat-cutters.

Foma Yegorovich looked at her and forgot his middle-aged wife, his unbeautiful children, his life, full of deprivations and difficulties, his harsh life of a tramp in foreign lands.

The sun set.

A cloud, black as charcoal, moved toward the east. The sky cleared. The sunset flared like fireworks. Its hot, glassy, raspberry flame illuminated the glassy pages of the magazine.

A black pool of mud which had almost dried up and was split into squares, like a highly polished strap, gleamed brightly at the feet of the American.

LVII

MARGULIES ran to the machine.
"Why the stop?"
"Water!"
"What's the matter?"
"No water!"
Every second was accounted for. The world's record depended on every second. The world's record hung by a hair.
"Oh, we'll never make it!"
Work stopped. The men froze in the poses in which the interruption had found them. They rested.
Kutaisov was shouting into the telephone:
"Hello! Water system! The chief of the repair staff of the 'Komsomolskaya Pravda' speaking. Why is there no water at the sixth sector? What? You say there *is* water? You did not shut it off? Dear comrade, how can you say that there is water when there is no water? What? But I tell you that there is none! But who *does* know? Excuse me, who is speaking? What is your name? Well, now, Nikolayev, remember that you will be personally responsible for what you say. So you maintain that there *is* water? Good!"
Scuffing his shoes, Korneyev was crawling over the boards into the plant. There, on the opposite side, worked another concrete-mixer of the sixth sector—the large stationary Ransome.
The enormous space, breached and cleft in all directions by red whirling beams of the sunset, gleamed with the moving shadows of men and wheels.
With the dull rustling sound of a whetstone, the large drum was turning slowly.

Korneyev put his hands to his lips as a speaking trumpet.

"Hey! You there! On the Ransome! Have you any water?"

He turned sideways and placed his hand to his ear.

"Going! Go-in-ng!"

The words flew, slow and echoing, from man to man, across the enormous space of the plant.

"O-o-ing . . . o-o-ing . . . o-o-ing . . ." the echo moaned through the eight-story building. The echo was counting the steel beams.

"Going!"

Korneyev rushed back.

"The water is going on the Ransome. The water system is in order."

Margulies walked around the machine.

"Going?"

"No."

"What is the matter?"

The operator jerked the lever back and forth. There was no water.

Ishchenko, Mosya, Nefedov, Triger, ran up.

"What's the matter? What has happened?"

"Is there a break in the water system?"

"No."

"Did something break?"

"No."

Margulies threw off his coat and rolled up his sleeves. He ran up on the platform, climbed upon the mount, and buried his head in the water tank.

He examined it attentively for a long time. He pounded the water gauge with his fist. He took a wrench out of his boot top. Straining frightful oaths through his teeth, he loosened and tightened nuts, touched bolts, knocked against the riveting, applied his ear to the walls. Everything was in perfect order.

He ran down from the platform and put on his coat without brushing the dust from it. He craned his neck.

"How did it happen?"

The operator shrugged his shoulders and spat loudly.

"It didn't happen at all. Simply, the water was going and suddenly it stopped—as if somebody had chopped it off. Plup—and no water!"

He took hold of the lever and began to jerk it with stupid stubbornness, forward and back, forward and back.

"David Lvovich," Mosya said piteously. "What do you say to such a thing? Just as if on purpose! Just as if to be mean!"

He dashed his fist against the post of the platform.

Khanumov was cracking his steely fingers, crushing the splinters into fine pieces, and throwing them under his feet furiously.

Margulies firmly knitted his thick brows, and, pushing people aside with his elbows, ran, stumbling, into the plant.

"What are they doing there?" he muttered. "What are they doing there? This famous repair staff! They took the responsibility for the water system, and now there is no water, and there's no one on the job! Who is in charge of it? Is it Semechkin? Where is this Semechkin?"

He stopped and cried out in a thunderous voice:

"Semechkin! Where is Semechkin? Who has seen Semechkin? Semechkin!"

He ran to the other side.

"Well, what's the matter? Why all this panic?" came the thick, disapproving little basso of Semechkin.

Margulies stopped. Semechkin's voice was coming from somewhere under the floor. Margulies looked down.

The floor of the plant had been taken apart here. A square hole yawned. Out of it, as if out of a theatre trap, slowly rose the figure of Semechkin in dark goggles, with his canvas brief case under his arm, taking his time and breathing heavily. His nose was spotted with red lead.

"What's the matter?"

"Are you—on the water system?"

"I am."

"Water!"

Semechkin crawled out of the trap, neatly brushed his leggings and knees, and, coughing importantly, said:

"Everything is in order. It's all done."

"What?"

"They are already putting it in. I have arranged for everything."

"Putting in? What are they putting in?"

"The metre."

"What metre?"

Semechkin clapped Margulies on the shoulder in a jaunty and somewhat patronising manner.

"Ekh, you! Industrialists! You are breaking world's records and you forget cost accounting. Well, it's all right, Boss. Don't worry. I have arranged for everything."

Margulies looked at him with narrowing eyes that did not waver. His face was as firm and hard as a rock.

"What did you arrange?" he asked slowly, emphasising each word. "What did you arrange?"

Semechkin shrugged his shoulders carelessly.

"I arranged to have the metre put in. In an hour and a half, it will be working. How else can you maintain cost accounting?"

"Was it you who ordered the pipes to be disconnected and the water shut off?"

Margulies was terrifying.

"Well, suppose? We have to audit with the ruble," Semechkin remarked in an authoritative little basso.

"Immediately . . . do you hear? . . . immediately . . ."

Margulies was choking.

"Immediately connect the pipes and give us water!" he cried piercingly, screaming.

Semechkin turned pale. His lips trembled.

"Under no circumstances. I am responsible for the water system."

"Fool!" Margulies thundered out. "Dummy! Idiot! Immediately! I order it immediately!"

"I would ask you, Comrade Margulies, not to express yourself like this."

Semechkin's little knees were bobbing up and down.

Margulies seized the end board and jumped down into the trap. A five-candle-power reflector lamp was burning there. Two water-system men were sitting on the ground and eating their supper of canned fish, which stood on a piece of newspaper. "Sturgeon in Tomato Sauce" Margulies read on the box. On the label was a pug-nosed sturgeon riding a bicycle. Madness possessed him.

The water pipe was unscrewed. One end of it was closed with a wooden plug. The thread of the other was covered thickly with red lead. A large metre lay on a pile of waste. Pieces of water pipes and tools were scattered everywhere.

"Connect it immediately!" Margulies said through his teeth.

Semechkin's dark goggles flashed from above.

"Put in the metre! Put in the metre first!"

"Immediately!"

"Don't screw it together!"

"I order you to screw it together!"

"I order you not to screw it together! I am in charge of the repair staff! I am responsible!"

"Screw it together immediately and give us water!"

Margulies caught the end board, pulled himself up with his muscles, swung out and sprang out of the trap. He moved menacingly upon Semechkin.

"Shut up!" Margulies cried out. "You moron!"

"I would ask you . . ."

"What? Wh-a-a-a-t?"

Margulies pulled a whistle out of his pocket. With trembling hands, he shoved it convulsively into his mouth. A long, piercing canary-bird trill passed through the plant.

"Hey! You there! The guard!"

A rifleman ran up, the butt of his rifle clattering against the boards.

"Do you know me, Comrade?" Margulies asked calmly.

"Yes, sir. You are the chief of the sixth sector."

"Correct."

Margulies nodded his head at Semechkin.

"Take him."

"This one?"

"That's the one."

The rifleman took Semechkin by the arm.

"Where shall I take him?"

"Put him in the fire-barn."

The rifleman regarded Semechkin with curiosity and a certain amount of compassion: the multitude of badges on the lapel of his coat, his socks, which were pinned to his riding breeches with large safety pins, the laces on his shoes, the terrible dark goggles, the red Adam's apple.

"Let's go, Comrade."

"You have no right!" Semechkin cried out, turning red. "I will not go anywhere. I am in charge of the repair staff. You will answer for this. I will write to the regional press!"

He tried to pull himself out of the rifleman's grasp, but the rifleman held him firmly. The dark goggles fell off his nose. Under the terrible goggles appeared small, blue, scrofulous eyes. They darted back and forth in fright.

"I go under compulsion!"

"Come on, come on, little fellow."

"Let him out in two hours," Margulies remarked over his shoulder.

He walked up to the trap, bent down and said calmly:

"Screw it together."

Margulies ran back to the machine.

The glowing track of the sunset was dimming slowly, yielding to the dove-coloured and lilac shadow of the distant Ural range.

"Water!"

With a clang the scoop started. The drum spilled.

Three hundred forty-three, Margulies noted in his mind.

"What time is it?"

Korneyev looked at his watch.

"Three minutes past ten."

"How long did we stop?"

"Twelve minutes. We still have one hour and fifty-seven minutes."

"We won't make it."

Margulies rushed to the middle of the planking.

"Boys!" he cried. "Lads! Get behind it! Push on it! Don't fail!"

Everything started from its place.

About the sector, low on the ground and high in the bright air, pale watery stars of thousand-candle-power lamps were lighted, one by one.

"Oh, they won't make it! They won't make it!"

Khanumov could not stay in one place. He kept walking back and forth along the length of the planking, throwing short glances at the operator. Suddenly he turned abruptly and ran up to Ishchenko.

"Ekh!"

He caught Ishchenko by the shirt.

"Listen, Kostya! The devil take you! . . . The two levers . . . one lifts the scoop, the other lets in the water. The difference is five to seven seconds. Connect them with a wire. It will give you the scoop and the water at once and you will gain ten seconds for each mixture. Ekh! I kept it for myself, but it's all right! Use it! Drink my blood! I'll lick you anyway, without it! My lads are better than yours!"

He turned sharply away and quickly walked past him, taking off and putting on his *tyubeteika* as he walked along.

Ishchenko stopped and knitted his brows. In an instant, he understood. Correct! Two levers—into one lever.

He ran to the planking.

"Machine repair! Who is on machine repair? Morozov, connect the two levers with a wire!"

"Gravel! Gravel!" Mosya cried, beside himself. "The gravel is coming to an end!"

Jerking, with short puffs of steam, the engine was coming up slowly. Vinkich and Georgi Vasilyevich jumped down from the first flat car. The hooks thundered out. The boards fell down.

"Here's the gravel!"

Georgi Vasilyevich was covered from head to foot with a white powder of rock-dust. His bedroom slippers, torn to tatters, presented a comic and pathetic appearance. Dirty sweat streamed down his face. In his head was the hellish noise of rock-crushers and the clanking of sieves. Before his eyes flashed the belt that ran smoothly from the huge, slow master-wheel to the small, frightfully quick crushers.

The distance between the master-wheel and the crushers was so great that the metre-wide transmission belt flying along the dizzying heights of the rock-crusher seemed to be no wider than a tape. And the rock-crushing machine itself stood like a gigantic coffee mill, and pale, fine sparks poured out of the smashed, chewed-up boulders.

"This is some day!" said Georgi Vasilyevich, puffing heavily and sitting down on the ground. "And some people!"

Korneyev ran by.

"Do you understand?" he said to Korneyev, his round excited eyes shining. "We prove to them—like two and two are four—that the gravel is indispensable. And they tell us that they have no right to exceed the norms! So we tell them if that's the case—the devil take you—then raise the norms! But they refer us to the plant management. We point out to them, quite reasonably, the necessity of maximum increase. And they, if you care to know . . ."

Korneyev looked around with eyes that comprehended nothing, pulled at his nose, looked into his empty cigarette case, and, saying, "Excuse me," ran on.

Kutaisov, straining his voice, shouted into the telephone:

"What? I don't hear you. You haven't any, either? But try to understand, my dear friend, that we must have twenty application blanks. Why, yes! Simple, ordinary, printed application blanks for entering the Komsomol. Yes. Ishchenko's entire brigade. What? I rang up the city committee. There are none in the city committee. The bureau? I rang up the bureau and there're none at the bureau. Well, at least fifteen. You haven't any? Ah, the jester take you altogether! I don't know what you have, in that case. What? I don't care if you used them all up! Print some new ones! You wait. We'll rake you over the coals . . . What? No, my friend. Whatever you do, please don't try to frighten me. I am not a little fellow. Please. If you like, complain to the Politbureau . . . Good-bye . . . Even to the Politbureau . . . Anywhere you like. Good-bye."

He hung up the receiver.

"Slobodkin!"

LVIII

IT was forty-five minutes past eleven.

Margulies was counting the mixtures under his breath:

"Three hundred eighty-eight . . . three hundred eighty-nine . . . three hundred ninety . . ."

The crowd was pushing toward the planking. The crowd was noisy. The crowd was counting the mixtures aloud:

"Three hundred ninety, three hundred ninety-one, three hundred ninety-two . . ."

". . . three . . ."

". . . four . . ."

". . . five . . ."

Sheaves of light beat down from the projectors on the roof of the plant. The projectors were placed in groups. There were six in each group—six blinding glass buttons sewed in two rows to each shield.

Figures with barrows ran in all directions over the brightly illuminated planking. Each figure emanated a multitude of short, radial shadows. The irregular stars of the shadows intersected, crossed each other, merged and parted in the distinct, hot, youthful rhythm.

The rhythm was calculated with precision to one second, and the brigade worked like a clock.

A barrow of gravel.

A barrow of cement.

A barrow of sand.

"Scoop and water!"

One turn of the lever. Now the scoop and the water fell simultaneously with one motion of the arm.

"They won't make it!"

"They will make it!"

The crash of pouring concrete.

"Three hundred ninety-six . . ."

"Three hundred ninety-seven . . ."

". . . eight . . ."

". . . nine . . ."

"Time?"

Korneyev held the watch in front of his eyes. The projectors beat into them. Korneyev shut off the light with the palm of his hand. He nervously pulled his nose, coughed. In his eyes were burning tears.

"Two minutes to zero hour."

"They'll make it!"

"They won't make it!"

In the darkness Nalbandov was walking toward the labour front. On all sides were the low, bright stars of lights. They interfered with his vision. He stumbled over stacks of lumber, over wire. He tripped, explored ahead of him with his cane.

Before him was light . . . and the dark mass of the crowd.

Fame! Was this fame? Yes, this was fame!

Nalbandov separated the crowd with his cane. He pushed into the crowd with a swinging shoulder.

The drum crashed.

"Four hundred!"

There was a dead silence in the crowd. The barrows rolled with a sinuous screech. The motor whined. Blue sparks flew out of the motor. With a clang and a screech, the scoop crawled up.

The drum crashed.

"Four hundred and one . . ."

"Zero hour," said Korneyev in a low voice.

But everybody heard his voice.

"They did not make it!"

"They missed it by one!"

"Ekh!"

Silence—and the weak noise of the smoothly stopping drum.

And in this silence the distant but clear voice of a horn suddenly resounded.

A French horn jerkily pronounced the introductory phrase of the march, shining and twisted like a snail, a happy phrase in the brass language of youth and fame. After it the entire orchestra struck up. The orchestra thundered out with the holiday puffing of tubas, the round, dull tom-tom of bass drums, the clash of cymbals, the cries of bassoons.

It was Khanumov leading his brigade.

It came nearer and nearer. It passed from lamp post to lamp post, from projector to projector. Now it appeared in the light, now it disappeared in the darkness.

It lost itself in the black chaos of turned-up earth, loaded with materials. It passed from plain to plain. It suddenly appeared in its full height on the range of a new mound which was encompassed by sheaves of light from below—from unseen projectors placed on the bottom of the excavation.

The horns of the orchestra gleamed. And Khanumov's golden *tyubeteika* gleamed as he carried the outspread banner on his shoulder. He was leading his brigade from the rear to the front.

"They did not make it!"

Ishchenko placed the shovel slowly on his shoulder. The projectors beat into his eyes from all sides. He sheltered his eyes with the palm of his hand. He turned to all sides. But everywhere were—faces, faces . . . He sheltered himself from the faces, from the eyes.

Slowly, his head drooping, he walked across the planking, his heavy shoulders bent forward, and moving his small, tenacious, bare feet mincingly. Behind him across the planking slowly walked the lads.

The machine stopped.

Mosya sat in the middle of the planking, his feet under him Turkish fashion, and his head on his knees. His arms were spread out.

Behind the machine, in the plant, the last sample cube of concrete was being poured into the wooden form for testing its durability. Here were the representatives of the laboratory, of the plant office, correspondents, engineers, technicians. By the light of the projectors, set on the floor like military helmets, they were signing the official documents with indelible pencil.

Ten samples of concrete—ten wooden boxes—carefully numbered and sealed, were being sent to the central laboratory for expert testing. In exactly seven days the hardened cubes of concrete would be tested. Only then would the quality be determined, and not until then.

The concrete would have to stand the pressure of a hundred kilograms per square centimetre. If it would not stand it and would crack, then all this work was for nothing. It would then be necessary to break up the flagstone and to pour it over again.

Margulies's fate depended on the quality of the concrete. Margulies was sure of it. The proofs were in his pocket. Nevertheless, he was excited. He was strained. Tables and formulas flashed mechanically through his mind. Feverishly he was turning over all of his knowledge, all of his experience. Pages and pages flashed and flashed.

Everything seemed to be in order. But—suddenly . . . Who knew? . . . Perhaps the cement was of bad quality, or the water had been apportioned incorrectly.

Margulies took a stub of indelible pencil and signed the document with a flourish.

Nalbandov was in charge of dispatching the cubes. He counted the boxes unceremoniously with his cane and gave the order.

The sounds of the orchestra reached his ears. He squinted and smiled sarcastically. He shrugged his shoulders.

"I see that you are not working here, but having a holiday. A carnival at Nice. Very interesting."

Margulies peered attentively into his face, yellow and illuminated from below as if it were a bit of sculpture, black-bearded,
full of sharp lights and shadows. Margulies wanted to say something, but at that moment he noticed a strange silence.

The motor was silent.

"What has happened? Excuse me . . ."

He ran to the machine.

Korneyev was leaning against the post, his face turned up,
talking with the operator. The operator was wiping his hands
with waste. The time-keeper was putting the papers together and
counting them.

"What's the matter? Why aren't you working?"

"New shift. This is the end. One mixture short. Four hundred
and one."

Margulies took off his glasses and rubbed his forehead with
the palm of his hand. He rubbed spots of concrete all over his
face.

"Wait . . . I don't understand . . . What time is it?"

"One minute past twelve."

Margulies quickly put on his glasses.

"But when did we begin?"

"Sixteen eight."

"Then what are you doing!!! Stop!!! What are you
doing!!!"

At break-neck speed, Margulies ran to the planking.

"Stop! Who told you to finish? Back to your places!"

The brigade stood stock-still.

"Motor!" Margulies cried, beside himself. "Moto-r-r-r!!! You
began at sixteen eight. Stoppage because of the cement warehouse—ten. Because of Semechkin's fault—eight. Smetana's accident—seven. Altogether—thirty-three minutes. We have thirty-
three minutes more!"

Ishchenko stood rooted to the ground. Mosya jumped to his
feet.

"Stop, stop! Motor! Back!"

"Turn back!" Ishchenko cried. "Come on, boys, turn back!

Listen to me! Back to your barrows! To your shovels! To your sterlings!"

His voice rose higher and higher until it reached the vibrating heights of a cavalry command:

"To your pla-a-a-c-c-e-e-s!"

"Ready! Begin!" Mosya cried, throwing the remnants of his voice into it. "Go! Go-o-o-o!"

Everything moved from its place, ran, mixed, went, struck out, flashed . . .

A barrow of gravel.

A barrow of cement.

A barrow of sand.

"Scoop and water!"

The drum spilled.

"Four hundred two . . . four hundred three . . . four hundred four."

"Too bad for Kuznetsk! They're way behind!"

Mosya flung down the barrow half-way. He ran to the machine, flew up to the barrier of the planking like a demon.

He tore down the poster. He tore it into tatters, and flung them into the air. Illuminated by the projectors, they fluttered and whirled.

He flew like a dart back to the barrow.

"Hur-r-ra-a-ah!"

"Boys, boys, boys . . ."

The crowd counted in chorus:

"Four hundred five, four hundred six . . ."

The magnesium flared up. The shutters of the reflectors clicked.

". . . seven . . ."

". . . eight . . ."

". . . nine . . ."

Margulies examined himself on all sides by the light of the projectors. He examined his knees, his elbows. He brushed off the dust. He twisted around and tried to see his back—to see whether it was soiled. He spat on his handkerchief and stealthily wiped his face. He polished the lenses of his spectacles. He cleaned his boots, wiping one against the other, stamped his feet, adjusted his cap.

Smiling subtly to himself, and looking no longer at the brigade, he unhurriedly walked to the superintendent's office.

There sat Nalbandov. He sat on a low plank bench, his fat back and the nape of his neck leaning against the plank wall. The ends of his black coat lay on the floor. He was playing indifferently with his cane.

The office was crowded, smoky, noisy. The tables were covered with yellow, bleached newspapers. The newspapers were covered with rusty, purplish spots of ink, scrawls and pencil marks. The tables were piled with account books, notices, documents, demands, orders, draughts.

Crouched on the floor, Shura Soldatova was pasting the wall newspaper "Za Tempy." Her hair fell across her eyes. She flung it back. She modestly pulled her tatterdemalion black skirt over her dirty, shiny, pink knees.

The clerks were clicking on the abacus, smoking, drinking cups of cold tea that had a strong drug-store taste of chlorinated water.

Kutaisov was swearing over the telephone.

Georgi Vasilyevich sat on a shaky stool that was too low for him, his elbows spread wide apart. On one corner of the table, he was writing an article in pencil. Leaning over his back, Vinkich was peering at the paper, running his fingers through his hair, hurrying him:

"Go on, go on, Georgi Vasilyevich! This is fine. Ah! That's what it means to be a real writer. And here you were pretending that you did not know how to write articles, that you were technically unprepared! And yet you understand these matters no worse than any superintendent!"

Vinkich was flattering him shamelessly, but he needed the signature of Georgi Vasilyevich. He needed a powerful name.

There would be a battle, and they would fight until blood flowed. He had already selected his weapon.

"Right, Georgi Vasilyevich! Right!"

Georgi Vasilyevich knew that Vinkich exaggerated his qualifications, but still he was very pleased.

"Well now, we'll remember the old days when I used to write for newspapers," he grunted. "Well now, well now, perhaps the old mare will not spoil the furrow."

His round eyes shone good-naturedly. He was in full swing. The pencil was running over the page. Vinkich was reading in a whisper:

" 'Recently we have noted two opposing currents of thought in the field of tempos for preparing concrete . . .' Very good, quite right. '. . . and in regard to the utilisation of concrete-mixers. On the one hand, several constructions were steadily increasing the number of mixtures. On the other hand, responsible engineers of certain of the largest constructions categorically opposed the increase of the number of mixtures, basing their opposition on the fact that such an increase in the quantity of mixtures might have a negative effect on the amortisation of expensive imported equipment.' Very good."

Vinkich glanced quickly at Nalbandov, and purposely raising his voice, said:

"Georgi Vasilyevich, in front of the word 'negatively,' place the word 'presumably.' "

He emphasised "presumably."

"Presumably negatively. Write presumably negatively. That's stronger."

"We'll make it presumably. If you like, we'll make it presumably. 'Presumably negatively . . .' Well, now . . ."

Nalbandov was deaf. He refused to hear. Amortisation and quality, he thought to himself. His glance glided carelessly over the room. Everywhere—newspapers, newspapers, newspapers . . . Newspapers spotted with portraits of heroes. Ribbons of heads. Columns of heads. Stairways of heads. Heads, heads, heads.

Loaders, concrete mixers, armature men, muckers, scaffolding men, carpenters, rigging men, chemists, draughtsmen . . . Old, young, middle-aged. Caps, *kubankas,* hats, visored caps, *tyubetei-kas* . . . Names, names, names.

Fame! Was this fame?

Yes, this was fame! This was real fame. It was precisely thus that fame was made. Fame was made "here," but it might be cashed in on—"there."

He glanced sideways at Shura Soldatova. Crouched on all fours and moving her tongue in a childish way, she was pasting a photograph of Margulies on the page of the wall newspaper.

Yes, this is fame, he thought, and I am foolishly letting it go by me. One must make a name for himself, a name, a name.

The name must be printed in newspapers. It must be mentioned in reports. It must be argued about, repeated in meetings and disputes.

It was so simple! All that was necessary to attain it was the technical level of the time. Suppose that level was low, elementary? Suppose it was a thousand times lower than the level of Europe and America, although it seemed higher?

The epoch demanded adventurism. And so, one must be an adventurist. The epoch did not spare those who fell behind or disagreed.

Yes, this was fame.

And to-day he let an opportune occasion slip past him.

What could be simpler?

One must be on the level of his time, take the business of record-setting in his own hands, organise it, move it, advertise it, be the first . . .

He had committed a tactical error, but it was not yet too late. There would be a thousand such opportunities ahead of him.

LIX

". . . four hundred twenty-nine . . ."

Korneyev did not take his eyes off the second hand.

"Zero hour. Thirty-three minutes. Enough. Finish."

Ishchenko carefully put down the barrow and wiped his face with the tail of his shirt.

"That will do. Stop the motor."

He lazily waved his tired arm at the operator.

The drum stopped smoothly.

The crowd shouted, "Hurrah!"

Without looking to either side, Ishchenko unhurriedly walked off the planking. The crowd made way for him.

Before him stood Khanumov.

In his golden, brightly gleaming *tyubeteika,* in russet leggings, red-headed, snub-nosed, with a face pock-marked as if by hail, he stood firmly with his weight on one foot, and leaning carelessly with his lifted arm against the pole of the unfurled banner.

Ishchenko dropped his eyes and smiled.

Khanumov also smiled, but immediately frowned.

"Well, Kostya . . ."

His voice sounded friendly, solemn, but at the same time portentous. He stopped. He sought but could not find suitable words. He stood there for some time in silence, and then stretched forth his arms to Ishchenko.

They embraced and kissed each other clumsily three times, covered by the cloth of the banner.

Three times Ishchenko felt on his lips the hard, harsh cheek of Khanumov, as rough as a board.

"Well, Kostya. . . . To-day you have attained great fame. A great victory. A world's record is nothing to sneeze at . . . In a word, good health to you! Accept my congratulations. You are the first on the entire construction. To-day you are the first. Four hundred twenty-nine mixtures as if it were one kopeck! A fine fellow you are, a good brigadier. You showed up Kharkov. You showed up Kuznetsk. In one shift you showed them all up. Very good indicators. Very good brigadier . . . for this snip of time."

Khanumov swallowed hard.

"You made four hundred twenty-nine mixtures," he suddenly cried out. "And against you, we propose a counter-plan of five hundred! Five hundred and not one less! If we do less than five hundred, we won't leave the place! We'll drop dead!"

He turned to his brigade.

"Is that right, boys?"

"Right! Five hundred! Five hundred fifty! We won't leave the spot!" the lads cried.

"Did you hear that, Ishchenko? Did you hear my lads? Make a note of it. Five hundred! Don't celebrate yet!"

"Don't count your chickens . . ." Ishchenko said darkly.

Khanumov examined him carefully from head to foot, but did not honour him with another word.

With dignity he walked to the side, stuck the banner into a pile of gravel, returned to his former place, and turned to the brigade:

"Comrades! Listen to my command. Every man to his place! To the barrows! To the shovels! To the ster-r-li-i-ings!"

His voice attained the vibrating heights of an inimitable cavalry command.

"Begin!"

Khanumov's brigade rushed to the planking.

Mosya entered the superintendent's office.

Korneyev sat sideways on the table. One foot hanging down, he was quickly writing with pen and ink a demand for additional norms of sand.

"Comrade Superintendent."

Korneyev did not hear.

"Korneyev!" Mosya cried at the top of his voice.

Korneyev turned around.

"Yes?"

Mosya sprang smartly to attention. He cast a quick, triumphant, hysterical gaze around him: at Vinkich, at Georgi Vasilyevich, at Margulies and at Nalbandov, at Shura Soldatova, at the clerks. He assumed a severe expression and reported formally:

"Comrade Superintendent, the third shift has finished its work. We have laid two hundred ninety-four cubes. We have made four hundred twenty-nine mixtures. Kharkov has been beaten. Kuznetsk has been beaten. A world record has been established. The average norm of production has been increased by one hundred twenty per cent. Brigadier—Ishchenko. Foreman—I."

Every one knew this perfectly well. It could very well have been left unsaid. But Mosya had been preparing this report for a long time. For a long time and passionately, he had awaited this moment. He had foretasted it. Now it had arrived—the moment of Mosya's triumph.

With a curt military gesture, he proffered the report to Korneyev.

"Good," Korneyev said indifferently.

He waved his pen in embarrassment. A large drop fell off and spotted his shoe. Korneyev glowered at it and wrinkled his face painfully. He put the piece of paper against the wall, and, without reading it, signed it. He merely asked:

"Did Khanumov begin?"

And that was all. In one shift, Mosya had laid two hundred ninety-four cubes, had shown unheard-of tempos, had beaten two world records, and *he* did not say a word, as if it were a matter of course.

Hurt, Mosya shoved the report into his pocket. He reported officially:

"Khanumov is in place. Shall I turn over the shift?"

"Turn it over."

"What norm for Khanumov?"

"Norm? . . ."

Korneyev's nose twitched. He looked quizzically at Margulies. "David! How many for Khanumov?"

"Forty-five mixtures per hour," said Margulies, yawning. "Maximum—fifty."

He yawned so heartily and with so much relish that his "maximum fifty" sounded like "may-u-ee-fty." Mosya could not believe his ears.

"How many, David Lvovich? How many?"

"I said—maximum fifty mixtures per hour," Margulies repeated calmly.

"David Lvovich, are you joking? How many does that make per shift?"

Mosya began quickly to multiply in his mind: five times eight —forty, zero down, four to carry . . . He looked at Margulies as if he were a madman.

"Four hundred mixtures per shift? We laid four hundred twenty-nine, and Khanumov four hundred?"

He laughed a low, insulting, bleating little laugh.

"Three hundred sixty. Maximum—four hundred."

Margulies again yawned for all he was worth. He could not restrain the yawn. Instead of "maximum four hundred," it sounded like "may-u-u-o-o-o-owa."

Nalbandov clutched his beard with his fist and, squinting sharply, aimed sideways at Margulies.

"Maximum four hundred?" Mosya asked again.

"Maximum four hundred," Margulies confirmed.

"David Lvovich!"

"Go, go!"

Margulies ransacked his pockets, but there was no more candy.

"Go. Don't delay Khanumov."

Mosya stood still.

"All right."

He went to the door, seized the latch, but again returned and took his place in the corner. He leaned his elbows on the board and began to tinker with a bit of tar between his fingers.

Outside, the music thundered. The parade beats of the march pulsed dully against the glass. The panes tinkled. Margulies looked at Mosya severely and quizzically.

"Well?"

"Do what you like, David Lvovich, but I won't go."

Margulies arched his brows.

"David Lvovich," Mosya said piteously. "Not I. Go yourself, David Lvovich, and talk to Khanumov. I will not go. They'll kill me!"

"What?"

"They'll kill me. Word of honour! What do you mean? Don't

you know Khanumov? Just see what's going on there. It will start trouble. They have a counter-plan of five hundred and not one mixture less. I will not go. Khanumov will not agree to less than five hundred."

Mosya sat down on the floor and tucked his feet under him.

"Do what you like. Go yourself."

"Tell them to forget about five hundred mixtures for the time being," said Margulies coldly. "The maximum is four hundred, not one mixture more."

"Go yourself!"

Margulies did not have time to rise. Mosya jumped quickly to his feet. He forestalled Margulies.

"Sit down!" he cried angrily. "Sit down! I will go myself."

Mosya walked out of the office with decision, but in a minute he ran back, breathless, and slammed the door behind him.

Outside the windows were excited cries and whistling.

"Oi! What's going on there! I only opened my mouth about four hundred . . . !"

Mosya sat down in the corner. He was pale.

"Go yourself, David Lvovich," he cried desperately. "Go yourself. They won't listen to me. Go yourself."

Margulies rose and walked out of the office. The latch clicked. He stopped on the threshold.

LX

THE crowd made way for him. Unhurriedly, he walked toward the machine. Khanumov stood in the middle of the planking, his short, crooked feet spread apart, and looked unblinkingly into his eyes. Margulies walked right up to Khanumov.

"Why don't you begin?" he asked in an ordinary tone of voice, offering his hand to the brigadier. "Zero hour, fifteen minutes. It's time, Boss, it's time."

Khanumov did not take his narrow, motionless eyes off him.

In the heliotrope mirrored light of the projectors, his face seemed utterly white.

"What is Mosya prattling about our norm, Boss?" he said in a quiet, hoarse voice that was almost unrecognisable. "Explain it, please. Be so kind! What is the norm?"

The brigade surrounded them in silence.

"The norm is from forty to forty-five per hour. No more than four hundred mixtures per shift."

Khanumov's eyes became even more strained and narrower.

"Kostya did four hundred twenty-nine—set the world's record. And I, who follow Kostya, am to do four hundred?"

"So far, any more is impossible."

"David Lvovich, you are joking, of course! Aren't you?"

"What a strange fellow! You're a strange fellow, Khanumov." Margulies peered closely at him with his tender, near-sighted eyes. "Under no circumstances, can we do more than four hundred. First we must test the quality. In seven days, we'll crush the cubes, test the durability. Then, if you like, even eight hundred . . . if the quality will permit . . . Do you understand?"

"Kostya can, and I cannot?" Khanumov asked with stupid stubbornness.

"Wait."

"David Lvovich? Five hundred?"

"Impossible."

Khanumov knew Margulies well. He knew that it was useless to argue. Nevertheless, he repeated stubbornly:

"Five hundred."

"No."

The brigadier looked around as if he had lost his bearings. From all sides, intent faces, immovable waiting eyes, looked at him.

Korneyev, Mosya, and Nalbandov came up. Khanumov smiled ingratiatingly.

"Four hundred fifty . . . Boss?"

Margulies shook his head.

"In time, in time . . ."

"Four hundred fifty? . . ."

"Stop bargaining, Khanumov. We are not in the market place. You're holding up the work . . . In time."

Khanumov's neck swelled.

"Five hundred!" he cried with all his might. "In that case, it will be five hundred and not one mixture less! Five hundred!"

He trembled with anger and stubbornness.

"Can't be done."

"What are you . . . what are you . . ." Khanumov muttered, breathing with difficulty. "What are you doing, David Lvovich? Are you trying to tear my soul out? Do you want to disgrace me before every one? Do you want to make a joke out of me? David Lvovich! You know me . . . You know me and I know you. Together, you and I laid the dam. We froze our hands and feet together . . ."

Nalbandov stood there, his arms behind his back, leaning on the cane. He squinted derisively and attentively.

Margulies curtly shook his head.

"Comrades! Boys!" Khanumov cried out with all his might, twitching all over. "Concrete men of the first unconquerable brigade! Do you see what they are trying to do to us?"

The brigade was sullenly silent.

"David Lvovich! Comrade chief of the sector! Margulies! Be human! Be a real human being! Five hundred!"

"Don't play the fool, Khanumov," Margulies remarked with annoyance. "It can't be done. Begin the shift."

"It can't be done? It can't be done? . . . Then . . ."

It was difficult for Khanumov to talk. He tugged at the collar of his shirt.

"Then . . . I'll tell you . . . Then . . . David Lvovich . . . Don't torture me . . . you know . . . I'll tell you . . . to all the devils . . . to the swine! To the dogs! To the dogs, to the swine! . . . There!"

Khanumov jammed his hand convulsively into his pocket, tangled it in the lining, and tore out cigarette case and lining together. Pale and trembling, he flung it on the boards of the planking.

"There . . . The engraved silver cigarette case for the dam . . . eighty-four proof . . . Take it . . . I don't need it . . ."

From the other pocket, he pulled out a silver watch and placed it beside the cigarette case.

"This watch was given to me . . . for the CES . . ."

He flung his *tyubeteika* on the watch.

"The *tyubeteika* . . . for the flagstone at the smithy!"

He suddenly sat down on the ground and began to tear off his shoes.

"The shoes, for the foundry-yard . . . Take them . . . Choke on them! . . . I don't need anything!"

Before Margulies could say anything, he had deftly pulled off the shoes and flung them aside.

"I am going to the devil's mother—away from the construction! Give me my time! I don't want to work with opportunists! Go hang yourself! . . ."

Margulies turned pale. Khanumov looked with dazed eyes around him and suddenly saw Nalbandov.

"Comrade Nalbandov . . ."

He was clutching at a straw.

"Comrade Nalbandov, you be witness! Be witness to what Right opportunists are doing here to a man!" he cried in anger.

All eyes turned to Nalbandov. Nalbandov stood there, surrounded by eyes. He saw these eyes, turned to him hopefully, prayerfully.

Here! The opportunity! Fame lay before him! All he had to do was to stretch out his hand and pick it up. The epoch did not spare those who fell behind, and did not forgive vacillation.

One or the other.

"David Lvovich," Nalbandov said in the midst of universal silence. His voice was calm and sonorous. "I don't quite understand you. Why don't you permit Khanumov's brigade to raise production to five hundred mixtures per shift? It seems to me that it is quite possible."

"Of course, it is possible! Correct! That's right! It *is* possible," the brigade shouted.

"You hear, David Lvovich, what this man—the chief engineer on duty—is saying?" Khanumov said quickly, jumping to his feet.

Nalbandov turned toward Margulies.

"I advise you to reconsider your decision."

"I do not need your advice," Margulies said roughly.

"I have the right not only to advise you, David Lvovich. In my capacity as assistant chief of the construction, I can order you."

Nalbandov emphasised the word "order."

"I do not wish to submit to your orders!" Margulies cried in a falsetto. "I am responsible to the Party for my orders."

Nalbandov shrugged his shoulders.

"As you please. It is my duty to point it out to you. But I think that your orders have a flagrantly opportunist character. Instead of taking advantage of results already attained, and utilising the experience of the previous shift to go further, you retreat or, at best, mark time. Thus you break down the tempos. Tempos, in the epoch of Reconstruction, decide everything."

His words fell into the crowd like unsnuffed matches into dry straw.

"I would ask you . . . you . . . without demagogy . . ."

Margulies clenched his fist and walked right up to Nalbandov. His jaw was shaking. He could scarcely contain himself. Making an incredible effort to remain calm, he said, enunciating each word sharply:

"Before I am certain of the quality, I will not permit the quantity to be increased. This is a construction, not a stunt. Do you understand?"

He walked away, adjusted his spectacles, although it was not necessary to do so, and said over his shoulder:

"Please do not stand in the middle of the labour front. You are interfering with discipline."

Then Margulies walked up to Khanumov, placed his slightly trembling arm on his shoulder.

"You, Khanumov, listen . . . You know me, Khanumov . . .

If I tell you it can't be done, then—it can't be done. Did I ever deceive you? You and I together, Khanumov, laid the dam. Well . . . are you—a child? Just think: we might have to tear down the entire flagstone."

Khanumov peered suspiciously into Margulies's face. He looked at it long and persistently, as if he were trying to read in it all the truth, all the most secret emotions, the most secret processes of his thoughts.

And he saw nothing on this pale, dirty, brightly illuminated face except friendliness, restrained love, good wishes, fatigue, and firmness.

"Four hundred fifty . . . what? . . . Boss! . . ."

Margulies shook his head.

"In time."

Khanumov bent down and began to pick the things up from the floor. The crowd made way.

Margulies walked unhurriedly into the superintendent's office. Mosya dogged his footsteps, loosely swinging his arms.

Margulies, standing, moved a loose-leaf pad toward him, and, breaking the tip of the pencil, quickly wrote an order forbidding the making of a mixture in less than one and two-tenths minutes. The sheet crackled as he tore it off and handed it to Mosya.

"Give it to Khanumov. For precise execution."

Mosya went out.

In a minute, Margulies caught with his trained ear the smooth noise of the drum that had started.

"Zero hour thirty-five minutes," said Korneyev.

LXI

SEMECHKIN sat on a bucket in the dark barn of the fire department. Yard-long rays from the projectors streamed through the long cracks.

By their light Semechkin was writing a dispatch for the regional and central press, exposing everything. The theme of his correspondence was the disgraceful treatment that had been accorded a representative of the press.

He spread out the papers on his knees, and wrote and wrote and wrote. He wrote at length. He wrote extensively. He wrote insinuatingly. He wrote without scratching out, with a multitude of parentheses, quotations, and dots.

His lips were trembling. He was pale. Beside him on the ground stood his canvas brief case, casting a mirrored reflection into the dark corner of the barn.

Trains thundered by. The barn trembled. The rays flickered rapidly across the shadow-bars. The shadows flickered from right to left and from left to right. The barn seemed to be riding forward and backward along the sector.

The bolt rattled and screeched. The rifleman looked into the barn.

"Are you writing?"

"I am writing," Semechkin affirmed with dignity, in a bass voice.

His dark goggles gleamed disapprovingly, reflecting the white electric light.

"Get your things together, little fellow, and get out."

Semechkin put the papers into the brief case and walked haughtily out of the barn.

The shadows of a train flashed by. The lads were running out of the light into the shadow. They had already thrown off their canvas overalls, had poured water on themselves, but they had not yet recovered from work.

Their chests were rising and falling exaggeratedly under their shirts. Their wet forelocks were hanging and creeping into their eyes. Their unfastened shirt sleeves were dangling.

"Ukh! U-u-ukh!" Olga Tregubova was squealing. "Ukh! Who will carry me to the barrack? I'll give him two kopecks."

She breathed heavily, blowing on her burning palms. Her eyes gleamed with desperate, enticing coquetry. Her small, feminine breasts were rising and falling under the impossible tatters of her holiday dress, which had become a rag.

"I'll give you ten kopecks. But leave me alone!"

Sayenko was lurching across the sectors.

He was skulking, wolf-like, from shadow to shadow, carefully avoiding street lamps and projectors. The black night, shot through with crackling sparks, flickered and shone around him like the hide of a wolf. He was stealing in by back ways, like a thief. From the sixth sector came the noises of the brass band. He avoided the sixth sector.

In the shadow of plants and scaffoldings stood the invisible riflemen of the guard and watchmen.

Night. He walked around the plants and scaffoldings.

The blast furnace led a night life, bright and deliberate, like sleep. The wondrous light illumined the emerging blast furnaces fantastically. At night they emerged and stood out more starkly than in the daytime. They were illumined wondrously from the bottom, from the top, and from the sides. Their rounded storys quivered in the mirrored light.

In the morning there had been eight storys. Now there were nine. The tenth was being put up.

Chained to the arm of the crane, a bent sheet of rusty iron dangled at a dizzy height. From the ground, the sheet of iron seemed no larger than a piece of broken tooth. But, as a matter of fact, it weighed a ton and a half. If it were to fall on some one's head, not even a wet spot would be left. The tenuous shadow of the sheet of iron was a broad jamb that swung over the bulging body of the blast-furnace. But at this height, it became a piece of broken tooth turning slowly around and around.

Supernatural, electric-blue stars burst forth from the insistent roar of acetylene torches. Radial shadows splattered. The green hands of the acetylene workers flared eerily. Masks hid their faces. From above, came the repeated salvos of pneumatic hammers, like the rat-tat-tat of machine guns. Little men and their tremendous songs ran back and forth. But they were the songs of giants.

Portable furnaces roared. Out of the ruby incandescence, men with long tongs extracted gleaming mushrooms of white-hot rivets. Each rivet smoked like the slow-match of a cannoneer. While it was being rushed to its destination, it changed colour. White turned yellow, yellow—pink, pink—a dark, thick raspberry.

With the lash of a pistol shot, the hammer crashed down on the raspberry head of the rivet. Sparks flew. Under the frightful blows, the rivet again changed colour. It became blue, dove-coloured, raven-coloured, and again white, but now a white that was cold, ferrous, like a tarnished button.

Sayenko shunned the blast furnace. He shunned the car of the "Komsomolskaya Pravda."

The green Pullman car with the rosette of Lenin stood on a side-track. It seemed to be buried deep in the ground. It was illumined within and without.

Sayenko walked around the car and peered through the windows. All the windows shone brightly, but there was only one man in the car.

The poet Slobodkin was standing in front of the composing-frame, composing-stick in hand, near-sightedly picking out letters for an application blank. He tied a string around the compact square of letters he had picked out. He carried it to the zinc table. He beat it with a brush. He was hurrying.

Sayenko walked around the side of the car. Behind his back, the green car with its stubborn bulges of Lenin's forehead still breathed of the iron smoke of Zlatoust, the ferns of Miass, cyclones, thunder storms and rainbows, the anthracite of Karaganda, the glitter of Chelyaba, all the freshness and power of the great Urals, all its route made in space and in time.

In the long shadow of the warehouse the gun of the sentry shone dimly.

Sayenko walked softly around the warehouse, his hands deep in the pockets of his wide trousers. He was trying to prevent the box of matches from rattling in his pocket. He made his way to a field.

The steppe night wound its watch of stars with the little carved key of the cricket.

The wound-up stars moved in all directions, crossing and meeting each other, rising and setting, but their movement was imperceptible.

Rails gleamed in the secret light of the risen moon. A train was passing. It was a long-run train. It approached an incline. The flat cars rolled slowly. On the flat cars heavy pieces of ore swayed, somnolently exchanging knocks with the wheels. Sayenko ran after a flat car, tried to catch hold of its side. In the shadow of the brakeman's box stood the dark figure of the brakeman.

Sayenko ran down the embankment, looked around, let two flat cars pass, then ran after another flat car.

The conductor's fur coat, a red lantern, and a rifle. The incline ended. The train gathered speed. The train ran past Sayenko.

His pockets rattling, Sayenko ran after the red lantern. He ran until he was exhausted. Finally, he fell behind.

The night and the lights flowed endlessly across his eyes. An airplane flew overhead. It was invisible. Only its bright signals flared. An imaginary strip of impetuous sound hung overhead.

The airplane flew over the steppe like a burning Primus oil stove.

LXII

SEROSHEVSKY was returning to the construction eight hours late. He had been delayed by a stop necessary because of the storm.

Seroshevsky was looking down through a slanted window. Three-quarters of the horizon was covered by the huge white wing. It looked like the seamed rubberoid roof of the warehouse.

Four letters were written on the wing of the airplane. The four letters stretched into the spaces of the night: A huge *P;* after it, somewhat smaller but still large—a *C*; and then a somewhat smaller *C*; and then a very small *C*.[1]

The airplane was landing, circling over the space occupied by the construction. Under its wing the starry field of the earth swayed and turned. The statistical table of flickering, pulsing lights stretched below. Thus the embers of a cooling, scattered bonfire pulse and play.

But there the colour is subdued, roseate, while here it was white, bright, electric.

Automobiles crawled like glow-worms. The moon-white steam of trains swirled up. Dotted lines, strips of streets and roads stretched in all directions, clashing and crossing each other.

Signals sparkled like drops of multicoloured syrups. Red of fire-barns, blue of open warehouses, green of railroad switches and semaphores. The bulging sides of hills, studded with lights, swam by.

Seroshevsky recognised the starry geometry of his complex enterprise. He solved the theorem by memory.

To the left was the mine. To the right, the blast-furnace. To the west, the socialist city. To the east, the carriers. In the middle was the sparkling box of the central hotel, the plant of the Coke-Chemical Combine, the slanted stacks of the scrubbers—the pipes of the organ that was being put together.

Illuminated by groups of projectors, objects in aggregate stood below obliquely, like chess figures carved out of ice. The lake glittered with painstaking minuteness. Everything was torn up, unfinished, scattered.

But Seroshevsky knew that this was merely the preliminary sketch. He looked down on the space of the construction as if it were an illuminated blue-print.

He saw it as it would look a year hence. In a year all these separate, torn details would be joined together, smoothed over, welded, integrated, polished. The construction would have become

[1] This represents in reverse order the Russian letters *C.C.C.P.*, the English equivalent of which is U.S.S.R.

a factory, and the factory would spread out with all its rivets, pipes, and cylinders, like a motor taken out of an automobile, a compact engine of internal combustion.

And the lake would be different, new. The lake would cover thirty square kilometres. The lake would change the climate.

In the cabin flashed the pink candy-bar of the lighted signal: *Attention*.

Seroshevsky grasped the arms of his chair. An amazing silence fell over the world.

Unnoticeably, something inexplicable occurred. The earth disappeared from the right window. Its place was taken by the recumbent sky—a huge, bright blue space with a lily of the valley blossom in the middle. It attracted irresistibly to itself the magic surface of the blue planet.

In the meanwhile, the left window was covered entirely by the star-sprinkled earth, which clung to it tenderly with its restored details—the roofs of illuminated barracks, the train signals, the crossings, the excavators, the projectors that were dug into the earth, the roads, the railroad tracks . . .

Thus before passing from the general to the particular, the airplane whisked up like the board of a swing, reversed the positions of the starry sky and the starry earth (the moon and the hotel), made one last circle, straightened out, and swooped down to the landing.

Grass ran under the wings. Landing flares blazed smokily at the ends of the wings. A painted polychrome of fire fell on the grass. The grass flared up. It smouldered and ran. It smoked and ran.

People ran.

Seroshevsky placed his leg in its russet puttee on the running board of the long automobile. The running board resembled a waffle. He pressed his foot against it as if it were a stirrup. The chauffeur pressed the throttle.

"Where?"

"To the plant office."

Seroshevsky dropped the collapsible dust goggles over his eyes. The projector blazed in the glasses—a magnesium flare. He clutched the side of the car and threw his brief case on the seat.

LXIII

NALBANDOV was sitting at his Swedish writing desk. He sat, his beard turned sharply toward the window, large and square like a wall. He tapped his cane against the xylonite floor.

It was possible to press two charges against Margulies.

The first: in violation of the exact demands of contemporary science, Margulies *permitted* the number of mixtures to be increased to four hundred and twenty-nine per shift, thereby endangering the quality of the concrete, and thus revealing himself to be a Left extremist.

The second: in violation of the resolution of the Party urging every possible effort to increase tempos, Margulies *forbade* a brigade to make more than four hundred mixtures per shift, thereby undermining the enthusiasm of the brigade and revealing himself as an opportunist of little faith and a Right extremist.

Both charges were just and could be corroborated by facts. They lacked only motivation: from what motives did Margulies permit on one occasion and forbid on the other? But—these were mere details.

And so—two contradictory charges were formulated. One could write a report, cold and deadly, like a pistol shot. There remained only one question: which of the charges should be selected?

To Nalbandov the first seemed the stronger, the more scientific. But its force depended upon the results of the qualitative analysis.

The second was less scientific, but it was more in the spirit of the times. It would present Nalbandov as the advocate of high tempos, and Margulies as opposed to them. Such a position would be impregnable, but its force again depended on the results of the analysis.

Should the results of the test prove negative, then the second charge would become a rapier-thrust against Nalbandov: it would be he who had demanded raising quantity at the expense of quality.

Should the results of the test prove positive, then the first charge would become a rapier-thrust against Nalbanov: it would be he who had demanded lowering tempos at a time when quality permitted their increase.

Dialectics!

Nalbandov pounded his cane angrily.

The inkwell increased to incredible proportions. It already occupied half the world. In its glassy pit airplanes could fly, trains could run, forests could grow, mountains could rear themselves.

Nalbandov seized the pen and wrote two reports. In one was the first accusation; in the other, the second accusation. He laid them side by side and studied them.

The telephone rang. The telephone was on the verge of bursting. Nalbandov did not go near it. He was thinking, concentrating feverishly.

No, after all, the first accusation seemed the more reliable. Science was science. One could always rely upon it. Good old academic science! Finally, there were the official instructions of the firm. Foreigners were never mistaken. They could not be mistaken.

Nalbandov tore the second accusation to bits and threw them into the waste basket. He took the first report and walked decisively toward Seroshevsky's office. He stopped before the door.

Perhaps it would not pay to start a case. Perhaps it would be best to destroy the report.

But then Margulies would triumph again. No! No! Anything but that! Nalbandov began to lose his self-control.

It occurred to him that, by submitting this report, he might be risking his reputation, his future. But suppose the laboratory analysis . . .

But he could no longer contain himself. He burst open the door with his cane and entered the office.

"Listen, Seroshevsky," he said in stentorian tones. "Here! Report!"

LXIV

FILONOV wrinkled his forehead painfully. He was trying to understand, to determine Semechkin's main thought.

In a dull, injured, little basso, Semechkin spoke sentence after sentence. The sentences were vague, long, full of venomous insinuations.

"Wait, my dear fellow . . ." Filonov said, turning red. "Wait . . . Tell it to me in order . . ."

Various people kept coming in and going out. The door kept slamming.

The incandescent lamp either dimmed to scarcely perceptible redness or flared up to the brightness of a projector. The makeshift electric station was breathing regularly, laboriously. The corners of the room either vanished in the darkness or struck the eye with all their details of placards, graphs, and stools. The old typewriter clattered and rang out like a motorcycle.

Ishchenko walked up to Filonov and placed a paper on the table. On a graph sheet torn out of an old account book, with the printed script of *Deb.* and *Cred.*, a declaration had been written, in indelible pencil, very carefully, each letter traced distinctly.

Filonov immediately grasped it in all its details by the light of the glowing lamp.

"Wait, Semechkin."

He read:

To the cell of the CSU (b) [1]
of the Coke-Chemical Combine
From the brigadier of the concrete
mixers of the third shift,
Konstantine Yakovlich
Ishchenko

DECLARATION

I petition to be accepted into the Party. I have finished my candidate status of six months. I have come to the socialist construction from the village, from the collective farm, illiterate. Here I liquidated my illiteracy, raised my political literacy, began my work as a mucker. Now I am brigadier of the concrete mixers of the third unconquerable shift. I am a shock-brigader. I have been carrying out my work with twenty to twenty-five percent in excess of the plan; here with the lads I have beaten Kharkov and Kuznetsk and the world record in the laying of concrete. Here I have understood that all workers who work for the socialist construction build for themselves, and therefore I consider that I should be in the Communist Party and my lads in the Komsomol to help and to carry out the general line of the Party.

K. Y. ISHCHENKO.

From under his arm Ishchenko took a package of Komsomol application blanks and placed it beside his declaration.

"Well, how is your woman?" Filonov asked hoarsely, opening his red mouth, on the upper lip of which, like shining black eyebrows, was his young moustache. "Has she had the kid?"

"Who knows? What with the world record and everything else, my head is aching all over. I'll go in the morning. Maybe it's already there."

"Well, well."

Filonov wearily turned Ishchenko's application blank sideways and wrote on the corner of it: "To be accepted. Filonov."

[1] Communist party of the Soviet Union (bolsheviks)

"She was in a bad way," Ishchenko remarked, smiling diffidently.

Margulies looked through the window of the art shop. The boys were sleeping in different corners, rolls of wallpaper under their heads. Shura Soldatova was sitting sideways on the floor, her feet under her. She was drawing a poster of Ishchenko in an airplane.

The airplane was large, like a seraph, with six wings, and of an unheard-of construction. Ishchenko's head stuck out of a small cabin-window, while his bare feet somehow managed to be outside. They hung over the fantastic, antediluvian landscape with its coal-age flora.

The grass was the height of trees. The trees were the height of grass. The jointed bamboo seemed to have been transplanted here from Lilliputian Japanese gardens, and the red utopian sun, half hidden by the river, gave no definite indication as to the time of day—sunrise or sunset.

Margulies tapped on the windowpane.

Shura carefully put the brush into the insulator cup, wiped her hands on her skirt, flung back her hair from her eyes, and went out to meet him.

They walked slowly along the sector.

She put her somewhat long arm, in its white sweater sleeve rolled up above the elbow, around his neck. He held on to the fingertips of this hand. He carried it on his shoulder as if it were a yoke. They seemed to be about the same height.

"What did they say at the hospital?" Margulies asked.

Shura shrugged her shoulders.

"Will they cut his hand off?"

"They don't know yet."

"It was all so stupid . . ."

"Have you eaten anything yet?"

He shook his head.

"You'll die, for a fact."

"I won't die. What time is it now?"

"Quarter past two."

"The dining room opens at seven."

"And sleep?"

"That's right. It wouldn't hurt to have some sleep. Let's take a little walk."

"You're a camel. The boys call you Camel."

Margulies laughed quietly.

They walked out of shadow into light and out of light into shadow. Where it was light it was day, but in the shadow it was night. They sought the night.

Around them were innumerable sources of light. The lantern over the tar-paper roof. The semaphore. The naked stars of the five-hundred-candle-power electric lamps. The projectors. The signals of switches. Fire barns. Automobile headlights. Bellows. The acetylene torches.

But everywhere was the constant presence of the almost unnoticeable, magic, lily of the valley radiance. Like a potion, it mingled with all things.

Shura gently laid her head on Margulies's shoulder.

"Listen, David. What happened to Korneyev?"

"Klava went back. She has a child and a husband there. It's a long story."

The small moon was in the middle of the light green sky, like a taut little bud of a lily of the valley that has not yet blossomed.

Shura Soldatova was silent for a while, thinking earnestly about Korneyev.

"Have you any children, David?" she suddenly asked, earnestly.

"No. As a matter of fact, I haven't even a wife."

"And haven't you ever had one?"

"Well, why not? Certainly I've had one."

"Where is she now?"

Margulies waved his arm.

"In a word, I had one, and now I haven't any."

She laughed.

"Aren't you ever lonely?"

"At times."

He pressed his head against her cool round arm and tickled her with the stubble of his unshaven cheek. They walked into the shadow of the warehouse and kissed tenderly.

In the shadow of the warehouse stood a watchman.

They walked down to the bottom of excavations and walked up to the crests of fresh embankments. They crawled through barbed wire and flung the wires of electric connections and field telephones over their heads. They landed in blind alleys and walked around the gigantic buildings of aggregates confined in cages of lumber and scaffolding.

"By the way, David, how old are you?"

"I'm an old man."

"Well, anyway, tell me."

"I'm afraid to tell you . . . Thirty-six."

"Pff! . . . Think of it, an old man!" Shura snorted contemptuously. "You're just a little boy."

"Do you know, that's right! As a matter of fact, I always feel like a little boy, like a seven-year-old child. Here my childhood comes back to me. Now as I walk around and look and see all these huge things around us, the noises, the smoke, the lights . . . Feelings . . . But I don't suppose you're interested in that."

"No, on the contrary, it's very interesting. Go on, go on."

"You see, I remember myself as quite young. Well, say about seven or eight. So we lived there at Ekaterinoslav . . . By the way, my father had a very interesting profession. He was a professor of calligraphy. Of course, we say that only as an affectation —that he was a professor. In a word, he taught fools how to write beautifully. On the street in front of our house was a glass show window, and in it on black velvet, lay a pink wax arm with a goosequill between the fingers. And over all was the speckled, grapevine shadow of acacia. All along the street were huge trees— like in a park. And in the summer everybody's head was covered with mosquito netting that reeked of oil of cloves. It was simply impossible to get away from the odour of cloves. To make a long story short, in 1905 there was a pogrom. Father was killed, and for some reason we fled to Nikolayev. And at Nikolayev we boarded a steamer at night. For the first time I was on a steamer.

As a matter of fact, it was a lousy little steamer, but to me it seemed huge, mysterious. Have you ever noticed that in childhood all things seem to be big? The rooms were huge, and the chairs and the sideboard and the pictures and the cats and the dogs—even sparrows, eggs, and pieces of sugar seemed much, much larger than they actually were. And suddenly—a steamer! Can you imagine it? I wanted to sleep. I was sitting on the bundles. My mother was running around. My little sister was crying. The sky was black, and white clouds of steam were lighted by the hanging lanterns as if by opalescent moonlight. And everything was tremendous—the lanterns, the smoke, the fear, the sky, Mother, the chirruping of the winches, the bales hanging in the air, the hold of the steamer, the smokestacks, the whistles . . . Especially the whistles were large, thick, long, cut off sharply, like sausages—hoarse basso whistles. But later I became accustomed and thought nothing of it. I began to grow—and the world began to shrink. Things, fears, people began to grow smaller. My mother became a little old woman. Chairs, which had been thrones, were transformed into small, hobbling, ramshackle furniture. Rooms, which had been chambers, became holes in the wall . . . I was outgrowing the world. But now suddenly I look around, and the world is outgrowing me again. Again I feel its hugeness. And the things around me are huge—plants, kilometres, tons, blast-furnaces, dams, lanterns . . . The world is outgrowing me. I walk around as I did in my childhood—a little fool—and I am astonished at everything. At times I am simply stunned . . . just as I was stunned by that magic steamer. By the way, all this resembles the night in the port at the time of loading—whistles, winches, the steam of the moonlight, and everything in general . . ."

"By the way, David, do you happen to be a poet?"

"No. But why?"

"Oh, nothing. I wish you would write me a bit of verse for the posters."

"You're a dumbbell, Shurochka!"

"You're a dumbbell yourself. What do you think? That I don't understand? I understand perfectly well. I have noticed it myself . . . Everything used to be so much larger. But now I'm growing out of everything . . . and not only out of things—out of a skirt or out of a jacket . . . But I'm creeping out of the world, somehow . . . It seems sort of crowded—can't quite fit in . . . But when I was young, it was quite the opposite."

"You're old, too."

"I'm not old! But I'm not too young, either," Shura said with conviction.

And suddenly flinging both arms around Margulies's neck, she nestled close to him, and, looking directly and frankly into his eyes, she said:

"Will you marry me, David?"

Margulies began to laugh.

"Well, that's a fine state of affairs! Why should I marry you, and not you me?" he lisped. "But will you marry me?"

Two straight, slender rays of searchlights issuing from one point moved along the starry dial of the sky. It seemed as if the starry clock were losing time and it was necessary to move the hands forward.

Time marched toward dawn.

Mr. Ray Roupe could not sleep. He suffered from insomnia due to old age. He worked at night. His small portable typewriter was clicking, but it was too stuffy in the room.

In checkered felt slippers and pyjamas, Mr. Ray Roupe walked out on the terrace of the cottage and looked at the low, distant panorama of the construction.

The night was unrecognisable. It gleamed, breathed fires, lights, thunders, smokes, fantastic constructions.

His senile imagination populated it and built it up according to his own taste.

He imagined it to be a port city. Here were bars, dancing palaces, cafés, the smokestacks of steamers, the din of loading, the screech of pulleys on lofty booms, the illumined towers of town-halls.

Multicoloured fires sparkled in glasses, stimulating thirst.

Light-signals hung over crossings. They hung like the boxes of sleight-of-hand artists, like small, three-story Chinese pagodas. Multicoloured globes jumped from section to section, magically changing colour. Yellow turned to green, green to red.

The sumptuously illuminated crowd revelled. Faint music swayed. In the distance resounded all this powerful symphonic orchestra of lights, odours, movement, passions.

Gusts of hot wind blew against Ray Roupe's eyelashes. The night was moonlit, starry.

"Babylon . . . Babylon . . ."

The terrace was like the deck of a ship. Ray Roupe swayed slowly . . .

"Woe to thee, Babylon!"

He was frightened. Nowadays, he always experienced fear at night. It was a consciousness of inevitable, imminent death. Well, ten, fifteen years . . . perhaps seventeen!

But then . . .

LXV

ON a shaky little oval table an open, illustrated magazine lay neatly beside an uncorked bottle of cognac and a small drinking glass. A fine, dark-red, straight Dunhill pipe and a tin of tobacco, left on the page of the magazine, were so yellow, so boldly lighted by the silken table lamp that they resembled a spendidly printed coloured advertisement of a tobacco firm. The air was filled with the pleasant aroma of Capstan.

Foma Yegorovich, tugging and pulling at his hair unceasingly, sat down at the table and placed his elbows upon the magazine.

He pressed his fingers into his head. With his elbows he pressed down all these things printed in blue so clearly and shiningly on the crackling white paper. Now they were no longer attainable. They were hostile and cold. And the less attainable they had now become, the more perfect, tangible, and natural they seemed.

One could easily stretch his arm toward them, touch them, take them. But each time, the fingers met an obstacle in the slippery surface of the paper.

The lamp flickered and went out, and flared up again like a cigarette. The bulging cherry-wood of the pipe gleamed brazenly. Two levels of cognac swayed rhythmically—the low level in the glass and the high level in the bottle. And all this was meaningless. It was desolation, organised into painted forms of china, furniture, walls, materials, travelling bags.

Youth, life, Maggie, the refrigerator, the cottage . . . All this had come to an end.

Foma Yegorovich gulped six glasses of cognac, one after the other, but it was a drop in the bucket. Then he began to pour the cognac into the aluminum cup of his shaving outfit. The cognac took on the flavour of soap and chocolate.

Throwing things and books around his room, Foma Yegorovich pulled a glass tube containing morphine tablets out of his suitcase. The broken edge of the vial cut his finger. He sucked it as he had been wont to do when he was a child.

The vial, with two tablets spilled out of it, lay on the page of the magazine, so yellow and boldly lighted by the lamp that it seemed the splendidly designed advertisement of a pharmacy firm.

Clenching his teeth, Foma Yegorovich drank one glass after the other and could not get drunk. Then drunkenness struck his head all at once and knocked him out. For a long time the dying lamp swam steadily in his eyes and could neither float by nor stop.

Foma Yegorovich ran out of his room into the corridor. The newspaper trembled in his hand.

The hotel was sleeping. At times the lamps in the corridor would begin to go out. They went out slowly, reflected in perspective in the black square-paned windows. Losing its strength, the light passed from tone to tone, from a bright white to a dark raspberry, without lustre. Finally it would go out entirely.

Then the windows of the darkened corridors were illumined immediately from the outside. Rays of projectors and construction lamps shone through them. The light lay in sharp, long, checkered diagonals. It broke on the corners and on the steps of the stairway. The drooping flags of the curtains hung somnolently and shroud-like in its mirrored radiance.

Out of the rooms came snoring, drowsy mutterings, heavy sighs, the jingle and creaking of spring-mattresses under the blows of turning bodies.

After a time the lamps began to flare up again, passing in reverse order from tone to tone, from dark raspberry, devoid of lustre, to the bright whiteness of blinding incandescence. The lamps went out and flared up and went out again, like cigarettes puffed at in darkness.

The makeshift electric station breathed with the burdened, uneven sighs of a flywheel that had to overcome an obstruction.

The lamps flared up and died down.

Foma Yegorovich ran through corridors, up and down stairs, stopped in front of windows, sat down on steps.

He carried the paper to every source of light and, bringing it close to his eyes, read the same dispatch over and over again:

AMERICAN BANK CRASHES

New York, May 28th. The epidemic of bank failures throughout America continues. The Commercial Company, a large Chicago bank, with deposits of thirty million dollars, stopped payment yesterday. The chairman of the board and the chief director committed suicide. The manager of the credit department was arrested. An investigation is being carried on.

"My money . . ." Foma Yegorovich muttered. "My money gone . . ."

Along the corridors, the stairways, in light and in darkness, people walked. They walked from work and to work.

Foma Yegorovich would run up to those he knew and to those he did not know.

"Excuse me . . . Comrade . . . One minute," Foma Yegorovich would say, stretching forth the quivering newspaper. "I do not read Russian very well. Would you please help me? There is some misunderstanding . . . I assure you, on my word of honour, that it is impossible . . ."

Some of them excused themselves and hurried on. Some of them stopped and took the paper with curiosity.

"Where? What? Oh, that Kharkov record? Three hundred and six mixtures? That's last year's snow. To-day we made four hundred and twenty-nine at the sixth sector. But what of it? Do you still think that it is impossible?"

Foma Yegorovich turned to the right and to the left. He reeked of alcohol. He walked up to people, and walked away, and came back again. He could not stay in one place. He tottered. He almost fell.

"No, no! That's not it! Not there! Read the dispatch from New York."

He pulled at his suspenders. He twisted them. He snapped them.

"Comrade, read the dispatch from America! This one, this one!"

"Oh, another crash?" the other would respond with disappointment.

"What is written there? What is written there? Please, I beg of you, read it aloud."

"What is written there? Nothing interesting. Well, a crash. Well, in Chicago. Well, the Commercial Company. Well, the deposits were lost. Well, they committed suicide . . . Good-night. It's time for sleep. Excuse me. It will soon be morning. Go to sleep."

Foma Yegorovich pounded on Margulies's door with his fist. It was dark in the room. No one responded. Foma Yegorovich returned to his own room.

With mechanical thoroughness, he began to destroy everything around him.

He began with the magazine. He tore out page after page and flung them on the floor. Steamers, palms, automobiles, cottages, clothes, watches, tennis-rackets, umbrellas, canes, collar buttons, clocks, cigarettes, tablets swirled and fell.

Swirling to the floor, and disappearing forever under the bed, went Maggie's golden hair, her fresh vegetables, her loaves of bread, her lemons and ham, her mouth, open for a kiss, her simple, inexpensive striped dress.

When not one page, not one desired thing remained, Foma Yegorovich turned to available things.

He broke pencils. He crushed the shaving outfit with his heels. He smashed wine glasses and water glasses. He tore the sheets into ribbons. He took chairs apart and smashed the mirrored wardrobe with their broken pieces. Things fled from him like the Philistines. He smashed them relentlessly with the bludgeons of broken chairs. He routed his enemies with such laconic precision, and with such long pauses in between, that the noise in his room did not produce the impression of any excess. It attracted no one's attention.

Sweat poured down his hot face. His head whirled. He lost his balance. He fell. He felt sick, stuffy. He broke the window and fell across his bed.

He laid his head on the pillow and began to shed the profuse, irrepressible, terrible tears of a man no longer young.

"My money . . . My money . . ."

Tears strangled him. His corn-coloured Ukrainian moustaches were sodden.

His feet lay on the floor. With his hand he clutched and clung to the nickel bars of his bed. The bed flew through the room, dragged him along, lifted itself in the air, flew, swayed, fell into an abyss.

LXVI

MR. RAY ROUPE was frightened.

Mr. Ray Roupe went into Leonard Darley's room.

"Leonard, are you asleep?"

Darley turned over, jumped up and sat down on the edge of

the bed. He was large, bony, clad in black silk pyjamas. He wrapped Scotch-plaid blankets around his legs.

Ray Roupe sat down beside him on the edge of the bed.

"Excuse me, Leonard . . . I awakened you. I forgot to ask you . . ."

He pursed his lips. After all, he was paying Leonard Darley pretty well, well enough to have the right to talk with him a bit at night.

"I forgot to ask you, Leonard, what you think about this crash in Chicago?"

Mr. Ray Roupe smiled subtly and brightly. He was sitting in a lighted room and talking with a living young man. He was no longer afraid.

Darley yawned unceremoniously and began to look for the cigarettes on the chair.

"I hope, Mr. Roupe, that this misfortune did not touch you personally."

"Oh, it seems you haven't a very high opinion of me, Leonard! Don't worry. I keep my money in reliable enterprises."

He nodded his head toward the window:

"I invest my money in the construction of this Babylon. It is profitable and absolutely safe."

He implied that he was one of the largest stock-holders of the construction company which had undertaken the building of this factory.

"Thus I am helping to build Babylon, so that later I may have the satisfaction of blowing it up . . . with my books. Leonard, do you see the paradox?"

With self-satisfaction, Ray Roupe rubbed his chin—his soft, good-natured chin that was like a suède purse.

"There is a dialectic in this. It is quite in the spirit of our new friend, Comrade Nalbandov. Isn't that so, Leonard? Oh, I know where to invest money . . ."

The old man was chatty, especially at night when he could not sleep.

Darley looked at the window. It was growing definitely lighter. He began to pull on his heliotrope breeches.

"To tell you the truth, I'm beginning to tire of this Asia, Leonard. The bathing season is beginning at the Lido."

LXVII

FOMA YEGOROVICH regained consciousness. He recovered suddenly, as if from an inner shock.

Something irremediable had happened in the world. But what?

The room was illumined by the pitilessly strong light of very early morning. But there was no sun in the room. Perhaps it had not yet risen.

Fragments of shattered things lay motionless on the floor. The window was broken, but it brought in no coolness. The air in the room was hot, immobile.

The dead silence of false dawn was over the world. The silence was terrifying. A deadly, oppressive fear clutched at Foma Yegorovich's heart. An irremediable silence had fallen over the world.

The silence stretched around an unpeopled earth for thousands of kilometres. It became clear to Foma Yegorovich that there was no longer any living creature on the entire planet, except himself—neither beast nor bird nor fish nor man nor bacteria.

The hotel was utterly dead, desolate, abandoned. Foma Yegorovich had been forgotten.

The silence hung on the frightful height of an unendurable, mechanical note. It was the monotonous, baying, tinkling sound of steam escaping from the valve of a boiler, drifting, dissolving.

The blood pounded in his temples loudly and distinctly. It pounded with such frightful slowness that between two of its blows one could easily pace the entire length of the corridor, graphed with the rapid footsteps of a man.

The silence paced the corridor ceaselessly, like a doctor.

I am dying, thought Foma Yegorovich.

His forehead was covered by thick, cold, sticky perspiration. The lilac darkness of oblivion advanced upon him from all sides. With a frightful exertion of will, he overcame it.

But what was happening? What had happened? He tried to recollect, but he could not. He strained his memory. Finally he remembered.

"Morphine!"

There had been tablets. But had he taken any? He could not remember. On the floor lay an empty bottle and a small aluminum cup.

In deadly horror, he flung himself on the floor and began to rummage among the wreckage, among the dead things devoid of all meaning. He was seeking the tablets, but he could not find them.

The silence hung on the frightful height of an unendurable note. It was joined by another note, even higher, and then by a third.

"Morphine! I have poisoned myself! The tablets! No!"

He rushed to the window.

A multitude of notes on the unendurable height moaned in unison.

The area of the construction stretched to the very horizon, illumined in all its details by the rosy-grey, skeletal light of the early dawn. It was ominously unpeopled and lifeless.

The useless lights of the lanterns and projectors, devoid of power, brightness and sense, glowed thinly and weakly, scattered over the entire earth as far as the eye could see. And all the earth, as far as the eye could see, was covered by pendant white snowflakes of steam.

The motionless landscape of the construction thundered without stopping, and its entire forest of pipes groaned like an organ shaken to its foundations.

The metallic voices of all the machines on the construction cried out. Engines, excavators, trucks, locomotives, tractors. Steam-whistles, horns, sirens.

It was a soul-shaking symphony of several thousand machines, an intense, uninterrupted moan of horror and despair.

On the window sill lay the vial of tablets.

Life!

Foma Yegorovich rushed out of the room.

One window which embraced the entire end of the corridor faced the west. Over its checkered screen a fiery curtain of bright yellowish-strawberry colour rose steadily. People ran through the corridors, down the stairways.

Foma Yegorovich rushed to the window. His shadow ran back and forth along the entire length of the glowing corridor.

In the immobile air resounded the sharp, shattering alarm of a fire-siren. One could hear the steady roar of a conflagration and the crackle of wood possessed by flames.

Foma Yegorovich sat down on the xylonite floor and leaned against the heated glass that reached to the very floor.

He was overcome by an irresistible compulsion to sleep. As a child, he used to fall asleep on trains at night in his father's arms. He could not move a finger.

He saw people running in front of the burning barrack. As he fell asleep, he recognised some of them. He smiled, but it was difficult for him even to smile. Margulies, Triger, Korneyev, Shura Soldatova, Mosya were running. In their hands were shovels. They began to dig. They were digging around the burning barrack.

From the red fire-truck a hose was being pulled. Water crackled. But the fire swung out and looped along the entire breadth of the burning building, like a piece of light, beautiful, strawberry-coloured silk.

Raging in an encompassing wall, the flames rose higher and higher until they merged with the sky.

With the crackle of ripping canvas, matter passed from one state to another, and this transition was accompanied by a rise in temperature so great that the windows in the hotel cracked.

Foma Yegorovich slept, and through his sleep he felt on his eyelashes the dark, burning, bitter, riotous heat of the conflagration.

LXVIII

EVERYTHING moved from its place. Everything started.
The same train that had brought Fyenya was taking Klava away.

The train moved from the east to the west.

The train marched along the route of the sun. But the sun caught up with it three times on its way to Moscow. Three times the shadow of the train fell back, lengthened, stretched out to the east, caught at the fugitive dry grass, as if unable to part with the Urals.

Biting her swollen, chapped lips, she wrote her letters on the hard, vibrating window table. She wrote them one after the other. She would break the pencil and run to the train porter for a penknife.

The letters were long, passionate, muddled, with a multitude of abbreviations, dashes, dots, scratches, incorrect transpositions and exclamation points! They were brimful of splendid descriptions of the landscape, the passengers, the weather, incidents in the car. They were full of promises, plans, compassion, tears, and kisses.

At every station, the military man with the rhomboids pushed his way through the crowd of seasonal workers and ran to drop these letters in the mail box.

Two hours after the departure, he had already been initiated into all the details of Klava's life. He knew about the impossible, coarse husband, about Korneyev whom she loved passionately, about her daughter, about Anapa. No longer embarrassed by the presence of strangers, she wept without hiding her face and without drying her tears.

He was genuinely touched. He sharpened her pencil. He offered her stamps and envelopes, of which there was a constant shortage.

By evening, the entire car was taking the warmest interest in her fate. She was touchingly frank. It was a heroic frankness, bordering on self-flagellation. People consoled her, entertained her.

The Germans started the phonograph for her. She listened to barking recitatives of negro choruses, to dull metallic chords of banjos, to shameless moans of Hawaiian guitars—all these sounds and voices from another, mysterious world.

She laughed through her tears. She roared with laughter, biting her lips. And, roaring with laughter, she wept. She was angry at herself because of her laughter and because of her tears. In the beginning she was angrier because of her laughter; later, because of her tears.

At first, yellow hillocks littered with shovels and gloves stretched away on all sides. The steppe over which the rainstorm had recently swept flickered, hot and oppressive. Hobbling clouds grazed on the steppe.

On one side, a nomad tent swam by, as if it were a *tyubeteika* thrown into the grass.

The gleaming black disc of the phonograph turned around and around. In the centre of the disc, the dog in front of the horn turned around. The needle bobbed up and down. The shining, jointed horn spoke mysteriously, abysmally.

Evening came. Every kilometre returned lost details to ravished nature. The first trees appeared.

Trees! Oh, how long since Klava had seen trees and how satisfying they seemed to her! How could she have endured for so long without trees?

At first one or two trees appeared. Then small, scattered groups gilded by the setting sun. The trees wandered along like new recruits who had fallen behind an army. Then the trees began to walk in scattered chains of platoons, of companies. Then, with the songs and whistles of nightingales, appeared regiments and divisions.

Shaggy armies of conquerors crossed the mountains. They were returning home, covered with the iridescent fame of the rainbow. Steely, raven-blue clouds lay on the mountains like firearms.

The train ran through the sparkling fire of the rain, through bright ferns, rainbows, freshness, ozone.

Gay electric lights were turned on in the train.

We move like a shadow from the west to the east.

We return from the east to the west like the sun.

We cross the Urals.

". . . to lower tempos means to fall back, and those who fall back are beaten. But we do not want to be beaten. No, we will not have it! This was the history of old Russia: it was continually beaten because of backwardness. It was beaten by Mongol khans. It was beaten by Turkish beks. It was beaten by Swedish feudal lords. It was beaten by Polish and Lithuanian gentry. It was beaten by English and French capitalists.

"It was beaten by Japanese barons.

"It was beaten because of military backwardness, cultural backwardness, governmental backwardness, industrial backwardness, agricultural backwardness. It was beaten because it was profitable to do so and because the beating went unpunished . . .

"That is why we cannot be backward any more."

We cannot! We cannot! We cannot!

A railroad shack or a transformer-box. Black and red. It clung to the crag like an ingot of oxidised iron. Above it—the slender feathered arrows of Ural fir.

Black and red—the colour of attack. The alarming label on the box of a trotilla.

A small night-light glowed in the stuffy compartment—a small, blue night-light, the shade of lungwort slightly tinged with rose.

Dawn! The train crossed the Urals.

Flickering across the windows from right to left, swirled the obelisk: "Asia—Europe."

A senseless post . . .

I demand that it be taken down!

Never again shall we be Asia!

Never! Never! Never!

On the meadows, among the mountains, yellow flowers, downy like ducklings.

A small moon melted in the green sky, like a tight little bud of lily of the valley.

Klava lay her wet face on a wet bunch of lilies of the valley. Through the lilies of the valley she looked out of the window.

The sprays of lily of the valley, having lost their proportions, flickered past like telegraph poles.

At the stations, children selling lilies of the valley! Everywhere the odour of lily of the valley!

The dawn filled to the brim with icy dew!

The clear clinking fillipping bubbling through the clay neck of the night.

The nightingales reverberate—reverberate all through the night until dawn.

They do not fear the train.

Road of lilies of the valley and of nightingales.

Ufa—Saratov.

Clouds, elevators, fences, Mordovian sarafans, water pumps, caterpillars, echelons, churches, minarets, collective farms, village soviets.

And everywhere, no matter where you looked—from right to left, and from left to right, from west to east and from east to west—the transmission poles of high tension wires marched on diagonals in open formation.

Six-armed and four-legged, they marched monstrously, like Martians, flinging checkered shadows over woods and mountains, over groves and rivers, over the straw roofs of villages . . .

Never again shall we be Asia!

Never! Never! Never!

I

(CHAPTER ONE)

A letter of the author of this chronicle to:

Comrade A. Smolyan, Special Correspondent,
Russian Telegraphic Agency,
No. 60 Central Hotel,
Magnitogorsk.

DEAR SASHA:

I have just received your letter. It was forwarded to me here
from Moscow. Thank you for remembering me. Double thanks for
the attention with which you are following my chronicle.

Following "our chronicle," I should say.

It approaches its end.

You ask: But where is the first chapter?

I have just begun to write it.

By rights, the first chapter belongs to you, my dear friend
and guide.

You taught me to see a garden in a drop of rain.

The first chapter is a dedication to you. I am restoring the tradition of long dedications, but I am perfecting it. I place the
dedication not at the beginning, where it is never read, but at
the end, where it must of necessity be read because it contains
the dénouement.

The dénouement depends on the quality of the concrete.

And the quality of the concrete cannot be determined for seven
days.

The time of the action of my chronicle is twenty-four hours.

Thus the unity would be violated if I were to look seven days
ahead.

Can one solve this difficulty?

Yes. The way out has been found. I include the dénouement

in a dedica.ion, and I place the dedication, not in the beginning, but before the last chapter.

Under the banner of a dedication, I place the dénouement in its place, and at the same time avoid violating the structure.

Under the banner of the dénouement, I shall compel the dedication to be read and your name to be remembered, for it is worthy of remembrance and gratitude.

And so, dear Sasha Smolyan, do you remember that day when you and I ran across the construction to the central laboratory in the socialist city at seven o'clock in the morning?

It was exactly seven days after the events described in this chronicle.

I hope that you will not chide me especially for having invented a thing or two here and there.

For example, the elephant. There really was no elephant. I made him up. But couldn't he have been? Of course, he could have been! More than that, he should have been! And the fact that he was not, was entirely the fault of the management of entertainment, which could not organise a good circus at the construction.

However, perhaps they have an elephant by now. If so, please write me about it.

As for the rest, I stuck to the truth as much as possible.

And so, the canvas curtains flew out of the room into the corridor after us.

We did not even attempt to shove them back. That was impossible.

Lifted by the draught, they flapped, flew, swirled, raged.

You and I had studied their behaviour thoroughly. We slammed the door on them, simply and roughly. They hung outside like grey banners.

On the hill, ore was being blasted. Frequent uneven explosions followed each other.

The air broke softly, in layers, like a slate.

At the entrance to the hotel stood woven Ural carts. They

were waiting for the engineers. Tails swished. Shaft-bows gleamed with painted rosettes. There was the strong odour of horses.

The sun burned with the speed of magnesium ribbons.

Through the black crêpe of the floating dust, the quicksilver bullet of the thermometer blinded us.

We ran at break-neck speed. We were afraid of being late.

The immense sultry air flamed in our faces with Asiatic fire, with the ammonia of the steppe and the horses.

The tar roofs of the barracks quivered in the sun as if they were covered with ether.

In the cool cellar of the laboratory was the odour of raw lime, cement, sand.

Near the hydraulic press stood all the principal heroes of this chronicle, except Nalbandov.

(Of course, it is not necessary to reveal the pseudonyms to you. You have guessed them long ago, and it is all the same to the readers.)

Korneyev looked impatiently at his watch. His slippers were faultlessly white. He had just painted them. Not a single spot had yet darkened their blinding morning whiteness.

With some uneasiness, Margulies was rubbing the lenses of his spectacles with a handkerchief.

Mosya, his legs folded under him, sat on the earthen floor, opposite the press, and did not remove his hysterical eyes from it.

Ilyushchenko came in. He sat down at the table and opened the large record-book.

Stooping, two workers brought in the first cube. They placed it carefully on the steel plate of the apparatus. They began to pump slowly.

The other steel plate pressed down upon the cube.

Margulies put on his spectacles. Cracking his long, thin fingers, he thrust his nose into the dial of the monometer and did not remove his near-sighted eyes from it.

The workers pumped. The arrow of the monometer moved with short jerks across the figures. It moved very slowly but irrevocably.

The cube firmly resisted the pressure.

Suddenly, a faint crack ran down its corner.

"Stop!"

Ilyushchenko walked up to the monometer.

"One hundred and twenty."

The cube had withstood the pressure of one hundred and twenty kilograms per square centimetre. This was more than sufficient.

Displeased, Ilyushchenko walked up to the table and recorded the figure in the book.

"Next!"

Thus, ten cubes were crushed. The results were the same with slight variations.

Semechkin walked up to Margulies, pompously cleared his throat—h'm . . . h'm . . . and pompously offered his large moist hand to him.

"Well, Boss . . . I congratulate you," he said in a thick basso. "We won."

"We ploughed together,"[1] said Slobodkin, in his round Volga accent.

Margulies stooped, and walked out of the cellar into the yard, into the blinding, sultry light.

Mosya ran after him, clapping his hands against the damp walls, against his knees, against his shoes, against the backs and heads of his comrades.

He was breathless.

When every one had left, Ilyushchenko walked up to the telephone.

"Central. Plant Office. Give me Nalbandov . . . Hello! Ilyushchenko speaking. Yes. Just now. An average of one hundred and twenty."

"Good."

Nalbandov replaced the receiver with precision.

He picked up a pen, dipped it into the inkwell, which had now

---

[1] an old Russian saying, repeated in various fables, indicating that credit is being claimed for work done by some one else

assumed its normal proportions, and wrote on a sheet of the pad, with a flourish: "Report of Illness."

His throat was tightly bandaged with a handkerchief.

We saw him again at five o'clock that evening. He was in an automobile—on his way to the station. He was leaning on the head of his huge orange stick and did not acknowledge our greeting. He had not noticed us.

While riding by the sixth sector, he likewise failed to notice a small fresh poster: In a barrow sat a frightful, black-bearded man with an orange stick under his arm, and around him were Lilliputian trees, gigantic grass and a red utopian sun.

All of this occurred seven days later.

But on the morning on which our chronicle ends, everything was still indefinite and disquieting . . .

Well, dear Sasha, at this point, permit me to wish you everything good. Forgive me if the beginning of my dedication sounds somewhat pompous, somewhat French.

But really, I am beginning to be affected by my extended stay in Paris.

Do you remember our talks about Paris?

Imagine! Paris is not what we thought it was. I have not found what I sought, what I dreamed of. But then, I have found something much greater.

In Paris, I have found the sense of history.

We are too young. We have not yet acquired this sense. But some of our advanced thinkers are already trying to awaken it in us.

And it is not for nothing that Gorky constantly repeats: Write the history of factories and plants. Write the history of the Red Army. Create the history of the great Russian proletarian revolution which is a thousand, thousand times greater and more splendid than the "great" French revolution.

May not a single trifle, not even the smallest detail of our inimitable, heroic days of the first Five-Year Plan be forgotten!

And is not the Jaeger concrete-mixer with which the shock-brigades of proletarian youth set world records, more deserving of being preserved in the memory of future generations than the rusty blade of the guillotine, which I have seen in one of the gloomy cells of the Conciergerie?

And is not the football sweater of the shock-brigader, the kerchief and ribbons of a young Communist girl, the passing banner of the shock-brigade, the childish poster with its turtle or its steam engine, or the torn canvas trousers—are they not a thousand, thousand times more precious to us than Danton's brown frock-coat, Demoulins' overturned chair, the Phrygian night cap, the order for arrest signed by the blue hands of Robespierre, the last letter of the Queen, and the faded tri-color cockade, ancient and light, like a dry flower?

I firmly press your hand. Until I see you again—soon,

Yours,

V. K.

Paris.

LXIX

IT was growing light.

They were standing at the little window of the telegraph office.

Vinkich stood in line. Georgi Vasilyevich was writing the telegram.

Mosya languished beside him. He had not dropped behind for a single step. He was here now. He shifted from foot to foot, peeked over his shoulder, bumped his elbow. His face was entirely covered with soot—he had been putting out the fire—and so now he looked like the devil himself.

Georgi Vasilyevich, laughing to himself, wrote:

"Brigade concrete-mixers set world record, beating Kharkov, Kuznetsk, making 429 mixtures during shift . . ."

Mosya read it rapidly over his shoulder, and pleaded:

"Georgi Vasilyevich . . . Comrade author . . . Brigadier Ishchenko, Foreman Weinstein."

"Never mind, we don't need that."

"Brigadier Ishchenko, Foreman Weinstein."

Mosya was almost weeping.

"Ishchenko and Weinstein. It's a fact. What do you lose on it? It *is* a fact!"

"Lose money," Georgi Vasilyevich said edifyingly. "We must take care of government money."

Mosya did not know what to do with himself. He turned around in one spot. He swung his arms desperately.

"It's a fact," he whispered hoarsely.

"Shall I really put in Brigadier Ishchenko and Foreman Weinstein?" Georgi Vasilyevich asked Vinkich and winked at Mosya. "But is it worth while? That is the question."

Vinkich looked solemnly at Georgi Vasilyevich.

"Put it in, Georgi Vasilyevich," Mosya whispered. "What do you care? The newspaper will pay for it. Put it in."

Georgi Vasilyevich leaned over the desk.

"All right. You win. So be it: Brigadier Ishchenko. I'll put it in."

"And—me?"

Mosya became little and burdock-eared, like a schoolboy. He spoke animatedly and ingratiatingly, as if to a teacher:

"Georgi Vasilyevich, and will you mention me, too?"

"What have *you* to do with it?" Georgi Vasilyevich asked imperturbably.

"What have *I* to do with it? I? But who else has anything to do with it!!!"

Blood rushed to Mosya's face. He shouted:

"Georgi Vasilyevich, to the devil with you! Don't make me swear!!! I beg your pardon, of course . . ."

"Well, all right, all right," Georgi Vasilyevich said soothingly. "I was joking. Can't you take a joke?"

He wrote quickly:

"Brigadier Ishchenko, Foreman Weinstein."

Mosya read his name over his shoulder, but he did not leave Georgi Vasilyevich until he saw with his own eyes the tired woman-clerk take the telegram, count the words with her pencil, write a receipt, and strike it with a long-handled stamp.

Then he cried:

"Well, I'm going, comrades!" And he rolled down the stairway, head over heels.

"What style!" exclaimed Georgi Vasilyevich, taking Vinkich by the arm. "Learn it, young man: 'Brigade concrete mixers set world record, beating Kharkov, Kuznetsk, making 429 mixtures during shift. Brigadier Ishchenko, Foreman Weinstein!' Homer! The Iliad!"

From behind the mountain, covered by the white smoke of explosions, appeared the sun. It was already as white and violent as at noon.

Ishchenko was breaking his way into the maternity ward.

They would not let him in.

On the blackboard opposite the name Ishchenko were incomprehensible letters and figures:

"Boy, 3½ kilo."

An elderly woman in a nurse's uniform pushed Ishchenko out of the hall.

"Go, go! Come back in two or three days. You can't come in now."

Ishchenko's face was swollen, capricious, surly. His hair drooped over his forehead.

"How can you do such a thing?" Ishchenko cried. "What do you mean I can't see my own child?"

"Go, go!"

"I'm the brigadier of the world record! I've been a member of the Party since this year!"

"Behave yourself! You can set world records, but you don't know how to behave yourself."

The woman smiled and quietly led the brigadier outside the door.

"Stop," said Ishchenko. "Wait. Tell me one thing. What is it there—a boy or a girl?"

"A boy, a boy. Three and one-half kilo."

"Three and one-half kilo?" Ishchenko asked suspiciously. "Isn't that underweight?"

"It will do for a start."

Ishchenko went out into the street. He walked all around the hospital barrack. He peered into the windows. The panes gleamed with blinding whiteness. He could see nothing.

But in one of the windows appeared a figure. It was Fyenya. Fyenya pressed her face against the glass. Her nose, forehead, and chin were flattened into five-kopeck pieces. Her bright pearly teeth gleamed. In her arms she held a bundle. She lifted the bundle and showed it to her husband.

Through the unbearable glitter of the glass, Ishchenko saw a small, red face with dim, vacant, little eyes, round and blue, like juniper berries.

The brigadier made signs with his hands, and shouted something, but Fyenya did not hear. She was pulled away from the window. An elderly woman was scolding her.

Ishchenko went off to one side and sat down in the shadow of the barrack. Tears choked him. He understood neither their cause nor their meaning.

The sun glowed with the speed of magnesium ribbons.

The alarm clock began to rattle in Margulies's room. It was half-past six. The alarm clock rattled like a tin of bon-bons.

Burning flies swirled around the alarm clock in loops. The flies crawled in herds across the yellow paper.

The alarm clock rattled and rattled and rattled until it was exhausted. No one stopped it.

Margulies was sitting with Shura Soldatova on a bench near the hotel. They were waiting for the dining room to open. Margulies held her hand in his own large hand. He held it as if he were holding a carpenter's plane. He was thinking of the cubes which would be crushed in seven days. The unbearably hot sun illuminated their dirty, tired faces. Margulies was almost falling asleep. His head was nodding. With difficulty, he struggled against the attacks of delicious, swooning sleep.

Vinkich walked out of the doors of the hotel. He walked toward Margulies.

Falling asleep, Margulies noticed the fresh newspaper sticking out of the pocket of the special correspondent's leather coat.

Falling asleep and smiling faintly, Margulies asked:

"Well . . . where?"

"At the Chelyaba tractor plant!" Vinkich cried.

"How many?"

"Five hundred four . . ."

Moscow, 1931-1932.

THE END

European Classics

Honoré de Balzac
The Bureaucrats

Heinrich Böll
Absent without Leave
And Never Said a Word
And Where Were You, Adam?
The Bread of Those Early Years
End of a Mission
Irish Journal
Missing Persons and Other Essays
The Safety Net
A Soldier's Legacy
The Stories of Heinrich Böll
The Train Was on Time
Women in a River Landscape

Madeleine Bourdouxhe
La Femme de Gilles

Lydia Chukovskaya
Sofia Petrovna

Grazia Deledda
After the Divorce
Elias Portolu

Yury Dombrovsky
The Keeper of Antiquities

Aleksandr Druzhinin
Polinka Saks • The Story of Aleksei Dmitrich

Venedikt Erofeev
Moscow to the End of the Line

Konstantin Fedin
Cities and Years

Fyodor Vasilievich Gladkov
Cement

I. Grekova
The Ship of Widows

Marek Hlasko
The Eighth Day of the Week

Bohumil Hrabal
Closely Watched Trains

Erich Kästner
Fabian: The Story of a Moralist

Valentine Kataev
Time, Forward!

Ignacy Krasicki
The Adventures of Mr. Nicholas Wisdom

Miroslav Krleza
The Return of Philip Latinowicz

Curzio Malaparte
Kaputt

Karin Michaëlis
The Dangerous Age

Andrey Platonov
The Foundation Pit

Valentin Rasputin
Farewell to Matyora

Alain Robbe-Grillet
Snapshots

Arthur Schnitzler
The Road to the Open

Ludvík Vaculík
The Axe

Vladimir Voinovich
The Life and Extraordinary Adventures of
*   Private Ivan Chonkin*
Pretender to the Throne

Stefan Zweig
Beware of Pity